"What do I get if I win . . . ?"

Saidh's voice was a little breathless as she asked.

"Ye'd do better to ask what I get when I win. Because I will," he assured her, running his fingers along the top of her neckline now. Leaning forward, he whispered against her ear, "I like to win."

His lips brushed the edge of her ear as he spoke, and were followed by a light nipping that made Saidh gasp and squirm on top of him.

Greer groaned at the action, his hands moving to her hips to still her. She didn't understand why until she became aware of the hardness suddenly poking the bottom of one thigh.

"Greer?" she whispered, staring down at his hands on her hips.

"Aye, lass?" he growled.

"I'm going to enjoy this game," Saidh breathed, raising her head to smile at him as she added, "and I like to win, too."

By Lynsay Sands

LYNSAY SANDS

THE Highlander Takes a Bride

AVONBOOKS

An Imprint of HarperCollinsPublishers

This is a work of fiction. Names, characters, places, and incidents are products of the author's imagination or are used fictitiously and are not to be construed as real. Any resemblance to actual events, locales, organizations, or persons, living or dead, is entirely coincidental.

AVON BOOKS
An Imprint of HarperCollins*Publishers*
195 Broadway
New York, New York 10007

Copyright © 2015 by Lynsay Sands
Excerpt from *About a Vampire* copyright © 2015 by Lynsay Sands
ISBN 978-0-06-227359-8
www.avonromance.com

First Avon Books mass market printing: August 2015

Avon Trademark Reg. U.S. Pat. Off. and in Other Countries, Marca Registrada, Hecho en U.S.A.
HarperCollins® is a registered trademark of HarperCollins Publishers.

Printed in the U.S.A.

10 9 8 7 6 5 4 3 2 1

THE Highlander Takes a Bride

Prologue

SAIDH HAD JUST CAUGHT UP HER SKIRT AND started to squat when she heard it: a man's short, sharp shout that sounded like a death cry. Cold creeping down the back of her neck, she let her skirt drop and straightened, ears straining. At first there was nothing. No running feet, no sounds of battle, nothing to tell her what had happened, and then she caught a high keening that dissolved into weeping.

Cursing, Saidh pulled her sword from the scabbard at her waist and started through the woods, following the sound of those heart-wrenching sobs. She recognized them, knew their source. She'd heard the same sobbing last night from the bedchamber next to the one she'd been given during her stay at Fraser Castle, the bedchamber the bride and groom had been carried to during the bedding ceremony that had followed the wedding feast.

Saidh shook the thought away and paid more attention to where she was going when a branch slapped back and hit her across the face. The spot they'd stopped to make camp was a lovely clearing, but Saidh had wandered far away from it in search of a place to take care of her needs. The distance was a habit with her. She'd learned that she needed to take herself far from camp did she want to avoid one of her brothers finding and somehow either embarrassing or scaring her while she was in the middle of relieving herself. They'd played that trick often enough in the past for her to have learned her lesson.

Mind you, she'd returned the favor a time or two. As the only girl among seven boys in the Buchanan brood, Saidh had quickly learned to defend herself. It had been that or turn into a sniveling, whiny little girl who ran constantly to her mama to tattle on the boys and that was not Saidh. Now sixteen, Saidh gave as good as she got, and had earned the love and respect of every one of her brothers because of it.

Saidh's thoughts died as she stepped into a small clearing. It was pretty, surrounded by a wall of tall, stately trees and with a low carpet of purple flowers making up the ground, but it wasn't the picture-pretty setting that had Saidh sucking in a gasp of air. Instead, it was the sight of her cousin, Fenella, sitting, sobbing next to her husband's prone body, her dark hair a tumbled mess about her round face, her gown torn and disheveled, and a bloody knife in her hand.

"Fenella?" she breathed, finally getting past her shock and moving toward her. "What happened?"

Her cousin lifted her head, peered at her briefly without recognition and then just cried harder and shook her head as she lowered it again.

Frowning, Saidh slid her sword back into its scabbard and squatted to examine Hammish. There was a large circle of blood on his chest with a hole in the middle, and he didn't appear to be breathing. Saidh felt her mouth tighten, and turned to her cousin to gently take the knife from her unresisting hands. After a hesitation, she tossed it to the side, then caught Fenella by the shoulders and gave her a gentle shake. "What happened?"

She was hoping Fenella would tell her they were set upon by bandits, or some other such thing. Instead, Fenella sniffled miserably and cried, "I killed him."

"Dear God," Saidh breathed releasing her to straighten and peer helplessly around the clearing.

"I did no' mean to," Fenella sobbed. "I jest could no' take his rapin' me again."

Saidh glanced back to her with a frown. "Raping ye? Ye're married, Fenella. He was yer husband. He—"

"He was a cruel heartless bastard who hurt and humiliated me all through the night," she countered bitterly. "By the time he'd finished with me, I was raw, torn and bleeding worse than if I had me woman's time." Her gaze shifted to her dead husband and she said quietly, "That was bad enough, but I could ha'e withstood it. I would ha'e withstood it." Crossing her arms over her chest, she lowered her head and almost whispered, "But then he turned me o'er and took me in unnatural ways, ways even more painful." She raised her head again, eyes round with a combination of horror and pleading as she added, "And he was going to do it again, right here in the woods like an animal." Her head swiveled to the fallen man again and she said miserably. "I could no' let him. I jest could no' bear it, so when I felt his dagger in his belt I—I did no' think, I . . ." Moaning miserably, she lowered her head again. "I jest grabbed it and—"

When she broke off and shook her head miserably, Saidh peered at the man on the ground. She believed Fenella. It was impossible not to after what she'd heard on her way to her bedchamber last night. Saidh had been a little the worse for wear at the time. Her brother Rory had goaded her into a drinking contest after their cousin's wedding feast. Saidh had never much cared for ale or whiskey and her brother knew it. However, she'd also never been able to resist a challenge, especially when it included phrases like "Ye're no afraid, are ye?" or "Ah, ye'd ha'e lost anyway, ye being a lass and all." Both of which he'd used last night when he'd apparently decided it would be fun to drink her under the table.

He'd lost the contest. Saidh had been swaying in her seat, but still upright when Rory had slithered off the bench to land in a heap under the table. She vaguely recalled the cheers and congratulations from the others as she'd got to her feet, then she had staggered away from the table, intent on reaching her room before she too fell to the drink. Her memory became clearer though when she reached the upper landing. With the laughter, chatter and music reduced to a dull roar, she'd paused on the landing as the sound of a woman's screaming had reached her ears.

Frowning, she'd stumbled down the hall toward

the sound, intent on helping whoever it was. Her feet had slowed and then paused altogether however as she'd reached the door. Even in her drunken haze, she'd realized it was the bridal chamber.

Swallowing the drink that tried to rush back up her throat, Saidh had hesitated, unsure what to do. She'd heard that the bedding could be painful the first time, but the screams coming from behind the door had spoken of agony. Surely it should not be this painful? It sounded as if Hammish was killing her poor cousin rather than merely consummating their marriage.

Saidh had raised her hand, intending to knock and check to see that all was well, but then the screaming abruptly ended.

"There," Hammish had grunted with breathless satisfaction, the sound coming muffled through the door, accompanied by a rustling. "Now we're well and truly married. Ye're mine, lass."

When Fenella had sniffled and mumbled something that could have been agreement, Saidh had sighed and turned away from the door to continue on to her own. She'd been grateful to do so. The landing had taken to spinning around her by then and Saidh doubted she would have been much help to Fenella if it had been necessary.

Still, she'd thought as she'd staggered into her room, if she were to judge by Fenella's screams, the bedding must be even more painful than she'd heard it to be and they really should warn a girl. Of course, if they did that, women would be much less eager to be wedded and bedded.

Saidh had just collapsed on the bed when the distant sound of screaming reached her ears again. She'd struggled briefly, trying to sit up, but unconsciousness was already rushing up to claim her, pulling her down into the soft bed with firm, dark hands.

That second round of screaming had been the first thing she'd remembered on rising, so Saidh had been more than relieved to find her cousin alive and well in the morning when she'd gone below to break her fast. Fenella had been pale and quiet, but when Saidh had asked her with concern if she was well, the woman had nodded and ducked her head as color flushed her cheeks. Conran had distracted Saidh then, calling her down to where he and her other brothers sat at the table so Saidh had left Fenella to join them. There was little she could have done for her cousin anyway. She was his wife now and belonged to Hammish as much as his horse, his castle and his sword. Women had little in the way of rights in this world.

MOUTH TIGHTENING AT THAT THOUGHT, SAIDH peered at her cousin with pity and breathed, "They will kill you for this."

"Aye." Fenella turned dead eyes to the prone man beside her and shrugged wearily. "Let them. I'd rather be dead than suffer again what he did to me last night."

Saidh bit her lip and peered to Hammish, the screams she'd heard the night before echoing through her mind. This was the first wedding she'd attended, but surely the breaching did not always cause the agony those screams had suggested. And she knew there was blood during the breaching, but what Fenella described sounded extreme. As for the part about turning her over and taking her in unnatural ways, Saidh knew exactly what her cousin meant. She had been raised with seven brothers after all, and they had taken great delight in telling her things they shouldn't in the hopes of embarrassing or distressing her. What Fenella described sounded like what Geordie called "copulation in the rear." Geordie had also said it was a sin, punishable by a gruesome death by mutilation, hanging or burning at the stake.

In truth, Saidh supposed Fenella had given the church's justice to her husband, and a kinder end than mutilation or burning at the stake. Perhaps even kinder than hanging, although she wasn't sure about that one.

Sighing, she turned back to her cousin and knelt before her again. "If ye tell the priest what he did—"

"Nay!" Fenella cried with alarm. "I could ne'er tell anyone he did that to me. Ever."

"Ye told me," she reminded her gently. "Mayhap—"

"Nay, Saidh. Please." She grasped her hands, squeezing them desperately. "Just kill me. I'll no' fight ye. Just slit me throat. Then ye can say ye found me o'er the body, we fought fer the weapon and ye killed me."

"Oh, Fenella," she said sadly, and pulled her into a hug. "I'll no' do that to ye."

"Ye ha'e to," she wept, clutching at the front of her gown. "Hammish's brother is as cruel as he, he'll no' let this go unpunished. He shall kill me anyway. At least if you do it I ken ye'll no' torture me first. Please, Saidh."

Saidh remained still for a moment, her mind racing. She understood why Fenella would ask it of her, but she simply couldn't do it. Her gaze swept the clearing, and then she released Fenella and straightened. "I ha'e a better idea."

"Nay. Just kill me, Saidh. Please," Fenella cried, scrambling to her feet to follow and then pausing abruptly when Saidh stopped and bent to scoop up a large branch from the ground at the edge of the clearing. It was a good six feet long, one end as big around as a man's arm, the other as small as her wrist. "What are ye doing? This is no time fer a fire."

Saidh turned to face her, took a deep breath and announced, "Ye were set upon by two men when ye got to this clearing. Bandits, poorly dressed, one tall and thin, one short and fat."

"I was?" Fenella asked with a frown, taking a step backward when Saidh stepped toward her.

"Aye. Ye and Hammish were. Other than that ye remember little," she added, raising the log.

"Oh," Fenella breathed, paling.

Saidh steeled herself against the sudden fear in her cousin's eyes and swung her makeshift weapon, catching Fenella in the side of the head. She watched her spin to the side and crumple to fall across her prone husband on the ground, then dropped the log, backed to the edge of the clearing and began to scream.

Chapter 1

"Oh, he's a beauty, Joan," Saidh murmured, peering down at the baby in her arms. Glancing up, she grinned at her friend and added, "Ye've done a fine job here. Cam must be most pleased."

"Aye. We both are," Joan said, beaming, and then her smile turned wry as she added, "Although he was less pleased when I commented that mayhap we should give little Bearnard here a sister."

"What?" Saidh asked on a disbelieving laugh. She knew Joan and Cam had been terrified of her getting with child to begin with, fearing she could die in childbirth. In truth, they'd done everything they could think of to avoid having the precious child she was holding. But now, Joan gave her a crooked smile and shrugged.

"It was not so bad. I survived it without even a hint of trouble so why not?"

Saidh shook her head with amusement and then glanced to the open shutters as a trumpet sounded from the wall.

"It sounds like we have company," Joan murmured.

"Mayhap 'tis Edith," Murine suggested, following when Saidh moved to the window.

"Aye," Saidh murmured as she peered out. She'd been rather surprised that the other girl hadn't been here with her and Murine for the birth. Saidh knew she'd planned to be when last they'd all visited. The four of them had become very close friends since meeting more than a year ago, which was just strange considering the circumstances under which they'd met. Saidh, Edith and Murine had been among more than a dozen women that Campbell Sinclair's mother had invited to the family castle to tempt her son into marrying again. She'd been hoping for a grandchild, but after the death of his first wife in childbirth, Campbell hadn't been the least interested in remarrying. His mother had decided that wouldn't do, and had invited every unbetrothed female she could find to Castle Sinclair in the hopes that one would tempt him to re-enter the matrimonial state. She hadn't warned him of her intentions though, planning for it to be a surprise. She, however, was the one who was surprised when Campbell arrived home with Joan in tow and announced they were married.

Some of the other girls had immediately hated Joan for stealing the man they'd hoped to win. But Saidh, Edith and Murine had ended up being the best of friends with her.

"Nay. It can no' be Edith," Joan announced, drawing Saidh's attention back to the conversation at hand.

"Why not? Did Cam no' invite her?" Saidh asked as she squinted her eyes to better see the traveling party some distance yet away from the castle. They were just specks in the distance at the moment.

"Does he no' like Edith?" Murine asked, offering a finger for the baby Saidh still held to grab on to.

"Oh, aye, he likes all three of you," Joan assured them both. "And he did invite her. But she was delayed and arrived late last night after we all retired."

"Edith is here?" Saidh and Murine said as one, turning to glance at her with surprise.

Joan smiled widely. "Aye. Cam told me when the little one there woke me up with his fussing for a feeding in the middle of the night."

"Well, where is she then?" Saidh asked with a frown.

"And what delayed her?" Murine asked.

"She is presently still abed. As I said, she arrived late," Joan said. "I am sure she will wake up soon, but as for what delayed her—" She paused to glance at the door as a knock sounded. "Come in."

The door opened at once, and Edith rushed in. Excitement coloring her cheeks and a happy smile on her pale face, she hurried to the bed to hug Joan. "Good morn! Sorry, I fear I slept late. But when I went down to break me fast, Cam said ye were awake so I came to see ye and the babe." She straightened and raised an eyebrow expectantly. "So, where is this grand babe Cam was bragging about last night?"

Her gaze swung to the two women by the window when Joan pointed their way. Edith's eyes widened, her smile growing with happiness as she rushed toward them now. "Oh! Saidh! Murine. I am so pleased to see ye both."

She hugged Murine first, but paused when she turned to Saidh and saw the bundle she held in her arms. In the end, she gave her a half hug from the side as she peered down at the baby.

"Oh," Edith breathed, reaching out to take one tiny hand in hers. "He is perfect."

"Do you want to hold him?" Saidh offered.

"Oh. Aye," Edith said eagerly and quickly scooped him from Saidh's arms. She settled him in the crook of her arm and smiled down at the babe, then glanced to Joan and said, "I'm so sorry I missed the birth. I wanted to be here for ye, and I would ha'e been were it no' for Laird MacDonnell."

Saidh raised an eyebrow in question. "What did he do to delay yer journey here?"

Edith grimaced. "He died."

"Oh." Murine looked uncertain as she tried to sort out how the man's death had delayed the other woman's arrival.

"Allen, Laird MacDonnell, is a cousin through our mothers," Edith said on a sigh. "But I think it was only the second or third time I'd seen him in me life and in the normal course o' events I would no' even have heard that he'd died were we not there at MacDonnell when it happened."

Noting the surprised expressions on the women around her, Edith moved to sit on the edge of the bed with Bearnard still in her arms as she explained, "We stopped there to rest on the way here. We only planned to stay the night and leave in the morning to continue our journey, but we woke to the news that he was dead and . . ." She shrugged helplessly.

"We could no' simply say 'sorry to hear that' and then mount up and continue on."

"Nay, of course not," Joan patted her arm reassuringly, letting her know she understood. "How did he die, Edith? Was he an old man?"

"Oh, nay," Edith assured her solemnly. "Allen was only four years older than I."

Saidh's eyebrows rose at this news. She knew Edith was twenty, the same age as herself, which made Allen twenty-four. Definitely not an old man. "Well, then what happened?"

"He drowned," Edith announced with a shake of the head. "Apparently, he liked to go fer a swim in the loch in the morn ere breaking his fast, and that morn . . ." She shrugged helplessly. "He drowned. They do no' ken why. He was by all accounts a fine swimmer, but that morning he just . . .

She grimaced and then explained, "I gather that his first became worried when he had no' returned by the time his lady wife was up to break her fast. Apparently, Allen made it a point always to join her at the table, but that morning he had no' yet returned. When I joined the table, Lady MacDonnell was asking after her husband, wondering why he had not yet arrived and whether she should no' wait fer him ere breaking her fast. His first sent someone to check to see if he was still swimming. The man returned with the laird's body over his horse." She sighed. "It was quite distressing. Aunt Tilda and Allen's lady wife were terribly upset." She shrugged unhappily. "So, as I say, we could no' simply mount up and ride on."

"Nay, and I would not expect you to," Joan said with understanding.

"We decided we should stay fer the funeral, expecting to be delayed a couple days or a week at most, but Aunt Tilda— Well, he was her only son. She decided he should lie in state in the village church fer two weeks so that his villeins and friends could pay their proper respects."

"Two weeks?" Saidh with dismay. "Bloody hell, he must ha'e stunk to high heaven by the time they put him in the ground."

"Oh, they did no' put him in the ground," Edith assured her. "He went in the family vault, and he did no' smell either." She paused briefly and then almost whispered, "They embalmed him."

"What?" Murine asked with amazement. "But the church frowns on that. They say 'tis pagan."

"Oh, aye, but they'll allow it for a fee," Saidh said dryly.

Edith nodded. "Me aunt got special permission to do it."

"Hmmm," Saidh muttered. "So ye stayed fer the funeral?"

"Aye." Edith grimaced. "Although I really wish we hadn't. Lady MacDonnell was inconsolable, but Aunt Tilda was worse. She kept saying that Allen was such a strong swimmer and how could this happen, and then she began looking at Lady MacDonnell as she said it. By the time of the funeral, she was treating Allen's wife most coldly and reminding anyone who would listen that Lady MacDonnell's previous husbands died unnaturally too."

"Did they?" Murine asked with interest and Saidh nearly grinned at her expression. There was nothing that could put color into the woman's cheeks like the possibility of good gossip.

"Apparently," Edith said. "They say her last husband, Laird MacIver, died just a month after they married when he was thrown from his horse. Broke his neck, he did."

"Oh dear," Murine and Joan said together.

"So two husbands dying in accidents," Saidh said dryly. "It does sound a bit suspicious."

"Hmm," Edith murmured in agreement. "But four dead husbands in as many years sounds even worse."

"What?" Murine asked with amazement. "Surely not?"

"Aye. She has been married and widowed four times."

"Well, what happened to the other two husbands?" Saidh asked, her interest now captured. There was nothing like a good murder mystery to pass the day.

"Well, the one before Laird MacIver was his uncle, Laird Connell MacIver. He died in his bed on the wedding night. He was old though," she added quickly. "They said he could no' handle the excitement o' such a young bride."

"Ohhhh," both women crooned with interest.

"And the first husband?" Saidh asked.

"That was Laird Kennedy. He was killed the day after the wedding. Attacked by bandits on their way from her parents' hold, where they'd held the wedding, to the Kennedy stronghold."

Saidh stiffened. "Lady MacDonnell was not born Lady Fenella Fraser?"

"Aye," Edith said with relief, and then smiled wryly and admitted, "For the life o' me I could no' remember her first name once I started to tell ye all what had happened. But that is it: Fenella." She nodded and then grimaced and added, "They are starting to call her the widowmaker though. Which is completely unfair really," she added firmly. "Fenella was with her first husband and injured in the attack that took his life. They found her unconscious and bloodied next to his body. As fer her second husband, the elder Laird MacIver was an ancient old man and everyone said the excitement of the wedding night with such a young bride had surely killed him."

"What of the younger MacIver laird?" Murine asked. "Was there any suspicion that it was no' an accident?"

"O' course there was, but the King sent men to investigate and they determined it was nothing more than an accident. Lady Fenella was entertaining his mother and aunt in the great hall when he left for his ride and the three women were still there when news came that his horse had returned without him. Lady Fenella herself went out with the riding party to find him, pulling his horse behind her own in hopes he could ride back. Of course, he couldn't. He was dead when they found him, his neck broken."

"Still . . ." Joan frowned and pointed out, "My horse threw me as well and that was not an accident. 'Twas a pin in my saddle, puncturing the horse's back so it would throw me."

"Aye, but yer horse went wild and ran madly through the woods the moment ye put yer weight on the beast," Edith pointed out. "By all accounts, Laird MacIver mounted in the bailey and rode out without any difficulties. The horse threw him when he was well into the woods. It could no' have been a pin in the saddle as was done with you."

"Nay, I suppose not," Joan agreed slowly and then shrugged and glanced at Saidh. Her mouth opened as if she meant to say something, but then she paused, her eyebrows rising abruptly. "Is all well, Saidh? You look . . ." She hesitated, apparently unsure how to describe how she looked.

Saidh couldn't blame her, since she wasn't quite sure how she felt. There was a knot in her stomach made up of a combination of emotions. The few she could pick out of that nauseating miasma were dread, fear, and anxiety. Swallowing the bile that seemed lodged in her throat, she forced a smile that failed miserably, shook her head and admitted, "Fenella is me cousin."

"Really?" Edith asked with interest and then grinned. "That means me cousin married yer cousin. We're related."

"Did ye no' ken she was married to the MacDonnell?" Murine asked with a frown.

"Nay," Saidh admitted and then sighed. "In fact, I did no' ken she'd married again at all after Kennedy."

"Not even the Laird MacIver?" Murine asked with amazement.

Saidh shook her head. "We attended her first wedding. In fact, we all traveled together on the way home. Buchanan is on the way to Kennedy land. They left with us the morning after the wedding."

"Ye were with them when Laird Kennedy was killed?" Murine asked almost breathlessly.

Saidh nodded silently.

"But if ye went to her first wedding, surely, ye were invited to the others?" Edith said.

"Nay," Saidh assured her, and then frowned thoughtfully and added, "Well, actually, we may ha'e been. But mother died shortly after Fenella's first wedding, and me eldest brother, Aulay, is laird now and does no' care for large celebrations. He may ha'e just sent a wedding gift with his regrets and neglected to tell the rest o' us about the weddings."

"That is probably it, then," Edith said on a sigh.

Saidh nodded, but her mind was back in a clearing where the Kennedy lay dead and her cousin confessed, *I killed him*.

"Damn."

Saidh glanced around with surprise at that curse from Murine. The woman never cursed. Spotting her by the open shutters, Saidh became aware of the sounds coming from outside. Shouts of greeting were joined by the *clop clop* of what sounded like at least a dozen horses. Curious, she walked over to stand beside Murine and look down at the busy scene below as well. There were not a dozen horses, but at least three dozen, and Joan's husband Cam was greeting a man who was dismounting. If she were to guess by his posture, Cam didn't like the man, which was a concern when the visitor had brought such a large contingent of men with him.

"I do no' recognize the banner," Saidh said with a frown.

"'Tis the Danvries banner," Murine said grimly.

"Yer brother's?" Saidh asked, glancing to the woman with surprise.

"Me half brother," Murine corrected, her voice giving away her contempt. Saidh wasn't surprised. She and Murine had become good friends, and she knew the woman absolutely loathed her half brother.

"Why would Montrose be here?" she asked quietly, afraid she already knew the answer.

"Papa must ha'e died," Murine said, a catch in her voice. Releasing a shuddering sigh, she shook her head and closed her eyes. "He has no' been well fer a while, but had seemed to turn a corner. I felt sure he would recover else I ne'er would have left him to come here."

"Mayhap not," Saidh said, though she suspected Murine was right. Biting her lip, she slipped an awkward arm around the other woman in support. It seemed the thing to do. She knew how much Murine adored her father.

"I suppose I should go below and find out one way or the other," Murine said after a moment.

"I'll come with ye," Saidh offered quietly.

"Thank ye," Murine whispered, and slipped her arm through hers to walk to the door.

GREER HEAVED A SIGH AT THE SOUND OF DISTANT hoof beats, and reluctantly opened his eyes. Through a frame of green leaves from the trees that surrounded the clearing he was reclining in, he could see that the sky was still a bright, pale blue above him with fluffy white clouds drifting slowly by. He took a minute to guess how much time he had before the approaching horse reached him, and then sighed and raised his head to peer down at the blond head bobbing over his groin.

"Ye'd best leave off that now, lass. We're about to ha'e company."

The blond maid removed her mouth from one of his favorite body parts and cast him a pouty look. "But I've jest begun."

"Aye, I ken. Trust me, I ken," he said dryly and sat up to tuck himself away inside his plaid. "But someone is coming, and by me guess ye've just enough time to straighten yer dress ere they arrive."

Clucking under her tongue with irritation, the woman stood and proceeded to pull up the top of her gown, covering the generous breasts he'd worked so hard to uncover. When she then began to struggle with the lacings, Greer stood to help. He finished with the task just moments before his squire, Alpin, rode into the clearing and brought his pony to a shuddering halt.

"Me laird," the boy cried, nearly throwing himself off his mount in his eagerness.

Greer reached out a hand to steady the boy and simply waited. Everything was a crisis with his new young squire and Greer had quickly learned not to let the boy's excitement raise his own.

"Lady Fenella sent me to find ye," the boy blurted. "She was wondering where ye are."

"O' course she was," Greer said dryly. He had arrived at MacDonnell only a week ago, just in time for his cousin's funeral. But it had quickly become obvious that the late laird's widow was a pain in the arse. She was forever weeping and whining and moping about the castle like some tragic ghost. And most often she wanted someone to weep and whine at. Since his Aunt Tilda was as good as accusing the woman of killing her son, and everyone here was keeping their distance until they sorted out what way the grass lay, he was the only one who had even spoken to her this last week. The woman had promptly decided he was her ally and had begun to trail him around like some poor starved puppy looking for a new home. In fact, that was why Greer had found Milly, pulled her up on his mount and slipped away from the keep. He'd been looking for a bit of respite.

His gaze slid to the maid, noting that her nipples were still erect and poking at the soft cloth of her worn gown. Seeing that he was looking, she ran one hand up her stomach to catch and briefly cup one round globe through the cloth, then licked her lips. The action made Greer's still erect cock throb under his plaid and he caught her by the arm to urge her away from Alpin and his horse, saying over his shoulder. "Tell her ye could no' find me."

"But what about the guests?"

Greer stopped walking and closed his eyes on a sigh. Guests. Of course there were guests now too. As if half the country hadn't just left after sticking about for two weeks and nearly eating MacDonnell out of its stores. Some stragglers were arriving too late to attend the funeral, but would still demand food and housing for the night at least. And as the new laird, he would be expected to greet and welcome them.

Milly's small hand closing around his cock brought his eyes open and down to see that she was standing sideways to him, her position hiding from Alpin that she had her right hand under his plaid. Greer groaned as her hand slid the length of his erection, and then rose its length again.

"Tell them ye could no' find me," Greer repeated in a growl as the maid pressed her breasts against his arm and repeated the gloving action with her hand.

"But—"

"Go!" Greer roared, his hips jerking involuntarily under Milly's attention. Trying for a calmer voice, he added, "I'll be back soon."

Alpin released a most put-upon sigh. The sound was followed though by a rustle that was probably the boy remounting his pony, and then the soft *clop clop* of the animal trotting out of the clearing.

Milly immediately dropped to her knees in the grass and ducked her head under his plaid to lay claim to the erection she'd been so eagerly fondling. Greer groaned and grabbed her head through the plaid for balance as she clasped his hips in her hands and began to move her mouth lustily over his organ.

Damn, the woman had some serious skill, he thought vaguely and then stopped thinking and gave himself up to the pleasure. Within moments he was roaring with release as he spilled himself down her throat.

"WHAT WAS THAT?"

Saidh shook her head at Murine's nervous question and reined in her mare, aware that the entire traveling party had done the same. Murine's brother's soldiers were all halted and peering warily into the woods around them, seeking the source of that pained shout.

"Ye do no' think Laird MacDonnell's ghost now walks these woods, do ye?" Murine asked worriedly and Saidh glanced to her with surprise.

"Nay. Of course no'. Do no' be silly, Murine," she said. Good Lord, she had enough on her plate without worrying about ghosties and goblins in the woods around the castle she was about to stay in.

If she stayed. Saidh added the thought grimly. It was not as if she had been invited. In fact, Fenella didn't even know she was coming. But after learning that Murine's brother, Montrose Danvries, was indeed at Sinclair to inform Murine that her father was dead and to take her to his home in England, Saidh had found herself asking if she might accompany them as far as the MacDonnell keep. Even she had been surprised by the words when they'd slid from her lips.

She'd been more surprised, though, when Montrose had agreed readily to the request. The man was an ass, selfish and dissolute. He rarely did anything that he did not gain from. But it had become quickly obvious that he had hoped to gain something after all. He'd apparently expected that she would be so grateful for his escort that she'd allow him liberties. Saidh had set him straight on that quickly with a move her brothers had taught her—she'd kneed him in the place it hurt a man worst. He hadn't spoken to her since.

"Do ye think Laird MacDonnell's death was an accident?" Murine asked quietly as the party started forward again.

"I do no' ken," Saidh said wearily. It was the question that had plagued her this entire journey.

"Do ye think someone may be murdering yer cousin's husbands?"

Saidh glanced at Murine with surprise. "What?"

"Well, she has lost four husbands in as many years. The king's men obviously do no' think she killed the first three, but now there is a fourth. Mayhap someone else is doing the killing. Mayhap she has a jealous admirer who wants her fer himself and is killing her husbands."

Saidh considered that as they rode forward. She almost hoped it was true. Because if it wasn't . . .

The king's men may have decided that Fenella was innocent and she could understand that. Fenella had not been alone when Laird MacIver the younger had been tossed from his mount and broken his neck. She was in fact with his family members, a perfect alibi. As for the senior Laird MacIver, he had been extremely old and might well have died from all the excitement of bedding a much younger and beautiful bride. But Saidh knew something the king's men did not know, and that was that Fenella had definitely killed her first husband. And knowing that cast suspicion on all of the men's deaths in Saidh's mind. She needed to find out for herself if

Fenella had had anything to do with the deaths of the Lairds MacIver senior and junior, and Laird MacDonnell. Because if she had, Saidh had saved her cousin that day at the expense of three men who otherwise would surely be alive today. Their blood would be on her hands.

The thought made her mouth tighten grimly as she followed Montrose's mount out of the woods and along the dirt lane toward the castle gate. She would find the answer, but after that she had no idea what she would do. Or even what she could do. If her cousin was killing men, was there anything she could do to stop her? Nothing that wouldn't include admitting her collusion in the death of Laird Kennedy. She may not have killed the man, but she had lent her aid in concealing who the murderer was. What kind of punishment was she likely to be dealt for that?

The question left Saidh in an unhappy silence as they reined in and dismounted at the foot of the stairs to the castle. A servant led them up the steps and through the keep door, explaining with a pained expression that, unable to find the laird, they had sent for Lady MacDonnell, who would surely greet them soon. He'd barely finished making those apologetic explanations when a soft rustle and the patter of footsteps drew their attention to the older lady descending the stairs. Allen MacDonnell's mother, was Saidh's guess as she looked over the still attractive woman. Certainly, it wasn't her cousin.

"Lord Danvries." Tilda MacDonnell smiled sadly as she crossed the great hall to greet them. " 'Tis a pleasure to see ye again. I trust ye found yer sister?"

"Yes. Thank you," Danvries said, his voice for once quiet and respectful rather than the bluff and arrogant booming sound it normally was. Turning, he gestured toward Murine and added, "This is my sister, Lady Murine Carmichael, of clan Carmichael."

"My dear," Lady MacDonnell took Murine's hand and clasped it gently in both her own. "I was sorry to hear o' yer father's death. It seems Scotland has lost two good men in short order."

"Aye," Murine murmured, her eyes glazing with the tears that had filled them every time someone had brought up her father since she'd learned of his death.

Lady MacDonnell hugged Murine briefly, and then stepped back, dashing tears from her own eyes before turning to include Saidh in her smiling welcome. "And is this another sister perhaps, or—"

"Ah, no," Montrose interrupted with a grimly satisfied smile that Saidh didn't understand until he added, "This is Lady Saidh Buchanan, and the reason we stopped again on our way home. She is a cousin and dear friend of Lady Fenella's and begged my escort so that she might see her cousin and offer comfort."

Saidh's mouth tightened at the bit about begging his escort. She'd never begged for anything in her life, and it had actually been Murine who had asked if they couldn't escort her to MacDonnell on the way home. Her irritation with Montrose was forgotten though when she noted that Lady MacDonnell's smile had frozen. In the next moment it dropped away altogether like so much ice slipping from an overhang to crash to the ground.

Face pale and eyes cold, she nodded stiffly at Saidh. "Ye will find yer cousin in her room. It is the third door on the left once ye reach the top o' the stairs."

Saidh hesitated, wanting to offer her condolences but suspecting they wouldn't be welcome. She had obviously been dismissed and was no longer welcome in the woman's presence, something Montrose was enjoying greatly, she noted with disgust.

Ignoring the man, Saidh murmured a quiet "thank ye" to Lady MacDonnell and turned to cross the great hall to the stairs.

Saidh didn't encounter anyone on her way up. Once outside the door Lady MacDonnell had said was Fenella's, she paused and listened, but heard no sound from within. Straightening her shoulders, she knocked sharply and waited for the softly uttered "Come in" before opening the door and stepping into the room.

It took one look to tell Saidh that this was not the master bedchamber where Laird MacDonnell and his bride would have slept. It seemed Fenella had already been moved to a lesser room and probably the lesser of the lesser rooms was Saidh's guess. The chamber was tiny, with barely enough space for the single bed and the hard wooden chair that sat in the corner. There was no fireplace at all which would make it a damned cold room in winter.

If she were to guess, Allen's mother had selected this room for Fenella and it appeared her cousin had not argued the point. But then Saidh supposed her cousin's position here was now probably rather precarious. She was no longer the Laird's wife, and had produced no heir to earn her any position in the household. Lady MacDonnell obviously had more power than her.

"Saidh?"

That bewildered, almost hopeful whisper drew her gaze to the woman on the bed and Saidh's eyebrows rose. This was not the sweet, round and rosy-faced Fenella she recalled from five years earlier. It was not even the pale, round Fenella from the morning after her wedding. This woman was thin to the point of emaciated, her face wan, and eyes red with recent and repeated tears.

"Oh, Saidh!" Fenella lunged off the bed and threw her arms around her in a hard, hungry hug of desperation. "Oh, thank God. A friendly face. I have missed ye so. What am I to do? Me husband is dead. I loved Allen so. I thought surely this time I would be allowed to live happily with him. How could he go and die on me like that? I am being punished, am I no'? God is punishing me fer Kennedy. I—"

Saidh silenced her cousin by covering her mouth. Her gaze moved warily to the door as she replayed Fenella's words in her mind and wondered how much she'd given away . . . and who might have heard.

Easing Fenella away, Saidh raised a finger to her lips and slipped quickly back to the door to ease it open. When a quick glance in both directions along the hall showed it to be empty, she let her breath out on a little hiss of relief and eased the door closed again.

Chapter 2

"*B*LOODY HELL," GREER MUTTERED AS HE RODE through the castle gates and saw the horses and men filling his bailey. There were a good thirty or forty soldiers that he could see, and English soldiers at that. It looked like a bloody invasion party, he thought, and then recognized the banner they rode under and grimaced with disgust. Montrose Danvries had returned, he realized. No doubt the man was on his return journey from collecting his sister. He probably hoped to spend another night at Mac-Donnell, eating his food and sleeping in one of the guest rooms. Greer just hoped it would only be one night this time. He didn't like the man.

Bringing his horse to a halt just inside the gates, he caught his arm around Milly's waist and lifted her off his mount, leaning to the side to set her down.

"Enter around the back o' the castle," he instructed. "I would ha'e a word with these men and I think it best they not see ye."

Milly nodded quickly and moved along the castle

wall toward the cover of the stables. Greer waited until he saw her disappear behind the building un-molested, then straightened and urged his mount forward. He had nearly reached the back of the widespread group of men and horses when he spot-ted Alpin and the stable master at the front of the group, talking with one of the Englishmen. There was no sign of his first, Bowie, though.

"Alpin," he barked.

The squire glanced around, then beamed with relief and rushed to his side as he dismounted.

"What the devil are all these Englishmen doing cluttering me bailey? And where is Bowie?"

"Bowie is inside with yer aunt and Lord Danvries, and these are Lord Danvries' men, me laird," Alpin said, and then allowing some exasperation to show through, added, "I did try to tell ye that we had com-pany approaching the castle. The men on the wall saw them some distance off and when they heard Lady Fenella had sent me to look fer ye, told me to tell ye about them as well . . . but ye would no' let me."

Greer considered reminding the lad, yet again, on how he was to speak to his betters, but then decided he couldn't be bothered just then. There were other issues of more import. "Do no' tell me that Lady MacDonnell has invited that blasted man to stop o'er again?"

"All right. I'll no' tell ye that," Alpin said with a shrug, and then added with some satisfaction, "But she did. Which ye might ha'e prevented had ye trou-bled yerself to return to the castle with me rather than throwing up Millie's skirts like ye were still a warrior fer hire and no' a laird now."

"Ye go too far, lad," Greer growled. "And one o' these days ye'll be sorry fer it."

Alpin did not look the least concerned. He merely shrugged and turned to walk back toward the stable, but Greer collared the boy and dragged him back. "Tell the stable master to do the best he can by the horses. Then ha'e Bowie settle as many men as he can in the barracks with our men. Send the rest into the keep. They can sleep in the great hall as they did last time. But tell Bowie to post more guards. I do no' trust Danvries."

"Aye," Alpin said with distaste. "The man's a skeevy whoreson."

Greer scowled at the lad with surprise. "Where the devil did ye learn to talk like that?"

"From you," Alpin said dryly and then turned and moved back toward the stable master and Bowie, who Greer saw was now there as well.

Shaking his head, Greer led his horse to the stables himself to tend the beast. The stable master would have enough on his plate trying to find places to put the English horses without having to tend his horse. Besides, Greer had no great desire to see Danvries again. In fact, he was wishing that he'd stayed in the woods for the rest of the day and night. Or that he'd returned earlier and had the gate closed on Danvries and his men ere they'd reached it.

"I'm sorry," Fenella breathed. Fresh tears were pooling in her eyes and she was wringing her hands miserably as she shook her head. "I am no' thinking straight. I ha'e no' done so since Allen's death. He was such a wonderful man, Saidh. Ye would ha'e liked him. He was so kind, and gentle and sensitive. He had the servants cut flowers fer me every other day and place them in me room."

She turned to gesture to several arrangements of dry and dead flowers along one wall of the room. Saidh supposed she'd had them brought from the master chamber when she'd been moved here.

"And he bought me the most expensive fabrics and lovely jewels," Fenella continued, turning back to her. "But best of all, he was just so sweet. He could tell I was terrified on our wedding night, and rather than force me to endure the consummation, he gentled me and told me it was all right, he would no' trouble me for his rights, ever. That I was free of them altogether if I wished. But if I came to desire to have children, I need only let him ken and we would do whatever I wished to accomplish it."

The tears in her eyes spilled over now, rushing down her cheeks in rivulets. "There can no' be another man as sweet and good as Allen in all of Scotland and England combined. And now he is gone." The last word was a long mournful cry and Fenella threw herself against Saidh to burst into another round of heart-wrenching sobs.

Saidh stood still for a moment, but then raised her hands to awkwardly pat her cousin's back. The woman had taken her completely by surprise. She had come here suspecting her of having turned into some sort of madwoman, bent on killing her husbands. Instead, she found a woman who truly seemed to be in deep mourning for a husband she appeared to have loved a great deal. Saidh didn't think anyone could be such a good actress to feign this distress.

Saidh remained standing there, rubbing Fenella's back until the woman's sobs gentled to soft sighs and hiccups, then urged her to sit on the side of the bed with her and took her hands in her own.

"What happened?" she asked quietly. "Until the other day I had no idea ye'd e'en married again, and then I learned ye've remarried three times since Kennedy, and each has died. What happened?"

Fenella blinked at her through red-rimmed eyes. "How could ye no' ken? I invited ye to each wedding."

"Did ye?" Saidh asked and frowned, realizing that she had probably hit the nail on the head when she'd suggested that Aulay may have received invitations and simply sent his regrets without mentioning it to her or her other brothers. She would have to have a talk with her brother about that when she returned to Buchanan. She understood that he disliked public affairs, but that did not mean she would not have wanted to attend. Okay, so she probably wouldn't have wanted to attend. Saidh hated feasts and weddings almost as much as Aulay, but still, it would have been nice to know her cousin was marrying . . . again and again.

"Aulay," Fenella said suddenly on a sigh, her thoughts obviously having run along the same lines as Saidh's. "I should ha'e realized he no' only would no' attend, but would no' bother to mention the events to the rest o' ye. Is he still so very self-conscious about his scars?"

"Aye," Saidh admitted quietly. Aulay had always

been a bright and happy lad, and had grown into a brave and handsome warrior the women had all fawned over . . . until the battle that had killed their father. Aulay had returned from the battle-field scarred in spirit and body, his handsome face halved by a sword blow that had nearly killed him. While his wounds had healed, he had yet to recover his outgoing and easy personality and Saidh began to fear he never would. Shaking away her worries about that, she squeezed Fenella's hands. "Tell me. I hear ye married Laird MacIver after Kennedy. How did that come to pass?"

"The king," Fenella said unhappily. "Old MacIver was a friend o' his and wanted me to wife so the king ordered it six months after I was widowed." She gri-maced with distaste and said, "I did no' want to marry again after what Kennedy did to me, but I had no choice. Me best hope at the time was that the MacIver was so old he could no' manage his husbandly duties."

"And was he?" Saidh asked, watching her face.

Fenella grimaced. "He tried. He huffed and grunted on top o' me fer a bit, trying to manage the deed, but then rolled off with a sigh and went to sleep. At least I thought he was sleeping and I went to sleep too. It was no' til morn that I realized aught was amiss. He was gray and cold and I realized I'd been sleeping with a corpse."

Saidh bit her lip to keep from saying "Ewwww." She was trying to work out what to ask next, when Fenella continued.

"Of course, then the king decided I should marry MacIver's nephew. It seemed a shame, he said, to let

a pretty young lass like me whither away fer want o'
a husband. But the truth was, the nephew was leering at me all through the wedding feast and I suspect the king saw it and decided to pass me down
to the nephew along with the keep and lands," she
said bitterly.

"The king attended yer wedding?" Saidh asked
to change the subject.

"He attended both weddings. MacIvers have
always been supporters of his and he wanted to
keep it that way," she said grimly.

"So ye married the younger MacIver," Saidh
prompted.

"Aye."

When she didn't continue, Saidh prompted, "And
how was he to husband? Was he kind?"

Fenella sighed and shrugged miserably. "He was
all right. At least he was young and healthy and
did no' stink like his uncle. But he was nothing like
Allen. He did want his husbandly rights," she said
unhappily, and then glanced up and confessed, "I
fear after Kennedy, I was afraid o' the marital bed.
The older MacIver did no' seem to notice, and I was
so scared I just lay still and waited fer the pain and
humiliation to start so was surprised when it was
so clumsy and . . ." She shrugged helplessly, as if
unsure how to phrase it and finally said, "Limp."

"Anyway," she muttered, her cheeks now flushed
with a bright blush. "The younger MacIver did no'
ha'e the same issue. He tried to go gently and slow,
but he did insist on his marital rights. And he was
nothing like Allen."

"Ye said that," Saidh murmured quietly.

"Well, 'tis true. Gordon MacIver was kind enough, but he was no' nearly as thoughtful and sweet as Allen. And the man was horse crazy. He was always off riding on that stallion o' his. I was no' surprised when he fell off the stupid beast and broke his neck. And I did no' grieve overly much," she confessed almost apologetically. "At least no' at first. But then when the king sent his men to investigate and I realized that they thought I had something to do with his death . . ."

"I am sure he did no' really think that," Saidh said quickly. "No doubt he was just making certain no one could raise questions later."

"Aye, mayhap," Fenella said dubiously and then shrugged. "Anyway, I was widowed again and stuck at MacIver. Gordon had died without an heir, but the king waited to see if I carried one. However, when my woman's time came and I told him that I was definitely not with child, he passed the title and estate to a second cousin of Gordon's or some such thing."

"And then the king arranged fer yer marriage to Allen?" Saidh asked.

Fenella shook her head. "No' at first. Fer a while I was allowed to return home to Fraser. I think he hoped people would forget about me first three husbands' dying," she admitted with a grimace. "But then Allen asked Father fer me hand in marriage, and he was all too eager to hand me o'er."

She sighed, and slipped her hand from Saidh's to fret at the fur on the bed. "At first, I was furious. I really did no' want to marry again," she admitted sadly. "I did no' ken Allen and how kind he was, and Mother pretty much had to drag me down fer the wedding ceremony. But in the end . . . he was the most wonderful man." She smiled gently, and then her smile faded and a new bout of tears welled up in her eyes. "But now he's dead too, and everyone is sure I somehow did it, when I was nowhere near the loch. I can no' swim, Saidh, ye ken that. I ne'er went near the loch. And I loved him, I would ne'er ha'e killed him. God is surely punishing me fer what I did. He gave me Allen just to take him away as punishment fer killing Hammish."

"Hush," Saidh hissed, glancing fretfully toward the door. Her cousin was going to get herself hanged for murder at this rate. Standing up, she urged Fenella to lift her legs onto the bed, saying, "Here. Why do ye no' rest fer a bit, hmmm? We can talk later."

Fenella sniffled and nodded and curled up on the bed, but when Saidh straightened to move away, she caught her hand, her eyes almost feverish with panic. "Ye'll be here when I wake up, will ye no'? Ye'll no' leave me?"

Saidh hesitated. Now that she was sure that Fenella had not killed her husbands, and she was sure, she would have rather gone on home than stay. But she couldn't say that to Fenella. The woman was obviously desperate for a friendly face. Besides, if she didn't stay to see her through this, the woman was likely to blurt her confessions about Hammish to someone else. Fenella needed her here.

"Aye. I'll be below stairs when ye wake. I'll no' leave MacDonnell," she assured her solemnly.

"Thank ye, Saidh. Ye ha'e always been there when I needed ye," Fenella said huskily.

Saidh merely nodded and then slipped free of her grip and headed for the door, murmuring, "Sleep well."

"OF COURSE, WE SHALL LEAVE IN THE MORN. However, 'tis up to ye as to whether Saidh leaves with us. It would be little trouble to escort her home to Buchanan if ye wish her gone, Lady MacDonnell. It is not far out of our way and 'tis the least we can do when you were kind enough to put us up on our way to collect Murine and now on our way back."

Greer just managed not to roll his eyes at Danvries's words. As far as he could tell, the man had left Tilda little choice but to put him and his men up either time. On his way north, the man had stopped, claiming he'd heard the news of Allen's death on his journey and had felt compelled to stop and offer his condolences since he had suffered a loss as well.

Of course, Tilda had been touched and sympathetic to the loss of Laird Carmichael. Misery loves company, after all. But once the lady had retired and Montrose Danvries had been in his cups, he'd shown that he had little love for his stepfather and held nothing but bitterness and resentment for the man. Mostly, it seemed because the Laird had not left Carmichael along with all its riches to him. Instead, the title of laird and the castle and land had gone to an actual Carmichael and a Scot.

Imagine that, Greer thought dryly and knew the greedy, grasping Englishman didn't care about the title or the people and had only been interested in the wealth he would have gained. No doubt Laird Carmichael had known that too.

"Oh, 'tis no' me place to decide if she stays or no'. Greer is laird here now," Tilda said quietly.

Greer stiffened at the words. It was the first time his aunt had actually deferred to him. Since he'd arrived she had been acting as lady of the manor and deciding everything as if she still ran MacDonnell. And, much to Alpin's disgust, Greer had let her. He wasn't sure why that upset Alpin, and couldn't even actually say why he had, or why the fact that she was now passing the baton of leadership on to him alarmed him, but he could see that he was not the only one surprised. If he were to judge by Danvries's face, the man had had no idea that the title and land had passed to him now. For some reason, his dismay made Greer want to smile.

Catching movement out of the corner of his eye, Greer glanced toward the stairs to see a woman descending. Short in stature, and curvy all over under the dark green gown she wore, she seemed almost to float down the stairs rather than actually tread on them. His gaze slid over the cascade of wild, dark curls around her heart-shaped face, and then found bow lips and bright green eyes and he felt his breath leave him.

The woman very much resembled the phantom lover he'd imagined in his youth as he'd lain abed at night, fiddling with himself under the furs. It brought memories to his mind of imagining her riding astride him, her head thrown back in ecstasy, long hair tumbling over her shoulders and half covering her bobbing breasts as he'd thrust up into her once, twice and then a final third time before his excitement had outstripped him. At that age, even his imagined lovemaking had been swiftly over. Fortunately, he'd improved much since then. At least Greer liked to think so. However, watching his dream woman reach the bottom of the stairs and start across the hall toward them, he wondered if he would do much better with her in the flesh than he had with her in his boyhood dreams.

"Here is Lady Saidh now."

Greer's eyes narrowed at his aunt's announcement. So this was the woman who was kin to Fenella and who Montrose Danvries had used as an excuse to stop on his journey home. And he was to decide whether she should be allowed to stay, or go.

"She stays," he growled and stood abruptly to leave the table.

"Greer? Where are ye going?" his lady aunt asked with surprise. She also sounded a little wounded that he would abandon her, but Greer didn't slow. He couldn't slow. He was now sporting a log under his plaid bigger than the one Milly had raised in the woods. If just looking at the woman caused that, he shuddered to think what her actually speaking might do to him. He needed to get away . . . and take care of the beast poking at his plaid. Maybe Milly could help with that. He could take her from behind, close his eyes and pretend it was Lady Saidh Buchanan he was thrusting into.

Just the thought made his cock harden further, pulling the skin painfully tight and squeezing his balls uncomfortably. Hell, he thought as he rushed out of the keep. Mayhap he should have said nay to the woman staying. She was a lady after all, not someone he could use for his pleasure and send on her way like the camp followers and Millys of the world.

Speaking of Milly, he thought wryly as she suddenly appeared before him, hands on hips, breasts thrust forward and a leering smile on her face.

"Me laird," she breathed, moving close and searching the front of his plaid until she latched onto his erection. Her eyes widened incredulously. "Oooooh, someone is in need o' me care."

She rose up on tiptoe to kiss him, but Greer found himself pulling back. She must have eaten onions since he'd seen her last for her breath was most unpleasant. And her face was dirty, he noted. She had dark smudges on her chin, her cheek and her forehead. Her hair was none too clean either, not flowing soft around her cheeks like Lady Saidh's, but hanging limp to her shoulders. The only good thing was that the combination was having a calming effect on his body. Rather than a log fit for the fire, he now had half that and still shrinking.

"What's the matter?" Milly asked with a frown.

"Nothing," he assured her, gently disengaging her hand from his body. "There is something I need to do is all. We'll talk later, lass."

Greer patted her shoulder and then headed to the stables to retrieve his horse. A nice dip in the loch sounded just the thing to finish cooling his blood. It would also have the added benefit of cleaning him up in case he was as filthy as Milly. After years of marching dusty trails, sleeping in muddy clearings, and tossing up the skirts of equally filthy lightskirts and camp followers as a warrior for hire, Greer was used to being dirty. But things had changed. He no longer needed to wield his sword to earn a meal and a place to sleep. He was a laird now with a castle, a bed and a bath. Perhaps he should start using that bath, sleeping in his bed, and acting like the laird he now was. Perhaps then he could woo and win a lady wife as sweet and delicate as Lady Saidh.

"BLOODY HELL!" SAIDH MUTTERED, YANKING THE brush viciously through her hair. She was not a morning person, and the love-hate relationship with her hair was due probably partially to her lack of patience when she woke. Actually, she supposed, her relationship with her hair was mostly hate with little room for love. In truth, she'd be happy to cut it all off if it wouldn't shock and horrify everyone from her brothers to the priest. Although, she supposed her brothers might not care. Most of them would have shaved their heads ages ago if Aulay wouldn't have a fit about it, and for the same reason. They had all inherited their mother's completely unmanageable hair—a thick, nasty, curly mess that seemed to knot the moment she finished unknotting it with the brush she was using.

Sighing with vexation, she gave up and tossed her brush across the room. It hit the wall and fell to the floor with a clatter that she ignored as she quickly began to lace her gown. She really should have a maid to tend to all of this, and in the not too distant past she'd had one, but shortly after leaving Sinclair last year, her maid, who had also been her nurse-maid before that, had taken ill and died. Aulay had not bothered to replace her, and Saidh had not asked him to. Partly because she had known and loved the woman for so long that she was irreplaceable, and partly because she was relieved not to have a maid harassing her at every turn, chasing her with a hair-brush, and grousing at her to wash her face, take a bath, and "Dear God, at least *try* to be a lady."

Saidh was not a good lady. She was not the most horrible one either. She could talk like one and walk like one when the need arose, but the truth was, she'd rather not. She'd grown up with seven broth-ers who had treated her like just another boy, and after having enjoyed that freedom for most of her life, she tended to resent losing it to ladylike ways when in public. That was why she didn't mind by-passing all the feasts and celebrations they were invited to. In fact, Fenella's first wedding was the last such public occasion she'd attended, and she'd gotten herself in trouble with the drinking game she and her brothers had held. Her mother had lectured her about behavior befitting a lady all the way home to Buchanan.

Saidh sighed as she finished with her lacings. That had been the last lecture her mother had given her before she'd died. She'd insisted she shouldn't join in drinking games, shouldn't share ribald jokes with her brothers, and shouldn't be wearing that "bloody" sword her brother Aulay had paid the blacksmith to make for her.

That thought drew her gaze to the chest at the foot of the bed where the specially made sword rested nestled in amongst her clothes. Saidh had not worn it since her mother's death, but wondered if she might not now. She wanted to go for a ride down to the loch, and it did seem that if she were going alone she should take the sword with her for protection. Especially with Montrose Danvries still here. If the man caught her alone she would not put it past him to try to punish her for kneeing him so efficiently in the ballocks. By her guess, the fact that she was Murine's friend would matter little to him. The man was a pig and Saidh felt nothing but regret that the girl was now going to have to live with the bastard in England. She also didn't understand how the late Laird Carmichael could neglect to make provisions for her in his will. No dower, nothing. He'd left the land and title to some cousin, and left her to the mercies of her half brother.

Shocking, really, Saidh decided grimly, especially since Murine had worshipped the man. She'd loved her father dearly, and mourned his passing with every bit of flesh in her body. Murine did not even resent him for not taking care of her in his will, saying only that he probably had thought she would be married and well cared for by the time he died.

Shaking her head, Saidh walked to the chest, opened it and pulled out the sword and the leather sheath and belt the blacksmith had also made for her. She would do her best to hide it in the folds of her skirt until she was out of sight of the castle.

The great hall was full of sleeping men when Saidh made her way below. Most of them were Danvries soldiers, she noted as she crept through their midst, headed for the keep doors. The sun was just beginning to peek up over the horizon when she stepped outside. Saidh was up early. She hadn't slept well last night. Actually most of yesterday after arriving here had not gone well. Laird Mac-Donnell had got up and marched out before she'd even reached the trestle tables, and while Murine had talked to her in the subdued tones she'd been using since learning of her father's death, Lady Mac-Donnell had been noticeably silent, and Montrose had alternated between smug and leering smiles. As for Fenella, after begging Saidh to stay, the woman had not even made an appearance.

Saidh had been relieved when the meal was over and she could escape above stairs to check on her cousin. That was when she'd learned that Fenella and Lady MacDonnell had had words shortly before Saidh and the Danvries party had arrived. Apparently, insults had been exchanged and then Lady MacDonnell had outright accused Fenella of being to blame for her son's death. Fenella now refused to come below and intended to remain in her room for the indefinite future.

Saidh had thought rather irritably that her cousin could have told her that before she'd agreed to stay. Why was she staying if Fenella was going to remain locked up in her room? Before she could work up a good head of steam over that, though, Fenella had started to sob on her shoulder again about the loss of her dear Allen and how God was punishing her for the sin of murdering her first husband.

While she had a very sympathetic soul, Saidh was not given to the vapors and weeping all over everyone. She was more the stiff-upper-lip-and-get-on-with-it type, so had no idea how to handle Fenella. Aside from which, the woman had only been married to Allen for a matter of weeks. Surely that was not long enough to have grown so attached that his death should cause this much distress? Saidh suspected that rather than weeping out of any real caring for Allen, Fenella was reacting more to how this would affect her life. Burying four husbands would make any man think twice—or ten times—about risking marriage to her. She may never be married again. Which meant she would be here at MacDonnell, dependent on the MacDonnell family for the rest of her days, unless she went home, which she had morosely told Saidh last night was impossible. Her father had told her on leaving with Allen that she was not welcome back should he die, so she'd best see he lived a long while.

Saidh wasn't sure if her uncle had meant what he said, or if he'd begun to suspect something was amiss with her husbands' deaths, but Fenella was sure he meant it. And since Allen's mother detested her and suspected her of having something to do with her son's death, and since the new laird appeared to be—and according to Fenella was—absent most of the time, staying here would surely not be a pleasant life for her.

Knowing that, Saidh hadn't a clue what to say to soothe the girl and had been relieved when she'd finally been allowed to remove herself from her cousin and find her own bed in the chamber Lady MacDonnell had given her for her stay. She hadn't known whether to be grateful to the woman for giving her the large, luxuriously furnished room she had slept in last night, or whether she should be offended on Fenella's behalf that her room was not nearly as pleasant. So Saidh had tossed and turned most of the night, her cousin's words playing through her head.

While the castle was asleep, the stable master was up and preparing Danvries's horses for the day's journey. Saidh shooed him back to his work when he moved toward her to see what she needed. She then saddled her own mare and led her out of the stables before mounting.

A quick word with one of the men at the gate pointed her in the right direction, and Saidh soon found her way to the loch where Allen had drowned. Finding a clearing, she reined in and simply sat staring out over the water, soaking in the beauty of the spot. She could certainly understand why Allen had liked to swim here on most mornings. It was serene and beautiful.

It was also the perfect place for a lover's tryst, Saidh thought idly as she watched the rising sun begin to dapple the water with light. She'd barely had the thought when a dark circle appeared on the surface of the loch. It then rose slowly, revealing the furry black head and shoulders of some unholy beast she'd never heard existed in Scotland. Heart stuttering in her chest and eyes wide, Saidh reached for her sword.

Chapter 3

SAIDH RELEASED A LITTLE SIGH, AND ALLOWED her sword to slip back into its sheath as the beast continued toward shore and the water dropped, revealing the most beautiful chest she'd ever seen.

Not fur but hair, she realized as the man lifted his hands out of the water to push the hair back off his face. Finding that less than satisfactory in freeing him from the clingy wet strands, he dipped his head back and let the water do the work for him so that when he straightened again, his hair was slicked back and running down his back rather than over his face and shoulders.

Laird MacDonnell. Saidh recognized him at once now that his face was no longer cloaked in wet hair. She eyed him as he continued forward, the water dropping inch by delicious inch to reveal more of his chest, then his stomach and then—

"Are ye just going to sit there gawking at me?"

Saidh blinked at that question, and forced her eyes back up to his face. The man had stopped walking and now eyed her with amusement, his hands disappearing into the water to prop on his hips below the surface. Shifting a bit in the saddle, she gave what she hoped was an indifferent shrug. "I've seven brothers. It's nothing I ha'e no' seen before."

Which was true, she assured herself. Although, truth be told, she'd never been as interested in seeing what lay beneath the water when it had come to her brothers. And she'd never found herself as breathless as one of those simpering ladies she detested just at the sight of one of their chests.

"I'm no' yer brother," the MacDonnell said dryly. "And a lady would turn her back."

"I'm no' a lady," Saidh responded without thinking, and then clucked under her tongue as she heard her own words and quickly dismounted and turned her back to the lake. It nearly killed her to remain that way, though, as she heard the splashing of water and movement behind her. Saidh so wanted to turn and take a peek at the man in all his glory as he finished coming out of the lake.

"Which is so unladylike," she lectured herself under her breath. Her mother would be most disappointed in her, she knew.

"What is so unladylike?"

Saidh stiffened at the amused question from very close behind her. She instinctively started to turn, but her mother's voice in her head made her stop. Sighing, Saidh shrugged in a way she hoped appeared nonchalant, and confessed, "I am. Or so me mother always told me." Wry amusement filling her voice now, she admitted, "I fear being raised with so many brothers made me less o' a lady than I should be. Me mother did her best to rein me in, but me father and brothers were o' little help in the endeavor and in the end . . ." She shrugged. "She was fighting a losing battle."

"Ye seem ladylike enough to me."

The voice had moved away again and she could hear the rustle of material. He had no doubt laid out his plaid on the ground and was now crouched beside it, pleating the cloth in preparation of donning it. At least that was her guess, and she imagined him in her mind's eye doing so, the rising sun glinting off his wide back. Shaking her head to remove the image, she cleared her throat and said, "I fear ye'll no' say that, once ye've heard me cursing like a warrior."

"Cursing?" he asked, sounding startled at the very suggestion.

Saidh grimaced, but nodded. "Aye. 'Tis a bad habit I learned from me brothers. And they ha'e taught me the most foul curses."

A sudden chuckle nearly had her turning again, but again she caught herself. Lifting her chin defiantly, she added, "I also wear English braies under me gowns so that I can ride astride. I ken no ladies who do that."

"English braies?" This time he sounded rather bemused.

Saidh nodded and then caught a bit of her gown in hand to lift it to knee level and reveal the bottom of the braies she wore beneath.

"Where the devil did ye come up with that idea?" he asked with what might have been shock.

"It was me mother's idea," Saidh admitted as she let the gown drop back into place. "First she tried to stop me from riding astride and running about, climbing trees and rocks with me brothers, but when that did no' work, she had the braies made for me."

"Yer mother sounds a clever woman," he decided, still sounding amused.

"Aye, she was," Saidh said sadly. "As a child, I always feared I was a great disappointment to her because o' me wild ways. But one day me da sat me down and told me that me ma had been just as wild when she was younger. That she'd worn braies under her own gowns, and had handled a sword like a warrior right up until I was born. He said I'd come by it naturally. When I asked why then she was so desperate to make a lady o' me, he said that 'twas because she feared there were few men like him who would be happy with such a woman to wife. That most lairds expected a lady, and so she'd curbed her own wildness to try to teach me to be the lady she knew everyone expected."

Silence fell when she stopped talking, and Saidh had to wonder why she'd even said so much to this man. He was a stranger, yet she was confessing things she'd not even told Murine, Joan and Edith, who were dear friends of hers.

"And the sword?"

Saidh stiffened when those words were almost whispered by her ear. He was behind her now, the heat of his chest warming her back and his hand now resting at her waist, just above her sheathed sword.

"I—" She paused and cleared her throat when that one word came out on a husky breath, and then tried again. "Me oldest brother, Aulay, had the blacksmith make it fer me birthday, years ago," she confessed and then grinned and added, "He said he got tired o' me brothers complaining that I'd taken their swords."

That brought a chuckle from the man and his breath stirred the back of her hair. Disturbed by his closeness, she moved away and turned, giving him a wide berth and avoiding looking at him as she walked to the water's edge.

"Is the bottom dirt or slippery stone?" she asked abruptly, peering at the dark surface of the lake.

"Dirt with small pebbles," he answered, his voice moving closer again. "It is no' slippery at all."

"Does the water drop off of a sudden or gradually deepen?"

"There are no sudden drops that I ha'e yet found," he responded and then asked, "Thinking o' swimming here?"

Saidh considered the possibility. It wasn't why she'd asked her questions, but the idea of stripping off her clothes and sinking into that cool, embracing water did sound tempting.

"Or trying to sort out if Allen drowned accidentally or was killed?"

That question made her whirl with dismay. "I'm quite sure Fenella did no' drown Allen."

"So am I."

Saidh blinked in surprise and then tilted her head. "Really?"

"Aye. There were no signs o' damage to the body.

He was no' hit over the head or any such thing, and she is no' strong enough to have held him under. Besides, she was at the castle when it happened. Allen had ordered a bath fer her ere taking himself here. Several servants were needed to carry up the tub and water and then to take it away, and they all swear she was in their room. And just as many swear that she was at the table in the great hall after that. She could no' ha'e killed him."

Saidh let out a little breath of relief. While she'd said she was quite sure Fenella had not killed Allen, and while she'd been telling herself the same thing, she was almost ashamed to admit even to herself that some small part of her had still wondered. It was all because of Hammish. She kept seeing Fenella in the clearing, the man's blood on her hands. Of course, the deaths of her other two husbands between Hammish and Allen had not helped either.

"So you think Allen's death was just a tragic accident?" she asked solemnly

"I did no' say that," the MacDonnell said quietly and she peered at him wide-eyed.

"You do no' think 'twas an accident?"

"She could ha'e hired someone to do the deed," he pointed out solemnly.

Saidh began shaking her head at once. Her thinking that the abuse her cousin had suffered on her first wedding night had driven Fenella insane and turned her into some kind of husband-killing mad-woman was one thing, but what he was suggesting was cold-blooded and preplanned. "Nay. I think she truly loved Allen."

"Do ye?" he asked curiously, and then admitted, "She claims to me that she did, but what else would she say?"

"I think she's being honest when she says it," she assured him, her voice firm.

"Why?" he asked.

Saidh briefly debated what she should tell him. She'd already confessed several of her own secrets to this man. For some reason, she trusted him, although she had no idea why. Perhaps he reminded her of her brothers. Still, she turned to peer out at the water before saying, "Fenella's first husband was quite rough with her on their wedding night. It left her terrified o' the marriage bed. Allen seemed to sense that about her and was verra kind. He did no' insist on consummating their marriage on their wedding night or any night afterward. He apparently told her that she need ne'er fear that he would touch her if she did no' want it."

"He ne'er claimed his marital rights?" the Mac-Donnell asked with disbelief. "I find that hard to believe. She is an attractive woman."

Saidh turned to face him and said firmly, "I believe her when she says he did no' claim them. She was too grateful fer it to be a lie."

He frowned and shook his head. "What about an heir? She would be expected to produce the next laird."

Saidh shrugged. "He apparently said that should she desire a child eventually, they would manage it in any way she chose. Perhaps he was giving her time to adjust to marriage and to learn to trust him."

The MacDonnell grunted at this, not looking convinced.

Saidh sighed. "I believe her, and I'm quite sure Fenella loved him fer it."

"She loved him fer *not* bedding her?" he asked dubiously.

Saidh nodded. "She also loved him because he was kind and considerate to her. She says he had the servants cut flowers and set them in water in their room fer her because he knew she liked them. That if he knew she wanted a bath, he would order it fer her at once rather than leave the task to her. That he bought her expensive fabrics fer gowns and lovely jewels. That he ordered cook ne'er to make the things she did no' like." She shrugged. "It sounds as if he—"

"Was too good to be true," the MacDonnell said grimly. "No man is that considerate. He sounds more a woman than—"

"What?" Saidh asked when he suddenly paused, his expression closing.

The MacDonnell hesitated and then shook his head. "Nothing."

Saidh frowned. He'd obviously thought of something, but while she trusted him enough to tell him her secrets, he apparently did not trust her with whatever he'd thought of.

"Can ye use that pig sticker?" he asked abruptly.

Saidh blinked and then glanced down to the sword at her waist when he gestured to it. A scowl immediately claimed her lips and she withdrew the sword from its sheath to show it to him. "It is no' a pig sticker. 'Tis a fine sword."

"'Tis short," he said with amusement, taking the sword from her to run his finger along the blade and test its sharpness. His finger came away with a fine line of blood on it and his eyebrows rose in what she guessed was surprise.

"I am short," she snapped, snatching back the sword when he held it out. "'Twas made to suit me."

"Aye, but can ye wield it or is it just a pretty bauble like the necklaces ye ladies like to wear?" he asked in a taunting voice.

Saidh narrowed her eyes on the man. "If ye had yer own sword here I'd show ye how well I wield it, MacDonnell."

"Hmmm." He considered her briefly and then walked over to collect a large, heavy-looking sword from a large boulder at the water's edge. He didn't raise it in battle, however, but merely smiled and suggested, "Meet me here after we break our fast and ye can show me then."

"Why not now?" she asked. Her blood was up and she was ready to battle right then.

"Because people shall wonder if we do no' soon return to break our fast," he pointed out, moving to mount a horse tethered to a tree several feet to the left of them.

Saidh stared at the large, dark animal with surprise. The beast had blended into the shadows cast by the trees and stood so silently she hadn't even noticed that it was there.

"Besides, I am hungry," he said with amusement as he turned the beast to face her. Tilting his head, he asked, "Can ye mount on yer own, or do I need to help ye?"

Saidh scowled at the arrogant man and slid her sword back into its sheath with a quick snap, then walked to her horse and hauled herself onto the saddle.

"I can see yer braies, me lady," the MacDonnell taunted as she settled astride her mare, her skirts rising to reveal her braies from the knees down.

"And I can see yer tarse," Saidh responded sweetly, and urged her mare out of the clearing as the man glanced down at himself with alarm. She'd been lying of course, his plaid had covered him properly, but his expression when he'd thought his penis was hanging out had been priceless.

A gusty laugh reached her through the trees as he realized her joke. It was followed by the drum of hooves as he set his stallion charging after her. Saidh promptly urged her mare to a gallop. She was determined to get back to the castle before him, but of course, that was impossible. She had a fine mare, but the MacDonnell's beast was absolutely huge. Its legs outstripped her mare's by almost double. She suspected her horse would look like a pony next to his stallion. Most horses would, she thought grimly as she caught movement out of the corner of her eye and realized he had not only caught up, but was about to pass her.

Saidh almost tried to gain more speed out of her mare to prevent that, but then eased up on the reins instead. She was not going to win this race anyway and would never abuse an animal in an effort to do so. Instead, she slowed down to a cant and let him charge past. Still, she was surprised when he slowed his own beast and fell back beside her.

"Ye ride well." He complimented her.

"I do," she agreed. "I fight well too. Ye'll be sorry fer yer challenge after we break our fast. I shall trounce ye."

"I shall look forward to yer trying," he said with a grin that made him ridiculously attractive.

Saidh scowled at the man, and then turned her face forward, determined to ignore him.

"Do ye like to dance?" he asked suddenly.

"Nay," she said succinctly, but wondered why he'd ask such a fool question.

"Do ye sing like a canary?"

"A canary with a broken neck," she responded.

"Can ye sew a stitch?"

"I sewed me brother up once, but then I was the one who cut him while we were practicing so it seemed only fair," she informed him with a wolf-ish smile. The truth was she could sew. She didn't even mind doing it. Sewing was a soothing activity, a good way to pass the time on a cold winter evening when ye were stuck inside with naught to do.

"Can ye . . ."

"Me laird," Saidh interrupted dryly.

"Aye?"

"I win," she announced and urged her mare to a gallop to charge over the drawbridge and through the gate into the bailey first. She heard another burst of laughter from behind her as she steered her mare toward the stables, and found herself smiling at the sound. But then was distracted when the stable master approached her as she reached the stables.

The man took the reins and grinned widely at

Saidh as she slid from her mount. "Ye go on in and break yer fast, me lady. I'll take care o' yer beast."

Saidh hesitated, but when she glanced around to see Laird MacDonnell riding into the bailey at a canter, she nodded, murmured her thanks and started across the bailey at a quick clip, eager to get inside and seated before he could. She'd only taken half a dozen steps, however, when she was suddenly caught about the waist and hauled up into the air. Saidh squawked in surprise, and glanced around with amazement at the MacDonnell. She hadn't even been aware that he'd changed direction and come after her.

"Allow me to escort the winner to the castle door," he said smoothly against her ear as he settled her in his lap.

Saidh wanted to roar at him to put her down, but didn't want to draw attention in the busy bailey so almost swallowed her tongue in her determination to still it. She sat unmoving and silent, very aware that his arm clasped her just below her breasts, the top of it rubbing against the bottom of those sensitive globes with every shift of the horse's hooves. She was also excruciatingly aware of the heat of his chest against her back, and that she seemed enveloped in the clean, male scent of him. She was slower to realize though, that the hardness against her bottom appeared to be growing larger and harder by the moment.

"Me laird?" she asked sweetly.

"Aye?" he growled by her ear, his lips brushing the tender skin and sending a shiver up her back that just annoyed her.

"I think ye might be enjoying this just a tad too much," she informed him. "That, or I'm sitting on yer sword."

He chuckled, his breath brushing her ear again. "Yer just sore that I made ye turn away and ye didn't get to see me tarse as I came out o' the water."

Saidh flushed as she recalled the way she'd gawked at him earlier, but merely shook her head and snapped, "Ye'd like to think so."

"Oh, I know so," he assured her and then reined in and lifted her down off of his horse at the base of the stairs. He also let his hand slide along the underside of her breasts under cover of releasing her, and Saidh gasped at the sensations the action sent racing through her. It left her weak kneed and unsteady so that she stumbled as she started up the stairs. Managing to keep her feet beneath her, Saidh hurried up the steps and escaped into the great hall with relief.

The MacDonnell had an entirely bewildering effect on her. She had liked looking at him as he'd come out of the water, had told him things she'd told no one else, and yet every time he got near, these odd sensations rose up in her, heat racing through her body in a confusing rush that made her want to punch him. Well, okay, maybe she didn't really want to punch him, but her feelings were definitely aggressive. It was most bewildering.

"Saidh!"

She glanced around the hall, surprised to note that the room was awash with people. Most of them were seated at the trestle tables, breaking their fast, but several servants were bustling about and Murine was on her feet at the high table, waving her over.

"Thank goodness," Murine said on a sigh, hugging Saidh when she reached her. "I was beginning to worry we'd leave before ye came to break yer fast. I thought ye were still abed," she added with a frown as she released her.

"Nay, I didn't sleep well and woke just as the sun broke so decided to go fer a ride," Saidh admitted as she settled in the empty space next to her friend. Frowning, she asked, "So yer leaving after ye eat?"

"Aye. Montrose wants to make an early start. We've a long journey ahead o' us," Murine added grimly.

Saidh eyed her friend's pinched face with concern. She knew Murine was not looking forward to living in England with her brother, and could not blame her. She disliked the man a great deal and suspected he would make Murine's life a misery without even trying. He had already proven himself to be a cold, heartless bastard by not sending for her when her father died so that she could attend the funeral.

That was something Saidh couldn't even imagine her own brothers doing. And not just because she'd have run her sword through them if they'd dared. They wouldn't even have considered it themselves. But then her brothers were good men. Montrose just wasn't, from what she could tell.

"Mayhap you could stay here until I leave," she said suddenly.

Murine glanced to her with surprise. "What?"

"Well, Lady MacDonnell seems to hate me, but she definitely seemed to like you well enough. Ye could stay and be a buffer between us until . . ." Saidh trailed off, a frown claiming her lips. She didn't know how to finish that. She had no idea how long she would be staying. Fenella had begged her not to go and she had agreed, but—Saidh suddenly glanced along the table in search of the woman. She'd hoped Fenella would leave her room for meals at least now that she was there. However, there was no sign of her.

"If 'tis your cousin ye're looking for, I think she took her meal in her room," Murine said quietly, and then added, "At least I saw a maid slipping into a room with a tray o' food on me way down. I do no' ken if 'twas her room, but I ken it was no' the master bedchamber and since e'eryone else is here it must ha'e been."

"Oh," Saidh murmured. She supposed it had been too much to hope that her presence would lure her cousin below. However, if Fenella stayed in her room all the time, why did she want her to stay at all? Cripes, she hoped her cousin wasn't expecting her to stay stuck up there in her room with her all day long. She couldn't stand that.

"Thank ye fer the offer," Murine said suddenly, distracting Saidh from her thoughts. "But I think 'tis better that I just travel on with Montrose." She smiled wryly and added, "I'm no' at all sure he'd agree to send an escort back to bring me home later."

"Me brother would arrange an escort fer ye," Saidh said solemnly.

"Aye, I ken." Murine smiled sadly, and then pointed out, "But this is no' yer home, Saidh. Ye can no' jest invite me to stay."

"Oh, aye," Saidh muttered, peering down at the trencher that had appeared before her between then and the last time she'd looked. The servants here were quick and quiet, she noted.

"Besides, Lady MacDonnell does no' hate ye. I talked with her last night and explained how sweet and kind ye are."

"Sweet and kind?" Saidh asked with a wince.

"Ye are," Murine said firmly. "Why jest look how ye cut yer visit short with Joan to come see that Lady Fenella was all right. And this when ye'd had no idea that she'd e'en married again once, let alone three times. 'Twas sweet and kind," she insisted, and then added, "And I told Lady MacDonnell that."

Saidh grimaced at the news.

"I think ye'll find she looks on ye much more kindly now."

"Well, that's something then," Saidh said with mild amusement, and then glanced sharply toward the door when it opened. She wasn't surprised when the MacDonnell entered. She *was* surprised, however, by the small storm of reaction that seeing him walking toward her caused in her body. It was like the great hall at Buchanan when she and her brothers had raced through playing one of their games. They had run about madly, jumping and tumbling this way and that, sending things flying and banging about the room like a storm before racing out again with Cook or some other servant chasing after them, shouting their heads off. Her body was presently the great hall and all the liquids in her body were she and her brothers causing an uproar.

"Laird MacDonnell is verra handsome," Murine said suddenly beside her.

Saidh merely grunted and turned her face down to her trencher as she tried to control her body's response to him.

"What is his first name, do ye ken?" Murine asked curiously.

Saidh shook her head. She hadn't a clue.

" 'Tis Greer."

Saidh stiffened as the MacDonnell breathed that by her ear. Straightening slowly, she turned to see that he stood directly behind her.

"Rear?" she asked, managing a blank expression. " 'Tis an odd name to give a boy."

"Oh dear," Lady MacDonnell's amused voice drew her head around to see the woman approaching the table from the doors leading to the kitchens. "No dear. His name is Greer. Greer. Not rear."

"Oh." Saidh smiled apologetically, even blinking her eyelashes innocently as if she'd truly misheard the name. "Well that sounds much better."

"Aye, it does," Lady MacDonnell agreed with amusement.

Feeling the heat at her back withdraw, Saidh chanced a glance around at Greer as he moved along the table toward the chair in the center. Much to her irritation, he looked amused rather than offended at her feigned misunderstanding of his name. Really, that smug smile just made her want to punch him . . . or not. She really didn't understand her reaction to the man.

"Saidh?"

"Hmm?" She turned to peer at Murine questioningly.

"I think ye'd best be careful while here," Murine said quietly.

"Careful o' what?" Saidh asked with surprise.

Murine hesitated and then admitted, "I had the oddest sensation along me arm when Laird MacDonnell stood behind ye. It was like there was some kind o' heat bouncing between ye. I'm thinking mayhap ye'd do best to avoid being alone with him while yer here."

"Oh." Saidh waved her concern away. "I'll be fine."

Murine looked as if she wanted to say more, but paused and glanced past her as Montrose stood up at the far end of the table. A sigh slipped from her lips, but she forced a smile for Saidh. "It looks as if we are leaving."

"Oh." Saidh stood when Murine did and accompanied her along the tables in the hall. They were halfway to the keep doors when Saidh blurted, "Murine, if ye're e'er in trouble or in need o' aid, do no' hesitate to write me at Buchanan or e'en to come there. Ye'll always be welcome."

"Thank ye," Murine said and paused to hug her. "Ye're a good friend, Saidh, and the same goes fer you. If ye're e'er in trouble or in need, me door will always be open to ye."

Saidh hugged her briefly, then stepped back with

a smile to walk her outside. She was surprised to step out of the great hall and find the bailey swimming with horses. The stable master had obviously been busy since she'd entered the castle. It made Saidh feel bad that she'd left him to tend to her mount rather than do it herself.

"Mount up, Murine. We do not have all day," Montrose snapped as he slung himself into his own saddle.

Murine smiled tightly, but moved to do as instructed.

Saidh watched her mount and then moved up beside the horse and rubbed the mare's muzzle as she commented, "Joan's tincture must be working, Murine. It seems to me ye've no' fainted once since the babe was born."

"Aye." Murine gave her a real smile. "I'll ha'e to write Joan and thank her."

Saidh nodded and stepped back. "Safe journey."

"Safe stay," Murine said solemnly, and then turned her horse to follow her brother out of the bailey, followed by the soldiers.

"Ye're worried about her."

Saidh tore her gaze away from Murine's stiff back and glanced at Greer as he paused beside her. The man was huge, something she hadn't really taken note of until now. He made her feel small and dainty in comparison, something even her brothers, who were all large men, had never accomplished.

She turned to peer after the last of the soldiers riding out of the bailey and nodded solemnly. "Her father made no provisions fer Murine in his will.

No' even a dower. She's dependent on her brother now and I fear he's no' the most caring o' brothers."

"Was her father no' Laird Beathan Carmichael?" Greer asked.

"Aye," she said and noted the frown that pulled at his face.

Greer shook his head. "He did no' seem the type o' man to leave his daughter penniless and dependent on a half brother like Montrose Danvries."

"Ye knew him?" she asked with surprise.

"I worked fer him a time or two," he admitted.

Saidh's eyebrows rose at this news. "Worked fer him at what?"

"I was a sword for hire ere Allen died and I inherited the title," Greer admitted without shame. "Laird Carmichael hired me on a time or two. I liked him," he added. "And I suspect someone is no' dealing honestly with Murine if she thinks she was left without resources."

Saidh frowned at the suggestion and peered back to the now empty drawbridge, thinking that perhaps she should write Murine and tell her what Greer had said. She wouldn't put it past Montrose to claim there was no dower and gamble it away instead. From what Murine had said, he'd gambled away most of his inheritance from his own father already. The only thing left was Danvries castle and the lands he rented out to farmers as far as she knew.

Aye, she'd write to her, Saidh decided and turned to start back up the stairs. She still hadn't broken her fast, and then she'd have to check on Fenella before she returned to the loch to cross swords with Greer.

Chapter 4

SAIDH DISMOUNTED IN THE CLEARING AND TOOK a deep breath of fresh air before letting it out on a pleased little sigh. She'd arrived first, which she hadn't expected as she'd mounted the stairs to check on Fenella. She'd felt sure her cousin would keep her for hours as she cried and moaned about losing Allen . . . and Saidh would have stayed for all of it, doing her best to console the inconsolable woman.

Fortunately, she'd come across Fenella's maid on the upstairs landing and on hearing that the other woman was bathing, had told the maid she wouldn't trouble her just then. She'd asked the maid to tell Fenella that she'd come to check on her, and that she would return later, when she was out of her bath. Then she'd hurried to her room to change her gown before almost skipping back downstairs and out to the stables to gather her horse and head to the loch.

Sliding her sword out, Saidh swung it a couple of times to loosen her muscles. She didn't think she'd have long to wait for Greer. He'd been in the practice

area with his men when she'd passed on the way
to the stables and she knew he'd seen her. She was
quite sure he'd follow when he had the chance. He
was the one who had suggested they battle after
breaking their fast after all.

Saidh swung her sword again, enjoying the
whistle of sound it made as it sliced the air, and
then glanced at the water and found herself moving
toward it. It was such a pretty spot, it was hard to
believe anyone had died here, let alone Fenella's
husband. Thinking about that made her wonder
what he had looked like. Had he favored Greer in
looks? Had he been tall, and strong and so well put
together? She wondered as she recalled Greer rising
out of the water as beautiful as some ancient god,
water droplets racing down his tanned skin.

Nay, not a god, she thought now. His skin had not
been perfect and unblemished. Scars had marred
his chest and arms. Probably his back too, she
thought. It was not hard to believe he'd earned his
living by his sword ere inheriting the title. But he
was still beautiful. The scars had added rather than
taken away from his looks, to her mind.

"If ye wish a swim instead o' a fight, I can wait."

Saidh whirled around with surprise at that comment, startled to find Greer not only there, but off
his horse and crossing the clearing toward her. How
had he arrived and dismounted without her hearing? The question blazed through her thoughts, but
she already knew the answer. She hadn't really been
present in that clearing in that moment, she'd been
off in her head in another moment in that clearing

and ogling the man's naked chest in her mind. He was obviously a distracting devil.

"I can swim another time," she said raising her chin as he drew close enough that she had to do so to meet his gaze, or speak to his chest.

"A shame. I would ha'e enjoyed watching ye strip away yer braies and gown and slip into the water," he said with a grin.

Saidh blinked at the words, her nipples tightening in response to the thought of removing her clothes under the hot gaze of this man and then letting the cool water soothe the heat his eyes caused. Scowling with irritation at her body's response, Saidh shook her head. "In yer dreams, me laird."

"Aye. Ye've done that and much more in me dreams," he admitted and then grinned at the blush that rose up into her cheeks.

Saidh didn't know quite how to respond to that, so was relieved when he took on a more serious expression and backed away to withdraw his own sword from his sheath. He didn't raise it though, but arched an eyebrow instead and asked, "Are ye going to fight like that?"

Saidh glanced down at her dress and then raised an eyebrow of her own. "Ye expected me to strip to battle with ye?"

"Jest yer dress. Ye've braies under it," he pointed out.

"Aye," she agreed, "But braies do no' cover me duckies."

"Duckies?" he asked uncertainly.

"'Tis what me youngest brother calls me teats,"

she explained with amusement and was interested to see the flush that suddenly rose on his cheeks as his gaze dropped to the items in question.

"I do no' mind if yer duckies are no' covered," he said, his voice almost a growl.

Saidh snorted at the claim. "I'm sure ye do no'," she said dryly and slid her sword back into her sheath, then bent forward and reached between her legs for the back of her gown. Straightening, she pulled the cloth with her and tucked it into the belt that held the sheath at her waist. It probably wasn't attractive, she acknowledged, but it would keep her skirts out of the way while they fought, yet her legs were decently covered by the braies still.

Satisfied, she withdrew her sword again and faced him. "Come on then. 'Tis time I trounced ye."

"Ah lass," he said with a slow smile. "I made me living wielding me sword. 'Tis you I fear is about to be trounced."

"We shall see," Saidh said, unintimidated, and lunged at him, swinging.

Greer met her sword with his own, his eyes wide with surprise at the attack. He fended another swing easily, but said, "Mayhap we should be using wooden swords fer this. I'd no wish to see ye hurt."

"Or mayhap yer afraid yer the one who will get hurt," she suggested, swinging again. As their swords met, she added, "But ye'll not. I ken how to control me sword, and this is just fer play, no' to injure ye."

"I'm glad to hear it," Greer said with amusement, getting in a couple of swings of his own that she had to block. Saidh fended him off easily enough and was winding up to swing at him again when her skirt suddenly came unraveled and tangled around her legs.

Startled, she stumbled back to avoid hitting Greer in an uncontrolled swing as she struggled to maintain her balance, and then gasped with surprise as cold water rushed over her foot one moment before she tumbled back into the lake. Saidh landed on her bottom, her head and chest briefly falling backward under the water. She gulped a mouthful of the stuff as she cried out in surprise, and then quickly pushed herself into a sitting position so that her head and neck, at least, were out of the water.

Spitting out more curses than water, Saidh floundered briefly and flailed about with both hands, slapping her sword wildly about as she tried to maintain some balance and keep from falling back in the water again. Then she stabbed her sword into the wet dirt beside her and clung to it to get to her knees as the loch tried to wash her out and away from shore.

Pausing on her knees, Saidh released the sword with one hand to push her hair off her face and scowled around until she found Greer standing several feet back, his chin hanging down onto his chest and his eyes as wide as chicken eggs in his head.

"Well?" she growled, glaring at him. "Are ye going to help me or no'?"

Greer's mouth snapped closed and he smiled that infuriating smile of his. "I'm no' sure. Are ye done waving yer sword about like a madwoman?"

"Ye can see 'tis buried in the dirt," she growled furiously.

"Aye. And tis a piss-poor way to treat such a fine weapon," he said at once.

"I shall clean and sharpen it when I get back to the castle," Saidh said grimly, frowning at the hilt of her sword now. Truly, thrusting it into the ground was no way to treat a sword as fine as hers, but she'd been desperate. She still was. Her gown was heavy, and the braies underneath were just weighing her down more. Aside from that, it felt like the waves washing around her were trying to take her out to the middle of the loch with them as they rolled away from her.

"Do ye ken the proper way to clean and sharpen a blade?" Greer asked with interest.

Saidh didn't bother to respond but simply shook her head and staggered to her feet in the water. It was much harder than one would think. The ground was soft beneath her, shifting with her movement and her gown was hampering her horribly. But she got upright and immediately pulled her sword from the ground. The moment she'd returned it to its sheath, Greer was there, scooping her up into his arms.

"I can walk," she said with irritation as he turned to carry her back out of the water.

"It did no' look that way to me," Greer said with amusement. He set her on her feet on dry land and then stepped back to look her over, before meeting her gaze and arching an eyebrow. "I think this means I trounced ye."

"Ye did no'," she argued at once. "Me gown unraveled and tripped me."

"I tugged yer gown from its mooring so that it would trip ye," he countered with not an iota of shame. When she gaped at him, he shrugged. "All's fair in battle, love. Ye use what's available to ye."

Saidh let loose with a string of curses that would have made even her brothers blush, though they were the ones she'd learned them from.

Greer, however, merely smiled more widely, shook his head, and murmured, "That mouth o' yers, lass."

"What about it?" Saidh barked, glowering at the man.

"I like it," he said so softly she almost missed the words.

Saidh stared at him with bewilderment. She was wet and cold, but for some reason his words and his expression sent a warm shiver through her body, and she was aware of the rise of those bewildering sensations that only he seemed to raise in her. A strange want and need that culminated in frustration and aggressive action. Responding to it, she reached for him.

Greer's eyes widened and he reached for her too, then released a startled curse when she suddenly hooked her foot behind his ankle and pushed with her hands to send him crashing onto his back on the ground. At least that was her intention. However, Greer had already caught her arms when she pushed and rather than just send him to the ground, she was dragged down with him.

Saidh landed on his chest with a grunt of surprise and then pushed herself up to glare at him, her damp hair hanging down, a dark curtain around their faces. But then she just lay there staring at him. She should be pummeling him with fists and words, berating him for cheating and making her trip and fall in the lake. Or alternatively, she should be getting up and leaving him lying there in the dirt while she rode back to the castle. Instead, she just lay there, staring into his beautiful dark eyes, her upper body half raised and her lower body flat against him, feeling every inch of heated flesh through their clothes.

Greer stared back briefly, but then his gaze dropped and she gave a start as he ran a finger lightly along the neckline of her gown.

"Ye must be cold," he growled.

"Aye," she agreed, surprised to find herself sounding breathless.

"I'll warm ye."

"Aye," Saidh murmured as his hand moved up to cup her head and draw her face down to his. His lips were warm and soft yet firm as they brushed over hers, and she held her breath at his first touch. When his tongue slid out to run along the seam where her lips met, she made a startled sound, her mouth opening involuntarily, and then gasped when his tongue immediately slipped past the open gates to explore her depths.

This was uncharted territory for Saidh. She had grown up with seven bossy, nosy brothers who seemed to follow her everywhere. No boy or man had ever dared to even try to kiss her ere this. It left her feeling awkward and uncertain now as to how to respond. Should she suck on his tongue as she suddenly wanted to, or was she supposed to stick her tongue in his mouth too? Saidh didn't have a clue, so did neither and simply held herself still above him until her arms began to tremble.

Greer suddenly broke the kiss and shifted, turning them both until she lay on her back on the ground and he rested on his side. He didn't go back to kissing her though. Instead, his gaze drifted down her body. Saidh watched his face, but then glanced down with surprise when he pinched one nipple through the wet cloth of her gown.

The material was old, which was why she'd changed into it. She hadn't minded if it got damaged during their battle. But, she saw now that the cloth was thin with wear and rather sheer when wet, she noted as she saw the dusky rose of her nipple through the material. Before she could be embarrassed by that, Greer ducked his head and covered the nipple with his mouth.

Saidh sucked in a deep breath, her back arching in response as heat encompassed the sensitive nib. She then moaned, and clasped his head with some vague intent of pushing him away when he began to suckle her through the material. Instead of push at him, though, she found her fingers tangling in his hair and clasping him closer, urging him on. She even moaned her disappointment when he broke off the caress and raised his head, but she relaxed and wound her arms around him when he kissed her again instead.

This time she did suck on his tongue when it invaded her. She simply couldn't resist it, and he did not seem to mind. At least, he didn't stop kissing her. Instead, they became more demanding, almost violent as he slanted his head over hers and thrust his tongue in and out and in and out. Saidh was so consumed by his kisses that she wasn't even aware that his hand was working busily at the neckline of her gown until he suddenly broke their kiss and shifted to close his mouth over her breast again, this time without the cloth there between them.

Saidh cried out at the rush of excitement shooting through her and curled around his head, her legs squeezing together as the heat hit her there. She felt his hand on her leg and then clasping her bottom, squeezing, but didn't care. And then he tore his mouth from her breast and kissed her again as his hand slid around to cup her between the legs and Saidh cried out into his mouth. Her legs clenched around his fingers, squeezing even as her hips shifted in response, and then that strange want, need, frustration welled up inside her like a cyclone and she was moved to violence again.

Catching Greer by surprise, she thrust him onto his back and quickly scrambled to straddle him and then simply stared down at him, bewildered as to what to do next. Saidh knew she definitely didn't want to punch him and suspected she never had, but she had no clue what she should do instead. So simply sat there on him, her hair a tangled mess around her shoulders and her breasts bared by her open gown.

Greer watched her expression warily for a moment, and then offered her a crooked smile. "I surrender. Do with me what ye will."

Saidh hesitated, knowing she should gather her dignity, cover herself up, get on her horse and return to the castle, but she didn't want to. She wanted more of what he'd shown her so far. She'd never known it could be like this between a man and a woman. And she'd never been a shy young thing. With seven brothers she'd had to fight for every little thing she wanted, and she wanted Greer.

His hands were on her legs, simply resting there. Saidh caught them and raised them, placing them over her breasts. "Show me what to do."

Greer's eyes darkened, and his hands tightened briefly on her breasts, but then he took a deep breath and started to shake his head.

"Please," Saidh said quickly. "You make me feel—I want . . ." She shook her head with frustration, and repeated, "Show me what to do."

Greer hesitated, but then began to caress her breasts, squeezing and kneading the soft globes and then pinching at the nipples.

Saidh moaned, and let her head fall back, simply enjoying the sensation. Completely unaware that she was shifting her hips against him as she did, rubbing her soft core against his hardness through their clothes. Greer continued to caress her for a moment more, then suddenly shifted them both again, forcing her onto her back. This time he came to rest on top of her, his legs urging hers open to cradle him as he settled between them.

Greer released her breasts to plant his hands on the ground on either side of her to take the worst of his weight as he then kissed her. His hips shifted against her as his tongue thrust into her, and his chest moved over hers, exciting her nipples to an almost painful degree even as his hardness rubbed repeatedly against the soft spot between her legs.

Saidh's body was tightening in response to the lovely friction, straining toward some glorious end she could only imagine, and then it was suddenly as if a dam in her body was torn away and pleasure and release stormed through her like a wildfire in a dry wood. Saidh screamed her release, her body convulsing and legs clenching around Greer's hips, as he continued to rub himself against her, and then he too stiffened and convulsed, a somewhat familiar roar sending the birds shrieking from the trees.

GREER ROLLED ONTO HIS BACK IN THE GRASS, PULL-ing Saidh with him to lie across his chest. She nestled there like a contented cat, almost purring her pleasure as she tucked her head beneath his chin. It made him smile, and he rubbed one hand lazily down her back as he caught his breath and pondered the amazing thing that had just happened. He hadn't enjoyed such a spectacular release in some time, if ever. Even more amazing to him was that he'd experienced it while they'd both had their clothes still on, him humping on her like a green lad without actually entering and merging their bodies.

What would it be like with her without their clothes?

That question was one Greer was almost desperate to know the answer to, and he'd have her braies off and her skirts up over her head right now in search of the answer if Saidh weren't a lady.

Saidh murmured sleepily, and shifted slightly on him, revealing one bare breast. Greer couldn't resist reaching down to run a finger lightly over the nipple. Saidh moaned, her back arching and the nipple growing and hardening under the touch, and his groin immediately tightened. The woman was so damned responsive.

She had caught him by surprise when she'd tripped him up and sent them both tumbling to the ground, but the action had smartened him up somewhat, reminding him of the situation and that she was a lady, not to be trifled with. He'd intended to get them both to their feet and behave himself, until she'd taken his hands in hers and placed them over her breasts, then begun to rock on him, her body sliding over his already burgeoning erection. He hadn't had the strength to bring an end to it then. But he'd had enough sense not to take her innocence. She was a lady whether she liked to admit it or not, and not just by blood. She might curse like a warrior, which he actually enjoyed, and she might wear braies and a sword, but she was as innocent as a babe for all that. While she'd been eager and responsive, and as passionate as could be, he was quite sure she'd never even been kissed before today. Certainly, she hadn't known what the hell she was doing, although she'd learned quick enough.

"Oh Greer," Saidh moaned, snuggling closer and he realized that his hand had found its way from her back down to her bottom and was squeezing and kneading the flesh while forcing her front against his hip. Her response was most gratifying, and he couldn't resist catching her nipple between thumb and finger and rolling it gently.

While Saidh gasped, and shifted, throwing one leg over both of his, instinctively rubbing her core against his hip, Greer was quite sure she was still asleep. Her leg shifted again, rolling over his cock then and he almost groaned aloud at the sensation, dismayed to find he was already hard again. Fighting the urge to roll on top of her, Greer forced himself to still both his hands. He desperately wanted to do what he had managed not to do the first time. It would take little effort to slide her braes down her hips and sink himself in all that wet heat he knew awaited him. He was quite sure Saidh would not only allow it, but engage in it eagerly, however she was a lady and deserved better than a roll in the grass . . . whether she'd enjoy it or not.

Determined to take the high road, Greer eased gently out from beneath Saidh and got to his feet, smiling faintly when she grumbled unhappily in her sleep at the loss of him. The smile died though when his plaid slapped wet against his thigh and he glanced to see the mess that this little adventure had left on his plaid. There was no doubting what the stain was, nor the one on the front of her gown, he realized with a frown as he glanced to Saidh and noted it. It would seem his plaid had risen as he humped her and they'd both received a portion of his pleasure when he'd found it.

It had been a hell of a lot of pleasure, he noted,

somewhat impressed with himself, and then he bent to scoop her up in his arms. They couldn't return to the castle in this state or all would know what they'd been about. He wouldn't see her ruined that way. He had plans for her that did not include leaving her reputation in tatters.

Saidh snuggled her face into his neck with a happy little sigh, her breath warm against his throat, and Greer found himself smiling once again. The woman was like a soft sweet kitten, nuzzling him like that, he thought as he started into the water. A kitten with claws was his next thought when the cold water reached her and she came awake with a squawk of dismay and began to fight for her release.

" 'Tis a'right," Greer soothed, continuing forward into the water. "We jest need to—" His words ended on a roar of pain as her nails dug into his neck and shoulder, and he instinctively loosened his hold, not thinking, just eager to escape the pain even if it meant dropping her in the water. But Saidh had no intention of going into the water, in fact that was what she was trying to escape and rather than drop like a stone, she stuck her feet into his leg and groin, dug her claws into his head and neck and tried to climb out of the water using him as the ladder.

Greer wrestled with her briefly, trying to disengage her and then simply threw himself forward so that they both went under. It didn't exactly have the desired effect, for rather than release him and lunge for the surface, Saidh tried to climb on top of him, pushing him down in the water as she struggled upward. He ended up facedown at the bottom of the

lake with her standing on his arse. Greer was about
to force himself to his knees and upward, uncaring
that it would knock her off and under the water's
surface again, when she was suddenly off his arse
and he found himself being tugged upward by a
hand tangled in his hair.

"What are ye trying to do? Drown yerself?" she
bellowed, yanking his head out of the water.

Greer sputtered out the water he'd swallowed
and pulled her hand from his hair as he found his
feet and straightened in the chest-deep water. He
then turned to glower at the woman. "Nay. Yer the
one who was trying to do that."

"Me?" she squawked with disbelief. "The last
thing I remember I was curled up on dry land, and
then I was suddenly plunged into ice cold water. I'm
no' the one trying to drown anyone. Ye were." Her
eyes narrowed on his still scowling face. "Did ye
drown Allen too? Lull him into a nice nap and then
toss him into the lake to drown?"

"O' course not. I'd hardly do to Allen what we
just did," he pointed out dryly, but his temper was
cooling now. Probably a combination of the ice cold
water and the fact that the woman much resembled
the cat he'd been thinking of her as, but a drowned
cat this time. Smiling crookedly, he explained, "I
made a mess o' both o' us when we found our pleasure. We could no' return to the castle in the state we
were in, so I thought it best we take a quick dip in
the water to wash it away."

He saw the bewilderment on her face, and knew
she didn't have a clue what he meant. Then she

scowled and said, "Well, next time warn a lass. I did no' ken what was happening."

Greer merely grunted, then caught her arm and began to drag her toward shore, knowing that getting out of the water with her wet clothes dragging her down would be a struggle without his aid. He scooped her up into his arms once they were only knee-deep in the loch, and then staggered under the weight. Damn, women's clothing was heavy as hell when wet, he thought grimly once he'd regained his balance.

"Thank ye," Saidh said once he'd set her on her horse, but he couldn't help noticing that she sounded more resentful than grateful.

Shaking his head, he moved to his own mount without comment.

Chapter 5

"WHERE HA'E YE BEEN?"

Saidh winced at Fenella's shriek and pushed her chamber door closed with resignation. Calmly she replied, "I came to check on ye this morn but ye were in yer bath, so I went fer a short ride."

"Short?" Fenella asked with amazement. "Ye were gone fer hours."

"'Twas no' that long," Saidh argued weakly, although she wasn't really sure. It had seemed like a moment and a lifetime all at the same time. What she'd experienced had been life altering, to Saidh's mind, and she couldn't wait to go back to the loch for more battle practice with Greer. If he was willing, she thought with a sudden frown. He hadn't said anything about meeting by the loch again.

"Did ye enjoy yer ride?" Fenella asked on a sigh.

"Oh, aye," Saidh answered with a smile, recalling how she'd straddled Greer, her hips shifting and body rubbing against his as he caressed her breasts. It had been a most enjoyable ride. Although she'd liked it better when he'd rolled her over and come down on top of her, his body pressing urgently against her own.

"Did ye get wet?"

Saidh blinked at the question. She had indeed gotten wet, but didn't think Fenella was talking about the dampness between her legs that her excitement had caused, and she hadn't told the girl about getting dunked in the loch.

"'Twas cloudy this morning and looked as if it might rain," Fenella explained. "Did it? Were ye caught in a rain during yer ride?"

"Oh. Nay." Saidh forced a smile and then raised her eyebrows. "What would ye like to do today?"

"Nothing," Fenella said miserably, dropping to sit on the side of her bed.

Saidh bit her lip, and then moved to stand in front of her and said gently, "Do ye no' think it would be good fer ye to get out o' this room and take some air?"

"Nay." The word was followed by a sniffle.

Afraid the woman was going to start in sobbing again, Saidh caught her hand and hurried for the door dragging Fenella behind. "Well, I do. Ye'll make yerself ill if ye stay in this room. I think a nice little walk would be good fer ye. Just a short one," Saidh added when Fenella began to protest. "A quick one in the bailey so ye can get some sun. That way yer maid can air out yer room while yer gone."

"But I do no' want to walk," Fenella complained, tugging ineffectually at her hand.

Mouth tightening, Saidh pulled her down the

stairs to the great hall. "Ye can no' stay abed in that room fer the rest o' yer life, Fenella. Ye're still young, and ye're no' the one who died."

"Nay, me husband did," Fenella cried as they reached the bottom of the stairs. She then jerked her hand from Saidh's and covered her face as she burst into tears.

"Damn," Saidh breathed, not knowing what the hell to do now. It wasn't like she'd been faced with this situation before. Her brothers weren't the sort to stand about sobbing fit to break yer heart, and despite all the trials and tribulations Joan and Murine had suffered of late, neither of them had done it either. Even on learning of her father's death, Murine had stood straight and tall, silent tears trailing down her cheeks that she'd dashed away before saying, "I should go pack." She'd then walked away, head high, shoulders straight. Saidh could tell she was hurting, but the woman hadn't broken down. She'd born her pain stoically, and Saidh wished to hell that Fenella was more like that.

Sighing, Saidh shifted sideways toward the woman, patted her back awkwardly and then said, "I'll fetch yer maid, shall I?"

She didn't wait for a response, but hurried toward the kitchens, sure the woman would be found in there, or, if not, that someone there would know where to find her.

It took a couple moments to round up the wench. Fenella's maid had slipped out to the gardens to pick flowers for her lady, hoping to cheer her. Saidh helped her carry the flowers back in, and led the woman into the great hall, only to come to an abrupt halt. Fenella was still there, but she was also sobbing in Greer's arms.

Saidh's gaze narrowed on the couple, and she crushed the flowers she carried, only realizing she was doing it when a thorn pricked her fingers. Relaxing her hold on the flowers, Saidh straightened her shoulders and crossed the great hall to the couple.

"I found Sorcha," she announced grimly as she reached them. "And look, she picked flowers fer ye."

Fenella pulled away from Greer far enough to turn and look at the flowers both women were carrying, then burst into renewed sobs and threw herself against Greer wailing miserably. For Greer's part, he looked rather like a deer in the face of oncoming riders. Body stiff and neck red, he stared down with horror at the woman sobbing all over the clean, dry plaid he'd donned on returning to the keep. He then turned his gaze to Saidh, eyebrows rising in question as he mouthed, "What do I do?"

Finding the anger that had gripped her when she'd first seen Fenella in his arms suddenly slipping away, Saidh grinned and shrugged.

Greer scowled at her for her lack of aid, then scooped Fenella up in his arms and started up the stairs, muttering, "Come, Sorcha'll put ye to bed."

Saidh grinned, but turned to dump the flowers she carried on top of the ones Sorcha already held, then backed away from the stairs. There was no damned way she was going to be stuck up in that room all day with the sobbing woman.

"Oh!"

That startled sound from behind her accompanied Saidh's trouncing on something soft. Whirling around, she saw at once that it was Lady MacDonnell's foot. The woman stood behind her smiling weakly as she raised her foot to rub the end.

"Oh, dear, I'm sorry m'lady," Saidh murmured, taking the woman's arm to help her maintain her balance. "I was no' watching where I was going."

"Neither was I," Lady MacDonnell admitted with a wry little twist to her lips. She gave up rubbing her injured toes and straightened with a little sigh and then glanced from Saidh to the trio disappearing up the stairs. When anger immediately darkened her face, Saidh decided some distraction was needed and asked, "Were ye going above stairs?"

Lady MacDonnell glanced to her, expression briefly blank and then she nodded. "Aye. I was going to fetch me maid to help me with some sewing."

"I can help ye," Saidh offered. "I'm no' the best seamstress in the world, but I can sew a straight line."

"Oh, is no' that sweet o' ye?" Lady MacDonnell beamed at her. "Well, if ye do no' mind and ha'e a few minutes to spare, I'd appreciate yer aid."

Saidh nodded at once and followed her to the chairs by the fire. She even managed a smile, which did not usually come to her expression at the thought of sewing. But in this case, she didn't mind at all. It meant she had an excuse to avoid Fenella until she'd spent the worst of her tears and calmed a bit. While Saidh had agreed to stay when Fenella had asked her to, standing about patting her cousin's back, saying "there, there" while Fenella sobbed all day and night was not something she really wished to do. She would wait until the woman had spent her tears and then try to offer her some comfort and distraction, but until then, sewing seemed a more attractive pastime.

Much to Saidh's relief the sewing Lady MacDonnell was tending to was simple mending. There were no fancy stitches for her to fret over, as straight lines were all that were required. They worked in silence at first, though it didn't feel awkward to Saidh. It was when Greer came back downstairs and cast a brief scowl at her on his way out of the keep that they began to speak.

"Oh dear, Greer appears annoyed with ye." Lady MacDonnell sounded most amused at the fact and Saidh bit her lip, then smiled and admitted:

"Aye, 'tis sure I am he is. I fear I left him to Fenella's damp mercies earlier."

"Ah." Lady MacDonnell said grimly. "I came up as he was carrying her above stairs. Crying on his shoulder again, was she?"

Saidh nodded, but lowered her gaze to the stocking she was mending and muttered, "Crying seems to be all she does."

"Aye, and 'tis damned annoying," Lady MacDonnell said, drawing Saidh's startled gaze. Smiling, the woman informed her, "I have verra good hearing, me dear."

"Oh." Saidh swallowed and nodded with a weak smile.

After a moment, the lady commented, "Ye do no' seem to care much fer yer cousin."

Saidh stared at the stocking in her hands and then sighed. "In truth, I'm no' sure whether I do or no'. I barely know her, m'lady."

Lady MacDonnell raised her eyebrows at that, and Saidh nodded firmly.

"She stayed with us fer a week or two when we were children while her mother was ill, and then I attended her wedding when I was sixteen. But other than those two times . . ." She shrugged. "This is only the third occasion that I've spent time around her."

"I see," she said thoughtfully, and then asked, "What was she like as a girl?"

"She was always crying then too," Saidh said with a grimace, and then to be fair, added, "But I suppose that was me fault."

"How is that?" Lady MacDonnell asked curiously.

"I grew up playing with me brothers. 'Twas what I'd always done, so when she arrived, I thought, 'Grand, another playmate,' and expected her to want to muddy her face, wrap a fur around her waist, climb the trees and swing from branches yelling war cries too."

"Muddy her face?"

"Aye, well me brothers and I liked to play at being warrior Britons, but we had no blue paint so made do with mud."

"Ah, I see," Lady MacDonnell sat back, grinning and nodding. "I imagine that was fun."

"Aye," Saidh assured her with a laugh, but the amusement faded quickly from her face and she sighed. "Fenella did no' agree. She was a little lady. I could be a dastardly Briton if I liked, but she would no'. In fact, she decided I could be the dastardly Briton warrior trying to kidnap and harm her, and me brothers could be her valiant guards who rescued her from me filthy pagan hands."

"Do ye no' ha'e seven brothers?" Lady MacDonnell asked with a frown.

"Aye."

"Well, those hardly seem fair odds," she said dryly. "One little Briton warrior against seven bigger boys."

"I won," Saidh informed her with a wolfish smile.

"Nay!" Lady MacDonnell said with disbelief.

Saidh nodded. "Me brothers got a severe punishment did they ever actually harm me, but I was no' bound by the same rule. After all, how much harm could a wee lass do?" she asked with feigned innocence. "So, while they tried to capture and pin me down without harming me, I was free to pull their hair, punch and kick to me heart's content . . . and I trounced all seven o' them."

Lady MacDonnell's eyes widened incredulously and then she burst into laughter.

Saidh smiled at her amusement, and added, "Fenella was most annoyed that her champions failed her so."

"Oh, I can imagine she would be," the woman said dryly.

"Especially when she began to cry and I got so annoyed I tied her to a tree and left her there through the nooning meal."

"Oh, my sweet Lord," Lady MacDonnell breathed

with admiration. "I do believe I like ye, Saidh Buchanan."

"Why thank ye," Saidh said with surprised pleasure. "Ye seem a right nice lady yerself."

They grinned at each other briefly, and then Lady MacDonnell picked up her mending again. "So Fenella has always been a crier when she does no' get her way."

Saidh glanced up with surprise, but then slow realization rolled through her. Fenella had cried every time she hadn't gotten her way as a child. When she'd first arrived, Fenella had expected Saidh to play with the dolls she'd brought with her. But Saidh hadn't been interested, preferring to run about with her brothers as she always did. Fenella had cried.

Her mother had then taken Saidh aside and suggested it would be kind to play dolls with her cousin. When she'd protested that she didn't want to play with dolls, her mother had insisted, saying that first she should play with the dolls with her cousin, and then the next day Fenella would play what she wanted to play. So Saidh had suffered through the doll business, but the next day, Fenella had refused to join her and her brothers in a game of hide-and-seek, and had burst into tears when Saidh had shrugged and simply gone out to play with them anyway. It was her day after all, and she didn't care if Fenella joined in or not.

Fenella had gone weeping to her mother, and Saidh had feared she would be stuck playing dolls again, but her mother had kept to her original rules. If Saidh wished to play hide-and-seek, then Fenella could either join in, or sit with her all day. Fenella had chosen to sit with Saidh's mother that day and for two days following, but on the third day had finally come out to play with them. That was the day they'd played at being Britons and Saidh had left her tied to a tree. She had paid for that by having to play dolls the next day after Fenella had gone weeping to Saidh's mother again and tattled.

And so Fenella's stay at Buchanan had gone. If she didn't get her way, she wept, which quite often got her her way. At least from Saidh's mother and brothers. Since Saidh was not a crier, her brothers were unused to dealing with a weeping female and did whatever they could to shut the girl up. Saidh, however, not being a crier, just found the copious tears annoying and did her best to avoid the lass during her long visit. She'd been greatly relieved when Fenella's father had come to take her home.

But she hadn't held any of that against Fenella when her family had gone to attend the girl's wedding to Hammish Kennedy. And Fenella didn't appear to bear a grudge either. They'd got along well enough then during the little time they'd spent together before the wedding, although Saidh had found herself feeling somewhat awkward and lacking next to the dainty, ladylike woman Fenella had grown into. She still did, she supposed.

Frowning, Saidh glanced at Lady MacDonnell and asked, "Do ye really think Fenella killed yer son?"

"Aye," Lady MacDonnell said at once, her expression hard, and then conflict crossed her face and she admitted, "I do no' ken. There is just something . . ." Sighing, she eyed Saidh and asked, "Do ye think she is capable o' it?"

Saidh turned her face down to her stitching. She knew Fenella was capable of it. She'd killed her first husband after all, but that had been under much different circumstances and after he'd abused her horribly. However, Fenella claimed Allen was nothing like Hammish Kennedy. In fact, from what Fenella had said, Allen had been the perfect man for her.

Raising her head, she said, "I suspect everyone is capable o' killing in the right circumstances, but from what Fenella has told me she truly loved yer son. She says he was most kind to her, and considerate."

Lady MacDonnell released a short laugh and shook her head. "He was kind enough to leave her alone in her bed and considerate enough to order the servants to do what would make her happy so that he did no' have to and was free to go on doing as he wished."

"Ye knew he was no' claiming his husbandly rights?" Saidh asked with surprise.

"Oh, aye," Lady MacDonnell said with a crooked smile, and then told her solemnly, "Me son ne'er lied to me, and told me years ago that he preferred the company o' men."

"Do no' all men prefer the company o' other men?" Saidh asked dryly.

"Not usually in their bed," Lady MacDonnell said in hushed tones.

Saidh stared at her wide-eyed. "Allen . . ."

Lady MacDonnell nodded sadly. "Allen was a

good son; smart, strong, an excellent warrior and laird, and ever kind and affectionate with me. He always did what was expected o' him, except in this one area, and I believe he would ha'e if he could ha'e, but he simply could no'. "

"He told ye this?" she asked with disbelief.

"As I said, he was ever honest with me," Lady MacDonnell said with a little sigh and then shook her head. "And I think he wanted me to understand. Ye see, he did no' want to be that way. 'Tis a dangerous and difficult life. The church considers it unnatural and has men like him burnt at the stake, or mutilated and then hanged," she pointed out.

"Aye," Saidh murmured. The church was very much against sodomites. Frowning, she shook her head. "Then why did he no' just . . ." She paused helplessly, unsure how to put it.

"Why did he no' just decide to prefer the company o' women?" Lady MacDonnell suggested quietly, and when Saidh nodded she announced out of the blue, "I detest fish."

Saidh blinked in confusion at what seemed a change in subject, but then said, "I do no' care fer it meself. I'd rather no' eat at all than suffer fish fer a meal. I prefer beef and chicken and suchlike."

"Aye. So do I," Lady MacDonnell admitted, and then asked, "But why do ye no' like fish? Did ye sit down one day and simply decide ye'd no' like it?"

"Nay," Saidh said on a laugh at the very suggestion. "I've naught against fish. 'Tis just no' to me taste. 'Tis too . . . fishy," she finished helplessly.

Lady MacDonnell nodded. "'Tis the same fer

me. And that is how Allen made me understand.
He did no' sit down one day and decide he did no'
like women and preferred men. Women were just
no' to his taste. He said, he realized that he was different when a lad began to moan on about one o'
the maids in the castle where they were squiring together. The lad was drooling after her rather large
breasts, saying they were the finest he'd ever seen,
and asked Allen if he did no' agree. Allen told me
that he then looked at the woman, but did no' think
she was all that fine or worth the other boy's lavish
comments. In fact, he did no' find her attractive at
all, although the other squire was attractive to him."

"Oh," Saidh breathed.

"He told me that he did no' wish to be that way,
that his life would be much easier if he were like
other men, so he'd tried to like women, but he just
did no' seem to have been made that way." Lady
MacDonnell's expression was terribly sad, her voice
soft as she admitted, "It tormented him terribly. He
felt shame and confusion and was sure he was a fail-
ure as a son. But he assured me that he would do his
duty and marry and present me with grandchildren
as was expected."

"Oh," Saidh repeated weakly.

"And so, he set about finding a bride," Lady Mac-
Donnell continued quietly. "I told him he must be
most careful in his choosing, that most brides would
expect him to claim his marital rights on a regular
basis and that he could wound their esteem with his
lack of interest. So he set out in search of one who
would not be wounded by his lack o' interest."

"Fenella," Saidh said with realization.

"Aye," Lady MacDonnell said solemnly. "Allen's own betrothed had died while still a child, but there were a surprising number of women in the same position. He met with many o' them to consider them as brides, but most were too eager and spoke o' wanting babes right away, and many babes to boot. And then he met Fenella, who seemed to shrink from his touch and avoid his gaze, and so he tried to find out more about her." Mouth tightening, she admitted, "There had been whispers when Hammish Kennedy lived, of his strange tastes and cruelties in the bedchamber, and there had been a great deal of talk and dismay at how much blood covered the bedsheets they hung in the hall the day after his wedding to Fenella."

Saidh swallowed and nodded as she recalled those sheets herself. She'd been rather horrified too. It had looked like they were the sheets of someone who had been dealt a mortal blow and bled out in their bed, and Fenella had been so pale the next morning.

"Allen suspected Fenella feared the marital bed and would no' trouble him o'er much for his presence in her bed," Lady MacDonnell continued sadly, "And so he married her at once and brought her home."

Saidh sat back in her chair, her mending forgotten in her hands. "Well, that explains his kindness in no' claiming his husbandly rights." She smiled crookedly and admitted, "Allen was right, Fenella was terrified o' the marital bed after her first marriage. Actually, I suppose they were perfect fer each other."

"Aye," Lady MacDonnell agreed.

Saidh tilted her head and asked, "And yet ye still suspect her o' killing him. Why?"

"Fer the most part, Fenella was fine. But sometimes she'd get this look in her eyes . . . a flatness, cold and empty," Lady MacDonnell said slowly, almost as if she was trying to understand herself what made her suspect the woman had killed her son. "And then there is the feather."

Saidh didn't hide her confusion. "The feather?"

Lady MacDonnell set down her sewing, her gaze far away as she explained, "The senior MacIver was an old and dear friend o' me husband's when he lived, and so I attended his wedding to Fenella," she explained. "I was still there in the morning when he was found dead in their bed. Fenella was . . ." She frowned and shook her head. "Well, she was crying, as usual. So meself and several of the other women still present offered to prepare the body fer burial."

Saidh nodded and simply waited for her to continue.

"We were washing the body," she said slowly. "I was working on his face and noted that his eyes were bloodshot."

"Oh?" Saidh didn't have a clue what that might suggest.

Lady MacDonnell seemed to realize that and explained, "Allen was no' me only child. I had three sons ere him, and all o' them died ere they reached a year in age, and all in their sleep. I thought it was me fault, that I was birthing weak babes, but then when Allen was a wee tot, just months old, I woke in the middle o' the night, suddenly anxious o'er him and went to check on him. I caught the wet nurse trying to smother him with a pillow. She confessed she'd done the same to each of my other sons."

"I'm so sorry," Saidh said sincerely, horrified at the tragedies the woman had suffered in her life. She'd lost four sons, all told now.

"Thank ye," Lady MacDonnell said solemnly. "But ye see, me three dead boys had bloodshot eyes too and once I kenned what the maid had done, I did wonder if it were no' somehow a result o' the smothering."

"And Laird MacIver had bloodshot eyes," Saidh said slowly.

Lady MacDonnell nodded. "O' course, that was no proof. Laird MacIver was an old man and his eyes were often bloodshot and rheumy."

"Oh." Saidh nodded again.

"But there was also a goose feather in his mouth, caught at the back o' his tongue," Lady MacDonnell added grimly.

"Ye think Fenella smothered him with a goose?" Saidh asked uncertainly and Lady MacDonnell gave a surprised laugh.

"Nay, me dear, Laird MacIver was wealthy and had had his pillows and mattress stuffed with goose feather and herbs to encourage sweet dreams," she explained.

"Oh." Saidh grimaced and then admitted, "Our pillows were stuffed with wool and rags."

"Ah." Lady MacDonnell said with a smile.

"So ye think Fenella smothered him with his pillow and one o' the feathers was somehow . . ."

"Sucked into his mouth as he gasped fer breath," Lady MacDonnell said quietly. "I now think 'tis a possibility. Although, at the time I just assumed the feather may have been loosed in his efforts to bed Fenella, and that he'd sucked it in then." She grimaced and shook her head. "The senior MacIver was an old man, after all, and 'tis doubtful she'd have had long to wait to be widowed anyway, so why would she take the risk and kill him? Besides, the senior MacIver was only her second husband and the first had been killed by bandits who had struck her down as well."

Saidh bit her lip and held her tongue.

"Even when Laird MacIver's nephew married her and then died so precipitously I did no' think she may ha'e killed either man. After all, the younger MacIver was out riding alone and she was in the castle with his mother and aunt, so 'twas no' as if she could ha'e done it."

"Aye," Saidh muttered, but she was recalling the pin in Joan's horse that had made it go wild and throw her.

"But now me own son has died, a fourth husband in as many years, and that does seem like a ridiculous amount of bad luck fer any lass to suffer." Lady MacDonnell shook her head and sighed. "Mayhap I am just looking fer someone to blame fer me loss. After all, fearing the marital bed made marriage to Allen the perfect situation fer her. She was the wife of the laird, Lady o'er all o' MacDonnell with wealth and position and a fine title. His death leaves her little but dependence on Greer's kindness."

Saidh didn't comment and after a moment, Lady MacDonnell muttered, "But I keep thinking, 'Four dead husbands . . .' and I remember that tale me father used to tell me about the scorpion and the frog when I was a child."

"The scorpion and the frog?" Saidh asked curiously.

"Aye." She smiled faintly. "Me father traveled to foreign lands when young and had many tales to tell. I used to love to sit at his feet or on his knees and listen to him tell them to me siblings and meself. One he liked to tell was about a scorpion who wished to cross a river. O' course, the scorpion could no' swim—a scorpion is apparently a large buglike creature that can kill with its sting," she explained, apparently noting Saidh's confusion.

"Oh," Saidh said with a grimace. She didn't care for bugs much.

"At any rate, the scorpion could no' swim and asked a passing frog to take him o'er the river. The frog refused o' course, saying the scorpion would sting him. But the scorpion argued that o' course he would no', else they'd both drown. So the frog allowed the scorpion to climb on his back and started to swim across the river."

"And the minute they reached the other side the scorpion stung and killed him," Saidh guessed with disgust.

"Nay," Lady MacDonnell said patiently. "He

stung him when they were only halfway across the river."

"What?" Saidh squawked. "The daft creature, why would he do a thing like that?"

"That's exactly what I asked," she said with a smile. "And, according to me father, the frog asked that as well. Why would ye sting me? Now we will both die, he says as they are drowning."

"What did the scorpion say?" Saidh asked curiously.

" 'Tis me nature."

Saidh stared at her blankly.

"And I wonder," Lady MacDonnell said unhappily. "Four weddings and four dead husbands. Mayhap that wedding night that made her so affeared o' the marriage bed did something else to Fenella, mayhap it twisted her thinking so that she can no' help but kill her husbands, just as the scorpion could no' help but sting the frog."

Saidh let her breath out slowly and sank back in her seat.

"But as I said, perhaps I'm jest looking fer someone to blame fer losing me sweet son. After all, we ken she did no' kill her first husband, and it does no' seem likely she could have killed her third." Lady MacDonnell shook her head and set aside her sewing. "I'm suddenly tired. I think I'll go ha'e a lie-down ere the sup." She smiled at Saidh and added, "And ye're no' to continue with the sewing without me. Why do ye no' go take a ride on yer mare, or a walk in the bailey? The fresh air will probably do ye more good than my nattering has."

"Mayhap I will," Saidh murmured, setting aside the mending she'd been working on. Standing, she said, "Good sleep," to Lady MacDonnell as the woman headed away, and then just stood there and watched her cross the hall and mount the stairs. Even after the woman disappeared from sight, Saidh continued to stand there looking toward the stairs.

Saidh knew she should really go check on Fenella, but didn't want to. In fact, she didn't think it was a good idea to get anywhere near her cousin until she'd had a chance to absorb and think through everything that she'd just learned. Sighing, she finally turned and strode out of the great hall, heading for the stables.

Chapter 6

"Oy!"

Greer gestured for his practice partner to stop, and then lowered his sword and turned to glance toward Alpin at that shout. He then followed the lad's gesture toward the stables in time to see Saidh disappearing inside. He'd ordered the boy to keep an eye out for her when he'd come out earlier, and the boy had done as told.

A slow smile curving his lips, Greer glanced around in search of his first. Bowie must have heard Alpin's call. The tall golden-haired man was already looking his way and now hurried over at his gesture.

"Aye, m'laird?" the man asked as he paused before him.

"Continue to oversee the men. I need to ha'e a word with Lady Buchanan."

"Aye, m'laird," Bowie bobbed his head and then turned toward the men to find they'd all stopped to see what was about. Scowling, Bowie began shouting orders at them to get on with it and Greer nodded with satisfaction and started away. The man had been his cousin's first, and he'd inherited him along with the rest of MacDonnell. Allen had made a good choice, however, Bowie was smart, strong and good at his job. He'd proven himself invaluable in helping Greer learn what he needed to as he took on the role as the new laird.

The thought made him sigh, but Greer shook his head and pushed aside the depressing thoughts of his cousin and his new position. He had other matters to attend to just now, and the most important one at the moment was Lady Buchanan.

He found her alone in the stables when he stepped inside. The stable master was nowhere to be seen and Saidh was in her mare's stall, murmuring soothingly to the beast as she saddled her. The sight brought a satisfied grunt from his lips. She knew how to tend to her beast and didn't mind doing it. That was good. Greer knew many ladies who would have stood about, wringing their hands as they waited impatiently for the stable master or one of the stable lads to arrive and do it for her.

"So ye're done yer sewing lesson with me lady aunt?" he commented idly, walking down to lean his arms on the stall she was in.

Saidh glanced around with surprise and then scowled at him. "She was no' teaching me. I was helping her."

"Helping her how? Ye told me ye could no' sew," he reminded her with amusement.

"Ye asked if I could sew and I said I'd sewn me brother up once after cutting him. I did no' say I could no' sew."

"Ah." Greer grinned, and opened the stall door to step inside. "Where are ye going?"

"I thought to go fer a ride," she announced.

"Alone?" he asked with a frown.

Saidh shrugged. "I ha'e me sword."

"Ye could ride me," he offered and when she turned a startled glance his way, realized what had come out of his mouth and clucked his tongue. "I mean ye could ride *with* me. I'd go fer a ride with ye." He wouldn't mind her riding him either, or his riding her too, but that hadn't been what he'd meant to say. His first offer had been a slip of the tongue.

Saidh finished with the saddle in silence, then stepped away from the horse and closer to him. Very close to him. So close he could see the faint freckles that dusted her cheeks and feel her breath on his chin as she peered up at him.

"I might like that," she said in a husky whisper. "I enjoyed our last ride."

Greer's eyebrows nearly leapt up into his hair at that. He was damned sure she wasn't talking about horses now. The lass had just admitted she'd enjoyed his touch and kisses and—well, of course he'd known that. She hadn't exactly been quiet when she'd found her pleasure, but in his experience ladies simply didn't boldly admit to such things. They blushed, and batted their eyelashes and gave nervous giggles and . . .

Saidh definitely was not like other women, he reminded himself. And he liked that about her. A lot.

Smiling, he slid his hand around her neck to cup her head, then lowered his mouth to cover hers in what he'd intended to be a gentle caress. But when

Saidh immediately slid her arms around his waist, pressed closer and let her mouth open to welcome him, he forgot his intentions and went a little mad. The sudden rush of blood to his head and groin did not aid him much in the matter. The lass played havoc with his thinking just with her unfettered response to his touch.

When she sighed into his mouth and tightened her arms around him even as she plastered her breasts against him, he found himself forgetting where they were and tugging at the neckline of her gown, eager to see and feel the soft globes crushed between them. Saidh moaned her complaint when he finally broke the kiss so that he could urge her upper body back to better work at her gown and then impatiently helped him to get the task done quickly. She even tugged the top right off her shoulders, baring herself to him.

"Oh, aye," Greer growled, covering them with his hands and kneading gently. "Aye."

"Kiss me," Saidh demanded, sinking one hand into his hair and tugging his head down.

Greer gave in to the demand, growling and raising his leg slightly when she instinctively sought her own pleasure by slipping one leg between both of his to ride his thigh as he kissed her. They both moaned as her leg rubbed against his erection and his thigh rubbed at the core of her.

He felt her tugging at his plaid and broke the kiss to glance down to see what she was trying to do, and Saidh gasped, "I want to feel ye too."

Greer started to back up then to make enough

room for her to remove his plaid, but paused as he bumped into her mare and it whickered gently. The sound made him blink in surprise. He'd quite forgotten where they were, and he didn't recall doing it, but had turned her against the stall door so that his back was to her mare.

Another tug drew his gaze to see that she was working at the pin at his shoulder that held his plaid in place and he quickly covered her eager fingers. "No' here."

"What?" She frowned with incomprehension. "But I want—what are ye doing?"

Greer grinned at her scowl as he pulled her gown back over her shoulders and began to do up her lacings. "The stable master could come back at any moment."

"What? Oh." He could tell by her expression that she too had forgotten where they were and the knowledge pleased him greatly. At least he was not alone in the effect they had on each other.

"Then come fer a ride with me," she whispered, taking over her lacings.

Greer was tempted, but shook his head. If he went with her now, it wouldn't be his horse he'd be riding at the first clearing they reached. "I've work to do."

Her eyes narrowed. "What work? Ye were offering to ride with me just a minute ago."

"Aye, but that's no' such a good idea," he said gently.

Saidh growled under her throat as she finished with her lacings, and then propped her hands on her hips. "I could jest punch ye, m'laird. I really could."

"It's no' punching yer wantin'," he said gently, understanding her frustration. He was feeling a fair bit o' that himself. Fortunately, he could take his out on his men in the practice field. She had nowhere to relieve her frustration, he realized and after a brief hesitation, urged her back up against the stall door again.

"What are ye—?" she began with surprise and then gasped when he suddenly wrenched her skirt up, snaked his hand down the front of her braies and sunk his fingers into the wet heat that already waited there.

"Oh," Saidh moaned with understanding and reached for him, trying to pull his head down for a kiss.

Greer tugged his head back and shook it in refusal, knowing that if he kissed her, he'd be lost. Mouth set grimly, he began to caress her, finding the small nub that was the center of her pleasure and running his finger lightly over and then around it.

"Oh," Saidh gasped. Closing her eyes, she clutched at his arms and shook her head from side to side as if in denial of the excitement he was stirring inside her.

"Greer, please," she groaned, pressing herself against him. Her nails were digging into his arms through the shirt he wore under his plaid, and her hips were shifting into his caresses almost urgently. "Please, kiss me."

Instead, he tucked her face against his chest with his free hand and then held her close as he slid one finger inside of her.

Saidh cried out then, the sound muffled by his

plaid and chest, and Greer found himself gritting his teeth and thought that this was the stupidest damned thing he'd ever done. Her flesh had closed around the digit, hot and wet and oh so tight, and he knew that was how it would feel around his cock, sucking him in, trying to keep him there as he thrust again and again, his hips bucking, his cock throbbing.

A sudden sharp pain at his chest was followed by Saidh's crying out against him and then grabbing at his hand to stop it moving, and Greer realized that he'd brought her to release and she was now sensitive to his continued caress. It also made him realize that he had been humping her hip as he worked to give her that release and was now as hard as a dead hen and aching something terrible.

Heaving a sigh, Greer eased his hand out of her braies and let her skirt drop around her legs again. He then stood still and waited. Saidh was holding him tightly, and Greer knew she was struggling to slow her breathing and regain her composure, mostly because he was doing the same. He was also hoping that if given a minute, his cock would stop throbbing and shrink again, at least enough that he could walk back out to the men as if he hadn't been doing what he'd been doing in here.

"Still want to punch me?" he asked after a moment, to distract them both.

Saidh gave a laugh and shook her head against his chest.

"Good," he murmured, running one hand lazily down her back and wondering what the meaning was behind what he'd just done. Greer was not the sort to find his pleasure and leave a woman with none. He always ensured his lovers enjoyed whatever time they spent with him. But this was the first time he'd sought to give a woman pleasure without seeking his own too. Especially when he wanted her so badly that his whole body ached rather than just his balls. She was a lady, of course, which made that impossible . . . so why had he done what he had instead of leaving her to deal with her frustration in her own way?

"I should go fer me ride and let ye get to yer work," Saidh said suddenly, distracting him from his thoughts. She stepped back out of his arms in a manner that seemed almost reluctant, which Greer liked. But he didn't like the thought of her out riding alone. However, his aching—and still rock-hard—cock told him that accompanying her would be folly.

"Ye can take me squire with ye," he decided suddenly.

Saidh paused next to her mare and glanced to him with surprise. "That's no' necessary."

"Mayhap, but 'twould make me feel better to ken yer no' alone do ye run into difficulties," he said with a shrug and slipped out of the stall to head for the stable doors. He was halfway to them when the stable master stepped inside and then stopped with surprise.

"Oh, m'laird," the man said, then glanced down to the items in his hands and explained, "I was just getting a poultice for the horse that cut her leg yesterday. Did ye wish me to saddle yer—"

The stable master paused abruptly, eyes widening as his gaze lowered back toward the items he carried, but paused on Greer's plaid. He didn't have to look down to know why. He was aware that he was still noticeably excited, his erection poking out the front of his plaid in a most obvious manner. He supposed he should be embarrassed, but wasn't. Life, he had learned, was full of such moments for everyone. There was no sense agonizing over them, so he smiled with amusement and said, "I doubt ye've a saddle to fit that."

The stable master blinked and glanced up with confusion, then seemed to get the joke and grinned. "Nay, m'laird. But I could make one special if ye'd like."

"Reins and a whip might come in more handy," Greer said dryly.

"Aye, for most men I think," the stable master said with amusement. "I might no' be plagued with so many children if I'd had reins and a whip fer me own tarse when I was younger."

Greer chuckled and continued past the man.

"So, ye'll no' be needing yer horse saddled?" the stable master asked, making Greer pause at the door and glance back.

"No' mine, but I'd appreciate it if ye could saddle Alpin's pony. He'll be accompanying Lady Buchanan on a ride."

"Ah." The stable master glanced to where Saidh was caressing her mare's nose in the animal's stall. He then glanced back to Greer's slowly lowering plaid and nodded wisely before meeting his gaze and saying, " 'Tis fer the best it's the boy who joins her, at least until ye've found those reins and a whip."

"That was me thinking too," Greer agreed dryly and then the two men laughed and he turned to stick his head out the door to bellow, "Alpin!"

"A LADY DOES NO' CLIMB TREES."

"Ye've told me that three times now, lad," Saidh responded dryly, shifting her foot up to the next branch and hauling herself upward.

"Aye, but ye're still doing it, so I thought mayhap ye had no' heard me," Alpin said sharply. When she didn't respond to that, he added, "I could climb up there to pick the apples and throw them down, ye ken."

"Then there would be no one to catch them," Saidh pointed out.

"I was thinking mayhap ye could stay below and catch them, as a lady should," he said, sounding much put upon.

Saidh plucked the apple she'd been climbing to and glanced down to see where the boy was before dropping it in his direction. Once Alpin had caught it, and set it with the others they'd already gathered, she started to climb down and asked, "Just how old are ye, Alpin?"

"Nine," he said proudly.

"Hmmm," she muttered, easing down another branch. "Ye act ninety."

"Laird MacDonnell says the same thing," Alpin announced with disgust.

"Then we are in agreement," Saidh said cheerfully, easing down another branch.

"I suspect the two o' ye would agree on a lot o' things," Alpin said sounding annoyed.

"I suspect yer right," Saidh said with a laugh and jumped to the ground. She took a moment to brush her hands together, then released her skirt from where she'd caught it up and stuck it through her belt for the climb, then beamed at the boy and said, "Is that no' nice?"

"Nay," Alpin assured her heavily. "I'm thinking 'tis a bad thing."

Her eyebrows rose in surprise. "Why is that?"

"Because ye both just go about doing as ye wish with little regard fer how a laird or lady should behave," he said firmly. "Someone needs to take the two o' ye in hand and teach ye— What the devil are ye doing now?" he interrupted himself to ask with dismay when Saidh moved over to the apples, caught her skirt up and knelt to begin placing the apples in the bag-type affair she'd made of her skirt.

"Gathering the apples we've collected," Saidh answered patiently.

"I can see that, but ye canna ride back like that," he said with dismay.

"Sure I can," she said easily. "I've two hands after all, one to hold me skirt up, the other to hold the reins."

"But ye can no' ride around with yer skirt up like that," he cried.

"I'm wearing braies under me skirt, Alpin," she pointed out dryly.

"I ken that," he said with disgust, "but ye do no' want the whole bailey kenning it. And ye surely can no' be planning to walk through the castle like that too. What if Lady MacDonnell or one o' the servants sees ye?"

She couldn't tell which idea horrified him more, the servants seeing it or Lady MacDonnell. Saidh shook her head. Truly, the boy acted like an old woman. He'd done nothing but nag at her since they'd started out on this ride. She shouldn't ride astride, he'd instructed. What the devil was she doing wearing braies under her gown? That wasn't proper. She shouldn't ride so fast. She shouldn't be jumping boulders or bushes on her mare. She shouldn't climb trees. Truly, Saidh felt sure if she had to listen to his nagging much longer, she might be tempted to kill the lad, and had no idea how Greer had managed not to before now.

Finished collecting the apples, Saidh stood and moved to mount her mare. The action was a bit awkward with only one hand available, but she managed it and then glanced around to see if Alpin was ready. He wasn't. The boy still stood by where the apples had been, hands on hips and glaring fiercely.

"Alpin," she said patiently, "If ye plan to accompany me back to the keep, I suggest ye mount up . . . else I'll leave ye behind."

"A lady should ne'er ride alone. There could be bandits or—hey!" he bellowed, and ran for his horse when Saidh set her mare to start moving.

Laughing, Saidh urged her horse to more speed, uncaring if the boy caught up or not. Really, he was a little pain in the arse and she didn't know how Greer bore it.

That thought brought Greer firmly to mind and Saidh sighed and relaxed in the saddle, unintentionally allowing the mare to drop back to a trot. That man, she thought almost dreamily and shivered as she recalled the pleasure he'd given her in the stables. Her body was still tingling from what he'd done, which she didn't understand at all, because the tingling hadn't lasted as long after that time in the clearing.

Of course, perhaps the dunking in the loch had put an end to it then, she thought now. There had been no cold water to cool her fevered body this time, and not only was it still tingling, she could feel the dampness still between her legs. She even felt more pool there every time she thought of Greer and what he'd done. He'd driven her out of her mind with his talented fingers and God it had felt good.

Although, she thought with a sudden frown, it would have felt better had he kissed her while he was doing it. Saidh had missed his kisses. Without those, it had felt less like something they were doing, more like something he was doing to her, and for some reason that bothered her. Had he enjoyed it at all? she wondered, and then glanced around with a scowl when Alpin rode up beside her and began to lecture, "A lady does not—"

Saidh didn't stick around to hear what she was doing wrong this time, but urged her mare to move faster and rode ahead again. She shouldn't have slowed down anyway, Saidh thought. She had no time to sit about fretting over Greer at the moment. She had to get the apples to Cook.

Saidh had considered what she'd learned from Lady MacDonnell and had come to the conclusion that she needed to talk to her cousin and ask some hard questions. The apples were supposed to help with that. Saidh was hoping if she got the apples to Cook quickly enough, he could make Fenella's favorite dessert, applemoyse, in time for the sup. Because Saidh was hoping that the dessert would disarm her cousin and make her speak more freely when she asked the questions she wanted to.

"Is the meal no' to yer liking?"

At Greer's question, Saidh glanced up from the piece of cheese she had been tearing to shreds and smiled faintly.

"Nay. 'Tis fine. I am just . . ." Shrugging, she set down the remainder of the cheese without saying that she was simply trying to sort out how she was supposed to ask her cousin if she had killed any of her last three husbands, without sounding like that was what she was asking. Saidh was sure if she went charging into the room sounding accusatory Fenella would shut down and refuse to speak to her at all. And she was already at a disadvantage, to her mind, since it had been too late for Cook to make the applemoyse in time for sup when she'd got the apples to him.

"Saidh?" Greer prompted.

"Hmm?" she glanced to him, noted his questioning expression and realized he was waiting for her to finish her answer. Sighing, she shook her head and muttered, "I was just thinking."

"About what?" he asked.

"About the scorpion and the applemoyse," she said unhappily.

"The scorpion and the applemoyse?" Greer echoed with bewilderment.

"Aye, I fear I was too late getting the apples to Cook and he did no' ha'e time to make the apple-moyse before the sup."

"I see," he said slowly. "And what has that to do with a scorpion?"

"Oh." Saidh frowned. "Well ye see, when Lady MacDonnell's father was on crusade there was this scorpion that wanted to cross this river."

"And did my aunt's father ken this scorpion?" Greer queried.

"No, he did no', dear," Lady MacDonnell said, leaning forward from where she sat on the other side of Greer. She smiled at Saidh around her nephew's body, and then shifted her gaze to him to explain, "Saidh is telling ye a story that me father brought back with him from the Crusades. It was told to him there. I do no' believe he e'en saw a scorpion him-self."

"Oh," Greer said with a smile. "I see."

Lady MacDonnell smiled then and stood. "I find I am still weary tonight. Perhaps my humors are out of balance. I think I shall retire and hope that rest helps fight off whatever ails me."

"I'll wish ye good sleep then," Greer said, stand-ing when she did.

"Thank ye, Greer," she reached up to kiss his cheek and pat his arm.

"Good sleep, m'lady," Saidh murmured.

"And to you, dear," Lady MacDonnell said with a gentle smile, reaching out to touch her shoulder affectionately as she passed.

Greer waited until Lady MacDonnell had reached

the stairs before retaking his seat. Flashing a smile at Saidh then, he said, "She appears to be becoming quite fond o' ye, and quite quickly."

Saidh noted his pleased expression, but merely shrugged. "I like her too."

"Good, good," he said happily.

"Why is that good?" she asked.

"Ne'er mind. Tell me about me aunt's father's scorpion," he suggested.

"Right." Saidh shifted sideways on the bench to face him and began, "Well, as I said, the scorpion wanted to cross the river, but could no' swim, and—"

She paused and glanced to the side when Bowie appeared behind Greer. He offered Saidh an apologetic smile, but then the first leaned over to murmur something she couldn't hear in the MacDonnell laird's ear.

"Excuse me fer jest a moment," Greer said apologetically to Saidh, then stood and followed his first out of the keep.

Saidh scowled after him, glanced down at her uneaten food, but then just pushed it away and stood up. She headed toward the stairs, thinking that she should go have her talk with Fenella, applemoyse or no applemoyse. But halfway to the stairs it occurred to her that Fenella was the one who had asked her to stay and could easily ask her to leave as well if she handled this incorrectly. That thought brought her to an abrupt halt. She didn't want to leave MacDonnell. She liked it here, she liked Lady MacDonnell, and she definitely liked Greer, and if she left she would not get to enjoy any more of his lovely kisses and caresses and—

Turning abruptly, she started back toward the table, deciding that she would talk to Fenella tomorrow . . . when she had the applemoyse . . . and had sorted out how to get the information she wanted without offending Fenella and getting sent away.

Saidh had only taken a couple of steps when she paused again. She didn't really want to sit on the hard bench, staring down at her uneaten food as she waited for Greer. She would sit by the fire instead, she decided, and turned in that direction only to stop again when someone tapped on her shoulder. Spinning back, she peered up at Greer. He was grinning. She scowled.

"Ye looked like a lost lamb the way ye were standing here first turning this way and then that," he teased.

"I was going to go above stairs and check on Fenella, and then thought to leave it until tomorrow and—" Saidh waved away the rest of her words, unwilling to explain the thoughts that had followed.

Greer merely nodded and suggested, "Come sit by the fire with me."

Nodding, she allowed him to walk her to the chairs by the fire.

"So," he said as they settled in the seats. "This scorpion?"

"Oh, aye." She paused briefly to gather herself, and then said, "The scorpion wanted to cross the river, but—"

"Why?" Greer interrupted.

Saidh paused and blinked. "What?"

"Why did the scorpion want to cross the river?" he asked.

"Well, I do no' ken," she said with irritation. "Yer aunt did no' explain that part."

"And ye did no' ask?" He seemed surprised.

"I am quite sure why he wanted across the river was no' important to the story," Saidh told him grimly.

"O' course, it is," he said scornfully. "A person's intent is always important."

"The scorpion is no' a person, he is a little buglike creature who can kill ye with his sting," she said with irritation.

"Still, if he wants to cross the river, there must be a reason," Greer said calmly. "Was there a lovely lady scorpion on the other side? Was he following his wife who already crossed? Did he—?"

"Fine," Saidh snapped. "He wanted to cross the river to escape the battling Crusaders."

"Ah." He nodded and smiled, eyes twinkling. "Very well, continue."

Heaving a sigh, she shook her head, regathered the thread of the story and said, "So the scorpion wanted to cross the river but could no' swim, so he asked—"

She paused abruptly and turned a warning look on Alpin when he suddenly appeared next to Greer's chair.

"Sorry," the lad muttered, and then turned to Greer and cleared his throat before saying, "If ye'll no' be needing me again this night, m'laird, might I retire?"

Greer appeared surprised at the request and narrowed his gaze on the boy, then reached out to press the back of his hand to Alpin's forehead. "Yer warm and flushed. Are ye no' feeling well?"

Alpin grimaced, but shrugged. "I'm sure I'm fine. Just a little under the weather."

"Go on then," Greer said firmly. "Ye can sleep on the foot o' me bed and take as many furs as ye need to stay warm."

"Thank ye, m'laird," Alpin whispered and turned to hurry toward the stairs.

"That was kind," Saidh commented quietly as Greer watched the boy go. "Most lairds would no' share their beds with their squire."

He smiled wryly and shrugged. "The lad is a good one. I'd ha'e let him sleep at the top o' the bed, but he kicks in his sleep."

Saidh bit her lip briefly, but then could not help it. "The boy nags like a fishwife."

"Aye, he does," Greer agreed with a grin. "But he's brave and hardworking and he grows on ye."

"Hmmph," Saidh said dubiously.

Greer chuckled at her obvious disbelief and began, "So, this scorp—" This time he was the one who was interrupted when the stable master appeared beside them.

Saidh dropped back in her chair with exasperation, but then stood and headed for the stairs. She no longer wanted to tell the tale of the scorpion and the frog anymore. Besides, she suspected she wouldn't ever get to finish the tale, but would be constantly interrupted again and again and, frankly, she was out of patience.

Chapter 7

"WHERE ARE YE GOING?"

Saidh was halfway up the stairs when that question and Greer's sudden appearance beside her gave her a start. Gripping the rail, she scowled at him for the scare, and said, "I'm going to me bed, m'laird."

"But what about the scorpion story ye were going to tell me?" he asked, following when she continued up the steps.

"I shall tell ye tomorrow. 'Tis obvious I'll no' be allowed to finish it tonight with all these interruptions anyway," Saidh muttered as she moved toward the door to her chamber.

"There'll be no more interruptions," he assured her.

"Ye do no' ken that," she argued, pausing at her door and turning to scowl at him.

"Aye, yer right," Greer admitted, then suddenly reached past her and opened her door.

"What the devil are ye doing?" she asked with surprise when he urged her quickly inside and then turned to close the door.

"No one would think to look for me here," he pointed out, then glanced around the room before catching her hand and leading her to the chairs by the fireplace. The fire was lit, though Saidh had no idea who had lit it. She had no maid to do it anymore. Yet, every night her fire was lit. It made her wonder if her maid had ever actually lit the fire at home or she'd just been wrong in assuming it was the woman who did it.

"Here, we shall sit here and ye can finish yer story," Greer said cheerfully, dropping into one of the chairs, and then tugging her to sit sideways in his lap.

"There is another chair where I could sit," she pointed out with a small smile.

"Aye, but this is nicer, is it no'?" he asked, running one hand lightly down her back, and the other catching her hand and beginning to toy with it.

It was, actually. Saidh liked it when Greer touched and held her, so she relaxed against his chest, and brushed a kiss over his cheek, and then whispered, "Aye," against his ear.

Greer's hand tightened on hers and then he growled, "Tell yer story, lass. If ye can."

Saidh sat back with surprise. "Why could I no' tell it?"

"Because I'm going to do me best to distract ye," he assured her with a slow, wicked smile.

Her eyes narrowed. "And jest how do ye plan to do that?"

"How do ye think?" he asked huskily, and ran his fingers lightly up the sensitive inner curve of her arm. "Why do we no' see if ye can tell the tale and finish it ere I make ye scream yer pleasure?"

Saidh shivered, her body already tingling and a heavy wetness beginning to pool low in her belly just at the suggestion. Voice a little breathless, she asked, "What do I get if I win?"

"Ye'd do better to ask what I get when I win. Because I will," he assured her, running his fingers along the top of her neckline now. Leaning forward, he whispered against her ear, "I like to win." His lips brushed the edge of her ear as he spoke, and were followed by a light nipping that made Saidh gasp and squirm on top of him.

Greer groaned at the action, his hands moving to her hips to still her. She didn't understand why until she became aware of the hardness suddenly poking the bottom of one thigh.

"Greer?" she whispered, staring down at his hands on her hips.

"Aye, lass?" he growled.

"I'm going to enjoy this game," Saidh breathed, raising her head to smile at him as she added, "And I like to win too."

He stared at her blankly for a minute, then threw his head back on a loud laugh, but Saidh covered his mouth to muffle it and shook her head as she muttered, "Ye'll ha'e 'em all up knocking on the door do ye carry on like that."

Greer sobered and pulled her hand away, murmuring, "Aye, and we would no' want that."

"No' if ye want to continue the game," she warned, and then rushed on, "So the scorpion wanted to cross the river, but could no' swim so he asked a passing frog to swim him across. But the—"

"Frogs jump, they do no' swim," Greer interrupted, beginning to lazily undo her lacings.

"Aye, they do so swim," Saidh argued, trying to ignore what he was doing.

"Prove it," he demanded, leaning forward to nibble his way up her neck as he continued to work on her lacings.

Saidh frowned and tried to think of a way to prove that frogs could swim, and then gasped as his lips found her ear and began to toy with it. "They . . . er . . ." she breathed, tilting her head toward him as he nibbled and licked at her ear. "That is . . ."

Her gown fell apart under his busy fingers and Saidh bit her lip as he pushed the cloth to the sides to get at her breasts.

"Lady MacDonnell said so," she gasped as his hands closed over her flesh.

"That is no' proof," he argued on a laugh, kneading gently.

" 'Tis her story, so if she says they swim, they swim," Saidh panted, twisting her upper body toward him and clutching at his shoulders as he tweaked her nipples and cupped her breasts by turn.

Greer looked thoughtful as he toyed with the round globes, but then nodded. "Fair enough."

"Aye," Saidh moaned, arching into his touch and then realizing what she was doing, gave her head a shake and picked up the thread of the story. "So he asked the frog, but the frog said, nay, he'd sting him."

"Who would?" Greer asked.

Saidh glanced down with confusion at the question just as he leaned forward to catch one nipple between his teeth and then suck it into his mouth. The sight alone was frightfully exciting, but the feeling . . . She moaned and shifted in his lap as he drew gently on the already hard bud, then gasped and arched her back as he suckled harder, drawing the entire dusty rosy aureole into his mouth and lashing it with his tongue.

"The . . . er . . ." Saidh shook her head to try to clear it and asked uncertainly, "What did ye ask me?"

Greer let her nipple slip from his mouth and ran his thumb lazily back and forth across the wet nub as he raised his head to give her a wicked grin. "Having trouble telling the tale?"

Annoyed at his gloating expression, she narrowed her eyes, her anger pushing back some of the passion he was so busily stirring in her. "Nay. Having trouble understanding the fool question. Who would what?" she finished, able now to recall his question.

"Who would sting him?" Greer said on a chuckle.

"The frog refused to give the scorpion a ride across the river because he feared the scorpion would sting him," Saidh said succinctly.

"Ah, I see." He nodded solemnly. "Thank ye fer explaining that. I was no' sure."

"Aye, ye were sure," she said dryly. "Yer just trying to slow me down to give ye more time to try to win this race."

"I'm wounded that ye think so little o' me, m'lady," Greer murmured, tugging her gown off her shoulders to pool around her waist, leaving her bare to his view. "Gawd, Saidh, yer a beautiful woman."

Saidh flushed with pleasure at the compliment, but gave a sniff and muttered, "Ye've seen it all before."

She thought he whispered, "No' like this," before he leaned forward to lave one breast.

Saidh determinedly steeled herself against the action and continued, "The scorpion argued that he'd no' sting him because he'd drown then too. So the frog—" Saidh paused abruptly as his hand suddenly slid up her thigh to cup her between her legs through the skirt of her gown. "You—I—"

Greer used his free hand to pull her head to him so that he could kiss her, and she moaned as he thrust his tongue into her mouth, emulating what he'd done between her legs in the stables with his fingers.

Saidh kissed him back briefly, but then turned her head away to moan, "That's no' fair. Ye stop me from talking doin' that."

"Yer right," he growled. "I'll no kiss ye again. Just turn in me lap, love, so we're facing each other."

Saidh shifted under his touch, her hands clenching on his shoulders now and gasped, "Why?"

"I want ye to ride me to yer pleasure. I like it when ye ride me like ye did in the clearing. Come, shift fer me," he pled, removing his hand from between her legs and nudging her hip.

Saidh hesitated, but then slid off his lap, catching her gown to keep it from falling to the ground as she did. Only rather than climb to straddle him in the chair, she grinned and then rushed out, "So the frog took the scorpion on his back and started to swim across the river."

"Bloody hell, now who's cheating," Greer muttered and caught her by the waist to lift her onto his lap himself.

Saidh straddled him, but her gown was caught beneath her and uncomfortably tight across her upper legs, so she raised herself slightly to pull the material from between them before settling to sit on him saying, "But halfway across the river the scorpion stung the frog."

"O' course he did," Greer muttered, tugging at the material of her gown to get enough of it out of the way that he could get his hand under to continue caressing her.

Desperate to get the story done before he could succeed, she rushed on.

"As the frog began to drown, taking the scorpion with him, he asked the scorpion. Why—eee," she ended on a small cry as his hand finally got beneath her gown and found her core. Shaking her head, she continued determinedly, "Why would ye sting me when it would mean yer own death too, and the scorpion said—"

"Lass?" Greer interrupted in a weak growl and she glanced to him, startled to see that his face had gone pale. He also wasn't caressing her, she realized. His hand was just pressed against her, unmoving.

"What?" she asked uncertainly.

"Where are yer braies?"

Her eyebrows rose at his sharp tone. "Well, I take

them off when I change fer sup. 'Tis no' as if I'm like to go riding at night," she pointed out reasonably.

"Oh, dear God," Greer groaned and lowered his head to rest his forehead on her breast, but not in a good I-want-to-suckle-at-yer-teat way. It was more a, God-has-forsaken-me-and-I-am-in-hell kind of despair he appeared to be acting out.

Saidh pursed her lips and eyed the man, but when he continued to remain as he was, appearing frozen, she shifted impatiently in his lap, and said, " 'Tis—"

"Do no' move." Greer almost roared the words. He lifted his head abruptly and snatched his hand out from under her skirts as if he'd touched hot coals. Spotting her startled expression, he opened his mouth, closed it, and then said more gently, "Pray, m'lady. Do no' move."

The man was obviously beyond distressed, though she had no idea why. He seemed to be upset that she wasn't wearing her braies, but she wasn't at all certain why. He'd slid his hand inside her braies and touched her just that afternoon, so it could not be that he was upset that she wasn't wearing them because he'd touched her so intimately.

Aware of a hardness poking uncomfortably into her bottom, Saidh hesitated, but really this was ridiculous and just how long did he expect them to sit like that? " 'Tis all right, I'm just going to . . ." She started to shift in an effort to find a more comfortable position and Greer groaned and then caught her hips in his hand and held her still.

"I swear, Saidh, if ye do that again I'll no' be able to stop meself," he warned through gritted teeth.

"All right," Saidh said soothingly, " 'Tis all right."

" 'Tis no' all right," he assured her grimly, lowering his head again. "I was counting on those braies and yer no' wearing them."

"I see," Saidh said weakly, but really didn't see at all. Did he prefer touching her through the braies? Or having to snake his hand down them? She had no idea, but she was growing weary of just sitting there, and really the game was no fun if he wasn't going to play it. All that lovely desire he'd stirred in her was now fading away. Sighing, she asked, "Shall I put me braies on now? Would that make ye feel better?"

"Nay," Greer growled. "What would make me feel better would be if ye'd sit still and let me think."

"What are ye thinking about?" she asked curiously.

"Fish," he said succinctly.

Saidh raised her eyebrows. "Why?"

"Because I detest fish."

"Really?" Saidh smiled. "So do I. Lady MacDonnell does too."

Greer merely cursed under his breath.

Saidh fell silent for another minute, but then cleared her throat and asked, "Why are ye thinking o' fish?"

"Saidh!" he snapped, then sighed and began to rub his temples and explained more gently, "Sweetling, I was counting on yer braies being on so that I could pleasure ye without taking yer innocence. But yer no' wearing yer braies, and I am struggling to keep from taking me pleasure, yer innocence be damned, so I am trying to control me passion by thinking o' dead smelly fish because they are the least passionate thing I can think o' and the one thing most likely to help me control meself."

"Oh," Saidh said quietly, but then asked, "Would it be so terrible if ye took yer pleasure? Ye've given me pleasure twice now and while I think ye enjoyed yerself the first time, I'm no' sure ye did in the stables. Surely ye deserve pleasure too."

"Dear God, ye swear like a warrior, fight like one too, but ha'e no survival instinct to speak o', lass," Greer said with despair, then caught her at the waist and lifted her off his lap and into the air even as he stood up. When Saidh's gown promptly slid over her hips and fell to pool on the floorboards beneath her, Greer looked as if he might weep. He also froze again and simply held her there in the air before him as his eyes roved hungrily over her bare body.

"Greer?" Saidh said softly.

He tore his gaze from his inspection of her body and raised his gaze to her face. "Aye?"

" 'Tis in me nature," she said solemnly and when he stared blankly, explained, "That is what the scorpion said to the dying frog, 'Tis in me nature." She smiled crookedly. "I win."

Greer released a breathless laugh and shook his head. "Nay, lass. I'm pretty sure I win."

"Nay. That is the end o' the story. I win," she insisted as he carried her across the room.

"It may be the end o' me aunt's story, but 'tis just the beginning o' ours," he assured her as he set her to sit on the end of the bed.

"But—"

"How long is the journey to Buchanan from here?" Greer interrupted, straightening.

Saidh frowned. "I do no' ken. Half a day, mayhap less."

Nodding, Greer turned and headed for the door, ordering, "Do no' move. I'll return directly."

Saidh stared after him with bewilderment as he slid from the room, then shook her head and dropped back on the bed with a little sigh. The man had obviously lost his mind. That was the only explanation that made sense to her. First he was touching and caressing her, then he was upset she wasn't wearing braies, then he started spouting things that made absolutely no sense and marched out ordering her not to move.

What the hell did he mean that she hadn't won? She'd finished the tale before he'd made her scream in pleasure. In fact, she was beginning to think he would never cause that now. And what was that nonsense about their story just beginning? What story was that?

More irksome to her, though, was his claim that she had no survival instinct to speak of. Saidh knew he meant because she'd as good as offered herself to him, but he was wrong. She was not an idiot. She knew ladies were supposed to save themselves for their husbands and that by giving herself to him she would be making herself unmarriageable. But it seemed to her that she wasn't likely to marry anyway. Her betrothed had died, and no laird was likely to want a woman as rough as her to wife. She'd spent too many years with her brothers, learned too many curse words and how to fight. She wore those precious braies under her skirts, rode astride like a man, and could fight like one too. She'd been given a taste of freedom growing up with her brothers as playmates, and doubted she could give up that freedom just to be some man's chattel.

So why not find her pleasure with Greer while she was young enough to enjoy it? Her brothers wouldn't think less of her for it, she was sure, and before she'd left for Sinclair for Joan's birthing, Aulay had told her that she would always have a home with him at Buchanan.

Sighing, she turned her head to peer at the door, wondering where the devil Greer had got to . . . and what he'd gone for in the first place? Perhaps he was fetching them food, she thought hopefully when her stomach made a deep growling sound. She'd been too busy fretting over Fenella to eat at sup and was now hungry. She was also a tad chilly, she noted, and sat up to glance toward the fire. A frown claimed her lips when she saw that the fire was half the size it had been when they'd entered her room earlier. It needed feeding too.

Slipping off the bed, she tugged the linen off to wrap around herself and walked to the fire to feed it some logs. She was kneeling on the fur in front of the fireplace, just using the iron to push the logs about and urge the fire to a happier glow when her door opened. Saidh glanced around to see Greer closing the door. He didn't have food, she noted unhappily.

Spying her by the fire and noting her expression, he asked, "What's the matter?" as he crossed the room toward her.

"I was hoping ye'd gone to fetch food," she admitted, setting the iron back as she straightened.

"I will later," he assured her coming to a halt. Smiling faintly, he reached up to remove the pin that held his plaid in place. "Ye look lovely even wrapped in a sheet."

"Do I?" Saidh asked vaguely, her attention caught by what he was doing as he set the pin on the table by the chairs and then gave his plaid a tug that sent it rushing toward the floor. Saidh stared wide-eyed at his now revealed calves and knees below the hem of his shirt, which ended at his thighs, and breathed, "Oh my, yer lovely too."

Greer chuckled at her words and then lifted his shirt, to tug it off over his head and Saidh simply stared at the appendage between his legs. It wasn't nearly as majestic as it had felt the few times it had pressed against her. It had felt as large and uncomfortable as a log when she'd been sitting on it earlier, but now it was kind of just hanging there all wrinkly and— Saidh's thoughts stopped abruptly as it began to grow, stretching and lifting toward her like a flower seeking the sun. Curious, she reached out without thinking to touch it, but Greer caught her hand before she could make contact.

Glancing up, she saw that he was staring at her with a sort of bemusement.

"Ye ha'e no a bone o' shyness in ye, do ye, Saidh?" he asked huskily.

" 'Tis hard to be shy with seven brothers barging into yer room at all hours," she said wryly. She tilted her head. "I suppose a proper lady would be shy?"

"Aye," Greer agreed. Reaching out he tugged her sheet loose and sent it tumbling to the floor on top of his plaid as he added, "But I like ye this way."

"Oh," Saidh sighed as he drew her into his arms. Her breasts touched his chest first, his coarse hairs there tickling them briefly before his warm skin pressed against them. Saidh slid her arms around his neck and raised her head expecting a kiss, and he gave her what she wanted and more. His mouth slanted over hers, his tongue thrusting as he slid his hands down her back, cupped her behind and scooped her up against him until he could kiss her without bending his head.

Greer kissed her again and again, moving his head first one way and then the other until she moaned and wrapped her legs around his waist. He broke the kiss then and lifted her higher to claim one nipple and Saidh's eyes fluttered open with surprise, and then widened as she saw that the room was moving around them. It took her a moment to understand that it wasn't the room moving. He was carrying her to the bed again, she realized and then he knelt to set her on the end of the bed without having to disengage her legs.

Saidh did that for him, allowing them to drop away on either side of him as he ducked his head to lave her breasts. Saidh moaned with pleasure and dug her hands into his hair, urging him on. She then groaned with disappointment when he stopped that, only to gasp in surprise when he began to trail kisses down her belly. The muscles of her stomach jumped excitedly and Saidh began to tug at his hair, unsure what he was doing and even less sure she liked it. But Greer caught her wrists and urged her to lie back on the bed, continuing to hold them to keep her from interfering as his mouth moved along one hip.

The man was strong, she thought vaguely as she struggled in vain to free her hands. And then suddenly he released her. Before she could reach for him though, his head dipped between her legs and Saidh froze in shock as his tongue rasped across that most sensitive skin.

"Greer?" she gasped uncertainly, grabbing at the sheet under her.

He didn't respond, at least not verbally, and Saidh bit her lip and struggled not to scream out with shocked pleasure as he urged her legs further apart and suckled at the nub at her core as if it were a nipple. Something pressed into her then, spreading and filling her before withdrawing to thrust back in again as he continued to lick and suckle her and Saidh groaned and gasped and panted by turn.

She wanted to move her hips, to thrust into his caresses, to fight toward the release she knew waited just out of sight, but he had her pinned and helpless to do anything except wait for him to give her that release. And then it rocked over her, like a storm rushing down from the hills and Saidh opened her mouth to scream. Before she could, his free hand was covering her mouth and muffling the sound.

Reminded that they weren't out in a clearing where no one would hear her, Saidh bit off the sound and closed her eyes as she sank into a boneless puddle on the bed. Her body was quivering, her heart still racing, her breath coming in heaving gasps, but her mind was floating in some far off land where pleasure reigned.

Saidh was vaguely aware of Greer moving, and a slight breeze replacing the heat of a moment ago between her legs and then something nudged at her opening before thrusting into her. This time it was something much larger than the finger she thought he must have been using earlier, something that sent pain screaming through her body, tearing away the gossamer wings of the pleasure she'd been enjoying. Saidh instinctively sat up with a roar and struck out defensively before he caught her hands to prevent further blows and she opened her eyes.

She stared at him, her chest heaving, her body aching where before it had known only pleasure, and Greer pulled her head against his chest and rubbed her back. "I'm sorry, sweetling. I thought it best to get it done in one push than to draw out the pain."

"What did ye stab me with?" she asked with confusion, not sure what had happened.

"Just me," he said solemnly and then eased his chest back a bit so that she could look down and see that they were joined, his body disappearing into hers.

"Oh," she said weakly. "I could ha'e sworn ye'd run me through with a sword."

Greer frowned. "I ha'e never taken a woman's innocence before. I had no' realized 'twould be that painful. Mayhap we should jest—"

"Nay," Saidh gasped, wrapping her legs around his hips to keep him in place when he started to withdraw, merely adding to her pain. "Just . . ." She closed her eyes briefly and shook her head. "Just stay put fer a minute."

"Saidh?"

She glanced sharply around at that call from what sounded like Lady MacDonnell out in the hall. The door rattled, but fortunately didn't open. Greer had dropped the bar, she saw. His forethought was impressive.

"Saidh, dear? Are ye all right?"

She squeezed her eyes briefly closed.

"Ye'd best answer or she'll ha'e the whole castle up here," Greer whispered by her ear.

Saidh nodded and forced her eyes open and called out, "Aye."

"Are ye sure? I thought I heard ye scream, lass. Should I—"

"I'm fine," Saidh said, forcing more conviction into her voice. "Truly, m'lady. I am sorry I disturbed ye. 'Twas jest . . . a nightmare," she finished wearily and leaned her forehead against Greer thinking that her words were not far from the truth. What had started out as a pleasant dream had certainly turned into a nightmare when Greer had thrust into her. Dear God, she'd heard that the first time could be painful, but this was—

"Would ye like to talk?" Lady MacDonnell asked now. "Mayhap 'twould help if ye told me about yer nightmare."

"Nay," Saidh said at once, turning to peer at the door with horror, almost afraid it would open any moment despite the bar across it.

Something brushed across one nipple and Saidh glanced down with surprise to see Greer's hand retreating. She followed it to his mouth where he licked the pad of his thumb, and then he lowered it again to brush it across the tip of the same nipple again. The warm wet, was quickly followed by cool as he brushed his thumb lazily back and forth, making the nub harden and rise and the aureole around it darken as it shrank and wrinkled, tightening in response.

Saidh swallowed as she watched, and then gasped as he did the same to the other breast, wetting his thumb and rubbing it lazily over her eager flesh. This time when she raised her face to peer at him, Greer lowered his head to kiss her, his tongue whipping out to continue to stir back to life the desire she'd thought had been killed by the joining.

"Would ye like a warm drink, mayhap? I could ha'e one o' the servants bring ye some mulled cider or spiced rum. Mayhap that would help."

"Nay," Saidh groaned when Greer broke their kiss.

"Did ye say nay or aye, dear? 'Tis hard to hear ye through the door."

Saidh gave her head a shake, trying to concentrate, and then sighed and called, "I'm so sorry I disturbed ye m'lady, and I appreciate yer kindness, but nay, I would jest rather get back to sleep."

"All right then, dear," Lady MacDonnell said and Saidh glanced sharply down again as Greer gave up on her breasts and reached between them to begin to caress the nub just above where they were joined.

Saidh bit back a gasp and clutched at his arms as he teased her passion quickly back to full life.

"But if ye change yer mind and need anything, I'm just up the hall, dear. And don't ye worry about waking me," Lady MacDonnell said through the door. "Ye just come see me if ye like. All right?"

"Oh, aye," Saidh gasped, raising her legs to wrap them around Greer's hips and dig her heels into his butt to give her leverage as she began to rock into his caresses.

"Very well then, good sleep, Saidh, dear. I'll see ye in the morn."

"Aye," Saidh almost cried the word as Greer eased himself out of her and then slid back in. There was surprisingly little pain this time, and much more pleasure as he continued to caress her and Saidh began to clench around his body, legs, arms and entire body tightening in an effort to keep him where it wanted him.

When Greer pressed her face to his chest, she turned her mouth to his skin, knowing he was offering her a way to stifle the sounds building up in her throat. Little whimpering gasps issued from her throat and were muffled by his skin as he continue to increase the pressure mounting in her, and then he suddenly withdrew his caressing hand, to clasp her hips and pull her hard into his last thrust. But Saidh was already tipping over the edge of the cliff into her own release, and she cried out against his chest even as he released a guttural sound that she suspected was a roar, murdered in its infancy.

Chapter 8

SAIDH ROLLED ONTO HER BACK AND STRETCHED lazily, but stopped the moment her body protested in several places. One of those places was not one where she generally experienced discomfort and it made her eyes shoot open as memory rushed through her of the night and what she'd done.

What *they'd* done, she corrected herself, and turned her head on the pillow to seek out Greer, only to find the space empty beside her.

Sitting up abruptly, Saidh glanced around the room, but every bit of evidence that the man had ever been there was now gone. His clothes no longer lay on the fur by the fireplace. Neither did the linen they'd left there last night. It was back on the bed, and covering her, she realized. But he'd also removed any evidence of the food and drink he'd gone down to fetch from the kitchens after their first time together. They'd eaten the food on the fur in front of the fireplace, or at least they'd started to, but had got somewhat sidetracked and had ended up with him tossing up her skirts on the fur . . . well, if she'd been wearing a skirt he'd have tossed it up, but she hadn't.

After that, they'd returned to the bed and Saidh had cuddled up against him and drifted off to sleep, only to wake some time later to his caressing her into a fever and then thrusting into her again.

Saidh dropped back on the bed with a little satisfied sigh. While the first time had been terrible—at least the breaching had—it had much improved after that. She'd still felt a twinge of pain a time or two as they'd mated, but Greer had driven her to such heights of passion before getting to that point that it had been easily ignored.

Just the memory of the things he'd done to her made a tingle burst to life at the apex of her thighs and Saidh closed her eyes on the bed coverings overhead, allowing herself to drown in the memories. After a moment, she slipped her fingers under the sheet and furs to touch herself tentatively, curious to know what he experienced when he did it.

It was actually the first time she'd ever touched herself there and Saidh was quite surprised at how soft and slippery she was. It didn't feel the same when she touched herself, though. She missed Greer's presence, the feel of his warm body against her, the intoxicating scent of him, the taste of him as he covered her mouth with his own.

Suddenly wondering where he was and what he was doing, Saidh withdrew her hand, and pushed the linens and furs aside to leap out of bed. She rushed to her trunk then, the only one she'd brought, and began to pull out and examine the few gowns she'd brought away with her from Sinclair, trying to decide what to wear. For the first time in her life what she wore mattered to her. She wanted to look pretty for Greer. Of course, that being the case, it would be a time when she'd left most of her gowns elsewhere.

She was muttering to herself with exasperation as she discarded gown after gown when a knock sounded at the door. Stilling, she glanced toward it with surprise, and then—thinking it might be Greer—she straightened and rushed to it, a smile breaking on her face. Fortunately, she retained enough good sense not to open the door wide, but to crack it open and peer around it, keeping her nudity hidden behind the wooden panel.

Much to her disappointment it was not Greer, but a servant at the door. Saidh stared at the woman blankly. "Aye?"

"M'laird ordered a bath fer yer pleasure," the maid said, offering a smile and curtsy.

"Oh," Saidh murmured, peering past the woman to the small army of servants behind her. Two bore a huge tub, and half a dozen others carried pails full of water. Her smile softened at Greer's thoughtfulness, and then she pushed the door closed, shouting, "Jest one minute."

Rushing back to the bed, she dragged the top sheet off to wrap around her body. Saidh started to turn away then, but her eye caught on a large stain of blood on the bottom of the bed. It was where he'd first taken her and breached her maidenhead, she realized with a grimace, and quickly threw the furs over it before yelling, "Come in."

The door opened at once, and Saidh whirled, and

then dropped to sit on top of the furs covering the stain as the servants began to bustle in with their burdens. They were quick about their business, and filed out of the room within moments, leaving a steaming bath in their wake. All of them left but the woman who had greeted Saidh on opening the door. She merely pushed the door closed behind the others and then turned to smile at Saidh.

"Lady MacDonnell said ye must ha'e left yer maid at Sinclair since ye arrived without one. She suggested I might take her place while ye're here," she announced and then added quickly, "If 'tis all right with ye?"

"Oh." Saidh hesitated. She'd happily made do without a maid this past year but she could hardly admit that. She was quite sure Lady MacDonnell would be horrified at her lack. However, she wasn't pleased with the idea of having one again. As much as she'd loved Erin, the maid had driven Saidh mad with her constant attempts to make her more a proper lady. She'd fuss forever over her hair, fiddling and fixing it into silly little ringlets and whatnot. As for the bath, the woman had been nothing but a bother there, wanting to fill it with all sorts of herbs, spices and flowers to make her "smell sweet" and then trying to wash her arms and legs for her as if she couldn't manage the task on her own.

Saidh did not mind help rinsing the soap out of her hair, but other than that, wanted no assistance when it came to bathing. She didn't feel like she could refuse the offer of a borrowed maid, though. Sighing, she stood and said, "I'd appreciate help rinsing the soap out o' me hair after I've washed it, but other than that need little in the way of assistance."

"As ye wish, m'lady," the woman said easily.

Relaxing a little, Saidh nodded and walked to the steaming bath.

"What is yer name?" she asked as she dropped the sheet and stepped into the tub.

"Joyce, m'lady," the woman said as she retrieved soap and a scrap of linen to offer to her.

"Thank ye," Saidh murmured taking the items.

"Yer welcome." Joyce started to turn away, but paused when she noted Saidh running the soap over the linen. She hesitated briefly, but then said gently, "It works out best if ye wash yer hair first. Then the water is fresh fer rinsing out the soap. As well it will dry a bit while ye wash the rest o' ye."

"Oh." Saidh peered at the soapy linen with a frown. Erin had always tried to get her to wash her hair first, but had never offered an explanation as to why so she'd waved away the suggestion. But what Joyce said made sense. She supposed 'twas easier to rinse yer hair in water that was not already soapy, and allowing it those extra moments to dry before getting out would be helpful too.

Smiling tentatively, Joyce asked, "Shall I take the linen and set it aside while ye wash yer hair?"

"Aye, please." Saidh handed it over and Joyce set it on a small stool that had been brought up and placed by the fireplace.

"Shall I jest straighten the room and make the bed while ye bathe?" Joyce asked as she returned and bent to pick up the sheet Saidh had discarded on the floor beside the tub.

"Nay!" Saidh said with alarm, then forced a smile and shook her head. "Jest put the sheet on the foot o' the bed fer now, Joyce. I prefer me bed unmade today."

Joyce's eyebrows rose, but she merely nodded and carried the sheet over to lay across the foot of the bed.

Saidh set to work washing her hair then, her wary gaze on the maid the whole time. The last thing she needed was to explain the bloodstain on the foot of the bed, but she started trying to come up with some explanation for it just in case.

"What would ye like me to do now?" Joyce asked, turning uncertainly toward her.

Saidh hesitated and then glanced toward the gowns strewn around the small chest she'd brought with her.

"I was trying to decide what to wear when ye arrived," she explained, nodding toward the mess she'd left. Clearing her throat, she added, "Mayhap ye can see what's clean and what ye think would look nice on me?"

"O' course." Joyce beamed at her, then rushed over to begin gathering up the gowns and Saidh returned to massaging the soap into her hair. After a moment, she then shifted her position in the tub, sticking her legs in the air to hang over the end so that she could lean her head back in the water and swish it around to try to remove the soap she'd just put in.

"I kept a couple of pails of water to help rinse yer hair."

Saidh gave a start at that announcement as she lifted her head out of the water and was able to hear again.

Joyce stood beside the tub once more. Smiling at her gently, she offered,"I could pour them over yer hair now to finish rinsing it."

"Oh . . . okay," Saidh said with a weak smile and then watched as Joyce proceeded to take an empty pail and set it between the two full ones that remained. She first poured in water from the steaming pail, and then water from a second not steaming pail. After testing the temperature, the maid nodded with satisfaction and straightened.

"Just lean yer head back a bit," Joyce instructed. "And here, hold this over yer eyes so none of the soapy water gets in them by accident."

Saidh accepted the fresh bit of linen and pressed it tightly to her eyes. She leaned her head back, a small sigh of pleasure slipping from her lips as warm water flowed over her hair and ran down her back.

"One more pail ought to do it," Joyce announced, and Saidh mumbled acquiescence and remained where she was. A moment later, another rush of water coasted over her head.

"There," Joyce said brightly and Saidh stiffened as she felt the woman gather her dripping hair, but relaxed when she said, "I'll jest wring out the worst of the water, and wrap a linen around it to help it dry and keep it from falling into the soapy water while ye finish yer bath."

Joyce did what she said as she spoke and Saidh

took the linen away and sat up slowly as Joyce finished wrapping the larger linen around her head.

"Thank ye," Saidh murmured.

" 'Tis me pleasure," Joyce assured her and took the damp scrap of linen she'd held over her eyes from her hand, replacing it with the soapy one. "I'll jest go sort through yer dresses now. Give me a holler if ye need any assistance."

"Thank ye," Saidh repeated, feeling rather bemused. She was beginning to warm to Joyce as a maid. She didn't irritate her like Erin did. Perhaps it was because she was younger than Erin. She didn't seem much older than Saidh was herself. Perhaps being younger, Joyce didn't feel the need to scold and harass her as Erin did.

"How long ha'e ye been a lady's maid?" Saidh asked curiously, beginning to wash her arms and shoulders.

Joyce chuckled softly. "I'm no' really. I work in the kitchens, but I've been asked to fill in on several occasions when there were large parties staying here and one o' the ladies was without her maid fer one reason or another."

"Ye seem to ha'e learned well fer someone who has only filled in on occasion," Saidh commented, rinsing her arms and shoulders.

"Aye, well, I seem to learn something new from each lady," Joyce said with a smile. "Lady MacKendrick was the one who taught me that the hair should be washed first, and how best to rinse it. She said if ye did no' get all the soap out, it made yer hair flat and dull. Lady MacKendrick is well admired for her fine hair."

"Tell me what else ye've learned," Saidh suggested as she lifted one leg out of the tub and began to soap it.

"Lady Buchanan is awake and taking the bath ye ordered fer her, m'laird."

Greer turned from watching two of his men at that announcement and nodded at Alpin as the boy climbed up to sit on the fence next to where he leaned. He smiled faintly at the lad, but merely grunted, "Good. Now we jest need wait fer Bowie to return from his swim."

"He's back," Alpin announced, nodding toward the stables.

Greer straightened away from the fence and turned to see the man in question leaving the stables headed their way. "Good. Then he can take over training while we go fer a swim ourselves."

"We?" Alpin asked with alarm.

Greer ignored him and waited for Bowie to reach them so that he could give his instructions.

"Why did ye say *we*?" Alpin asked warily when Greer had finished and Bowie moved away with a nod.

Greer turned to the lad. Grabbing him by the arm, he urged him off his perch and asked dryly, "Are ye no' the one who used to carp at me that I should bathe more often?"

"Aye, but ye were given to go for weeks without one while we were at battle if I did no' carp," Alpin muttered as Greer dragged him away from the fence. "And I meant in warm water in a tub inside, no' in a freezing loch with all manner o' fish and critters in it."

"Bathing indoors is fer ladies and bairns . . . and mayhap fer men in the winter," Greer allowed reluctantly, but then rallied and added, "But when the weather is fine as 'tis now, a warrior prefers the loch."

"'Tis no' fine today," Alpin argued as Greer pulled him toward the stables. "There is a chill in the air."

"Just a hint o' fall hailing us ere summer starts her death cries," Greer said with a shrug.

"'Twill be me death cry yer hearing if ye make me swim in the loch," Alpin muttered with disgust as the stable master appeared at the mouth of the stables with Greer's horse in tow. "I am already down with fever and should be abed."

"Aye, I ken ye are," Greer said sympathetically as he swung Alpin up onto the saddle. He then mounted behind him and took the reins with a "thank ye" for the man before urging the horse toward the drawbridge. "And that is why I decided *we* shall go swimming rather than meself alone."

"Ye're trying to kill me," Alpin moaned, slumping in the saddle before him.

Greer rolled his eyes at the dramatics and shook his head. "Nay. I'm trying to help ye. Ye're too hot, lad. 'Twill boil yer brains do we no' get the fever down and I'm hoping a cold swim'll do the trick. Otherwise, 'twill mean leeches and poultices fer ye."

"No' leeches," Alpin gasped with horror. "I hate leeches."

"I ken ye do," Greer acknowledged sympathetically. Mouth firming, he then added, "But I've grown rather fond o' yer sorry little arse nagging at me, so if the swim does no' work, we'll do whatever we ha'e to, to see ye well. Even leeches."

Alpin groaned and slumped closer against him and Greer frowned at the heat pouring off the boy. He was really quite concerned about the lad. It had been dawn when he'd woken the last time in Saidh's bed. Greer had been terribly tempted to wake Saidh for another round of passion, but she'd looked so peaceful sleeping, and he was concerned that he would just add to the discomfort that she would no doubt suffer today, so had forced himself from Saidh's bed, gathered anything that would speak of his presence in her room and had dragged himself back to his own.

His bedchamber had seemed empty when he'd entered and Greer had quickly changed and headed below. He'd intended to go out and collect his horse to ride out to the loch for a quick dip to clean himself up before breaking his fast. But one look at the empty stall where Bowie kept his horse had told him that unless he wanted company, he should wait to take his own swim. His first, he had noticed, liked to swim early in the morning as well. He'd come across the man on more than one occasion down at the loch.

Clucking impatiently under his tongue, Greer had trudged back into the keep to break his fast, but it had been a tiresome business. He hadn't swum yet to build up his appetite, and Lady MacDonnell, Saidh, nor even Alpin were at the tables. He knew Lady MacDonnell hadn't been feeling well the night before and so was probably having a lie-in, and he had kept Saidh up half the night with his desires so she would sleep late. But Alpin's absence had been troublesome and after searching the bailey and castle, Greer had returned to his room and found that it wasn't empty after all. The boy had been huddled under a mountain of furs at the foot of the bed, shivering madly.

A quick feel of his forehead had only deepened Greer's concern and he'd rousted the boy from sleep and harried him downstairs to break his fast, making sure he ate heartily despite his protests. He'd then gone to the kitchens to order the cook to put water on to heat for a bath, then returned to Alpin and told him to go back above stairs, grab some furs from his bed, and huddle outside Lady Saidh's door. At the first sound that suggested she was awake, he was to run down to the kitchens and tell them to take up the bath. Then he was to come out and let him know.

The boy had done as told, Bowie had returned, and now Greer intended to make Alpin submerge himself in the cold loch water, even if he had to hold him down to get it done. He knew the common belief right now was that you should close all the windows, bundle the ailing individual up and stoke the fires in the room high to boil out the fever, but Greer had met a rather wise old healer once who had told him that was the wrong way to go about it. That a fever too high could damage the head and ye were better to do what ye could to cool the body than to heat it further.

Since that healer had saved his life when he was quite sure no one else could have, he was wont to listen to her advice and cool Alpin down. If it didn't work . . . well, then he'd try something else.

"THERE YE ARE."

Saidh peered into the mirror Joyce held before her. Eyes widening in surprise as she took in her reflection, she breathed with amazement, "Why ye've made me pretty without fussing hardly at all."

Joyce laughed and set the mirror aside. "M'lady, God made ye pretty. I jest brushed out yer hair and put in a couple o' wee braids to keep it out o' yer face during the day."

That was exactly what she'd done. Joyce had taken a few strands of hair on one side to make one long thin braid, and then done the same on the other before drawing both back to weave them together at the back of her head. Each braid held the rest of her unbraided hair off her face. It was most sensible. She would battle better with her sword without her hair getting in the way . . . and yet she looked pretty. . . . and ladylike, she marveled. And it had not even taken long or needed a lot of fuss.

Saidh smiled happily at the woman and stood up. "Ye're very good at this, Joyce. I'd be happy to have ye to maid."

"Ah, ye're too kind, m'lady. I did little," Joyce said, but beamed with pleasure.

Smiling, Saidh reached out to squeeze her hand in gratitude, and then turned to lead the way to the door, thinking that she would enjoy Joyce as her maid much more than she ever had Erin, and wondering if she could convince Lady MacDonnell or Greer to let her take her with her when she left. Lady MacDonnell was hardly likely to be eager to part with such a gem.

Thoughts of Lady MacDonnell reminded her of the woman knocking at her door last night to check on her after Greer had stabbed her with his cock and set her off bellowing. The memory made her bite her lip. She had been quite rude to the woman, leaving her standing in the hall to talk through the door, but had had little choice at the time. She really should apologize for it now though, she decided.

"How is Lady MacDonnell today?" Saidh asked as she opened her chamber door and led Joyce out into the hall.

"She is ha'ing a lie in, but I think is feeling better than yester eve," Joyce said solemnly.

"And Laird MacDonnell?" Saidh asked, trying not to sound too eager.

"Oh, he seemed fine and fit this morn," Joyce assured her. "Ha'e no' seen the man smile so wide since he got here. I'm sure he has no' been afflicted by whatever Lady MacDonnell and wee Alpin have."

"Alpin is ill?" Saidh paused and turned to the woman with surprise.

"Aye," Joyce said with a little sigh. "And he appears to ha'e it worse than Lady MacDonnell. She is merely tired, but wee Alpin was flush and shivering something fierce this morn when the laird dragged him down to break his fast."

Saidh turned to start down the stairs with a

frown. She found the news that the squire was ill surprisingly distressing considering what a pain in the arse the lad had been.

"Oh, I almost forgot," Joyce said suddenly as they reached the bottom of the stairs. "The cook asked me to tell ye that he made that applemoyse fer ye first thing this morn and 'tis ready whenever ye want it."

"Oh." Saidh's frown turned into a grimace. She'd quite forgotten about her plan to sweeten Fenella up with the treat and then try to sort out if she was like the scorpion and killing was just in her nature.

Well, Saidh thought, she had to break her fast anyway. She could take the applemoyse up to Fenella for them both to break their fast with.

"Thank ye, Joyce," Saidh said quietly as she led her to the door to the kitchens.

Cook was a large, florid-faced man who always seemed to be smiling from what Saidh could tell. He greeted her cheerfully, presented the applemoyse with pride and a pleasure that only seemed to grow when he realized she wanted it for her cousin. Saidh left the kitchens with the applemoyse and the distinct impression that the cook, as well as the rest of the servants in the kitchens, quite liked Fenella. None of them seemed to think she'd had anything to do with Allen's death, and while they loved Lady MacDonnell they all felt it was a shame that in her grief, the woman was blaming "poor wee Fenella."

Saidh pondered that as she headed back above stairs, wondering if they weren't right. After all, Lady MacDonnell herself had even suggested that might be the case. Of course, Lady MacDonnell didn't know that Fenella's first husband's death was not an attack by bandits. Just as Saidh hadn't known about the feather in Laird MacIver's mouth, which wasn't conclusive evidence of anything, but certainly made a body wonder.

Saidh paused at her cousin's chamber door, but before she could raise her hand to knock, it flew open and Fenella grabbed her arm and dragged her into the room.

"Where ha'e ye been?" Fenella cried, slamming the door and whirling to face her.

"Fetching ye the applemoyse I had Cook make special fer ye," Saidh said warily and held out the treat.

"I did no' mean now, I mean all yesterday after the nooning and in the even—" She paused suddenly, nose twitching and then peered down at the dessert. "Applemoyse?"

"Aye." Saidh held it out to her. "'Tis still warm from the ovens."

"It smells delicious," Fenella said on a little sigh.

"Aye. I took Alpin out with me yesterday and we found and picked the apples fer ye."

"Ye did?" Fenella asked with surprise.

Saidh nodded and shrugged. "Well, I remembered how fond ye were o' applemoyse and I thought it might cheer ye." She grimaced and added, "I gave them to Cook hoping he could make them in time fer ye to ha'e with sup last night, but 'twas too late, so he made it up first thing this morning."

"Oh, Saidh. That was kind o' ye," Fenella said, offering her a smile.

Saidh smiled back and then glanced around and moved to set the dessert on a very tiny table in the corner of the room that she hadn't noticed on her previous visits.

"I planned to check on ye last night after the sup, but I was no' feeling well and went to bed early instead," Saidh said as she turned back. She wasn't lying, she hadn't been feeling well when she'd left Greer in the great hall and stomped to the stairs to retire. She'd been cranky as an old hag. And she *had* gone to bed early, just not alone.

"I suspected ye were no' feeling well," Fenella admitted with a frown. "I ken ye had nightmares. I heard ye screaming yer head off and then Lady MacDonnell checking on ye." She grinned suddenly and added, " 'Twas rude o' ye to leave the old cow in the hall and no' e'en open the door when she'd dragged herself from her bed to look in on ye."

"Oh," Saidh said weakly, guilt flowing over her again at just how rude she'd been. She really needed to check on the woman after she left Fenella, and thank her again for her concern. Pushing that thought aside, Saidh glanced to Fenella and then waved her to the dessert. "Come, break yer fast. They were made special fer ye."

"I ha'e already broken me fast," Fenella confessed as she joined her by the table. "But I'll no' pass up applemoyse. You should ha'e some too though. Ye're the one who went to find the apples."

"Thank ye," Saidh murmured and scooped up a treat.

"Come." Fenella moved back to her bed and settled on it, then patted the space beside her. "We'll ha'e to eat here since Lady MacDonnell has seen fit to gi'e me such a small room there is no place fer furniture." She scowled bitterly and then added, "I suppose I'll ha'e to find another husband unless I wish to sleep in this hard cell fer the rest o' me life."

Saidh glanced to her with surprise. Just the day before Fenella had been moaning and weeping all over Greer's chest, sobbing that Allen was her true love and she would never get over him. Now she was planning to remarry?

Fenella caught her expression and scowled. "I ha'e to be practical, Saidh. I'm a young woman now dependent on the kindness o' me dead husband's family who suspect me o' killing him."

"Greer does no' seem to think ye killed Allen," Saidh said quietly.

"Nay." Fenella sighed. "He is verra kind too, and handsome in a rough sort o' way, and seems just as thoughtful and considerate as me Allen was." She lifted her gaze thoughtfully to the ceiling, and then tapped her chin briefly before murmuring, "I bet he would no' trouble me with his base needs either. Perhaps like Allen, he is above all that too."

Saidh pursed her lips, unsure what to say. She could tell Fenella that Allen had left her alone out of lack of interest rather than because he was "above all that." But that just seemed cruel. There was no need for her to know that now. But neither did Saidh think it was a good idea to assure her that Greer had some very strong base needs indeed, and a strong appetite for them. She might want to know how she knew, so didn't comment on it at all, and simply changed the subject.

"Fenella, tell me about yer marriages." Saidh winced as the words came out of her mouth. The question wasn't accusatory, but it certainly hadn't been as nonchalant as she'd hoped, or suggestive of a desire to chat and giggle about men the way women do either. But then, Saidh wasn't the sort to chat and giggle . . . well, usually, she acknowledged to herself. She had chatted quite a bit with Joan, Murine and Edith, and had even giggled with them a time or two, something she'd never done before.

Actually, she realized, Joan, Murine and Edith were the first female friends she'd ever had aside from her mother, who had been both friend and mother to her. Goodness, chatting and giggling with females, wearing her hair in this fancy style . . .'Twas as if she were growing out of the boyish ways she'd always embraced and turning into a girl, she thought with dismay. Next she'd be rubbing berries into her cheeks and on her lips, and going without braies.

Never! She thought grimly, but then reconsidered as it occurred to her that it would make it much easier for Greer to tumble her if she didn't wear braies under her skirts. He could just lift her skirt and his plaid and—

"What do ye want to ken? I already told ye about them."

Saidh blinked at those words and found Fenella peering at her almost resentfully. She hesitated, trying to think of a diplomatic way to find out what she needed to know, but really, there didn't seem to be one. Besides, it did seem to her that catching Fenella by surprise was more likely to give her the truth than beating about the bush and hoping the truth would fall out. Sighing, she sat up straight, looked her in the eye and asked, "Did ye ken Lady MacDonnell attended yer marriage to the senior MacIver?"

Fenella blinked in surprise. "Nay. Did she?"

"Aye. In fact, she is one o' the women who helped wash and prepare the body fer burial."

"Oh." Fenella grimaced. "They all thought I should help, but I did no' ken what to do. Besides, I'd just lost me husband and was no' sure where things stood or what would happen to me next. I was in no fit state fer it."

"I'm sure she understood that. But, ye see, the problem is—and the reason Lady MacDonnell suspects ye o' ha'ing something to do with Allen's death, is that while she was washing the MacIver's face, she noted that his eyes were bloodshot, and that there was a goose feather in his mouth, both suggestive that he may ha'e been smothered with a pillow."

Fenella sat frozen for a long moment and then launched to her feet and rounded on her furiously. "Ye think I killed me husbands," she accused grimly.

Saidh stood up, shoulders straight, and met her gaze firmly. "I ken ye killed the first one," she reminded her quietly. "What I'm trying to do now is reassure meself that ye did no' kill the others as well. Four dead husbands in four years does seem like a lot o' bad luck fer one bride to suffer."

Fenella's shoulders sagged abruptly and she shook her head, saying sadly, "Oh, Saidh. Ye too?"

Saidh's gave up her stiff stance and sighed. "Fenella, I just—"

"Get out," Fenella interrupted quietly.

"I—"

"Get out!" Fenella roared, and then hurried to the table to grab up the applemoyse and turned to throw it at her. "And take yer damned food with ye."

Saidh instinctively ducked, then turned to see the applemoyse a crushed mess that was slowly running down the door behind her. She didn't stop to collect it, or clean the mess. That was Fenella's problem. She'd made it, she thought grimly as she slipped from the room.

Saidh paused in the hall after pulling the door closed, then hesitated. She had intended to check on Lady MacDonnell after seeing Fenella, but really wasn't in the mood. Still, the lady had been kind to her, and had even dragged herself from her sickbed to check on her last night when she'd screamed. And, as Fenella had pointed out, she had been rude in not even opening the door to her. Of course, she hadn't been able to at that point. She'd been naked and pinned to the bed by Greer's large body. Still, she should thank the lady for her concern and apologize to her for causing it.

Sighing, Saidh turned and headed for the lady's room.

Chapter 9

"M'LAIRD?"

Greer slowed to allow Bowie to catch up to him, but did not stop walking toward the castle. Nor did he look away from Alpin's pale, sleeping face. If he was sleeping, he thought grimly. The lad had screamed his fool head off when Greer had carried him into the loch, and much like Saidh, Alpin had tried to climb him to get out. But the boy was half Saidh's size. Greer had had little difficulty in keeping him from scratching his face off and holding him in the water. He'd kept the lad there until the boy had calmed and seemed to go to sleep, and then he'd pressed his cheek to his forehead to test his temperature. It was the only dry part of Greer by that point, but he hadn't been able to tell if the soaking had done the lad any good. He supposed he'd have to wait and see on the matter.

At the moment, he was more concerned by how still and silent the boy had remained on the ride back to the castle. He was eager to get him stripped of his wet clothes and tucked up in bed, which was why he wasn't stopping for his first to speak to him.

"The men reported just moments ago on seeing a traveling party approaching," Bowie announced, hustling to keep up with him. "They think they carry the Buchanan banner, though the party is far enough away they are no' sure yet."

"What?" Greer stopped walking to turn on the man. "But 'tis no' e'en the nooning yet. I did no' expect them ere the nooning."

Bowie shrugged helplessly. "Mayhap, 'tis no' them. The men can no' be sure at this distance."

"Oh, it's most like them," Greer said grimly and turned to continue walking. "Warn Cook and tell him to make sure all is ready, then send someone to the chapel to let Father ken."

"Aye, m'laird." Bowie said and hurried away as Greer continued with his small burden.

"I CAME TO CHECK ON LADY MACDONNELL," SAIDH murmured when the lady's maid responded to her knock on the woman's chamber door.

"Oh, Saidh, that is so sweet." Lady MacDonnell's voice floated to them and her maid smiled and stepped back to allow her to enter.

She stepped into the room to find Lady MacDonnell sitting wrapped in furs by the fire, cupping a mug of something steaming in front of her face.

" 'Tis one o' Helen's tinctures," Lady MacDonnell said with an expression that was a cross between a grimace and amusement. "They taste vile, but work. I already feel better."

"Well, that's the important thing," Saidh said firmly as she moved to settle in the chair across from the lady. "I'm glad to find ye feeling better. I was concerned. And I felt bad too fer no' opening the door when ye came to check on me last night. I fear I . . ." She frowned and then said carefully, "In truth, I could no' seem to get up. I felt as if a great weight were pinning me to the bed."

"Oh dear," Lady MacDonnell said with concern. "I do hope ye're no' coming down with what I ha'e. Mayhap Helen should make ye a tincture too."

"Nay," Saidh said quickly. She could smell the swill Lady MacDonnell seemed to be avoiding having to drink and was quite sure the smell alone was vile enough to scare a body into healing itself rather than be forced to swallow it. Forcing a smile, she assured her, "I feel much better this morn, although I gather Alpin has taken ill."

"Greer's little squire?" Lady MacDonnell asked with alarm. "Oh no, what a shame. He's such a sweet lad."

Saidh wrinkled her nose at the claim, thinking she wouldn't exactly describe him that way.

"Helen, make a tincture for Alpin and we shall go check on him," Lady MacDonnell instructed now.

"At once, m'lady," the maid murmured and slipped from the room.

"Here, let me help." Saidh jumped to her feet, reaching for Lady MacDonnell's drink as she started to struggle to stand.

"Thank ye, dear," Lady MacDonnell murmured, quickly shedding the furs she'd been bundled in to reveal that she was dressed underneath. Free of the furs, she then reached for her drink and when Saidh gave it up, turned and dumped it in the fire with a shudder. "Dreadful stuff. I'd rather be sick than drink that muck, but do no' tell Helen. 'Twill hurt her feelings."

A soft laugh burst from Saidh, but she nodded quickly. "Yer secret is safe with me, m'lady."

"I knew it would be," Lady MacDonnell smiled at her, then turned to lead the way to the door, saying, "I truly am feeling much better today, but Helen likes to fuss. And in truth, I did no' feel sick last night, so much as just terribly tired, but that seems to have passed with a good night's sleep." Pausing at the door, she turned to inspect Saidh before shaking her head and opening the door. "I can see yer nightmares did ye little good last night, though. Yer looking a wee bit pale and tired this morning."

"Oh." Saidh flushed. "Well, I suppose I am a little tired."

"Well, then I recommend a good night of uninterrupted sleep," Lady MacDonnell said as she led her into the hall. "So, where is young Alpin? I hope Greer did no' make him sleep on the cold great hall floor last night with him feeling poorly."

"Nay. Greer sent him to sleep in his room on the foot o' his bed," Saidh assured her.

"Good, good," Lady MacDonnell said, starting up the hall. "I always did like Greer. He seems rough and gruff on the outside, and no doubt he's merciless in battle, but he's a good heart and kind to children and animals, and that's always a good sign." She glanced to Saidh and added, "Ye could do worse than a man like Greer to husband."

Saidh's eyes widened incredulously. "Oh, I—I mean he—is he no' already betrothed?" Saidh asked weakly. She'd just assumed he would be. Most nobles were betrothed while still in their swaddling, or not long afterward. She had been. Fortunately, the nasty bastard Ferguson she'd been betrothed to had been kind enough to drop dead ere claiming her.

"Nay. His father ne'er troubled to arrange a marriage fer Greer," Lady MacDonnell said grimly. "Greer's father was no' a kind, considerate man. 'Tis a wonder Greer turned out so well with him as an example. Or mayhap 'tis no' such a wonder after all, perhaps he learned how no' to behave from him."

"Perhaps," Saidh murmured as they reached the door to Greer's room and Lady MacDonnell opened it and led the way in.

Alpin was not huddled at the foot of the bed, he was tucked into the center top of it like a little lord. He also wore what appeared to be one of Greer's tunics, the sleeves rolled and rerolled so that they were above his hands. There was a damp cloth on his head, and a maid sat at the bedside, feeding him broth.

"Alpin, me dear," Lady MacDonnell crooned, crossing quickly to the bed. "I heard ye'd taken ill."

"Aye." The boy sat up with a grin. "But I'm better now. 'Twas horrible, the laird made me go in the loch to try to bring down me fever. I thought I'd die from the cold, but it seems to ha'e worked. I feel much better now."

"The laird said ye were to stay lying down," the maid said crossly, pushing at his chest.

"But I'm better now," Alpin protested, trying to stay upright. "Really I am."

"I fear yer maid and Greer are right, Alpin," Lady MacDonnell said gently, settling on this side of the bed to smile at the boy. "Ye should really lie down. Ye may feel better just now, but I suspect 'tis just a brief respite because Greer managed to get ye cooled down. I can see he is truly worried, else he would no' ha'e dressed ye in his own clothes and gi'en ye his bed."

"Aye." Alpin glanced down and ran his hands over the soft cloth of the shirt he wore. He was silent for a minute and then glanced up and asked worriedly, "Ye do no' think he'll ha'e to take me to the loch again, do ye?"

"Pretty bad, was it?" Lady MacDonnell asked sympathetically.

"Verra bad," he assured her, and then looking cross, added, "I tried to tell him ye did no' treat a fever that way, but he would no' listen."

"And yet it appears to ha'e brought yer temperature down," Lady MacDonnell pointed out.

Alpin shrugged discontentedly, and Saidh smiled with amusement at the confusion of expressions that covered the boy's face in quick succession. She then glanced curiously toward the open window shutters when she heard a commotion from outside.

"It sounds like we ha'e company," Lady MacDonnell said mildly, and Saidh moved to the window to peer out. She was too slow, however. The bailey was quiet again with little to see but soldiers and servants moving quickly about their business.

"Where is Greer?" Lady MacDonnell asked the maid as Saidh turned back to the room.

"He went to talk to the priest about something or other," the maid said with a shrug. "He said he'd return directly."

"Oh, good," Lady MacDonnell said and then they all glanced to the door with surprise when it suddenly burst open and men began to pile into the room.

For a moment, Saidh thought they were under attack. She even reached for her sword before she recognized the man at the head of the group. Tall, wide shouldered and with long dark hair half covering the scar on his face, he spotted her and rushed forward. It was like being run to ground by a bull. All Saidh had time for was to brace herself before he swept her off her feet and crushed her to his chest, growling, " 'Tis all right, wee Saidh. We're here now. We'll kill the bastard and take ye home."

"Aulay?" Saidh gasped with what little air he'd left her capable of breathing in. Pushing at his shoulders in a desperate search for more air, she managed to gain herself a little space, and asked with bewilderment, "Who are ye going to kill? And what the de'il are ye doing here?"

"Did ye really no' think we'd come when we got that message?"

Saidh turned with confusion to eye her brother Dougall at that growl. Second oldest and as big and strong as Aulay, Dougall could have been his twin except for the fact that he was unscarred. "What message?"

"Ne'er mind that," her third oldest brother, Niels growled, pulling her out of Aulay's arms and into his own. "Are ye all right, lass? Did he hurt ye horrible?"

"Let the lass breathe, Niels," her fourth oldest brother, Conran, snapped, tugging her away from him. "Ye've each about mauled her like a den o' those bears grandfather was always carping about battling."

"Grandfather ne'er saw a bear," her fifth oldest brother, Geordie, said with disgust. "Father said they were all hunted and killed here long ere grandfather was e'en born."

"Aye, more's the pity," her sixth oldest brother, Rory agreed on a sigh. "I wish they had no' done that and we still had some wandering about. I'd love to wrestle one."

"It'd tear ye limb from limb," Geordie said grimly.

"Would no'!" Rory snapped. " 'Tis more like I'd—"

Recognizing that a battle was imminent if she didn't intervene, Saidh put two fingers in her mouth and let loose with a loud, piercing whistle. Silence immediately fell, broken only when her youngest brother, Alick, grinned and said, "I wondered when ye'd shut them up."

Saidh ignored that and scowled at the seven very large men surrounding her like a circle of trees. "Now, if I've yer attention, mayhap someone could explain just what the bloody hell ye're all doing here?"

"Dear God, she swears like a warrior too," Alpin said with dismay into the silence that followed. "'Tis like Laird MacDonnell, only in Lady Buchanan's skirts."

Her brothers immediately all began shouting again and Saidh turned to cast an exasperated glare at the boy in the bed for causing it. Her head then whipped toward her brothers with surprise as she was caught by each arm and hauled toward the door. Saidh allowed herself to be dragged for a couple feet out of sheer surprise, but then began to struggle.

"WHAT DO YE MEAN THEY WENT UP TO ME ROOM?" Greer asked with confusion, turning away from the empty trestle tables in the great hall to stare at Bowie. "I told ye to seat them here, serve them drinks and tell them I would only be a moment."

"Aye, but they asked where their sister was, and Lady MacDonnell's maid happened to be passing and said that she'd gone to look in on Alpin with your Aunt Tilda, and the Buchanans just . . ." He shrugged helplessly. "I could no' stop them. There were seven, and they moved so quick they were halfway up the stairs before I e'en realized they were—" He paused and glanced toward the upper landing with wide eyes when a loud crash came, muffled, from one of the rooms. "Dear God, ye do no' think they're holding yer aunt responsible and attacking her. Do ye?"

Cursing, Greer hurried for the stairs. He took them two at a time, aware that Bowie was on his heels. If he hadn't already been told the Buchanans had gone up to his room, he would have known where they were by the loud bangs and curses coming from it. Truly concerned now for Saidh, Alpin and his aunt's well-being, Greer charged through the door, only to come to a startled halt.

Alpin lay in the bed where he'd left him, sitting up with excited color in his cheeks. Both his Aunt Tilda and the maid he'd left to tend Alpin sat on the sides of the bed. The three of them were staring wide-eyed at the chaos at the foot of the bed. There were three men, rolling on the floorboards, clutching their groins and moaning, another just getting painfully to his knees, and three more trying to subdue an apparently furious Saidh while avoiding her swinging fists and kicking legs.

Greer opened his mouth to bellow, but then paused and winced as Saidh suddenly lashed out a leg at one of the three brothers circling her. She got him with a kick to the groin that Greer could feel down to his very soul. He had to actually fight the urge to cross his legs and cover his own groin in sympathetic pain.

"God's teeth, that had to hurt," Bowie muttered behind him, and Greer gave himself a shake and started forward.

"What in the bloody hell is going on here?" he roared.

"See! I told ye," Alpin said excitedly. "They sound jest like each other. 'Tis the very thing she said."

Greer scowled at the boy briefly, but then recalled he was ill and probably delirious and started to turn back to Saidh and her brothers just as he was tack-

led to the floor by the two still standing men. He hit
the floor hard, the air briefly knocked from him, and
was just beginning to get it back when Saidh suddenly let out a roar and launched herself on top of
her brothers, who, sadly, were on top of him.

Greer groaned as the air left him again, sure this
time that it would not return. As he waited to die,
he heard Saidh bellowing, "Leave him be, ye great
gouks! He's naught to do with this!"

For some reason that made him smile and he
opened his eyes to see that she had one brother in a
headlock and was viciously twisting the ear of the
other. Damn, she did not fight fair, he thought with
a grin.

"Good morn, sweetling," he said when she
glanced his way and their gazes met over the heads
of her brothers.

Saidh blinked, then grinned at him and managed
a breathless, "Good morn, m'laird."

"He's everything to do with this!" the man whose
ear she was trying to twist off growled. "We came to
rescue ye from him, ye witless cow."

"Oh dear," Lady MacDonnell breathed as every
last man in the room suddenly went still as if holding their breath in the face of a storm. Even the
moaning and rolling stopped.

"Now, Saidh, love," the man she had in a headlock said quickly. "Dougall did no' mean that."

Saidh remained frozen for a moment, and then
suddenly thrust herself off of the three men, pop-
ping back to her feet with impressive speed. She
withdrew her sword and slammed the flat side of it

against Dougall's arse just as quickly and growled, "Let 'im up or I'll skewer ye, Dougall Buchanan."

Greer glanced to Dougall as the man released a heavy sigh. Resignation crossing his features, the man then stood and offered his brother a hand up as well. Free of their combined weight, Greer got quickly to his feet, watching with interest as Dougall took a moment to brush himself off. Since he'd landed on Greer, there wasn't really anything to brush off, so he suspected the man was either trying to come up with a way to ease his sister's upset at his insult, or he was delaying facing her in the hopes that her temper might cool a bit. Perhaps it was both, Greer thought with amusement and started toward Saidh.

He immediately found his way cut off by seven large, grim-faced men. Even the ones who had previously been rolling on the floor were suddenly upright and blocking his way, though a couple were grimacing in pain and wincing as they did it.

Greer raised an eyebrow. "Which one o' ye is Aulay?"

The last man Saidh had taken out with a kick to the groin moved forward. His jaw tightened as he did, but otherwise he showed no sign of the discomfort he must be feeling. Greer found that rather impressive since he knew men who would still have been, not only rolling on the floor, but weeping copiously as well. The only thing he could think was that either these men were used to such blows, or they were eunuchs.

"I'm Aulay, Laird Buchanan," the man snarled

with a fierce glare made more fierce by the scar that divided one side of his face.

Greer nodded. "Ye got me invitation then?"

"What invitation?" Saidh asked, unconsciously lowering her sword and stepping closer to the backs of the men between them.

"'Twas no' an invitation. 'Twas a call to battle," Aulay snarled.

"Aye, a call to battle," one of the other men growled, and all seven of them moved a threatening step closer.

Greer eyed the men warily and pursed his lips, trying to recall what he'd written. At the time, he'd been rather eager to return above stairs to Saidh's room and had rather rushed his way through it so that he could pass the message on to one of his men. He'd wanted the message delivered at once to set things into motion. It was possible he'd—

"Ye said ye'd ruined Saidh," Aulay snapped.

"What?" Saidh squawked.

"Aye," one o' the men assured her. "He said he'd ruined ye like a gooseberry pie left out in the rain."

"The hell I did," Greer snapped, embarrassed at the very thought that someone might believe he'd write such utter nonsense. "I wrote nothing about gooseberry pie."

"Oh, nay," the man agreed apologetically. "Ye just said ye'd ruined her. I added the gooseberry pie for effect."

"Oh, leave off, Alick," one of the other men snapped. "Do ye always ha'e to sound like a troubadour?"

"What the devil's wrong with sounding like a troubadour?" the man asked with affront. "'Tis a much-valued skill."

"Enough," Aulay barked, bringing immediate silence. He then glowered at Greer, which would have been more effective if Greer hadn't seen him roll his eyes in exasperation just moments before. The man wasn't the emotionless warrior he showed to the world.

"Ye ruined me sister," Aulay accused.

"Aye, but I plan to marry her. And I asked fer yer blessing in the message."

"And then ye added that with or without it, ye'd marry her anyway," Aulay snapped.

"And I will," Greer assured him.

"The hell ye will," Aulay snarled and the other men all growled like hungry dogs and moved in closer on another threatening step.

"Ye handled yer brothers most masterfully."

Saidh dragged her attention from the men surrounding Greer and glanced around with surprise to see that Lady MacDonnell had stood and moved to her side without her noticing. Smiling crookedly, she murmured, "Thank ye. But I ha'e an unfair advantage as I told ye."

"I did notice that they tried very hard to subdue ye without hurting ye, while ye were unhampered by such a restraint," Lady MacDonnell said with a grin. "Still, they are seven fine, strong lads, and I was quite impressed," she assured her, and then patted her arm and said, "I think I should like it verra much if ye'd call me Aunt Tilda from now on."

"Oh," Saidh said with surprise, and then smiled and nodded. "Thank ye, m'lady . . . I mean Aunt Tilda."

Lady MacDonnell nodded and then patted her arm once more. "I also think ye should take control o' the situation again ere these men decide yer future fer ye. Men often do what they think ye want and get it wrong without yer guidance."

"Aye," Saidh said on a sigh. She'd been so flummoxed by the bit about marriage, that she'd simply stood there afterward, completely bemused. Thanks to Aunt Tilda, she wasn't bemused anymore, though. Sticking two fingers in her mouth, she let loose a piercing whistle like the one she had earlier.

The men fell silent and turned to peer at her.

"I am no' ruined," she said firmly.

"Aye, lass, ye are," Greer assured her solemnly. "Well and truly, thrice or four times by me count." He frowned. "Surely ye recall last night?"

Her brothers turned back to him growling and Saidh rolled her eyes, glared at Greer, and asked dryly, "Are ye *trying* to get yerself killed?"

"Last night?" Aulay asked suddenly. "But we got the message last night."

"Aye, I sent it ere I went back up to Saidh's—"

"That is why ye left me sitting naked on the bed?" Saidh asked with disbelief. "To write me brothers?"

"Well I could hardly take yer innocence without first making provisions to protect ye," he pointed out reasonably.

"I do no' need protecting," Saidh snapped.

"Just a minute," Dougall said. Scratching his

head, he faced Greer and asked, "Do ye mean to tell us that ye wrote to tell us ye'd ruined our Saidh, and that ye were wedding her, and *then* went up to do the actual ruining?"

"The man's daft," Geordie muttered when Greer nodded.

"Aye," Alick agreed. "Ye can no' marry a daft man, Saidh."

"I am no' marrying anyone," Saidh said shortly.

"Well ye ha'e to marry someone if ye're ruined," Conran said reasonably.

"I am no'—" Saidh bit off the denial, her jaw clenching, and then asked, "Conran, are ye ruined?"

"What?" he asked with surprised amusement. "Nay, o' course no'."

"And what o' you, Rory? Are ye ruined?"

"Don't be daft, Saidh," he said with a shake of the head.

"What of the rest o' ye? Dougall? Niels? Geordie? Alick? Are any o' ye ruined?" Before they could answer, she added, "Because I've seen e'eryone o' ye, save Aulay, backing giggling maids into corners and tossing up their skirts at Buchanan. So why am I ruined fer tossing up Greer's plaid?"

"She did no' toss up me plaid," Greer assured her brothers when they all turned to glower at him. Just as they began to relax, he added, "I took it off meself the minute I got back to her room."

"Ye really are trying to get us to kill ye," Alick said with wonder.

"Mayhap he hopes to escape marrying Saidh that way," Rory suggested grimly.

"I am no' marrying anyone," Saidh snapped.

Sighing, Aulay moved over to take her hands. Expression gentle, he peered into her eyes and said, "Love, if he ruined ye, ye'll ha'e to marry."

Saidh frowned. "Do you see me as ruined, Aulay?"

"Nay, o' course no', but—"

"Do any o' ye?" she asked turning her attention to her other brothers. "Do ye somehow see me as less because I did what ye all do?"

"Nay, o' course not," Alick said quickly.

"Ne'er, loving," Rory assured her.

"We do no' blame ye," Dougall added. " 'Tis all our fault fer treating ye like ye were just another brother."

"Aye, we should ha'e made ye watch from the sidelines while we played tag, hide-and-seek and Briton warriors," Conran decided.

"Or she could ha'e been the fair maiden we kidnapped and tied up," Niels suggested.

"And we should no' ha'e let ye climb trees."

"Or ride astride."

"And we definitely should no' ha'e taught ye how to fight and curse."

"Do ye dislike me that much?" she asked with dismay, and received seven blank stares in return. "Would ye wish me to be like Fenella? Weeping and whining all the time?"

"Nay, Saidh," Aulay said quietly. "We would no' change ye fer anything. The lads are jest trying to say that this is our fault, no' yers."

"There is no fault," Saidh insisted wearily. "I am

unbetrothed, likely to spend the rest o' me life at Buchanan as an unmarried woman. What is so wrong with me seeking a little pleasure along the way?"

"Ye'll no' be at Buchanan as an unmarried woman," Greer said with a frown. "Ye'll be here at MacDonnell married to me."

"I'll no' marry ye jest because ye think ye've ruined me," Saidh said firmly.

"That is no'—I mean, I—"

When Greer paused with frustration, Alpin sighed and muttered, "He's murder with a sword and a fair hand at swearing, but can no' talk worth cow dung."

"Everyone out!" Greer growled.

"I really do no' think it would be good to move Alpin just now. He's a bit warm again," Aunt Tilda said when no one moved. "And I'd prefer to stay to watch o'er him."

"Well, I'm no' leaving," Aulay announced firmly.

The other brothers didn't speak, but merely crossed their arms as one and arched an eyebrow each as if challenging him to try to remove them.

"Ah, hell," Greer muttered and pushed through the men to catch Saidh by her wrist and draw her over to the side of the room to afford them at least a semblance of some privacy.

Pausing, he turned to face her and then scowled and gestured to the sword she still held in her hand. "Could ye put that away, lass? I'm no' armed and do no' want to be skewered if I say this wrong."

Saidh glanced down at her sword with surprise, then slid it quickly back into its sheath. She then

crossed her arms and cocked one eyebrow, unconsciously imitating the stance her brothers had
taken.

Greer shook his head, but then took her hands in
his and said solemnly, "I am no' marrying ye because I ruined ye. As I mentioned, I wrote to yer
brother about me intention to marry ye before I
ruined ye. So ye see, the truth is, I *really* wanted to
ruin ye."

Saidh stared at him blankly and Greer frowned.

"Nay, that's no' right. I meant to say, I really
wanted to marry ye, no' ruin ye."

"Why?" Saidh asked, withdrawing her hands
from his.

Greer hesitated. "Why what?"

"Why do ye want to marry me?" she explained
and he groaned.

"Ah, lass. Are ye really goin' to make me—"

"Why?"

"I'm no good with this talking business," Greer
said with disgust.

"Why?" Saidh repeated, not backing down.

"Yer a hard wench, Saidh Buchanan," Greer
growled.

"Aye, she is," Rory agreed from across the room,
proving they could hear everything.

"'Tis part o' her charm, I think," Aunt Tilda commented lightly.

"Aye, 'tis," Greer agreed dryly and then told
Saidh, "And I mean that."

"And that's why ye want to marry me?" Saidh
asked with disgust. "Because I'm a hard wench?"

"Nay," he said solemnly. He paused to take a breath, and then took her hands again and said, "I'm no' going to lie and claim I love ye, lass. We've no' known each other long enough fer that. But I like ye something fierce. And I want ye e'en worse. I think ye'd make me a fine wife and that we'd deal well with each other."

"Could ye no' tell her ye think she's beautiful or something nice like that?" Alick complained into the silence that followed.

"She kens I do," Greer said gruffly, meeting her gaze as he added, "I proved it to her last night, repeatedly . . . and I'll prove it to ye every night if ye'd just marry me," he added, squeezing her hands.

Saidh stared at him as she silently debated the matter. She was glad he wasn't claiming to love her. She wouldn't have believed that. She was glad that he liked her though, and was quite sure she liked him too. She definitely liked the things he'd done with her last night, and the promise of doing it every night was a tempting one indeed. More important, she too thought that they would deal well together. So long as he didn't try to change her.

"Ye'll no' fuss at me fer wearing braies and riding astride?" she asked.

"Nay," he assured her.

"Ye'll no' try to make me give up me sword?"

"Never," he assured her. "I like that ye can defend yerself. I'll worry about ye a little less."

"What about me cursing?" she asked.

"I'll teach ye a few I think ye may no' ken," he responded.

Saidh considered the matter briefly and then nodded. "All right then."

"Aye?" he asked with apparent surprise. "Ye'll marry me?"

"Aye," Saidh said and then gasped in surprise when he snatched her up in his arms and planted a kiss on her. He just as quickly set her down though, and turned to Bowie, who had remained safely by the door since entering. "The priest should be waiting below, go fetch him."

"The priest?" Saidh asked with dismay. "Surely we can wait to talk to him?"

"There's nothing to talk about. He's waiting to perform the ceremony," Greer told her.

"But—"

"Come along, dear. Me maid and I shall make ye pretty fer the ceremony," Aunt Tilda said cheerfully, appearing at her side and urging her toward the door.

"But—" Saidh repeated weakly and glanced back toward Greer as she was ushered out of the room. The last thing she saw, before the door closed, was her brothers moving to surround Greer.

Chapter 10

" 'Tis quite unusual fer the proof o' innocence to be on display at the actual wedding feast."

Saidh blinked at Aunt Tilda's words and tore her
gaze from her husband to glance at the bloodied
sheet that hung over the banister. Heaving a sigh,
she said, "Aye. I'm no' sure whose idea that was.
Probably one o' me brothers."

"Do ye mind?" Aunt Tilda asked gently.

Saidh shrugged. "No more than the fact that half
the castle probably heard me brother bellowing
about Greer writing to tell him he'd ruined and was
marrying me."

"Hmmm. No doubt the other half of the castle
were told about it within minutes afterward," Aunt
Tilda said dryly.

"Aye," Saidh agreed wryly and turned to find her
husband again. He was seated on a bench across
from Dougall at one of the lower tables. The rest of
her brothers were gathered around the pair, laughing and cheering them on as they chugged back

whatever they were drinking. All eight of the men had been seated at the high table just moments ago, but then her brothers had stood as one and dragged Greer down there to challenge him to a drinking contest. She had no idea why they'd dragged him away for it. She didn't mind them having the contest. They could have held it here at the high table without her fussing.

And they knew her well enough to be aware of that, she realized suddenly. What the devil were they up to?

"I suppose the proof o' innocence means we can bypass the bedding ceremony," Aunt Tilda said thoughtfully, and then glanced to her in question. "Unless ye want one?"

"Oh, nay." Saidh waved the idea away. She'd seen it at Fenella's wedding and thought it a great deal of fuss and nonsense for nothing. That thought made her glance toward the stairs as she wondered if Fenella knew about the wedding and feast. She must, of course. Her maid would have heard when she came below to collect Fenella's sup if not before, and had no doubt told her mistress. Saidh wasn't terribly surprised, though, that Fenella hadn't made an appearance to offer even feigned well wishes. She'd thrown the applemoyse at her just hours ago, after all, and that after seeming to suggest she was considering Greer as a husband for herself. No doubt Fenella's nose would be out of joint now.

"I find meself a little weary again tonight. Mayhap I'll retire early," Aunt Tilda said suddenly. Smiling at Saidh, she added, "And since that is the third time ye've yawned in as many minutes, mayhap ye should too. It may be good fer ye to get in a little nap ere Greer joins ye."

"Mayhap I will," Saidh said, stifling another yawn and rising when Lady MacDonnell did. She paused then, though, glancing uncertainly toward Greer and her brothers. "Do ye think I should tell Greer?"

"Nay." Lady MacDonnell chuckled. "Let him have his fun. He will be up soon enough."

Nodding, Saidh walked with her toward the stairs.

"I hope ye do no' mind not sleeping in the master chamber on yer first night as lady here," Lady Mac-Donnell said with concern a moment later as they started up the stairs. " 'Tis just with Alpin so ill—"

"I do no' mind at all," Saidh interrupted to assure her.

"Still, it seems a shame to spend yer wedding night in the guest room ye've been using."

"I do no' mind," Saidh repeated firmly. " 'Tis a nice room, and as ye said, there is no sense in moving Alpin when he's unwell."

"Aye," Aunt Tilda murmured with a frown. "Speaking of the lad, I suppose I'd best check on him ere I retire. His fever was definitely back before we moved below for the feast. I told Marian, the maid who was sitting with him," she explained. "I told her to fetch me if he got worse, so hopefully he has no', but I'll feel better checking on him anyway."

"I can do that, if ye like," Saidh offered.

"Thank ye, but nay. I want to talk to Marian anyway. Let her know I am retiring so no' to look fer me below."

Saidh opened her mouth to tell her that she could tell the woman that for her, but then gasped in surprise when Lady MacDonnell stumbled on the steps and crashed into her. The hand Saidh had been trailing along the rail tightened instinctively on the wood, saving her from a bad fall. She also reached for Aunt Tilda with her other hand to ensure she didn't tumble past her. The woman was surprisingly heavy and Saidh grunted at the full impact of Aunt Tilda's weight as it sent her falling back as far as her arm would straighten, before they then swung toward the railing, crashing into it with enough impact that it produced a cracking sound.

For one moment, Saidh feared the railing would give way and they'd both plunge to the great hall below, but it held and she was able to regain her balance, and then help Lady MacDonnell to find her own.

"Goodness," Aunt Tilda breathed once they were both safely on their feet again. "Fer a minute there I thought I'd be joining me Allen sooner than expected."

"So did I," Saidh admitted quietly. "Are ye all right?"

"Aye," Aunt Tilda assured her, but then scowled down at the steps and said, "Be careful though. There is something slippery on the steps. Probably Marian spilled some of the soup she fetched for Alpin. Or mayhap Fenella's maid spilled something as she carried up her food," she added in a mutter, and then shook her head and stepped carefully onto the next step as close to the wall as she could get to bypass whatever was on the wood. "I shall have Marian clean it up while I sit with Alpin."

Saidh peered down as she traversed the next couple of steps, but they were still a few steps from the landing and the light from the torches in the upper hall didn't reach there. The steps in question were in shadow.

"Well, good sleep, Saidh," Aunt Tilda murmured pausing on the landing and turning to hug her and press a kiss to her cheek. "I am glad to ha'e ye in our family."

"Thank ye," Saidh murmured, hugging the woman back. "Good sleep."

She waited until Lady MacDonnell had slid into the master bedchamber, and then covered a yawn with her hand and continued on to her own room. Her gaze slid to Fenella's door further down the hall as she paused at her own and Saidh's smile faded. She had resolved little, talking to her cousin, and was still left wondering if she had killed her husbands. It was a matter that she needed to put to rest, if only in her own mind.

Sighing, she pushed into her chamber and then paused to glance around. The room was softly lit by flickering flames in the fireplace. A tray with cheese, bread, fruit and what appeared to be mulled cider sat on the table between the two chairs by the fire. It was all quite lovely and Saidh found her smile returning.

Reaching up, she undid the lacings of her borrowed gown as she crossed the room. Then paused by the chairs to remove it. She laid it across the back of the nearest chair with a small grimace. The gown was beautiful, but a pale yellow that had never suited her coloring. However, when Lady MacDonnell had proudly presented it, announcing that she'd worn it for her own wedding, Saidh hadn't had the heart to refuse the offering. Unfortunately, Lady MacDonnell was a larger woman than her, and had been even in her youth. The gown had been too large, hanging unattractively from her shorter, thinner frame, the bodice sagging and shoulders constantly wanting to slip off. Lady MacDonnell had pinned it in several places to rectify the problem, but the pins had slipped halfway through the ceremony and Saidh had spent the rest of the ceremony and the following feast constantly pulling the shoulders back into place and tugging at the bodice to keep from revealing more of herself than she wanted to.

Ah well, Saidh thought, as she turned to move to the bed in only the shift Lady MacDonnell had given her to wear under the gown. She had never much been concerned about fashion anyway. Besides, Greer had seemed to quite enjoy how revealing the gown had been at times.

Chuckling as she recalled the way his eyes had lit up, filling with promise each time it had happened, Saidh lifted the edge of the linens and furs and slid into bed. Hopefully she would manage at least a half hour sleep before the boys finished with their game, and then . . .

Sighing, she curled onto her side with a smile and fell asleep imagining Greer waking her with soft kisses and caresses.

A loud crash and a burst of laughter startled

Saidh from a sound sleep. Sitting up abruptly, she glanced around with confusion to see her brothers stumbling into the room, bearing a dead stag on their shoulders.

Saidh blinked and tilted her head. Nay not a dead stag, but Greer with stag antlers fastened to his head by a cloth that looked suspiciously like a woman's stockings. They had been wrapped around the center of the stag horns, set on the top of his head and then tied under his chin to keep them in place, she saw, as her brothers bumped about to get him through the door and his head fell, hanging toward the floor.

"Bloody hell, ye killed him!" Saidh roared, tossing the linens and furs aside and flying from the bed in a fury.

"Nay," Aulay said on a laugh and put out one hand to halt her forward motion. Leaving Greer to her other brothers, he urged her out of the way and added, "He's no' dead, just plumb fou'."

"Dougall drank him under the table," she realized with a sigh. She should have thought to warn Greer that her brothers were fond of drinking games and had become quite good at them over the years.

"Actually, he drank Dougall under the table," Aulay admitted, sounding rather impressed.

Eyebrows rising, Saidh glanced back to the brothers now laying Greer on the bed and realized that there were only six of them. Dougall was missing. No doubt snoring under the trestle table where he'd fallen, she supposed.

"And then Rory challenged him and yer husband damned near drank him under the table too."

Aulay was definitely impressed, Saidh thought, and smiled with satisfaction.

"He did no'," Rory protested, and then stumbled and dropped onto the bed on top of Greer.

Saidh scowled and propped her hands on her hips, waiting for Rory to get up. Instead he merely released a loud snuffling snore.

Her other brothers immediately burst out laughing and turned toward the door.

"Oy!" Saidh bellowed. "Yer no' leaving Rory here."

"Nay, o' course we're no'," Conran said as he sailed out the door.

"We'd ne'er do a thing like that to ye, lass," Geordie assured her on his heels.

"Sorry, Saidh," was all Alick said as Niels hustled him out, pulling the door closed behind them.

"Aulay," Saidh growled, turning on her oldest brother.

"Settle yerself, lass. I'll take him away," Aulay soothed, then moved to the bed, turned Rory, and then lifted him up and slung him over his shoulder. "Get the door fer me, lass."

Saidh quickly opened the door.

"I'd apologize that yer new husband is in no fit state to tend to the consummation," Aulay said as he started toward her with his burden. Pausing beside her, he bent slightly to kiss her cheek and then straightened and continued out adding, "But since the two o' ye already enjoyed that last night and the proof is in the hall, there seems little need."

Saidh scowled at her brother's back, and then slammed the door behind him and turned to glare at her unconscious husband, her brother's laughter reaching her muffled through the door. Sighing, Saidh shook her head, then walked around the bed to get back into her side. She didn't lie down, but sat and pulled the linens and furs up to her waist, then turned her gaze on her husband.

The man looked ridiculous with the stag horns on his head. Actually, it was the cloth tied under his chin that made him look like an utter arse, Saidh decided. She hesitated, but then pushed the linens and furs down again and shifted to her knees beside him to quickly undo the ridiculous horns and remove them. Shaking her head, she tossed them to the floor, grimacing at the clatter they made. She'd probably just woken up the entire castle with that action, she thought with regret. At least, those who were sleeping—Saidh added the thought as she became aware of the music, laughter and chatter filtering up from the great hall.

There would be a lot of people with sore heads come the morning. Her husband included, she supposed. Saidh tugged a couple of the furs out from under her husband, threw them over him, and then climbed under the linens and furs again. Curling onto her side, she heaved a little sigh and closed her eyes. This was not how she'd expected her wedding night to go.

GREER OPENED HIS EYES, AND THEN PROMPTLY closed them again with a groan as light stabbed through them and straight into his skull.

"Bloody hell, what happened?" he muttered, covering his eyes with his hands and rolling onto his side.

"Ye drank Dougall under the table, and almost did Rory too afterward, but no' quite."

Greer blinked his eyes open again and found himself staring at a rather large, hairy leg sticking out from under a green, yellow and black plaid. Startled, he pulled back and sat up at the same time, seeing the leg was attached to Aulay Buchanan's body. The man was sitting on top of the furs and linens next to him, back against the headboard, legs crossed at the ankles, and arms crossed on his chest.

"What the de'il are you doing in me bed?" Greer asked with irritation.

"Well, first, I do no' believe this is yer bed," Aulay said calmly. "Although, since yer laird here, I suppose ye could argue that e'ery bed in the castle is yer bed."

Frowning, Greer glanced around and realized he wasn't in the master chamber, he was in Saidh's room, in Saidh's bed, and fully clothed.

"Where's me wife?" he growled, getting out of bed and moving to close the shutters. His head was pounding something fierce and the sunlight streaming into the room was not helping.

"She's below breaking her fast," Aulay announced, and then added with amusement, "And nay she does no' ken I'm here."

Finished with the shutters, Greer nodded and turned to eye him. "Why are ye here?"

"To welcome ye to the family," Aulay announced, swinging his legs off the bed and getting to his feet. He walked to the door, opened it, and then paused and swung back to add, "And to tell ye, do ye hurt our Saidh, I'll no' be the only Buchanan seeking to put yer head on a pike."

He didn't wait for a response, but slid out of the room, pulling the door closed silently behind him.

Greer released a small breath and then glanced down at himself. He was a muckle mess, his plaid half unpleated and hanging askew, his shirt stained with what appeared to be whiskey. Greer supposed he'd passed out with his whiskey in hand. That, or Saidh's brothers had poured their drinks on him after he'd passed out.

Grimacing, he left the room to head to his own.

"Oh Greer, good morn, son," Aunt Tilda said with a smile as he entered his room. "Did ye sleep well?"

He glanced to where she sat at Alpin's bedside, nodded and asked, "How's the lad?"

"Still feverish," Lady MacDonnell said with a sigh, reaching to caress the sleeping boy's head.

Greer frowned and then opened his chest to retrieve a fresh shirt and plaid. Slinging them over his shoulder, he then walked over to feel Alpin's head. He was warm, but not as bad as he'd been the day before and Greer relaxed and straightened. His gaze shifted to his aunt. "There's no need fer ye to sit at the boy's bedside. One o' the maids can do it."

"Oh, that's all right," Lady MacDonnell said with a smile, brushing a strand of hair off Alpin's forehead. "I do no' mind."

Greer bent to kiss her cheek lightly, murmuring, "Thank ye."

Straightening, he then headed for the door. "I'm heading to the loch to clean up. I'll no' be long."

"Ye should really order a bath up here instead. Ye'll catch yer death swimming in that cold loch," Aunt Tilda said quietly.

Greer opened his mouth to respond, and then paused abruptly as he recalled that her son had drown in the loch. In the end, he merely murmured, "Mayhap next time," and slid out of the room.

He didn't see Saidh at the table when he passed through the great hall to reach the doors. Her brothers were all there though, and every one of them was smiling or laughing as they ate and talked. It seemed they were not affected by the excessive amounts of drink they'd imbibed last night. Even Dougall, who had been the first to pass out, was chuckling at something one of the men said, looking completely untroubled by the same throbbing Greer was suffering.

Scowling to himself, Greer headed outside.

"Good morn, m'laird," the stable master said in greeting as he led Greer's horse out of the stables. "I saw ye coming and thought ye might be after yer wife and want yer horse."

Greer had taken the reins and started to mount, but paused with a hand on the saddle horn and one foot in the stirrups to glance to the man with surprise. "After me wife?"

"Aye. She left on her horse but moments ago," the man said with a nod. "Headed toward the loch, it looked to me."

Greer nodded and mounted his horse, his mood suddenly lifting a bit.

Saidh dove under the water and swam for a distance, then surfaced again. The water had felt ice cold when she'd first entered the loch, but she'd adjusted rather quickly and was now enjoying herself. She'd come here because it had seemed a better idea than staying at the keep and knocking her brothers' heads together. If she had to listen again to them chuckling about the fine trick they'd played on Greer last night, Saidh thought she could happily run at least one of them through. The bastards had deliberately set out to leave him an unconscious mess. Had he succeeded with Rory as he had with Dougall, then Geordie had intended to challenge him next. Saidh was not sure how they'd phrased the challenge to ensure he accepted, but whatever it was had apparently been effective.

"Ye should ne'er swim alone. If nothing else, Allen's death should tell ye that."

Saidh spun in the water to peer to shore, her eyebrows rising when she saw Greer sliding off his mount.

"Aye? And so ye ne'er swim alone then?" she asked dryly as she watched him tether his beast next to her own at the edge of the clearing. He then walked over to set a clean plaid and shirt on a boulder by the edge of the water.

"Oh, aye, all the time," he admitted with amusement as he began to remove his plaid and shirt from last night. "But I should no'."

"Then I shall make a deal with ye," Saidh offered. "You ne'er swim alone and I will no' either."

"Done," Greer agreed easily, tossing his plaid and shirt aside and pausing to prop his hands on his hips and contemplate her. "Are ye naked lass?"

"No more naked than ye are," she assured him, her gaze sliding over his body. If the man was standing there posing in the hopes of raising her lust with his magnificence . . . well, it was working, she admitted to herself with derision. Really, God had gifted him with a fine body. "Are ye just going to stand there all day, or will ye be coming in?"

"Oh, I'll be coming," he assured her with a wicked smile and started into the water. He walked out until the water was just above his knees, then raised his arms and made a shallow dive under the water's surface.

Saidh watched the water between them, trying to spot his approach, but didn't see him until he suddenly splashed up out of the water directly in front of her.

"Good morn," he growled and she felt his arm slide around her waist under the water, and then he dragged her against his chest and claimed her lips. Saidh smiled against his mouth and wrapped her arms and legs around him to keep from swaying in the water. Feeling his erection bob against her bottom, she pulled back from his kiss and arched an eyebrow.

"How are ye feeling this morn, me laird?" she asked sweetly.

"Better now," he said with a grin, shifting his hands down to clasp her bottom and squeeze gently.

"And did ye enjoy playing with me brothers?" she asked dryly.

"No' nearly as much as I enjoy playing with you," he assured her, shifting her slightly. Saidh's eyes widened when his erection rubbed against her and then was caught between them.

"How did they convince ye to play their drinking games?" she asked a little breathlessly as he shifted her to rub against him again.

"They said ye could drink all o' them under the table and surely I wanted to prove I was a better man than ye," he admitted wryly.

Saidh chuckled and shook her head. "I have drunk all o' them under the table, all but Aulay," she added. "And only one at a time."

"Ah," he said dryly and then shrugged. "If nothing else, they seem to hate me a little less now. At least only one o' them threatened to kill me this morning."

"Aulay?" Saidh asked with amusement.

"Aye," Greer said wryly. "Although he did include the others in the threat, saying they'd all come after me if I hurt ye."

Saidh tilted her head and eyed him with interest. "Ye do no' appear to be overly concerned by the threat."

"Because it's no' a worry, since I ha'e no plans to hurt ye," he assured her solemnly.

Saidh stared at him silently, and then tightened her legs around his waist and stretched up to kiss him.

Greer kissed her back briefly, but then pulled back to point out. "Ye ken we've yet to consummate the marriage?"

"That is no' my fault," she pointed out dryly. "I was waiting patiently abed last night when me brothers carried yer drunk arse in and dropped ye on the bed, antlers and all."

"Antlers?" he asked with a start. Greer had been carrying her toward shore, but paused now to peer at her with amazement.

Saidh nodded. "Ye had antlers strapped to yer head. The strapping was tied under yer chin like a bairn's bonnet. Ye looked quite ridiculous," she added.

"Yer brothers must ha'e done it," he said grimly as he continued out of the water, and then added, "They do no' seem to like me much."

Saidh nearly laughed at his confounded expression as he said that. She managed not to though, and simply pointed out, "Ye seem surprised."

"Aye, well, e'ery one likes me usually . . . except mayhap the men I've killed," he allowed thoughtfully.

Her eyebrows rose. "Ha'e ye killed many men, then?"

"Oh, aye," he said as if it was of no account. "I would ha'e had to be verra bad at what I did to earn me coin if that were no' the case."

"Oh, aye, ye were a sword fer hire," she recalled as he stopped in the middle of the clearing. Saidh waited until he'd set her on the plaid he'd discarded earlier, and then leaned back on her elbows and asked, "What was that like?"

Greer was silent for a minute, his gaze sliding over her naked wet body. Once he'd looked his fill, he turned his attention back to her face and arched an eyebrow. "Would ye rather I talk or get to the consummating?"

"Can ye no' do both?" she taunted.

"O' course. I just did no' think ye'd want me to," he said as he dropped to his knees beside her. "Since it would mean no' being able to kiss ye."

Saidh's eyes widened at that announcement and she sat up. Slipping one hand around his neck to urge him toward her, she whispered, "Ye were right," against his lips, and then slid her tongue out to run along them.

Releasing, a low growl, Greer slid his arms around her and covered her mouth with his in a slow, sweet kiss that left them both breathless and clinging to each other.

"I need ye, lass," Greer groaned, urging her back to lie flat on his plaid, his hands now moving over her body, caressing every inch revealed to him.

Saidh shifted restlessly under his touch, her hands covering his and giving a brief, encouraging squeeze before moving on to touch him. One hand slid up his arm to find and massage his chest, but the other dropped to the knee beside her and began to run up it. She'd nearly reached the stiff erection poking up between his legs when Greer gave off caressing her to snatch the hand away.

"'Twill be over ere we've begun do ye—" his words died on a startled gasp as Saidh suddenly sat up, letting her other hand drop to claim the prize the first had failed at grasping. Holding him firmly, she prevented any protest he may have offered by kissing him.

Greer hesitated, and then opened his mouth to kiss her back. Saidh sighed her pleasure into his mouth as his tongue plunged inside, and was so distracted by his kisses for a moment that her hand remained still, merely clasping him. When she did recall what she'd intended to do and started to slide her hand tentatively along his sheath, Greer broke their kiss.

"But—" Saidh began in protest, and then snapped her mouth closed in surprise when he abruptly caught her by the waist and turned her in front of him so that she knelt with her back to his chest. "What—?"

Saidh nearly bit her tongue off with surprise when he plastered his chest to her back, his arms snaking around her body so that he could cup and caress a breast with one hand, while the other slid down between her legs.

"Oh," Saidh moaned, pushing back against him as his skilled fingers slid between the folds of her womanhood to find the nub it hid. When his fingers then began to dance lightly over the sensitive flesh, she shifted into the touch, gasping, "Oh, husband."

Greer nipped and then suckled at her neck in response, then removed the hand at her breast to urge her face around for another kiss. Saidh responded eagerly, alternately thrusting her own tongue out to meet his, and then retrieving it so that she could suck on his instead. All the while her hips were riding the caressing hand between her legs, her bottom pressing and rubbing against his rock hard erection where it was caught between their bodies and then moving forward again into his touch.

When he suddenly broke their kiss, Saidh moaned in protest, then gave a gasp of surprise when he pressed on her back, forcing her forward on her knees. Releasing the stranglehold she hadn't realized she'd had on his hands, Saidh reached out to catch herself, hands flat on the ground, and then she cried out with surprised pleasure as he suddenly thrust into her from behind.

Already on the verge of succumbing to her pleasure, his suddenly filling her pushed Saidh over the edge and her surprised cry was followed by a scream of pleasure that sent the birds flapping in the trees overhead.

Greer froze, his erection planted deep inside her as her body convulsed around him. But he didn't stop caressing her, and, finding herself extremely sensitive there of a sudden, Saidh braced herself on one hand and started to reach back with the other to urge his caressing fingers away, but then gasped in surprise and quickly returned her hand to the ground to brace herself as he withdrew and then thrust into her again. Much to her amazement, after three or four thrusts, the excitement that she'd thought was spent began to build in her again, stoked by both his touch and his erection sliding in and out of her.

Planting her hands more firmly and shifting her knees a little further apart to adjust to a more pleasing angle, Saidh began to push back into his thrusts almost violently, demanding the release that lay just out of reach. She had nearly found it again when Greer suddenly withdrew both his hands and his body. Saidh glanced sharply over her shoulder, ready to bellow at him for it, then gasped instead when he caught her by the hips and flipped her like a bairn in a cradle. She landed on her back with an "oomph" and then simply stared in amazement when he caught her by the ankles, lifted her legs and thrust into her again from this new position.

Saidh simply gaped at the man's face where it was framed by her ankles, not at all sure she liked this position. Apparently, he wasn't as pleased with it as he'd thought he'd be either, because just as quickly as he'd changed positions earlier, he released her ankles, then caught her by the waist and lifted her up even as he sat back on his haunches. Now she was straddling his lap and she was able to wrap her arms around his shoulders and hold on as he raised and lowered her with his hands on her bottom.

Her breasts rubbed against his chest with each motion and while he wasn't able to caress her with his fingers this way, his cock did that for him, rubbing against her core each time he withdrew. Saidh liked it, especially when he began to kiss her as well . . . although, she soon had trouble concentrating on the kissing, and began merely to suck on his tongue almost desperately as her body pulled into a tight ball of anticipation.

This time they both found their pleasure almost at the same moment, Saidh barely beginning to cry out with release before Greer joined in with a bellow that was probably heard all the way back to the castle. They rode out the waves together, clinging to each other like children lost in a storm, and then Greer tumbled backward, taking her with him to lie on his chest in the safety of his arms as they both struggled to regain their breath.

Chapter 11

SAIDH SMILED AND LAY STILL FOR A MOMENT, EN-joying the warmth of Greer's embrace. But restlessness soon moved her to raise her head to peer at him. Finding his eyes closed, she tapped his chin. "Are ye sleeping?"

"I am trying to," he said dryly and blinked open sleepy eyes.

"How can ye sleep after something like that?" she asked with amazement.

Greer arched his eyebrows and countered, "How can ye not?"

Saidh chuckled at his expression and pushed away from him to get to her feet. "I feel most wonderful and wide awake meself."

"While I am spent," he muttered, his gaze warming as it ran over her body.

Saidh grinned at his expression and turned to saunter down to the water's edge, putting an exaggerated sway in her walk as she'd seen a maid or two do to tempt her brothers.

"Oh, lass, yer like to wake the beast do ye keep that up," Greer warned.

"And what beast would that be, m'laird?" Saidh asked, glancing back with a sassy smile. She let her gaze drop to his groin and arched her eyebrows. The man was well set in that department. At least he was if she was to judge by the glimpses she'd had of her brothers over the years. None of them were shy or overly concerned about being seen in all their glory. If she were to believe their bragging, they were all well endowed, a Buchanan trait. From what she could tell though, Greer was easily their equal. Still, she couldn't resist pinching his manly pride and teased, "Surely ye do no' mean that wee thing?"

"Och!" He was on his feet in a trice and rushing toward her.

Laughing, Saidh turned and started into the water. She'd barely taken two steps into the cold liquid when he caught her from behind and swept her up into his arms. Greer didn't stop there, but carried her quickly forward until he stood knee deep in the cold water.

"Take it back," he ordered, holding her out over the water.

"Take what back?" she asked innocently, unconcerned. She'd intended to swim after all.

"Wife," he growled in warning and Saidh's smile changed, softening with wonder.

"I *am* yer wife now," she said softly and when confusion filled his expression, explained, "We've consummated the marriage. We're truly husband and wife now."

Smiling faintly, he nodded, drawing her against his chest. His voice was a soft growl as he agreed, "Aye. We're man and wife now."

They smiled gently and leaned toward each other to share a kiss. Their lips never met, however. The sound of snapping branches followed by whinnies from their horses made them both glance sharply toward the beasts as the mare and stallion shifted nervously away from the edge of the clearing.

Saidh wasn't surprised when Greer suddenly turned and carried her quickly out of the water. The moment he hit dry land he let her legs drop. Once she was on her feet, he also removed the arm from around her back and then he abandoned her to hurry to his plaid and grab up his sword. Saidh was already doing the same thing herself, snatching up her own sword from where she'd left it. She then moved toward the horses even as he did.

"Do ye see anything?" she asked when he paused at the head of his stallion and peered at a fixed spot in the trees.

"Nay, you?" Greer responded and cast a quick glance her way. At least she suspected it was only supposed to be a quick glance, however his eyes locked on her and stayed, his expression turning from grim concern to flabbergasted dismay. "What the devil are ye doin' woman? Get dressed!"

Saidh rolled her eyes at his distress. She didn't point out that he was naked, or that bandits jumping out at them while she was in the middle of dressing would be worse than being seen naked. Nor did she point out that the dress would only hamper her ability to fight. She did think all those things though and mutter under her breath about them as she strode impatiently to her clothes and snatched them up.

The moment he saw that she was doing as requested, Greer turned his attention back to the woods. Saidh scowled at his back, then stabbed her sword into the ground so that the handle would be easily accessible should an attack happen while she was trying to dress, then she tugged on her chemise.

During the brief seconds that her vision was obscured by the soft cloth sliding over her face, Greer disappeared from the clearing.

Checking the woods, no doubt, she thought with irritation as she snatched up the dress next. She didn't bother doing up stays or even troubling to tug it into place. The moment it was on and had dropped over her hips, she snatched up her sword again and strode after her husband.

When Greer stepped out of the woods as Saidh reached the horses, she paused to run a soothing hand down her still nervous mare's nose as she peered at him in question. "Anything?"

"Nay. It may ha'e been a stag or some other beastie," he said with a sigh and ran a hand around his neck as if to soothe tensed muscles.

"Ye do no' sound like ye think that's the case," she said solemnly and he grimaced.

"Me stallion's no' a nervous beast. He only reacts as he did to a threat. A simple stag or doe would no' make him dance away from the woods."

"Hmmm," Saidh murmured and peered at her

mare. Her horse was well trained and not prone to nerves either. In fact, if Saidh were to judge by her behavior, she'd have said the mare had reacted as if a human had been approaching rather than an animal. Glancing back to Greer, she suggested, "It could ha'e been one o' me brothers. Or even a couple or more. They all like to swim. They may ha'e come in search o' the loch, saw that we were here and what we were about and headed away without interrupting."

Greer snorted at the suggestion. "I suspect yer brothers are no' the type to discreetly slip away. In fact, I'd venture to say they would ha'e taken pleasure in interrupting us."

Saidh grinned at the words and nodded. "Aye. They would," she agreed with amusement and then shrugged. "Then mayhap it was one o' yer men. I ken Bowie likes to swim here."

"Aye, he does, but I left him to watch o'er the men in practice," Greer said. "He is no' the only one who likes to swim here though." Giving up on his neck, he headed for his plaid, adding, "That being the case, I suppose it was foolish to behave so out here. We should return to the keep."

"Aye," Saidh agreed and quickly unhitched her mare from the tree both horses were fastened to and mounted. "I'll race ye."

"What? Wait!" Greer bellowed when she started to turn her mount toward the woods. When she paused and glanced to him in question, he pointed out, "I still ha'e to pleat and don me plaid."

"I ken," Saidh grinned widely. "That means I might actually beat ye back."

Greer shouted at Saidh to wait for him, but she didn't obey. It seemed she hadn't taken that part of her vows seriously. That or she hadn't heard him over her own laughter, he thought with irritation as he quickly laid out his plaid and began to pleat it. The woman was . . . well, she was magnificent, he acknowledged, some of his anger slipping away and a smile caressing the corners of his mouth as he quickly made clumsy pleats in his plaid. Damn, she had passion aplenty, a hell of a temper and more courage than most of the men he'd walked into battle with over the years. Few of them would have had the balls to take on the seven Buchanan brothers at once, or to face off against him with swords even in a friendly battle. The woman seemed to have no fear and she didn't half enjoy life, she did so fully.

Greer had never met a woman like Saidh before. She took his breath away . . . and he couldn't believe he'd been lucky enough not only to find her, but to win her.

Shaking his head, he acknowledged that his life had certainly taken an unexpected turn. If someone had suggested to him even weeks ago that he'd be a wealthy laird with his own castle and a woman like Saidh to wife, he would have laughed himself silly. This was not something he'd even allowed himself to dream of as a mercenary defending other lairds' lands. Yet here he was, a man who had it all.

For some reason that thought tugged a thread of fear inside Greer. He had so much . . . and so much to lose. Leaving the plaid only half pleated, he threw himself down on it and quickly tugged it into place.

The large pin he used to secure it wasn't even fully fastened before he was on his feet. He finished that task as he strode to his horse.

Once on the beast's back, Greer sent him out of the clearing at a run. That thread of fear was becoming a whole skein and it suddenly seemed urgent to him to catch up to Saidh as quickly as he could.

Greer was in such a rush he nearly trampled her. It was his mount that saved the day, slowing despite his urging and coming to an abrupt halt almost before Greer saw the mare next to the body on the path. In fact, he was lucky he didn't sail off the beast's back and break his neck tumbling arse over heels. He managed to keep his seat, however, and instead threw himself from the mount to rush to Saidh's side and see what was about.

At first, he thought mayhap she'd tumbled from her mare, but then he spotted the arrow sticking out of her side as he dropped to his knees beside her and his heart nearly fell out of his chest. It certainly felt as if it dropped down to somewhere in the vicinity of his stomach.

"Saidh?" he barked, grasping her shoulders and raising her upper body off the ground. Her head lolled backward, hair trailing on the dirt, but she released a small moan too and Greer could have wept at this sign that she still lived.

" 'Tis all right," he assured her, scooping her up in his arms. "I've got ye. I'll get ye home and we'll patch ye up, and ye'll be fine."

She wasn't awake to hear his reassurances, but Greer needed to say them. He needed to hear and believe them. He simply couldn't fathom the thought of losing her already. Repeating his reassurances over and over, he carried her to his horse and somehow managed to mount while keeping her pressed to his chest . . . though were anyone to ask him he couldn't have said how he'd done that.

Greer didn't bother about her mare, but left it to follow, or not, as it chose. He was halfway back to the keep before it occurred to him that Saidh might be upset with him did she wake up to find he'd lost her mare. He glanced around anxiously then, relieved to see that it was behind them. The mare was smaller and slower and couldn't keep up. She was a good distance behind but she was there, hurrying after them and that was enough.

Greer rode across the bridge, through the gates and straight for the stairs to the keep. He spotted Saidh's brothers by the stables, but ignored them even when one of them called out to him. He was too busy at that point deciding whether to ride his beast straight up the stairs and into the great hall or not. In the end, it was the fact that he couldn't sort out a way to open the door while in the saddle that made him decide to rein in at the base of the stairs. Pressing Saidh tight to his chest, he catapulted out of the saddle and hurried up the stairs and inside.

It wasn't until he was charging into the master bedchamber that he recalled Alpin was in the bed. He almost turned then and carried her to the room they'd slept in last night, but a moan from Saidh changed his mind and he hurried forward and laid her gently down. He then reached over and gave Alpin a shake.

The boy moaned but otherwise didn't respond, and Greer gave him another, much harder shake. "Alpin!"

"Aye. What? M'laird?" Alpin opened drowsy eyes to peer at him blankly. "What is about, me laird?" He gave his head a shake and struggled to sit up. "Do ye need something m'laird? Is it time fer battle? Shall I fetch yer sword?"

"Nay." Greer pushed the boy back on the bed. His fever was obviously affecting his thinking if he still thought them out on the mercenary trail. "Where are Tilda and Helen?"

"Tilda?" Alpin peered at him blankly.

"My aunt Tilda," Greer said impatiently. "She was sitting with ye when I left. Her maid is a fair hand at healing. Where are they?"

"Oh." The boy's expression cleared a bit, but he shook his head and glanced around the room. "I'm no' sure. Lady Tilda was here when I woke earlier. She made me drink a tincture her maid had mixed fer me." He grimaced and gave a small shudder. "Vile stuff, but she made me drink e'ery last drop. I fell back to sleep then and . . ." He shrugged helplessly. "I do no' ken where or when she left then."

Greer growled with frustration at that and turned to hurry to the door. Opening it, he glanced out and spotted a maid walking up the hall.

"Fetch me Helen," he ordered.

"Aye, m'laird." The woman rushed off and Greer closed the door and returned to the bed to check on

Saidh. Alpin followed his actions with wary eyes that widened with alarm when he noticed the woman in the bed next to him. Confusion covered his face.

"Why is Lady Saidh abed?" Alarm filled his expression and he added, "Ye're no' thinking o' tupping her right here next to me?"

Greer glanced to the boy with exasperation. "Does it look as if she's in any state to be tupped?"

Alpin glanced back to her and his eyes widened again. "Oh dear . . . is that an arrow sticking out o' her duckie?"

"Aye," he muttered, peering at the spot where the arrow had pierced her breast. There didn't appear to be a lot of blood around the wound. He wasn't sure if that was a good thing or not. He just knew they had to get the damned thing out and sew her up. He couldn't lose her after just finding her.

"Ye shot her?" Alpin asked with dismay.

"Do no' be daft," he snapped and then straightened from the bed with a curse and muttered, "Where the hell is Helen?"

"What happened?"

Greer glanced around at that sharp question to see Rory rushing into the room with Aulay hard on his heels.

"Me laird shot me lady," Alpin announced in a woebegone tone, his words slightly slurred.

"O' course I didna," Greer snapped, scowling at the boy. "Why the devil would I marry her and then shoot her with an arrow?"

"Cause ye came to yer senses," Geordie suggested dryly as he strode into the room now too.

"Aye," Dougall agreed grimly as he followed. "Ye woke up this morn, came to yer senses and realized ye could no' keep a fine woman like Saidh happy so ye decided to be rid o' her."

"That or ye realized she has a fou' temper and is as like to beat ye as look at ye, do ye tweak her temper," Alick suggested entering now as well.

"I did no' shoot me wife with an arrow," Greer said grimly and scowled suspiciously at Rory when he moved to the door and stopped Niels and Conran as they would have entered. After murmuring to the two men briefly, both Niels and Conran turned and rushed away.

"Look at him, lads," Aulay growled impatiently, capturing Greer's attention again. "He has a sword but no bow or quiver. Besides, he's fair distraught. He did no' do this."

"Thank ye," Greer said dryly, and then roared, "Now will one o' ye go find Helen to aid me wife ere she bleeds to death?"

"No need," Aulay said soothingly. "Rory's tending to her."

"What?" Greer glanced around to see that Rory was at the bedside, bent over his wife. Alarm racing through him, he hurried to grab the man's arm and pull him away from her. "What the devil are ye doing? Ye're like to do more damage. Let her be. Helen'll tend her."

"Leave him, MacDonnell," Aulay said firmly, pulling him away from the other man. "Rory kens what he's doing. He trained with our healer at Buchanan."

Frowning, Greer tugged his arm free. "Fine but I'm no' leaving her."

"Nay. O' course no'. But at least move out of the way so Rory has room to work," Aulay said quietly.

Greer almost refused, but recognized the sense in the suggestion and gave a grudging nod. He then moved quickly around the bed to Alpin's side. But he wasn't happy about it. Half the bed and Alpin were now between him and his wife.

"I got yer satchel," Niels announced, rushing back into the room.

"Thank ye." Rory accepted the bag and set it on the bed. He began to pull out weeds and tinctures, and then suddenly paused to hand a bottle to Niels. "When Conran returns, put six drops of this in the water I sent him to fetch."

Niels nodded as he took the bottle. "Six drops. Aye."

"Six drops what?" Conran asked, rushing into the room with linens and a bowl of water he was sloshing everywhere in his rush.

Shaking his head, Greer turned his attention back to Rory in time to see that he was quickly cutting away the cloth of Saidh's gown around the arrow, baring her breast and the arrow shaft that stuck out of it. Greer stared at the wound, concern seeping through him, then glanced down to Alpin when the boy sucked in a deep breath and then let it out again on the word, "Pretty."

Noting that Alpin's gaze was fixed on Saidh's exposed breast, he scowled and slapped a hand over the boy's eyes. He then scowled at the seven Buchanan brothers now ranged around the bed also staring at Saidh's naked breast.

"Stop gawking at yer sister's duckies," he growled, using the term he'd now heard both Saidh and Alpin use in reference to breasts.

"She's our sister," Dougall pointed out with disgust. "We're looking at her wound, no' her teat."

"Aye," Geordie agreed. "Besides, 'tis nothing we've no' seen before. We all used to swim naked in the loch at Buchanan."

"She did," Niels agreed. "Mind ye, she was twelve the last time she joined us. Our ma put an end to it after that."

"Aye, and she was flat as a sword then," Alick commented.

"Hmmm," Dougall murmured in agreement. Pursing his lips, he then shook his head. "Who'd ha'e thought she'd grow into such a fine figure o' a woman? Eh?"

"Aye. She was a scrawny child," Aulay said with fond reminiscence. "She did fill out nicely though. Makes a maun proud to call her sister."

"Get out, the lot o' ye!" Greer snapped furiously.

"We're no' going anywhere," Dougall snarled.

"This is me castle now," Greer growled. "Get out!"

"We're staying right here. She's our sister," Alick said defiantly.

"Aye, but she's *my* wife," he countered.

Geordie snorted at the claim. "She's no' been yer wife fer e'en a day yet."

"He's right," Dougall said grimly. "Ye carry no weight with us when it comes to authority over Saidh. Ye're lucky *we're* letting *you* stay."

Greer growled and lunged around the bed at the

man. He'd barely grabbed him by the scruff when he found himself under a pile of Buchanan flesh.

It was pain in her chest that stirred Saidh to consciousness. She blinked her eyes open on a moan, only to immediately close them again as a new sharp pain shot through her, this time stabbing through her head as the light entered through her eyes.

"Sorry, lass. I had to break off the end of the arrow shaft."

Saidh forced her eyes open again to stare at her brother blankly. "Rory?"

"Aye."

"What—" She'd been about to ask what happened, but becoming aware of the shouting and thumping around her, asked instead, "What the devil is all that racket?"

"Just the boys helping yer husband work through his upset. He was muckle distraught," Rory told her with an amused glance over his shoulder at the men rolling about on the floor. From what she could see it was six against one, but her brothers obviously weren't trying to hurt him, else they'd be doing more than rolling around the floor piled on top of each other like some huge ball of yarn. Still, as surprising as she found what she was seeing, Rory's words surprised her more.

"Greer? Distraught?" she asked dubiously.

"Aye." Rory smiled. "I think he has feelings fer ye, Saidh. He was all but wringing his hands in distress and acting womanish."

"Greer was?" she asked with amazement. "The big braugh man I married yesterday?"

"Aye," Rory assured her as he bent to peer at the now shortened shaft in her breast. Saidh forgot about her husband when she took note of the arrow shaft protruding from her chest. The sight brought back to mind what had happened to her. She'd been racing back to the keep, determined to beat Greer to the stables, when it had felt as if someone punched her in the chest, hard enough that she'd been thrown back and lost her seating. She'd spied the arrow as she tumbled from the saddle, and then she'd hit the ground head first and pain had exploded through her skull. She didn't recall anything after that until waking here.

"Damn. Someone shot me with an arrow," she muttered with dismay.

"Aye." Rory paused and peered at her solemnly. "Did ye see who 'twas?"

Saidh shook her head. "I had just left Greer by the loch pleating his plaid. I was racing to beat him back to the castle so was keeping a sharp eye on the trail ahead to be sure my mare was no' injured." She frowned. "I saw no one. I did no e'en realize what had happened when I was first hit. I only knew when I saw the arrow as I fell."

"Hmmm." Rory looked disappointed and she couldn't blame him. She was rather disappointed herself that she couldn't name who had shot her.

"How bad is it?" she asked with concern as she eyed the wound. There didn't appear to be a lot of blood, just a bit slowly seeping out around the arrow. That would no doubt change once the missile was removed, she thought, and then glanced sharply at Rory. "Ye broke off the tip o' the shaft."

"Aye," he admitted mildly.

"Ye're thinking to push it the rest o' the way through rather than pull it out the way it went in?" she asked with dismay.

"Saidh." Sitting on the edge of the bed, he took her hands in his. "The arrow near went through on its own. The tip is poking against the skin o' yer back. One quick shove and it should pop out the back and be easily retrieved."

Feeling the sweat of fear begin to push its way out of her body, Saidh almost begged when she said, "But can ye no' just pull it gently out the way it went in?"

"I could," he allowed, "But I risk doing more damage, especially if the arrowhead is a swallow-tail design, and since we do no' ken who shot ye, or what sort o' arrow they used, I'd rather no' risk it."

"Bloody hell," Saidh muttered, recognizing that what he said was true. If it was a swallowtail arrow-head, the barbs might catch on something coming out and do serious damage. It would be like pulling two hooks through her body, hoping it came out at the exact same angle as it went in . . . which wasn't likely.

Breathing out an unhappy sigh, she started to shift in an effort to sit up, but paused when agony immediately shot through her. She took a moment to let the agony pass, and then glanced to Rory. He stood waiting patiently, knowing her well enough to not offer aid until she asked for it. Saidh had always got cranky with her brothers when they'd tried to help before she admitted she needed it. She didn't like it when they treated her as weaker than them just because she was female.

"Ye'll need to help me sit up," she said quietly.

Rory let out a little relieved breath, his body relaxing, which was when she realized he'd been tense as he waited. He also then bent to help her sit up.

Once sitting, Saidh could better see what was going on at the foot of the bed. Most of the men were still rolling around on the ground, but two were now rolling around on their own, cupping their groins. Three were, she corrected herself silently as Geordie suddenly rolled free of the pileup with a groan of pain. It seemed Greer had taken lessons from watching her, she thought with amusement as he and Aulay and Dougall continued their struggle.

And her brothers were treating him as gently as they did her, she noted with affection. She would have to thank them for that later, Saidh thought. She had no fear that her husband couldn't take care of himself, and she didn't think he needed her brothers to go lightly on him, but she was glad that they were. It was a sign that they liked him.

"Ready?" Rory asked.

Saidh shifted her attention to her brother. He was seated on the side of the bed, apparently ready to push the arrow the rest of the way through her body. When she nodded, he lifted a piece of linen he'd folded several times and with it in the palm of his hand, pressed the linen against the broken tip of the shaft and then began to push on the arrow. Saidh couldn't help it, she immediately began to bellow in pain and instinctively leaned back away from his efforts.

"Saidh!" Greer roared and was suddenly on his

feet, shaking off her brothers like a dog shaking off water. Charging to the bed, he knocked Rory to the floor, bellowing, "What the devil are ye doing to her?"

" 'Tis all right, husband," Saidh said weakly, and then paused to savor the word. Husband. He was her husband.

" 'Tis no' all right. He's supposed to be mending ye, no' injuring ye further," Greer snarled, glaring at Rory as he got to his feet.

"He is," Saidh said quickly, recalled to the situation. "The barbs on the arrow could cause damage they avoided when the arrow went in. 'Tis safer to to push the arrow out rather than pull it back the way it came."

Greer relaxed a little, but didn't look happy. Dropping onto the side of the bed, he peered at the arrow shaft with disgruntlement, and shook his head. "I ken ye're probably right and it has to be done, but . . ." He swallowed and met her gaze, expression helpless. "I do no' like the idea o' anyone hurting ye. E'en fer yer own good."

"Trust me, I'm none too pleased meself," she said with a crooked smile, and then cleared her throat and said, "Mayhap ye could help and hold me still while he does it? 'Tis instinct to pull back when he pushes. 'Twill go faster and less painful do ye help keep me in place while he does it."

"O' course," Greer murmured and then hesitated, looking unsure how best to help with that.

"We can help too," Aulay said quietly.

Greer gave himself a shake and then seemed to

regather his wits. Glancing to her eldest brother, he nodded. "Aye. Aulay, if ye could get behind her shoulder on this side and brace her so she can't back away."

Nodding, Aulay moved up to the head of the bed and placed his hands firmly on Saidh's uninjured shoulder.

Greer then turned his gaze to the other men, but settled on her second oldest brother, Dougall, as he said, "Dougall, if ye'd kneel behind Alpin on the bed and help brace her other shoulder . . ." He didn't bother finishing, Alpin had already sat up to shift out of the way and Dougall was even now climbing to kneel half behind the boy and half behind Saidh. Placing his hands carefully on her upper arm and back, Dougall nodded that he was ready.

"Good, then I'll hold her about the waist and—" Greer had slid his arms around her as he spoke, but paused and glanced around uncertainly as he realized there was no way Rory could get at her to push the arrow through with him on the side of the bed.

"'Tis all right. I can straddle her," Rory said quickly, and did just that, climbing onto the bed and moving to straddle Saidh's lap on the bed.

"We'll hold her legs so she does no' kick ye off to stop ye," Geordie announced and the rest of the brothers bent over the bed to grab her legs and feet to hold them in place.

"Good, good," Greer muttered and slid his arms around Saidh again, careful to keep his upper chest enough to the side that he didn't risk bumping the shaft sticking out of her chest, or blocking Rory's ability to do what he needed to do. Once he had Saidh in a firm embrace, he pulled his head back enough to see her face. "Ready?"

Saidh glanced at all the men surrounding her. Men she loved, all there to keep her still, and gave a weak laugh. "Do ye really think ye need seven strong men to hold down little me?"

"Eight," Alpin corrected drawing everyone's attention to the fact that he now knelt at her side, one small hand on her back, the other just above Greer's arm on her front . . . pretty much cupping the bottom of her injured breast.

"Lad, ye'd best move yer hand else ye might lose it," Aulay said with amusement as Greer growled deep in his throat.

Flushing, the boy quickly shifted his hand to rest between her breasts, muttering, "Sorry."

Aulay nodded and then turned his gaze to Saidh and said, "As fer needing so many to hold ye down, love. We ken yer strength. We've wrestled with ye."

"Aye," Geordie said dryly. "Yer powerful strong when yer blood's up, Saidh. 'Tis best we take precautions."

"Hmm," Saidh muttered and shook her head.

"Put yer arms around me and try to keep them there," Greer instructed. When she did, he added, "Scream all ye want to, love. Ye've a right to."

"Trust me, I will," Saidh assured him with little humor and then roared in shocked pain and tried to buck backward as Rory suddenly thrust forward on the arrow shaft without any warning at all.

Of course, with so many holding her in place, Saidh couldn't back away. In fact, she would have sworn that Aulay and Dougall pushed her forward into the thrust and Greer pulled her in the same direction doing the same thing. Whatever the case, pain exploded in her chest and then her back as the arrow tore through the undamaged skin there.

"It's through!" Saidh heard Aulay bark above her bellowing. "Pull it out from yer side, Dougall."

"Carefully, and straight out. Do no' bend or twist it," she heard Rory caution as her roaring turned into a whimper and blackness rushed in to claim her.

Chapter 12

GREER EYED DOUGALL'S EXPRESSION OF GRIM concentration and almost held his breath as the man slowly pulled the arrow out through Saidh's back. It seemed to him they all breathed a sigh of relief when it was done. Dougall pitched the weapon aside, and then he, Aulay and Alpin released their hold on Saidh and moved out of the way.

Greer started to lay her back on the bed then, but Rory stopped him with a hand on his shoulder.

"Nay. Keep her upright. I need to clean and bind her both front and back," the man said.

Greer nodded, and raised Saidh upright again. Holding her still, he gazed at her unconscious face, frowning at how pale she seemed. His gaze then shifted to her wound as Rory barked orders to the others to hand him strips of the clean linen Conran had fetched. While there had been little blood when the arrow was still present, there was certainly blood now. It was as if the arrow had acted as a cork in a bottle, now that the cork had been removed, blood was pouring out a thick, dark red and Rory was pressing linen into the wound both front and back trying to staunch the flow.

"She'll be a' right, will she no'?" Greer asked with concern as he watched the man work.

"Aye. She's strong," Rory said reassuringly, throwing the already blood soaked swatches aside and grabbing the fresh ones Niels held out. "The bleeding is already slowing."

It didn't look that way to Greer, but he held his tongue and merely watched as Rory continued to press linens against her wounds.

"Did ye put the tincture in the water as I ordered?" Rory asked, lifting up the edge of the linen he'd pressed to the front of her wound and then pressing it firmly back again.

"Aye," Niels assured him. "Six drops."

Rory nodded. "Then dip two folded linens in it, but do no' wring them out ere ye give them to me. I'll need to clean the wound ere I sew her up."

"Are ye all right, me laird?" Alpin asked suddenly.

Greer glanced to the boy with surprise. "Aye. O' course."

His squire merely looked dubious at the claim. "Ye're looking pale enough I'd think ye were the one losing the blood."

The comment made Rory glance sharply at Greer and the man frowned. "If ye're going to faint, let Aulay take o'er holding up Saidh and—"

"I'm fine," Greer snapped, sitting a little straighter and tightening his hold on Saidh. He was feeling a bit off, but was damned if he was going to faint away like a puling woman in front of these men. He was just alarmed at how much blood Saidh was losing. It seemed a hell of a lot to him.

Rory eyed him for a moment longer, then merely turned his attention back to Saidh. After a moment, he replaced the now blood red and sodden linens with the tincture-soaked ones Niels gave him. As he pressed the wet material to her wound, he muttered, " 'Tis good she's sleeping fer this. This tincture stings like a son o' a bitch and the sewing up part would no' be a pleasure to endure either."

Greer merely grunted and shifted his gaze to Saidh's face. Her head was lolling back, her face upraised as if waiting for a kiss and he gently pressed one to her lips, then leaned his forehead on hers and closed his eyes. He had no desire to see Rory pressing a needle and thread into her flesh and back out again. Whether she would feel it or not, he suspected he would if he watched, so kept his eyes closed and merely held her silently as Rory finished cleaning and then began to sew the wound.

Judging by the shuffle of feet moving away from the bed, Greer was not the only one who had no desire to watch this part of the procedure and found it ironic that warriors like himself and these men could be so squeamish about mending a body, when they had no issue with causing such injuries. That thought brought him back to the question he hadn't allowed himself to consider ere this. Who had shot Saidh with the arrow?

"Did ye see who shot her?" Aulay asked suddenly, his thoughts apparently turning in the same direction.

Greer opened his eyes and lifted his head, but steadfastly refused to look to see what Rory was doing as he answered, "Nay. She raced off and left me by the loch, pleating me plaid. I found her lying on the path moments later when I gave chase. There was no one around, jest her and her mare."

"Could it ha'e been bandits?" Dougall asked.

Greer considered that, but frowned. "I suppose. But Bowie has no' mentioned any issues with bandits around here, and if 'twas bandits, they were brazen. Where I found her was no' far from the castle. Another hundred feet and she'd ha'e been out o' the woods in full view o' the men on the wall."

"Conran, go fetch Greer's first so he can ask him if they've had trouble with bandits of late," Aulay ordered.

Greer didn't comment on the order. While he was sure Bowie would have mentioned such an issue if there was one, it was better to be certain. Besides, he wanted to have him send men out to search the woods for any clue as to who may have done this. Chances were they wouldn't find anything. It wasn't as if the culprit would have left a scroll with a signed confession lying about, but they may have dropped something or . . . hell, he just didn't know what else to do.

"Do ye really think 'twas bandits?" Niels asked and Greer could hear the doubt in his voice.

"Nay," Aulay said on a sigh. "They'd gain nothing from shooting her except drawing attention to their presence."

"Mayhap she came upon them in the woods and they feared she'd give their presence away anyhow," Alick suggested.

"Then they'd be more likely to take her than shoot her on the spot," Dougall growled. "That way they'd have something to ransom, or a good raping at the very least."

Geordie snorted at the suggestion. "Rape our Saidh? She'd ha'e gutted them fer trying."

"It had to ha'e been bandits," Alick said suddenly. "Who else would want to hurt our Saidh?"

Greer peered at his wife, his arms tightening instinctively around her. His mind was stuck on Dougall's comment about the bandits raping her. The idea was an appalling one: this strong, passionate woman held down and raped by a group of filthy bandits. He was quite sure Geordie was right and Saidh would gut a villain or two did they try, but if there were a lot of them, or they took her by surprise, or if they even just got lucky, she could have been overcome.

He shuddered at the thought, suspecting that for a woman as strong and proud as Saidh, such an attack would leave her broken in spirit as well as body. Greer would rather suffer the tortures of hell than witness such an eventuality.

"There."

Greer glanced around at Rory's weary comment to see that he'd finished not only sewing the injuries closed, but had bandaged her as well while Greer was lost in his thoughts.

"Ye can lay her down, now," Rory said as he shifted off of her and got off the bed.

Greer hesitated, oddly reluctant to let her go, but then sighed and lay her gently back on the bed, only to stiffen and frown when he saw the state the bed was in. While someone had thought to push the furs down the bed and out of the way, both the upper and lower linen were now soaked with blood and the water with the smelly tincture in it.

"Hey!" Alpin cried in surprise when Greer suddenly scooped Saidh and the top linen off the bed, leaving him uncovered.

"The bed has to be changed ere ye both sleep," Greer announced as he turned and strode across the room. "Bundle yerself up in the furs and come sit by the fire until 'tis done."

"Alick—" Aulay began.

"I'll fetch some maids to change the bed," Alick said before Aulay could finish giving the order.

Greer merely grunted a "thanks" as he settled in one of the chairs by the fire and arranged Saidh in his lap. He wasn't leaving her side until she was up and about and well again, and then he would only leave her side if at least two of his men—no four, four of his men were there to guard her. He wasn't going to risk losing his bride again. Today was the last day she would suffer harm in any way.

SAIDH OPENED HER EYES WITH A LITTLE SIGH AND peered at the sleeping boy beside her. Alpin, she realized. Lying on his side facing her and sound asleep. The boy looked sweet as could be in repose. One could almost forget the pain in the arse he could be when awake, she thought, and smiled faintly, only to frown in the next moment as it occurred to her to wonder what the boy was doing in her bed.

"Oh, there ye are. Ye're awake."

Saidh followed that voice to the woman seated in a chair on Alpin's side of the bed. Lady MacDonnell was leaning forward in the seat, beaming at her as if she'd just done something incredibly clever by opening her eyes.

"M'lady," Saidh said uncertainly, and then her eyes widened slightly as her gaze slid past the woman and she took note that she wasn't in her room, but the master bedchamber.

"I thought we'd agreed ye'd call me Aunt Tilda," Lady MacDonnell said gently and then tilted her head and frowned slightly. "Ye look confused, dearling."

"I—aye, I am," Saidh admitted almost apologetically. "Why am I—" She started to turn on her back, intending to sit up, but stopped abruptly when her movement sent pain shooting through her arm and chest. She glanced toward the shoulder where the pain seemed to be situated, but all she could see was the heavy cloth of what she guessed was a sleeping gown.

"Oh dear, I fear that knock ye took to the head may ha'e done some damage," Lady MacDonnell said, sounding concerned.

Saidh glanced to her with amazement. "Knock to the head?"

"Aye. Yer brother, competent as I am sure he is, was so busy tending yer shoulder he ne'er e'en looked to see if there was aught else wrong with ye. It was my Helen who found the bump on yer head.

Ye must ha'e hit it as ye fell from yer mount," she added with a frown. "I can't imagine that whoever shot ye troubled themselves to then kosh ye in the head too."

"Shot," Saidh breathed, her memory returning. Someone had shot an arrow into her as she was heading back to the castle. She'd woken up here in the master bedchamber where Rory had forced the arrow through her back and . . . well, she must have fainted. She didn't recall anything after that.

"Are ye remembering now?" Aunt Tilda asked with concern. "Ye look as if ye might be."

"Aye," Saidh smiled at her weakly and relaxed back onto her uninjured side in the bed. "Someone shot me with an arrow as I was returning to the keep and Rory removed it."

"Good, good." Aunt Tilda smiled and sat back in her seat again. "Head wounds can be so tricky and then ye've slept fer so long . . . for a moment I feared it had done some permanent damage."

"How long was I sleeping?" Saidh asked curiously.

"Three nights and two days," Lady MacDonnell said solemnly. "This is the third morning, and I can tell ye we've all been worried sick. Why, Greer refused to leave yer side the first two nights and days. Last night, though, I insisted he go find some sleep. As I pointed out, it would do little good if ye woke up only to have him drop across ye with exhaustion and relief the minute ye opened yer eyes. I promised to send for him though if ye woke while he was no' here, so I guess I'd best—"

"Nay! Wait," Saidh protested when Lady Mac-

Donnell stood and moved toward the door. When she paused and glanced back with surprise, Saidh hesitated, but then flushed and admitted, "I ha'e to relieve meself and I'd rather—"

"Oh, o' course ye do. Where is me head?" Lady MacDonnell muttered, rushing back to the bed. "Why ye must be full to burstin' after sleeping so long. Shall I fetch a basin, or do ye think ye can manage the garderobe do I help ye?"

"The garderobe," Saidh said, though she wasn't at all sure she could manage it. Still, it was that or here in the room with Alpin in bed next to her. Even the thought of that was too distressing to bear, so she took a deep breath and forced herself upward on the bed into a sitting position. It was harder than she'd expected and not just because of the pain it sent shooting through her chest and arm either. She was alarmingly weak after so long asleep, or perhaps it was the blood loss, she thought as Lady MacDonnell bent to help her sit up.

"All right?" Aunt Tilda asked once they had her sitting up in bed.

Saidh hesitated, waiting for her pain to ease and the room to stop spinning. Dear Lord, she felt like hell: weak, nauseous and she was starting to sweat just from the effort to sit up. How the devil was she supposed to make it to the garderobe? She wasn't even sure she was going to make it to her feet.

Apparently, Lady MacDonnell had some doubt that she could manage it as well, because she suddenly said, "Helen left a basin. Perhaps we should just—"

"Nay. I'm fine," Saidh said determinedly and then forced a smile. At least she hoped it was a smile. It felt more like a grimace on her face. Setting her teeth, Saidh held her breath and shifted her feet off the bed, so she was sitting on the side of it. Relieved to manage that part so easily, she smiled at Aunt Tilda. "If ye could just . . ."

She let her words trail away. Lady MacDonnell was already shifting to a half crouch beside her to draw her good arm over her shoulder.

"On three," Aunt Tilda said and then counted off. When she reached three, Saidh lunged upward even as Lady MacDonnell pulled.

"There," Lady MacDonnell gasped, once they were both upright.

Saidh merely grunted and closed her eyes. The room was spinning like crazy now and she was quite sure she was swaying on her feet.

"Are ye sure ye'd no' rather I fetch the basin and—"

"Nay," Saidh interrupted, forcing her eyes open and sucking in a deep breath to steady herself. "I can do this."

Aunt Tilda didn't argue, she simply waited until Saidh started to shuffle forward and moved with her, taking as much of her weight as she could.

The master bedchamber was a good-sized room, but it had never seemed as large to Saidh as it did that morning as she struggled to get out of it. Dear God, the walk to the door seemed like miles, and getting there seemed to take forever, but they did finally reach it. When they paused for Aunt Tilda to open the door, Saidh reached out to press her hand on the wall and lean against it as she tried to catch her breath. She was panting as if she'd just run all the way from the loch, and her back, her whole body, was damp with sweat.

"Here we go," Lady MacDonnell said as she pulled the door open wide.

Sighing, Saidh shuffled forward again, trying not to think about just how far away the garderobe still was. It was at the opposite end of the hall. By her guess she had to travel at least three times the distance she'd just traversed, possibly five or six times and she was beginning to seriously doubt she could manage it. Chances were she'd collapse before she got halfway there and then further humiliate herself by relieving herself there on the hall floor.

"Saidh!"

Pausing, she glanced up sharply to see Greer rushing toward her from the open door of the room she'd occupied since arriving.

"Ye were supposed to fetch me if she woke," Greer growled as he scooped Saidh off her feet.

"I was going to, dear," Aunt Tilda assured him. "But she needs to use the garderobe. Once we'd tended to that, I would ha'e fetched ye. I promise."

Greer had been about to carry her back into the master bedchamber, but paused abruptly and turned to head down the hall instead. "I'll take her. Ye should go and get some rest, Aunt Tilda. Ye sat up with her all night. Thank ye fer that," he added.

"Aye, thank ye, Aunt Tilda," Saidh said over Greer's shoulder, managing a smile despite the fact that her mind was now racing with the worry that her husband was taking her to the garderobe. How embarrassing was that?

" 'Twas my pleasure, dear," Aunt Tilda called out just before Greer paused and shifted her so that he could open the door to the garderobe.

Saidh swiveled forward again to glance around with alarm as he carried her inside the tiny room. There were two garderobes at MacDonnell. One large one with a long bench with several holes in it where many could tend their needs at the same time, and then this one, a very narrow cubicle with a small bench seat and one hole. It was not made to house two people, but Greer didn't seem to care. He was obviously aware of it since he had to maneuver carefully to avoid banging her head or legs into the walls, but it didn't stop his entering.

Saidh breathed a little sigh of relief when he set her on her feet. She then peered up at him expectantly.

Greer raised an eyebrow and frowned at her expression. "Do ye need me to lift yer nightshirt fer ye?"

Saidh blinked in dismay. "Nay!"

"Then what are ye waiting fer? Get to it," he said with a frown.

"I am waiting fer ye to leave and give me some privacy," Saidh said dryly.

That made him frown. "But what if ye need me?"

"I do no' think I need help with this task me laird husband," Saidh said solemnly. "But ye can wait outside the door and I'll shout if I do."

"Verra well," he said unhappily, but hesitated

briefly, then bent to press a kiss to her forehead. "'Tis happy I am to see ye up and about, Saidh," he said huskily. "I was verra worried about ye."

"Thank ye," Saidh murmured, but he'd already turned and slipped out of the room.

Sighing, Saidh shook her head, hiked up her sleeping gown and sat down. She was thankful to be able to do so and not just because her need to relieve herself had become a desperate one. Saidh was also more than grateful to be off her feet. She really was pathetically weak just now, and was quite sure she never would have made it to the garderobe without Greer. Even with Aunt Tilda helping her. Hopefully this was a temporary situation, she thought, as she finished her business and stood to open the door.

Greer must have been watching the door. Saidh had barely begun to push it open when he finished the task for her. The moment she stepped out into the hall, he scooped her back up into his arms.

Saidh settled against his chest and let her forehead rest against his throat. She found herself inhaling the clean, woodsy scent of him and smiled as she did it. He smelled delicious, like the clearing by the loch.

"Ye've been swimming in the loch," she murmured.

"I slipped away fer a quick dip last night when Aunt Tilda sent me away to sleep," he admitted and then wrinkled his nose and admitted, "I would no' ha'e slept otherwise. Rory got some o' that vilesmelling tincture of his on me while he was cleaning yer wound. After two days of it in me nose, I was glad to make a quick run down to the loch to wash it away.

Saidh murmured understandingly and then stiffened when he added, "Mind ye, you still reek of the stuff, but there's nothing we can do about that just now. I doubt Rory would be happy did I take ye down and dunk ye in the loch, even to remove that stench."

"Mayhap ye should anyway," Saidh said with a grimace. She'd been aware of the sickly scent clinging to her, if only on the periphery of her mind, but most of her attention had been on getting to the garderobe before this. However, now that need had been tended to, it was impossible to ignore the stench coming off of her. It was really rather unpleasant.

"Do no' tempt me, lass," Greer said with a teasing smile. "Yer brother Rory would probably drop some poison in me ale fer punishment did I do that. One that would keep me in the garderobe for a day or two."

That comment made her grin with amusement. "Someone told ye o' the time he did that to Dougall?"

"He did himself. Yer brothers ha'e spent a lot o' time at yer bedside with me while ye were sleeping and we talked some," he said quietly, and then added, "Rory and I were planning to sit with ye again last night. We only left ye because Aunt Tilda and Aulay insisted we needed sleep else we'd be no good to ye when ye did wake up." Frowning, he added, "Speaking o' which, Aulay was supposed to be sitting with Aunt Tilda. Why did he no' carry ye to the garderobe?"

"Aulay was no' there when I woke up," she told him. "It was just me, Aunt Tilda and Alpin in the room."

Greer slowed to glance at her with surprise. "Really?"

"Aye."

He shook his head with disgruntlement. "I would no' ha'e thought yer brother the sort to renege on his agreements, and he vowed to me that he'd sit and guard ye through the night."

"And I did," Aulay announced, drawing their attention to the stairs as he stepped onto the landing. "I only left but moments ago because yer Aunt Tilda asked me to fetch her some cider, and as ye can see, I was quick about it." Pausing next to Greer, Aulay reached out with the hand not holding the cider and caressed her cheek affectionately. " 'Tis good to see ye up and about, lass. We were beginning to despair o' ye e'er waking."

"I kenned it! No faith at all in me skills as healer, brother."

Saidh shifted to glance over Greer's shoulder at those words and smiled when she saw Rory approaching. "Good morn, brother."

"Good morn, sister," he responded as Greer turned with Saidh to face him. Rory then reached out to place the back of his hand to her forehead and nodded with satisfaction. "No fever."

"Did I have one?" she asked with a frown. "Is that why I slept two days and three nights?"

"Nay. Fortunately, ye managed to avoid the fever that often follows such wounds. I just wanted to be certain ye had no' developed one while I slept," he said with a crooked smile, and then added, "And ye slept so long because ye lost so much blood. Yer body needed to build it back up."

"Oh," Saidh murmured as Greer turned to continue to the master bedchamber. Both Aulay and Rory followed.

As Greer carried her into the room, he announced, "Saidh would like a bath."

"Absolutely no'," Rory responded at once.

"E'en if I promise no' to get me wound wet?" she asked over her husband's shoulder as her two brothers followed them into the room. "I smell fair fou', Rory. I can barely stand to smell meself."

"A bath'll no' improve that," he told her with amusement. "It's me tinctures and salves that smell so bad and I'm going to be slathering them on ye repeatedly and often until ye heal."

Saidh grimaced at this news and then glanced around as Greer paused and bent to set her in the bed. Alpin was still sound asleep, she saw. He was also extremely pale and the sight made her frown. "Is he still feverish?"

"Nay," Rory murmured, moving around the bed to peer down at the boy. "His fever broke yesterday afternoon, but he's still weak and like to sleep a lot for the next couple o' days as he recovers."

Saidh nodded and then glanced toward Aulay and the drink he held. Her mouth was as dry as old bones in a crypt. "Since Aunt Tilda has gone to find her bed, do ye think I could ha'e her cider, Aulay?"

"O' course." Aulay moved up next to Greer and

held out the drink, but Rory leaned across the bed to snatch it away before she could even think of taking it.

"Nay. She has no' eaten or had anything to drink fer two days and three nights. Cider is too rich fer her stomach just now. Fetch some broth from Cook. 'Twill be all she can stomach jest now."

Saidh grimaced at the words. She hadn't been hungry until Aulay had mentioned food, but now that food had been mentioned, broth seemed a poor offering indeed.

Casting her a sympathetic glance, Aulay nodded and slipped from the room. No doubt to fetch the dratted broth, she thought on a sigh and glanced at Rory as he settled into the chair on Alpin's side of the bed.

"Wife?"

Saidh turned to Greer, smiling faintly at the title. She was his wife now. They'd consummated the marriage by the loch before she'd been injured.

"Did ye see who shot ye?"

Saidh's smile faded at the question and she grimaced and shook her head. "Nay, but then I did no' get much chance to look. 'Twas most unexpected and knocked me out o' the saddle." She frowned. "Is me mare—"

"She's fine. She was standing beside ye when I found ye," he assured her. "She followed us back to the keep and is safely in her stall."

Saidh nodded and relaxed at this news. She hadn't really worried that the mare would run off—she'd had her for years and she was a faithful beast—but whoever had shot her might have shot her mare as well.

"Greer had his men search the woods fer bandits afterward, but they did no' find anything," Rory informed her.

Saidh's eyebrows rose. "Do ye ha'e trouble with bandits here at MacDonnell?"

"According to Bowie, nay," Greer said with a frown. "But who else would want to shoot ye?"

"Mayhap 'twas an accident?" Rory suggested when Saidh remained silently frowning over the question. "A stray arrow from a hunter?"

"Mayhap," Greer murmured, but he looked doubtful and she couldn't blame him. Peasants generally weren't allowed to hunt in the laird's woods and few would risk their laird's wrath to do so, especially so close to the castle. But if it wasn't bandits or a hunter's stray arrow, who had shot her?

Saidh shifted uncomfortably as that question drifted through her head. There was only one person she could think of who might want to shoot her. Fenella had been very angry when Saidh had started asking her questions about the deaths of her husbands . . . and then too, before she'd got upset with Saidh, Fenella had mentioned something about possibly marrying Greer herself. No doubt the news that he had married Saidh had come as something of an unpleasant surprise.

"Barely awake but moments and scowling a'ready. That's our Saidh."

Saidh glanced toward the door with surprise at that happy croon to see Geordie leading Dougall, Alick, Niels and Conran into the room. Every one of them was grinning, even Dougall, who rarely smiled.

"Aulay said ye were up," Niels announced as her brothers moved up to the bed and took turns hugging her.

"About time too," Dougall groused as he bent to give her an almost painful squeeze of greeting. Before releasing her, he muttered, "Ye scared us all silly with that nonsense. Do no' do it again."

When Saidh smiled faintly at the order and nodded, he straightened and stepped aside to let Alick take his place and greet her.

"Did ye ask her if she saw who shot her?" Geordie asked as Niels replaced Alick to give her a hug.

"Aye. She did no' see," Greer said glumly.

Silence reigned briefly as the men all stood about staring at her with varying expressions that ranged from concern to displeasure and then Dougall ran a hand over his shaved head and glanced to Greer to say, "Then it looks like ye've go' us fer company fer a bit."

"At least until we sort out this business," Geordie said with a nod that the others echoed.

Much to her surprise, Greer didn't look the least upset by the suggestion, but nodded as well and murmured, "Thank ye."

"No need to thank us," Dougall said firmly, patting his shoulder gently. "She's our sister. We want whoever did this as much as ye do, and we're happy to help."

Saidh blinked in amazement at this. The last she knew, Dougall hadn't cared for her husband. Or at least, he'd acted as if he didn't. Now he was treating him as if he were an old friend or something. What the devil had happened while she was sleeping?

"We can take it in shifts," Dougall announced. "Two with her at all times during the day, and two outside yer room at night."

"I was thinking four men when I thought it would be me soldiers," Greer admitted. "But I've seen the way you lads fight and two o' ye ought to do it."

"Hold on," Saidh said with a frown as her brothers preened under the praise. "What are ye talking about?"

"Yer guard," Alick explained. "Ye'll ha'e two o' us with ye at all times until we sort out who shot ye and ensure they can no' do it again."

Saidh gaped at them. She was going to have guards? Like she was some puling female who knew not how to defend herself? Oh, they had another think coming if they thought she was going to allow that.

"Ye'd ha'e done better to keep that information to yourselves and simply let her think ye enjoyed her company. Now she'll fight us," Aulay said dryly from the doorway, drawing their attention to his return and the fact that he must have been there for a bit to have heard the conversation. Shaking his head, he moved into the room and set a bowl of what she supposed was broth on the bedside table.

"Damn right, I'll fight it," Saidh snapped. "I ha'e no need o' a guard to protect me and ye should all ken that. Ye're the ones who taught me to defend meself."

"Saidh, someone shot ye," Alick pointed out reasonably.

"Aye, and me having two o' ye riding at me side

would no' ha'e prevented that," she snapped impatiently.

"She's right," Dougall said with a frown. "Whoever shot her probably kens she can defend herself. They'll no' attack outright, but continue to try sneaky attacks like that arrow."

"Aye," Greer frowned and nodded. "Then 'tis best she remain in the keep."

Saidh gaped at him with dismay. "What?"

"Aye. Mayhap 'twould e'en be best to keep her up here where we can control who gets close to her," Geordie suggested.

"That'll no' help us sort out who shot her, though," Aulay pointed out. "We shall ha'e to let her out o' the room, and even out of the keep eventually unless we want to move in here."

"Aye, but we can no' risk her getting shot or otherwise injured again by using her as bait," Greer said with a scowl.

"It may be the only way to put an end to this," Aulay said solemnly and then quickly added, "But let us worry about that later. She is too weak to e'en consider that right now."

Saidh simply sat and glared as her husband and her brothers continued to discuss their plans to keep her safe. They seemed to have forgotten she was there, and were definitely oblivious to her hot eyes boring holes into their heads and bodies. If she weren't so damned weak, Saidh would have got up and thrashed the lot of them. Unfortunately, she was suddenly exhausted, which was just pathetic to her mind when she'd just woken up after sleeping two days and three nights.

Mouth set with displeasure, she shook her head and then scooted further down the bed so that she could lie down again.

Let them plot and scheme, she decided as she settled on her uninjured side and closed her eyes. She would concentrate on regaining her strength and then thrash them all and go where she wished. She had no intention of being locked in her room like some sad maiden who could not look after herself.

She fell asleep to the drone of their plotting voices.

Chapter 13

"Mill!" Alpin crowed triumphantly.

Saidh shifted her gaze down to the nine-men's morris board between them and nodded. "Aye, ye've got a mill," she acknowledged, and then peered to the boy seated on the bed across from her and pointed out, "But I've got two sleeping brothers."

Alpin's eyes widened and his head swiveled toward the two men seated in the chairs by the fire. Noting that Niels and Conran both were now slumped in their seats, snoring loudly, he grinned widely. "So ye do. That trumps a mill any day."

Chuckling softly, Saidh scrambled off the bed and headed for the door. "Come on then, before someone comes to check on us or otherwise mucks up me plans."

"Ye want me to come?" Alpin asked with surprise.

"Aye, o' course." Saidh paused at the door and glanced back in question. "Do ye no' want to? I thought ye were as sick o' being stuck in here as me."

"I am, but I did no' think . . ." Letting the sentence

end unfinished, he shoved the game board out of the way and crawled across the bed to hurry to her side.

Smiling, Saidh waited until he reached her, then cracked the bedchamber door open and peered out cautiously into the hall.

"What is it ye put in their drinks?" Alpin asked in a curious whisper.

"Ye saw that, did ye?" she murmured, watching a maid traverse the hall, headed for the stairs.

"Aye," Alpin breathed.

"Some o' Rory's sleeping tincture. I snuck it out o' his bag last night when he went to fetch more mead to replace what ye'd spilled."

"I only spilled it because ye knocked me arm and— Oh," he said as he realized it had been a deliberate jostle, and then he frowned. "Why did ye no' jest spill yer own drink instead o' knocking mine all o'er me?"

"Because he might ha'e suspected something if 'twas me mead spilt. No' that I'm no' clumsy at times, but with ye spilling yers I figured he'd be less suspicious," she explained, and then caught his arm and urged him out into the now empty hall.

"Where are we going?" he asked in a hushed whisper as they crept along the hall to the top of the stairs.

Saidh smiled faintly at the question. Alpin sounded as excited as a lad heading out on his first hunt. She couldn't blame him. She was pretty excited herself. While it had only been three days since she'd woken after taking her injury, it felt like forever since she'd left the bedchamber. The men were being ridiculously protective and she was heartily sick of it.

"We're both still weak, so will jest slip out to the garden behind the kitchens fer a bit o' fresh air this time," she murmured, eyeing the activity in the great hall below with a frown.

"How are we going to get there?" Alpin asked, sounding dubious.

Saidh sighed. She hadn't really thought that far ahead. She supposed she'd just hoped they could simply walk down the stairs, through the great hall and then the kitchens and that no one would question them. That might have worked with the servants, but there were more than just servants in the great hall. Aunt Tilda was seated by the fire sewing, and Geordie and Dougall were presently at the tables talking quietly.

"We could use the secret passage," Alpin said suddenly and Saidh stiffened, then turned to peer at him.

"What secret passage?"

"There's a secret passage and stairs going below," Alpin explained. "Laird MacDonnell showed it to me shortly after we came here. He said 'twas a secret only the laird and his first usually kenned, but he was telling me so that were there ever an attack and the battle was no going well, I could get the ladies out to safety."

Her eyes widened at this news. "Where does it come out?"

"Several places. There's a door that opens into the pantry, another in the gardens and then there's a tunnel that leads all the way out past the outer walls and opens into a cave by the loch."

Saidh stared at him blankly for a minute, then a slow smile spread her lips. "Show me."

Nodding, Alpin turned and led the way back to the master bedchamber. When he reached to open the door, she stopped him and urged him aside to do it herself. Easing it open, she peered inside and saw that both Niels and Conran were still snoring fit to wake the dead. She relaxed and urged Alpin in. Saidh was about to follow when the sound of a door clicking closed up the hall caught her ear. Turning sharply, she peered in that direction, but there was no one in the hall.

Frowning, she hesitated, but then shrugged and slipped into the master bedchamber. She eased the door closed, then glanced around for Alpin. The boy had grabbed one of the torches from the wall and now held it over the low burning flames in the fireplace to light it.

" 'Tis dark in there," Alpin whispered for explanation as she joined him.

Saidh merely nodded, not surprised. The secret passage at Buchanan was dark as a pit as well. She supposed all secret passages were.

Straightening with his now lit torch, he turned to peer at the wall next to the fireplace, then reached up and pressed on a smaller stone at his chest level. There was a grumble of sound as a portion of the wall slid inward and Saidh glanced nervously toward her brothers, but both remained soundly sleeping.

Letting her breath out with relief, she gestured

for Alpin to lead the way, then followed him into the narrow passage.

"We have to push it closed," Alpin whispered once they were both inside.

Saidh nodded and turned to press both hands to the large stone door, surprised when it took the lightest push to make it close. Large as it was she'd expected it would be a harder task. It must have some kind of weight and pulley system, she supposed.

"This way," Alpin said, turning to head up the dark, narrow corridor.

"I am surprised ye're willing to show me the passage," Saidh commented quietly as she followed him. "I thought ye did no' approve o' me fer yer laird's wife."

"'S truth, I did no'," Alpin admitted in a wry little voice. "But I've change me mind."

"Ha'e ye?" she asked with interest. "Why? I'm still no much o' a lady. I curse and carry a sword and ha'e a filthy temper."

"Aye, but so does me laird," he said on a sigh, and then added, "But I think me laird loves ye."

Saidh stopped walking at this news and stared at the boy's back as he continued forward, the torch leaving him in silhouette. His words had knocked the wind from her. Greer? Love her?

The boy said he *thought* Greer loved her, Saidh's common sense pointed out. It wasn't as if Greer had confessed it to the lad or something and it was a certainty. Still . . . what if he did? For her husband to love her would be . . . well, she thought that would be just fine. Wonderful in fact. Because she suspected she was coming to love the big, stupid stubborn man herself. How could she not? He'd done nothing but fuss over her the last three days since she'd woken from her long sleep.

While she and Alpin occupied the bed, Greer had taken to sleeping on a pallet on the floor next to her to remain close. He was usually awake and gone by the time she woke in the morning, but always returned to share the nooning meal with them, and then again at sup. Afterward, Greer didn't retire below to drink with the men, but sat and played chess or nine-men's morris, or any number of other games to entertain them.

The first night, Saidh had been too tired to play and left it to him and Alpin while she dozed in the bed, listening to their quiet voices. The second day she'd managed to stay awake and play a game or two against him. Much to her amazement he'd won more games than her. He had a fine strategic mind. She'd also asked him questions about his time as a mercenary and he'd regaled her with tales of battle and life as a soldier until she'd begun to nod off. Then he'd urged her to lie down and had tucked the linens and furs around her, pressing a kiss to her forehead before settling into his furs on the floor next to her. Saidh had lain silently for a bit, then turned onto her side. She'd been just drifting off to sleep when she'd felt his hand clasp hers where it rested on the edge of the bed.

Last night the three of them had played games, laughed and chatted for hours before exhaustion had again made her settle in bed and snuggle down to sleep. He had again tucked the furs about her and settled onto his pallet. He'd also taken her hand again and Saidh had drifted off to sleep with a smile on her face.

"Besides," Alpin continued, unaware of how his comment had affected her. "I've been thinking."

Forcing herself to start forward again, Saidh murmured, "Oh? And what ha'e ye been thinking?"

"Well, me ma and da are both very proper. Ye'd ne'er catch me ma cussing or wearing braies under her gown," he assured her in a dry voice as he led her around a corner to the left. "As fer me da, he ne'er loses his temper or swears either. But . . ."

"But?" she prompted curiously.

"Well, they are me parents, so 'tis probably a sin fer me to say this, but they're no' good nobles."

Saidh remained silent, not sure what to say to encourage the boy to continue. Sharing a sickbed with the boy, she'd seen the scars on Alpin's back and knew someone had whipped him viciously and repeatedly. She was positive Greer would never do it, so could only think it must have been his parents.

"Me mother seems sweet. She simpers and keeps her eyes lowered. She is always proper in company. But she lies near every time she opens her mouth and she's definitely less than proper when she raises her skirts for me da's first."

Saidh stopped walking again, her jaw dropping in shock.

"As fer me da, I ha'e ne'er e'er heard a cuss slip from his lips, and he ne'er loses his temper, e'en the time I accidentally broke his favorite inkwell, which was a gift from the king and one o' his most prized possessions. He just smiled coldly, grabbed his whip and punished me, the whole time just smiling that cold smile. Then he ordered one o' the maids to clean the blood away and put some salve on me back and walked away."

Saidh's mouth tightened at this and she continued walking again, thinking that if she ever met the boy's father—

"And I ken he lies too. He has made deals with others and not held up his side o' the bargain. He cheats our villeins all the time and there is naught they can do about it." He sighed unhappily and shook his head. "Laird Greer would ne'er do that, and these last six months since me father convinced him to take me on as squire he's ne'er raised a hand or whip to me either. Not e'en the time I near killed his horse by feeding him green apples. And he loves his horse," he assured her, glancing over his shoulder to meet her gaze for emphasis.

Saidh nodded in acknowledgment. She wasn't surprised to hear that Greer was fond of his stallion. She had had her mare for several years now and loved her dearly.

"So, after thinking on it," Alpin continued, "it occurs to me that proper behavior does no' make a good laird or lady. It does no' make them kind or brave or good to their people, and it does seem to me that being good is more important than no' wearing braies or cussing."

"I see," Saidh murmured with a faint smile. "So ye've decided to forgive me me lack as a lady."

"That's just it," Alpin paused and turned to face her in the narrow space to say earnestly, "Ye *are* a fine lady, m'lady."

Saidh snorted at the suggestion and waved at him to continue, but he stayed stubbornly where he was and told her, "Yer brothers and m'laird all stayed at our bedside the first two nights, refusing to leave ye."

Saidh nodded. Greer had mentioned something about that the morn she'd woken up. He'd also said they'd talked so she wasn't surprised when he continued.

"And yer brothers spent a lot o' time talking about ye, telling tales about the things ye'd done and such. How ye nursed yer mother during the illness that took her life, tending her yerself rather than let her maid do it. How ye whipped the smithy at Buchanan when ye found out he was beating his wife and children. How ye jumped in the moat after a village girl who had tumbled in, and saved her life. How ye snuck food and coin to a young villager with child when ye learned her husband had died leaving her with naught." He paused and shook his head. "And I could tell ye did no' like the gown Lady MacDonnell insisted ye wear to the wedding, but ye wore it anyway, just to please her."

Uncomfortable under his admiration, Saidh shrugged. "'Twas the right thing to do."

"Aye. But no' e'ery so-called lady would think so. Me own mother once fired a new maid because she decided she was too ugly to ha'e to look at. And she is mean as can be to me gran. I ken she would ne'er nurse her were she to fall ill." He nodded firmly. "Ye may curse and wear braies under yer gown, and ye may carry a sword and fight like a man, but ye've a noble heart, and are a true lady fer all that."

Saidh grimaced and turned her head away, embarrassed to find herself having to blink away a sudden welling of liquid in her eyes. Good Lord, she could take an arrow to the chest without shedding a tear, but a pain-in-the-arse boy gives her a compliment and she turns into a weeping female. Disgusting, she thought with a little irritation.

Sighing, she glanced back to Alpin and gestured for him to continue. "We'd best keep moving, else me brothers'll wake ere we even make it out o' the castle."

Nodding, Alpin turned and started forward again. Saidh followed, but after a moment of silence said, "I'm glad ye no longer think I'll be a poor wife to yer laird, Alpin. And I think ye're a fine squire to him as well."

"I try m'lady," he assured her. "Although I think me lecturing him on how to be a proper laird most like annoys him."

"Nay, he likes it," Saidh said with amusement.

"Really?" he asked glancing back again.

Saidh nodded, and then realizing the light from the torch didn't reach her and he probably couldn't see her nodding her head, she said, "Aye. Think on it, Alpin. Did he no' like it, do ye think ye'd still be his squire?" She smiled faintly, and added, "Besides, 'tis probably good fer us. We could both use a little polishing."

"Oh," Alpin breathed and turned to continue

walking again, moving more quickly now. "Then I shall continue to endeavor to help."

Saidh merely smiled to herself. She suspected the boy would have continued to endeavor to help anyway. She doubted he could help himself. Fortunately, she was growing fond of the boy and didn't mind the idea of his nattering at her. They reached the stairs quickly and moved cautiously down them.

"There is an entrance here to the kitchens," Alpin whispered as they reached level ground again. Raising his torch, he pointed to a wooden lever in the wall. "See that lever there?"

"Aye," Saidh whispered leaning back against the wall of the passage. She was relieved to be done with the stairs. While she'd felt fine and fit lying and sitting about in bed, she found the small walk and traversing the stairs had wearied her.

"If ye pull on it, the wall slides in and ye can slip into the kitchens."

"Good to ken," Saidh murmured. "How much further is the entrance to the gardens?"

"This way," Alpin said, which wasn't really an answer to the question, Saidh thought but didn't say so, and merely followed when he continued forward. However, she was nearly ready to call a halt and request that they rest when he finally stopped several minutes later. Sighing with relief, she leaned against the wall again and watched as he set the torch in a sconce in the wall.

"Are ye feeling all right?" she asked with concern when she noted that he had to use both hands to lift the torch and that they were trembling a little.

"Aye. Just tired," he admitted and then added with irritation, "'Tis a ridiculously long passage."

Saidh gave a small laugh. "I suspect it did no' seem so long when me husband showed ye through it the first time?"

"Nay," he agreed, sounding surprised.

Pushing herself away from the wall, she patted his arm and reached for the lever to open the door herself. "We are both still weak. We need to build our strength back up and lying about in bed is no' likely to do that. A bit o' sun and fresh air will help though."

"Let us hope so. We still ha'e to travel back up those stairs, and I suspect going back up'll no' be as easy as coming down," he said unhappily.

"We can rest on the way back up if necessary," Saidh reassured him and then stepped back as she pulled the lever and the wall opened inward. Fresh air immediately rushed through the opening and they both inhaled deeply.

"I feel better a'ready," Alpin announced and she could see his grin in the sunlight pouring through the doorway.

Smiling, she leaned out to peek about and be sure there was no one nearby. Finding this part of the gardens empty, she relaxed and stepped out into sunlight and fresh air for the first time since being shot.

"Oh," Alpin breathed as he followed her. His gaze slid over the fruit trees that filled this end of the garden and he sighed happily. "'Tis like entering paradise."

Saidh chuckled at the words, but silently admitted that he was right. Blue skies, bright sunlight, green grass, apple trees, and singing birds . . . it *was* like paradise. Funny how, after a few days without it, they now recognized the beauty they normally took for granted. Striding forward, she moved to the lower branches of the nearest tree. "Apple?"

"Aye, please!" Alpin almost hopped up and down with excitement. She suspected he actually would were he not so tired.

Reaching up, she plucked two of the ripest apples she could see among those low enough for her to reach, then walked over to hand him one. "Where shall we sit to eat them?"

"In the shade o' the tree," Alpin decided and led her back under the branches to settle against the trunk of the tree.

Saidh sat down next to him and they fell silent as they ate their apples.

"How long do ye think yer brothers'll sleep?" Alpin asked suddenly.

Considering the question, Saidh tossed her apple core away, and then stifled a yawn before admitting, "I'm no' sure. An hour or two. Why?"

"I was just thinking it would be nice to nap here under the tree," he admitted with a chagrined expression.

Saidh chuckled softly at the admission, but understood his embarrassment. She would not mind napping here either. Which meant they'd gone to all this trouble to escape the bedchamber only to sleep in the grass. Shaking her head, she pointed out, "Geordie and Alick may sleep for an hour or two, but that does no' mean Aulay or Dougall may no' go up to check on us ere that."

"Aye," Alpin agreed on a little sigh as he tossed his own finished apple aside. "For all we ken they may already ha'e done so and discovered us missing."

"Nay," Saidh assured him. "Were that the case, we'd ha'e heard Aulay bellowing at Geordie and Alick fer letting us escape."

"All the way from here?" Alpin asked dubiously.

"Aulay's fair loud when he wants to be," she said dryly and then suggested reluctantly, "I suppose we should think about heading back in now."

"Already?" Alpin groaned.

"I suspect it'll take us much longer to mount the stairs than it did to come down them," she said quietly. "Especially if we ha'e to stop and rest a time or two."

"Oh, aye," Alpin said on a sigh, and then asked, "But can we come out again tomorrow?"

"If ye help me sneak more o' Rory's sleeping tincture, we can," she said as they both stood up.

"His satchel is probably in his room. We could stop and sneak some now, on the way back to the master bedchamber," Alpin suggested as he watched her brush down her skirts to remove any grass or leaves that may have attached themselves to her. "That would save us ha'ing to try to distract him later."

"Is there an entrance to his room from the passage?" she asked with surprise as she straightened.

"There's an entrance to e'ery room on that side o' the hall."

Saidh considered the setup of the upper floor and then frowned. "Windows."

"What about them?" Alpin asked, tilting his head curiously.

"The passage is along the outer wall, but there are windows there," she explained, "How—"

"The passage floor is six or seven feet below the windows. The floor o' the passage slants down-wards when ye first step out o' the master bedcham-ber. Did ye no' notice?"

"Nay," she admitted, a little surprised that she'd missed that detail.

"There are stairs from the other rooms, very narrow stairs cut into the stone, but because it starts on the side wall and then turns to follow along the outer wall, they just slanted the floor for the entrance to the master's bedchamber."

"Hmmm," Saidh murmured and decided she'd have to pay closer attention on the way back in. Shrugging, she glanced to him and raised an eye-brow. "Ready?"

He snorted at the question. "I ha'e been waiting fer you. Are ye done fussing with yer gown?"

Saidh wrinkled her nose at the lad, and placed a hand at his back to urge him toward the still open passageway. "Ye'd do well with a bit o' fussing o' yer own. Ye've a leaf stuck to yer arse. 'Twill gi'e us away do me brothers see it."

"Nay!" Alpin stopped walking and turned to try to see his backside as he brushed at it. "Is it gone? Did I get it?"

Saidh grinned to herself with amusement and continued walking toward the passage entrance. She'd only been teasing him. There was no leaf on his plaid.

"Saidh!"

She thought he'd realized her trick when he yelled her name, so was taken completely by surprise when he slammed into her back, sending her crashing forward. Her head hit and bounced off the castle wall as she was plastered against it by his weight. The blow sent up a roaring in her skull that nearly blocked out the sound of Alpin's grunt of pain and the thud of something heavy hitting the ground behind them.

"What?" she began with confusion, raising one hand instinctively to her forehead and pressing the other against the castle wall as she tried to push away from it. But Alpin was still pressed to her back . . . and then she felt him begin to slide to the ground behind her.

Forgetting about her head, she glanced around and tried to grab at him. Her eyes widened in alarm when she caught a glimpse of bright red blood on his back.

"Alpin?" she said sharply and then spotted the collection of large stones on the ground directly behind him. It looked like one of the merlons had come down from the battlement along the top of the castle wall . . . and Alpin had received a glancing blow by the stones as they fell. Actually, she would have been crushed by them had he not suddenly crashed into her, Saidh realized as she saw where the stones rested. He'd saved her life . . . and been injured in the process.

Cursing, she released her hold on Alpin and let him slip to rest against the backs of her legs. She then shifted out from between him and the wall as carefully as she could before turning and dropping to her knees to examine him. He had landed crumpled on the ground and she could see that it wasn't just his back that had been injured, for there was blood on the back of his head as well.

Mouth tightening, she turned him over. He had been terribly pale ever since the fever had felled him, but now he was as white as death.

"Alpin?" she said, patting his cheek gently. When she got no response, Saidh glanced around in the hopes that one of the servants may have come out into the garden in search of an herb or vegetable for the sup, but it was empty. She had to get him help herself, but feared leaving him there on his own. What if another merlon fell?

She wasn't taking that chance. She'd have to take him to help. That wouldn't have been a problem a week ago, she would have merely hefted him over her shoulder and carried him around to the kitchens. But right now she wasn't sure she had the strength to heft a kitten over her shoulder. Hell, just getting her own weight back up the stairs had seemed like a major undertaking moments ago; carting around a boy who must weigh four or five stone . . .

Grinding her teeth with frustration, Saidh turned back to Alpin and set to work.

Chapter 14

"WE'VE BEEN O'ER THE AREA SIX TIMES NOW, Greer, and found nothing."

Greer sighed at Aulay's more than reasonable words and gave up examining the ground to move back to his mount. His brother-in-law was right, of course. He'd had the men search the woods repeatedly and had checked here several times himself before this, but today he and Aulay had checked and rechecked the area six times with nothing to show for it. There wasn't even a crushed patch where the archer might have waited. He should have been satisfied that he'd done all he could, but he wasn't. Greer felt as if there was something they were missing . . .

But that might have been simply because he was desperate to find something, anything that might point him in the direction of who had shot his wife. Frankly, to his mind, the best thing would be to find traces of a camp where bandits may have been, or even some sign that a peasant had been hunting in the wrong area. Either would please him. At this point, Greer didn't think he'd even be angry at the hunter if he came across one. He'd just be relieved to know that this occurrence had been a one-time event and unlikely to be repeated.

However, without some evidence of something, he was forced to consider that it might have been a deliberate attack. That meant having to continue to do whatever was necessary to keep Saidh safe.

Greer grimaced at the thought. Recovering from the wound and loss of blood as she was, his new wife was growing restless at being kept to the bed-chamber, and he could not blame her. He was tiring of being in there himself and he was only there during the nooning meal and in the evenings. Greer very much feared that if he didn't clear this matter up quickly, she would rebel and neither he nor her seven brothers would be able to keep her in the master bedchamber.

"Perhaps we should be looking in a different di-rection," Aulay suggested now. "Mayhap we should check the arrow again to be sure there is no' some marking or something else we missed that may help us sort out who it belonged to."

Shaking his head, Greer quickly remounted and took up the reins of his horse. "We ha'e done that at least twenty times now. There were no markings, no nothing. 'Twas as common as can be, a broadhead arrow with gray goose fletching."

"Aye, verra common," Aulay agreed, sounding as frustrated as Greer felt, and then he suggested, "Then mayhap we should try the other side of the path."

Greer shifted impatiently, his gaze fixed on the spot where he'd found Saidh lying beside her mare. "Nay, the angle of the arrow was very slight, but suggested it was shot from this side. To have been shot from the other side of the trail she would have had to have been riding backward on her mount and shot after she passed the archer."

"I did no' really see fer myself," Aulay admitted with a frown. "I mean I saw the wound and the arrow protruding from it, but did no' notice at the time if 'twas at an angle." He slapped his leg impatiently. "Are ye sure o' the angle?"

"The wound on her back is closer to her arm than 'tis on her front," he explained.

"Aye, but Rory pushed it through. 'Tis possible he changed the angle a bit as he pushed it through," Aulay suggested and then shifted with frustration and said, "Nay. He is too careful to ha'e done that."

"He is," Greer agreed and then pointed out, "Besides, the arrow was already pressing against the skin of her back ere he forced it through. That is why he pushed it through rather than . . ." His voice trailed away as he considered his own words. The arrow had been pressing against the skin of her back, the bulge visible. It had hit with enough impact to travel nearly all the way through her body before stopping . . . which meant it had been shot from a relatively short distance; certainly the archer had to have been closer than the area he'd searched repeatedly the last three days.

Cursing, he urged his horse forward, moving slowly along the trajectory he had guessed the arrow had to have taken to hit her at the angle it had. He heard the *clop, clop* of Aulay's horse and knew the other man was following, but Saidh's brother didn't say anything, merely trailed patiently after him. When Greer suddenly reined in and dismounted, Aulay did as well, and moved up next to him when he stopped.

They both stared at the compressed grass next to the large oak tree to the side of the path. It was the size and shape of a body.

"Someone laid in wait," Aulay said grimly.

"Aye," Greer agreed, but frowned even as he said it and pointed out, "But if they'd shot her from the ground, the angle of the arrow would have been upward as well as to the side."

Aulay murmured in agreement and walked around to the top end of the spot, eyeing it solemnly before suggesting, "Mayhap they lay in wait here, then stood when they heard her mare coming and shot her from a standing position."

That made sense, Greer acknowledged, and the possibility scared the hell out of him. It meant it hadn't been a hunter mistaking her for a deer or some other such animal. No one would mistake the gallop of a horse for that of the much smaller deer. It also made it less likely to have been bandits too. They did not, as a rule, hang about waiting to shoot women in the woods. They would have taken her, or robbed her, not just shot her off her horse and fled, and Greer was quite sure there had been no one here in this spot when he'd found Saidh. He would have noticed them.

Someone had tried to kill his wife. They had lain in wait and deliberately shot her with lethal intent.

The thought floated through his head like a bird of prey winging through the air, and sent a shudder down his back. Whirling, Greer rushed back to his horse, mounted and turned him toward the castle. He had a sudden desperate need to ensure himself that Saidh was well and safe.

Greer didn't need to look back to see if Aulay was following. The man was right beside him, racing his horse through the woods, his expression as concerned as Greer was sure his own was. He had found many things to like about the Buchanan men the last couple of days, but the one he appreciated the most was how much they all loved their sister. They would help him keep her safe, he knew, and that was the only good thing he could think of at that point.

Greer and Aulay raced their horses through the bailey, sending merchants, servants, children, dogs and even a chicken or two scrambling to get out of the way. At the stairs, they dismounted and raced to the double doors together, each pushing through one to get inside. Greer spotted Dougall and Geordie at the trestle tables, noted that both men got abruptly to their feet in alarm at their rushed entrance, but didn't slow in crossing the great hall. He had to see for himself that Saidh was okay.

Apparently Aulay was feeling much the same way, for rather than stop or even slow to explain to his brothers, he kept pace with Greer until they reached the stairs. He only fell back a couple steps then because as wide as they both were in the shoulders they would not have managed the stairs side by side. But he followed on his heels and was only a step behind him when Greer reached and opened the door to the master bedchamber. Both men skidded to a halt just inside the door, however, as their gazes found first the empty bed and then the two men sleeping in the chairs by the fire.

Greer released a string of curses then that would have had Alpin in an uproar. It also woke up the two men in the chairs.

"What's about?" Niels cried, lunging to his feet, one hand grabbing for his sword even as Conran did the same.

Greer ignored them and turned to head back downstairs, his only thought to find his wife. The fact that the men were sleeping and that Alpin too was missing from the bed told him that she had not been taken, but had somehow arranged their escape. Although he hadn't a clue how she had managed it, he was quite sure she was somehow behind the fact that both brothers were sleeping. They cared too much for her to have simply dozed off while they were supposed to have been guarding her.

"What's happened?" Dougall growled, pausing on the steps and turning sideways to let him pass when he reached the man.

"They've escaped," Greer snapped, hurrying past him and then Geordie too when the man made way.

"Who's escaped?" Geordie asked with confusion.

"Saidh and Alpin, o' course. Who else would be wantin' to escape?" Dougall pointed out grimly and

Greer glanced back to see that both men were now following him with Aulay, Niels and Conran on their heels, Aulay still bawling out the younger men for failing at guarding their sister.

Greer had just stepped off the stairs when an alarmed shout from the direction of the kitchens caught his ear. He turned and rushed through the swinging doors. The stillness in the hot and steamy room brought him up short as he entered. The kitchen was generally bustling with noise and activity, but now every servant stood as if frozen and the only sound was bubbling from the pot over the fire. Greer scanned the room and had just spotted Saidh across the room when someone crashed into his back. He stumbled under the impact, but then continued forward, moving more quickly the closer he got to his wife. Her hair was a wild mess about her pale face, blood trickled from a new wound on her forehead, and she was dressed in only her chemise.

"Greer," she cried with relief when she saw him approaching. But rather than rush to him, she began to drag something along the uneven stones of the kitchen floor. "Fetch Rory. We need him."

Greer glanced down with confusion to the sack she was dragging. Not a sack, he realized on examining the material. Her gown. Shaking his head, he asked, "What—?"

The question died on his lips as she stopped and released the edges of the gown she'd drawn up to form the makeshift sack and the cloth dropped, allowing a small pale arm to drop out between the folds to lie unmoving on the floor.

"Alpin?" he asked with dismay.

"Aye," she said as he bent to remove the cloth that now covered the boy. "He saved me."

Something in her voice gave him warning. Glancing up sharply, Greer saw her beginning to teeter and quickly straightened to catch her against his chest as she fainted.

Closing his eyes, he briefly pressed her close, then scooped her up in his arms and turned back the way he'd come, pausing when he saw that Dougall, Geordie, Niels, Conran and Aulay were all there.

"Aulay—" he began.

"I'll bring the boy," the eldest Buchanan assured him before he could ask. He then glanced to Geordie. "Go find Rory and tell him to bring his medicinals."

"Thank ye," Greer said grimly and carried his wife out of the kitchens.

SAIDH OPENED HER EYES SLEEPILY AND GRIMACED as she became aware of the low throbbing in her temple. Good Lord, she'd thought she'd got past that. Her head hadn't ached since the third day after she'd been shot and had fallen off her horse. Her back was throbbing something awful too, and she realized she was lying on her back.

She immediately turned on her side and found herself peering at Alpin's sleeping face, a sight she'd woken up to several times during the last couple of days. It wasn't until she became aware of movement and noticed that Alpin wasn't under the linens and furs, but lying on top of them and that Rory was

working over him that she recalled why her head
hurt again.

"Is he going to be all right?" she asked anxiously,
sitting up.

"Aye. Fortunately, the stones only sheared him
as they fell rather than hit him full on. The head
wound is just a grazing."

"But he fainted," she protested with a frown. "A
mere grazing would no' ha'e—"

"I imagine it was the wound to his back that made
him faint," Rory interrupted.

Saidh shifted her gaze to Alpin's small back and
bit her lip. More than half of it was skinned from
shoulder to almost his hip. "How bad is it?"

Rory grimaced and removed the bloody cloth
he'd been cleaning Alpin's wound with. He dipped
it in a basin of water, wrung it out and then returned
to his work and finished grimly, " 'Twill heal."

Saidh sighed unhappily, knowing from the way
her brother had said it that the boy was in for a long,
painful recovery. Swallowing, she whispered, "He
saved me."

Rory paused and glanced to her in question.

"I was standing where the rocks fell. He pushed
me out of the way," she explained solemnly.

"Yer forehead?" Rory asked.

"I hit it on the castle wall as he knocked me forward. If he hadn't . . ." She didn't bother finishing
the sentence, but took a breath and asked, "Where
is me husband?"

"Up on the battlements with Aulay and the other
men, examining the merlons to see how they were

dislodged," Rory answered as he returned to his work.

Saidh nodded, but then just as quickly frowned. "How did they ken about the merlon? I did no' get the chance to tell Greer ere I fainted."

"Alpin awoke when Aulay picked him up. He told him about the merlon falling and where it happened as he was carried up here," Rory murmured, concentrating on his task.

"And then fainted again when ye set to work on him?" she asked, feeling for the poor lad.

"Nay. I gave him some o' me sleeping tincture so he could sleep through me cleaning his wound. There was no need fer him to suffer through it."

"Oh, thank ye," Saidh breathed, grateful that he had. She watched silently as he worked, then asked uncertainly, "Was Greer verra upset that we'd slipped our keepers?"

"Aye," Rory said shortly, and then paused to give her a cold glare. "As are the rest o' us." When Saidh looked away, he added, "Saidh, we were trying to protect ye from exactly what happened today. Ye should no' ha'e—"

"I ken," Saidh interrupted on an unhappy sigh. "We should no' ha'e done it."

"We?" Rory asked dryly. "By me guess 'twas ye who did it and Alpin jest got dragged along with ye."

"I did no' exactly ha'e to drag him," she protested. "He was as sick o' this room as I am."

"He is but a lad," Rory snapped. "Ye're a woman, full grown and supposed to ken better."

Saidh shifted uncomfortably and muttered, "Aye,

well how would you like to be locked up in a room fer days on end with men to constantly guard ye?"

"How would ye like to be dead?" he snapped back. "Because 'tis only by the skin o' Alpin's back that ye're not."

Saidh glanced to the boy guiltily and then lowered her head unhappily. Rory rarely got angry. He and Alick were the last two to ever lose their tempers. But he was furious right now and she could not even blame him. Alpin would not be in the state he was presently in if not for her determination to outwit and escape her jailors.

She grimaced to herself and picked at the fur covering her lap as she worried over what this meant. If Rory was this angry, how angry must Greer be with her right now? She'd nearly got his squire killed. Cowardly as it might be, she really didn't want to find out just how angry her husband was with her just then. In fact, she'd be happy to avoid having to deal with him until he'd had a chance to let his temper cool. In that regard, she could only envy Alpin. At least he was asleep and would not have to face Greer's anger. That thought made her still and then she glanced at Rory and said, "Me head is paining me something fierce."

"I am no' surprised," Rory said with little sympathy. He didn't even glance up from his efforts to clean Alpin's wound.

Saidh scowled, but then cleared her throat and asked, "I am sure rest would help ease it. I do no' suppose I could ha'e some o' that sleeping tincture o' yers?"

He straightened and eyed her through narrowed eyes.

Saidh held her breath and tried to look pitiful. It wasn't a natural state for her, however, and she suspected she just looked brain-boiled.

After a moment, Rory returned to his work, saying mildly, "Unfortunately, I somehow lost a goodly portion o' me sleeping tincture and ha'e precious little left. I am no e'en sure what I ha'e left will be enough to keep Alpin from suffering as he heals, so I fear I ha'e to say no." He paused and glanced her way as he added sweetly, "Howbeit, I do ha'e a tincture fer pain. It tastes vile, but it might help."

"Nay," Saidh muttered with disgust and lay back in the bed. It served her right for even considering taking the coward's way out . . . which was completely unlike her. Saidh was no coward. She'd stood fierce and proud in the face of her brothers' anger many times over the years, and couldn't say why this time was different. She wasn't afraid of Greer. No matter how angry he got, she knew, to the bottom of her heart, that he would not harm her. In truth, she didn't even think it was fear that she was experiencing. She just didn't want to see the disappointment and accusation on his face that she knew she deserved.

Saidh heard the men's voices coming from the hall and quickly sat up again. If she had to face Greer, she would do so upright. She'd rather have been out of bed and on her feet, but there wasn't time for that. She'd barely got into a seated position before the door opened and Greer led her brothers in. Every last one of them was there, she noted, and knew from experience that once her husband got done berating her, they would line up to take a turn at bawling her out as well.

She steeled herself against what was to come as the men walked to the bed, then gasped in surprise when Greer suddenly bent, tugged the linen and furs aside and scooped her up. When he then turned to carry her out of the room, she thought she understood. He didn't want to wake Alpin with his bellowing. She glanced over his shoulder, expecting to find her brothers all trailing behind, preparing to blast her. However, they had all gathered around the bed to talk quietly with Rory.

Perhaps they were letting Greer give her hell on his own before going at her, she thought with a frown and then glanced around as her husband turned into the room she had stayed in when she'd first arrived at MacDonnell. Greer strode inside, paused long enough to kick the door closed, then carried her to the chairs by the fire and sat in one, settling her in his lap.

Saidh raised her chin proudly as she waited for the scolding to start, only to gasp in surprise when instead he covered her mouth with his own and kissed her almost violently. She was just getting over her surprise enough to kiss him back when Greer tore his mouth away and pressed her close, muttering, "Thank God ye're all right."

"Alpin saved me," she breathed guiltily.

"Aye, and I'll reward the boy fer it too. He's a good lad," he murmured into her hair.

"Aye," Saidh agreed, guilt mixing with confusion now. "I thought ye'd be angry with me."

"I am," he growled, framing her face with his hands and pulling her back so he could meet her gaze.

Her eyes widened at the tortured expression on his face.

"But I'm so damned relieved ye're all right. When I found the crushed grass and raced back only to find ye missing, I thought me heart would stop in me chest."

"I'm sor—" Saidh's apology died in her throat as he kissed her again, his tongue thrusting into her mouth and demanding a response. After a brief hesitation, she slid her arms around his neck and kissed him back. It seemed she wasn't going to get a scolding. At least not from Greer. Her brothers were another story, but she could worry about that later: right now her husband's hand had found her uninjured breast and was kneading eagerly as his mouth worked on hers, his tongue whipping her into a frenzy.

Moaning, Saidh shifted slightly in his lap, her upper body twisting just a bit to press more firmly into his caress and her hands digging into his long hair to urge him on. The man could make her burn so easily, a kiss and light caress and her body went up like tinder.

She felt him tug at her chemise and released her grasp on his hair to help him. But she paused and grunted into his mouth with pain when he began to wrench the cloth off of her shoulders, sending pain through her injured back and chest. Greer broke their kiss at once and eased back from her with concern.

"I'm sorry, I forgot. Are ye all right?" he asked, turning his head to peer at the bandages revealed by his actions.

"Aye," she breathed and forced a smile. "I'll just . . ." She didn't bother to finish the sentence, but gently eased herself out of the chemise and let it pool around her waist. Saidh glanced down at herself and grimaced then. Her bandages crisscrossed over her injured breast, going over her shoulder, under her arm and around her waist above and below her other breast, leaving little more than the nipple of her uninjured breast on view. Not very attractive, she decided, and then gave a start when Greer suddenly bent his head and claimed the nipple poking out from between the strips of linen.

"Oh," she breathed with surprise, leaning back over the supporting arm he had around her waist. She then gasped and wiggled in his lap as liquid fire slid through her body, dripping down to pool between her legs.

"Husband," she moaned, clutching at his head with one hand and his shoulder with the other as he drew on the sensitive nipple and then flicked it with his tongue. She felt his free hand sliding up her leg under her skirt and began to find it difficult to catch her breath. By the time his hand reached her thigh, she was panting shallowly and wiggling like mad, but when his hand finally found and cupped her between the legs, everything in her seemed to stop.

Greer let her nipple slip from his mouth then and raised his head to kiss her again, and Saidh let out her breath into his mouth and kissed him back, then gasped that air back as his fingers spread the soft folds they'd been covering and slid in to find her warm, wet depths. Saidh shuddered and moaned wildly as he began to caress her, her body involuntarily moving in response to his touch, eager for more.

When Greer thrust a finger into her, he thrust his tongue into her mouth at the same moment and, in her excitement, Saidh nearly bit down on it. She managed to stop herself in time and satisfied herself by sucking on it instead until Greer withdrew it and broke their kiss. He withdrew his invading finger at the same time and returned to letting them lightly dance over her flesh, the touch more teasing than satisfying.

Saidh blinked her eyes open only to find him watching her face.

Biting her lip, she clutched at his shoulders, her hips moving to the music his fingers were strumming. But after a moment, she couldn't bear either his stare or his teasing touch anymore and she groaned, "Husband, please."

He immediately slid a finger inside her again and Saidh arched and bore down on the invasion, "Aye. Please."

Greer withdrew his finger and bent to nibble her ear before whispering, "Promise ye'll no' slip yer guard again."

Saidh stilled with confusion, slow to understand. Blinking, she peered at him in bewilderment.

"What?" she asked uncertainly and then sighed and closed her thighs around his wrist and arm as he slid a finger inside her once more.

"Promise ye'll no' slip yer guard again," he repeated, nipping at her ear.

"Aye," she groaned, riding his wonderfully talented hand.

"Promise," he insisted, his fingers stilling.

Saidh blinked her eyes open, scowling with frustration. "I—"

"Promise," he repeated. "I'll no' lose ye, Saidh. I'm happy with ye to wife. I want ye here, in me arms, like this. So vow ye'll no slip yer guard and put yerself at risk again."

Saidh shifted unhappily. "The falling stone was no' an accident?"

He shook his head solemnly. "And nor was the arrow. We found proof."

"What proof?" she asked with a frown.

"I'll explain later," he said solemnly. "For now, promise me that ye'll no—"

"I promise," she interrupted. "I'll no' slip me guard and put meself at risk again."

Greer breathed out a relieved sigh and kissed her forehead. "Thank ye."

"Ye're welcome," Saidh whispered, then gasped in surprise when he caught her about the waist and lifted her off his lap.

"What—?"

"Straddle me," he instructed, holding her aloft.

Saidh hesitated, glancing to the bed. "Should we no' just go to bed and—"

"Ye can no' lay on yer back or front," he pointed out. "'Twill be easier here fer ye. Ye'll ha'e to ride me."

Saidh peered at him at that suggestion. She would ride him. She would control how hard or fast they went and how deep he went. The idea was an attractive one. Smiling, she spread her legs to straddle him as he eased her back onto his lap again.

"I'm no' sure I like that smile," Greer said with amusement as she tugged his plaid up out of the way. He then closed his eyes and sucked in a sharp breath when she shifted forward until his hardness pressed against her damp flesh.

"Ye feel so good," Saidh breathed against his mouth, rocking against his erection so that it caressed the nub his fingers had toyed with earlier.

Greer growled against her lips, then claimed them with his own and thrust his tongue into her and Saidh sucked on it eagerly as she rocked against him again, caressing him with her body, even as she pleasured herself with his. She felt Greer's hands clasp her bottom, but resisted when he tried to shift her so that he could slip inside. She quite liked this and wasn't willing to stop now. She was in charge this time.

"Wife," he protested, breaking their kiss to trail his mouth to her ear and then her neck.

"Husband," Saidh breathed, urging his head to continue down until he clasped the nipple of her uninjured breast again. "Aye," she groaned, moving more firmly against him as he began to suckle. That made him groan around the nipple and then nip at it, and Saidh began to shift against him more urgently, chasing the release she wanted.

It was an accident when he suddenly pushed inside her. Saidh rose just that little bit too much and his erection was suddenly pressing into her as she lowered herself. She stopped briefly with just the head inside and then raised herself again and lowered just that little bit, teasing him as he had her before she dropped until the bottoms of her thighs slapped the top of his.

Greer released a guttural groan then and held her in place briefly, but then reached one hand between them to caress her as the other hand began to lift and lower her again. She realized only then that he could have taken control at any moment, but had allowed her to tease him. She didn't care. She stopped thinking altogether then, stopped worrying about rhythm, and teasing him. Her body was in pursuit of its pleasure and left her mind to take a hiatus as it began to move of its own volition, pressing into his caress and thrusting into his invasion with an eagerness that matched the tightly wound need building inside her. When it exploded inside her, she clawed at his back and froze with him deep inside to ride the waves. She was unsure which triggered Greer's release, but in the next moment his cry joined hers and they rode the waves together.

Chapter 15

"*Y*E SAID YE FOUND PROOF THAT THE ARROW was no' an accident?"

Greer lifted his head from Saidh's uninjured shoulder and sat back in the chair to peer at her. The quaking that had taken over his body as he'd poured himself into her was just beginning to slow, but she already looked fully recovered. He couldn't help thinking it was damned unfair how women came away from such passion feeling energized and frisky, while a man, at least this man, came out feeling as if he'd been run over by a full contingent of mounted warriors and was in need of recovery time and a nap.

"Aye," he said finally. "We found a spot where the grass was pressed down. Obviously someone had been laying there fer a good while. But ye had to be shot from a standing position for the angle the arrow entered ye."

"So they laid in wait and then stood to shoot as I rode into view," she murmured quietly.

Nodding, Greer caressed her cheek, marveling that he had been lucky enough to find her. With most women he would have had to explain what it meant. He also would have had a terrified, sobbing woman on his hands. Not Saidh. She looked annoyed rather than weepy and afraid.

"And the merlon that fell?" Saidh asked now.

"There are chips at the edges of the stones and in the bits of mortar that remained behind," he said solemnly.

"So, someone chiseled the stones free and pushed them off," she said on a sigh.

"Aye, but then we already suspected that was the case anyway ere we went to double-check."

"Why?" she asked with surprise, and then guessed, "Because ye kenned the arrow was no accident?"

"Nay, because when Aulay was carrying him above stairs, Alpin told him that he saw someone on the battlements, pushing at the stones just ere they started to fall," Greer explained, and then added, " 'Tis the only reason he managed to get ye both out o' the way in time. Had he seen it e'en a heartbeat later we might ha'e lost both o' ye."

"Did he see who it was?" she asked quickly.

"Nay." Greer sighed unhappily. "The sun was in his eyes. All he saw was a black figure. He could no' say if 'twas man or woman or even a child."

"Oh." Saidh lowered her head with disappointment, and then turned her gaze to where her fingers were toying with the hair on his chest and whispered, "I am sorry. Had I realized, I ne'er would ha'e taken Alpin and—"

" 'Tis done," Greer said solemnly, covering her hands with his own. "Ye're sorry and ye've vowed it'll no' happen again. Leave off fretting o'er it."

"But Alpin—"

"I am guessing ye did no' drag him out there with him protesting the whole way," Greer interrupted dryly.

"Nay, but still—"

"Saidh," he said gently, halting her words again. Taking one hand from hers, he caressed her cheek. "I can see ye're suffering some horrible guilt o'er this. Ye feel responsible fer Alpin's getting hurt, do ye no'?"

"Aye," she breathed unhappily.

"Well, don't," he said firmly. "Alpin chose to join ye in escapin', and probably most eagerly. 'Twas foolish. Ye both got hurt and could ha'e been killed, but ye weren't. And I ken Alpin will no' blame ye fer his injuries. Ye needs must let it go now. Regret and guilt are useless emotions that hold ye in a past that's already gone . . . and if there's one thing I've learned, it's that allowing yerself to be dragged down by the past helps no one. It jest keeps ye from ha'ing both feet in the present where ye should be.

"Now," he said, catching her at the waist and lifting her so that he could stand up. "Aulay'll be waiting fer us below. Let us straighten our clothing and go talk with him. We need to sort out a way to catch whoever is behind these attacks before they try again."

Saidh's eyes widened at the news that she was going to be allowed below, but she didn't comment, merely turned her attention to quickly cleaning herself up and then dressing. Fortunately, the maids were continuing to supply this room with a basin of water and fresh scraps of linen for ablutions. At least, the basin on the stand was full of water. Saidh quickly used it to clean herself up, then dressed and went downstairs with Greer.

Aulay was already seated at the trestle tables as Greer had said. Her other brothers were there too, all but Rory, who was apparently still upstairs with Alpin. Whether he was still working at cleaning his wound, or just sitting with the lad to be sure he was well, she didn't know.

"How is yer head?" Aulay asked as Saidh settled at the trestle tables with them.

"Fine," Saidh said with a shrug. " 'Twas a trifling wound at best."

Aulay narrowed his eyes and shook his head. "I do no' ken why I ask. Ye're jest like the lads."

"What's that supposed to mean?" Dougall asked, stiffening.

"It means e'ery last one o' ye could stand there, yer hand sawn clean off, and blood gushing from the stump, yet each o' ye'd still say ye were fine and 'twas a trifling wound."

"Aye, we would," Niels allowed with a grin, but then pointed out, "And so would ye."

"True enough," Aulay admitted with amusement and then turned to Saidh again and said, "So, who ha'e ye angered since ye left Buchanan?"

"What?" Saidh asked with surprise. "What do ye mean?"

"Well, no one was trying to kill ye at Buchanan," he pointed out in a perfectly reasonable tone of voice. "So, it stands to reason 'tis someone ye encountered either at Sinclair or here."

Saidh snorted with disgust. "Oh, aye, blame me. It must be me own fault someone is trying to kill me."

"Well . . . aye," Geordie said dryly. "None o' the rest o' us ha'e ever had someone try to kill us," he pointed out and then glanced to Aulay as if for agreement only to freeze briefly as his gaze landed on their brother's scar. Tearing his gaze away, he quickly tacked on, "Outside o' battle o' course."

"Geordie's right, Saidh," Dougall said in a rumble. "None o' us ha'e had anyone stalking us with murder in mind, but this culprit is the second one to try to kill ye."

"The second one?" Greer asked, glancing to her sharply.

"'Twas nothing," Saidh assured him and then turned to her brothers to add, "I was no' the intended victim last year at Sinclair."

"Ye were!" Conran countered. "Ye told us yerself that the villain was going to kill ye and Jo both."

"Joe? Who is this Joe?" Greer asked with a frown.

"A dear friend of mine," Saidh told him before saying impatiently to her brothers, "And I was only a target because the killer wanted to claim I was the killer. It was no' because I was unliked or anything of that ilk."

"Well, it wasna because ye were liked either," Alick said apologetically. "Else she'd ha'e tried to find someone else to kill and blame fer her murders."

Saidh scowled at her younger brother for the comment and said grimly, "I was in her way and handy."

"What the devil are ye all talking about?" Greer exploded. "Who tried to kill Saidh? And who is this man, Joe?"

"Jo is no' a man, she's Lady Jo Sinclair," Saidh explained. "And she—"

"We are getting off topic," Aulay interrupted before Saidh could warm up to the tale. "Ye can explain about the Sinclairs and such later. At present, we need to sort out who would want to kill ye now."

"Perhaps 'tis another case like the one Saidh just mentioned," Lady MacDonnell said and Saidh glanced around to see the woman standing behind her. Aunt Tilda smiled down at her briefly, and then continued, "Mayhap this is another case where 'tis no' that they do no' like ye, but that yer in the way or some such thing." She raised a hand to squeeze Saidh's shoulder and added, "That makes more sense to me than anything else. I can no' imagine anyone disliking and wanting to kill ye, lass."

"Thank ye," Saidh breathed on a little sigh and reached up to squeeze the hand on her shoulder. As much as she hated to admit it, it was a bit distressing to have her own brothers suggesting she was unlikeable enough for people to want to kill her . . . even if she was.

"I do no' ken," Conran said dubiously. "She can be a real pain in the arse at times."

Saidh growled at him and started to rise, but Lady MacDonnell squeezed her shoulder gently, urging her to settle back down on the bench, and said, "Oh, go on with ye, Conran Buchanan. I ken ye love yer sister. Ye all do. Why I'd venture there is no' a man at this table who would no' give his life fer her."

The men all grumbled, but nodded reluctantly and Aunt Tilda's smile widened. "There ye see! A woman who inspires that kind of loyalty and love surely could no' ha'e an enemy who wishes to kill her fer her own nature. Nay, I would look fer someone who would benefit from her death, or who sees her as being in their way."

Silence reigned as everyone at the table considered that.

"I can see I've given ye all something to contemplate," Lady MacDonnell said dryly. "Why do I no' ask Cook to send out some pasties and drinks fer ye to enjoy while ye think on who might benefit from Saidh's death? Hmm?"

She didn't wait for an answer, but turned to head for the kitchens.

"Soooo," Geordie drawled, glancing between Saidh and Greer. "Who would benefit should Saidh die?"

Greer shook his head with bewilderment. "No one."

"There's no ex-lover somewhere who may think they'd ha'e a chance with ye should she die, is there?" Aulay asked.

"O' course no'," Greer said with a scowl and then he grimaced and added, "Ere Saidh the only women I was with were lightskirts. Ladies ha'e little interest in mercenaries."

Aulay nodded and then said almost apologetically, "I had to ask."

"I suppose," Greer acknowledged and then rubbed the back of his neck and said, "In truth, I think Aunt Tilda is a long way off the beaten path with that suggestion. There simply is no one who might profit from Saidh's death."

"What about Fenella?" Alick asked suddenly, drawing all eyes his way.

Greer scowled at him, and then said staunchly, "I ha'e ne'er touched Fenella, and ne'er would."

Alick waved that away. "I ne'er thought ye had, but mayhap she feels that Saidh is taking her place and that were she no' here, she would still be lady o' the castle."

"Do no' be ridiculous," Geordie said with disgust. "From all I ha'e heard since we got here, Fenella was no longer acting as lady when Saidh arrived. She had retreated to her room and stayed there. We ha'e no e'en seen her since arriving."

"Aye, but . . ." Alick paused, frowned, apparently trying to marshall his thoughts, and then pointed out, "She may no' be right in the head. I mean, Lady MacDonnell is sure her son's drowning was no' accidental and that Fenella was behind it."

Saidh's eyebrows rose slightly at this comment. As far as she knew the servants were not gossiping about Aunt Tilda's suspicions regarding Fenella. In fact, from what she'd learned since arriving, most of them were most sympathetic toward Fenella. She'd concluded that while Aunt Tilda had felt comfortable enough to share her suspicions with Edith and then herself, she had spoken to few others about it. But it looked like she'd vented them to Alick as well.

Saidh supposed she shouldn't be surprised. Alick was a good listener.

"And ye ha'e to consider," Alick continued now. "Our cousin has seen four husbands into the grave in four years now. That jest has to be more than bad luck," he said, shaking his head. "And if she killed them, who is to say she has no' killed others and might try to kill our Saidh too?"

"But why kill Saidh?" Conran asked. "She'd no' gain from her death."

Alick shrugged. "Mayhap she is jealous o' Saidh's happiness, or something. As I said, I do no' think she's right in the head, staying up in that room all day and night. There's something wrong with her."

"Wife?" Greer said suddenly. "Ye're biting yer lip. What are ye thinking?"

Saidh gave a start at Greer's solemn voice, realizing only then that she had indeed been chewing anxiously on her lip. For one moment she thought perhaps she shouldn't say anything, but someone had tried to kill her twice now, and Alpin had been terribly injured in the last attempt. What if it was Fenella behind it? And what if the next time Greer was hurt, or one of her brothers? What if they even died? She could never suffer that on her conscience, knowing that if she'd just said something . . .

Sighing, she reluctantly admitted, "The morning me brothers arrived, Fenella did mention that ye were verra kind to her, and that mayhap ye'd be as . . . er . . . considerate about the marital bed as Allen. I think she was considering ye fer her fifth husband."

"What?" he said with dismay, and then scowled and asked, "And did I ha'e any say in this?"

Saidh patted his arm soothingly. "I think she thought because ye were kind to her, ye may be interested in—"

"The only kindness I showed her was no' pushing her away when she sobbed all o'er me plaid, which she did repeatedly and often," he said with disgust. "Other than that, we've barely e'en spoken. If she thinks that is kindness, and a sign that I might marry her, the lass really is no' right in her head."

"Perhaps we should speak to her," Aulay suggested quietly.

Greer frowned, but nodded grimly. "Aye."

"I'll do it," Saidh announced abruptly and stood up. She'd come here to find out whether Fenella had killed her husbands or not, and then had instead tiptoed about, not wanting to upset the woman. The sad truth was, Saidh was seriously uncomfortable around weepy women. It was not in her nature to go about weeping and wailing over life's cruelties and she had no idea how to deal with women who did. But it was past time she sorted the matter one way or another. Especially now that Fenella was under widespread suspicion of being behind these new attacks.

"Nay," Greer said firmly, catching her arm. "Ye'll go rest. Aulay and I'll speak to her."

Aulay raised an eyebrow at being roped into speaking to the woman with Greer, and arched an eyebrow. "Afraid she'll cry on ye again?"

Greer scowled at the suggestion, but said, "Aye,

and that I'll strike her dead if I deduce she is behind these attacks."

"Ah," Aulay said with amusement, getting to his feet as Greer scooped Saidh up into his arms.

"What are ye doing?" she cried with surprise and began to struggle, kicking her legs and pushing at Greer's chest with her good arm as he started toward the stairs. "Put me down."

"I am carrying ye up and putting ye to bed. Ye should be resting, ye're still healing."

"I can walk," she protested with a scowl.

"I ken it," he assured her. "But I like the feel o' ye in me arms."

Saidh blinked at this claim, her struggles stopping as he started up the stairs. "Ye do?"

"O' course I do, ye daft woman. Why do ye think I married ye?"

"So ye could tup me without me brothers killing ye?" she said dryly.

He chuckled at the suggestion and reminded her, "I am the one who told them I'd tupped ye."

"Aye, ye did," she said with a small smile. "More fool ye. I ne'er would ha'e told them or demanded marriage from ye. I'd ha'e just enjoyed ye while I could and then gone about me business."

"I ken that too," Greer said, not looking pleased. "I realized it the morning yer brothers arrived. Ye'd intended to take yer pleasure and then abandon me." Peering down his nose at her, he shook his head and said conversationally, "Yer a cruel wench, wife. 'Tis no wonder someone is trying to kill ye."

"Oy!" she bellowed in surprised offense and

began to kick her feet and push at his chest again. This time though, he opened his arms, dropping her. Saidh gasped in surprise as she fell through the air, but before she could do more than that, she landed on something soft. She peered around with surprise to see that while she'd been distracted, they'd reached the bedchamber she'd originally stayed in and that they'd made love in before joining her brothers earlier. He'd dropped her on the bed, and managed to do it in such a way that she'd landed sitting up, saving her wound.

She turned to raise an eyebrow at her husband. "Why am I here?"

"To rest while yer brother and I talk to Fenella," he answered, and then bent at the waist, pressing his hands on the bed on either side of her hips so that he could claim her lips in a sizzling kiss that had her slipping her arms around his neck and clinging to him. By the time he tore his mouth away to kiss his way across her cheek, she was breathless and terribly excited.

"I'll return shortly to tell ye what we learn and finish this," he murmured in a husky voice, nipping at her ear.

"Finish what?" Saidh asked weakly as he nibbled at her neck. Her brain appeared to be having some difficulty processing what he was saying at that moment.

"This." His hand slid under her skirt and along her thigh until he could lightly brush his fingers against the already dampening skin between her legs.

"Oh," Saidh moaned, reaching to catch his hand

as he started to withdraw it. "Can we no' finish this first?"

Chuckling, Greer tugged his hand free of her hold and gave her another kiss, this one quick and hard. He then removed her clinging arms and said, "Yer brother's waiting in the hall. But I'll be back."

Saidh let her hands drop to her sides and watched him walk to the door. Once he'd slipped out and pulled the door closed behind him, she lay back with a little sigh, then grimaced and quickly rolled to her side as pain shot through her back. She'd forgotten her wound.

The sudden opening of the door again when it had just closed startled her, and Saidh sat up with surprise, but relaxed when Greer merely stuck his head in to tell her, "Geordie and Dougall will be outside the door. Shout do ye need them."

He didn't wait for a response, but then pulled the door closed once more.

Saidh stared at the door for a minute, then lay down on her side again and closed her eyes. It had been after the nooning when she and Alpin had snuck out to the gardens, and while she'd lost consciousness, she didn't think she'd been out for long. Rory hadn't been far enough in cleaning Alpin's wound on his back for much time to have passed. Of course, she had dallied with Greer in here briefly, and then sat below, so by her guess, the afternoon was somewhere between half and three quarters done. Time enough for her to enjoy a wee nap before the sup. Well, time enough for a very short nap and, hopefully, some houghmagandie with her husband.

The thought made her smile as she allowed her eyes to close, but the smile faded when a rustling sound reached her ears. Blinking her eyes open, she listened briefly. Were she asked to describe it, she would have said it sounded as if a great huge snake were slithering through the rushes on the floor. The problem was, she couldn't tell where it was coming from. Sitting up, she peered around the room, but there was nothing and no one to see.

Frowning, she pushed her hair behind her ears and listened carefully, but couldn't really tell where it was coming from. It almost seemed to be coming from all around her . . . or beneath her, she thought suddenly and quickly slid her feet off the bed intending to get up.

Saidh stopped short, however, when a startled gasp sounded as her feet landed on something much softer than the hard floor with its scattering of rushes. Leaning quickly forward, she peered down to see that she had her feet on Fenella's gown-covered rump.

Chapter 16

"I'M SORRY IF I STARTLED YE," FENELLA SAID quietly, glancing up at her. "Do ye think ye could lift yer feet so I can finish getting out from under the bed?"

Saidh briefly considered pushing down more firmly and holding her in place as she demanded an explanation, but this was a Fenella she had never met before. She appeared subdued and her expression was actually apologetic, something Saidh did not think she'd ever seen on the woman's face. Relenting, she lifted her feet to sit cross-legged on the edge of the bed as she watched Fenella finish dragging herself out from under the bed.

Once out, her cousin got to her feet and began to brush at her gown and skirts, trying to remove the bits of debris stuck to her. Plucking irritably at the pieces that wouldn't brush away, she muttered, "Yer maids ha'e been lax about their job. 'Tis filthy under that bed."

"Hmm," was all Saidh said, although she could have pointed out that she had only been lady here for a very short time and that Fenella herself had been lady before that.

"Ye should order them to clean out the rushes in the room, including those under the bed and lay fresh ones," Fenella instructed, giving up on her gown with a grimace.

"I shall consider it," Saidh murmured, and then raised an eyebrow. "Would ye care to explain what ye were doing under the bed?"

Fenella hesitated, her gaze moving reluctantly to Saidh and then sliding quickly to the door, almost with longing. Saidh supposed the girl would rather leave than give explanations, but much to her surprise, Fenella sighed, her shoulders slumping, and then asked politely, "Might I sit with ye?"

Saidh's eyebrows both rose up almost into her hairline at this. She wasn't used to Fenella requesting permission for anything. Actually, her cousin almost seemed a stranger in that moment; quiet, polite and with an air of resignation that didn't really suit her.

"Sit," Saidh said simply and shifted a bit away when Fenella perched on the edge of the bed beside her. She waited a moment, but when Fenella didn't speak, asked, "What are ye doing in here?"

"I was in the hall when Greer picked ye up and started to carry ye upstairs. I ducked in here, thinking he'd take ye to the master chamber. I had the door cracked. I was going to slip back to me room as soon as he took ye in there, but instead he brought ye this way and—" She grimaced. "I jest panicked. First I ducked down on the other side o' the bed, then I scooted under it just ere he brought ye in."

Fenella shook her head and then peered down

and laced her fingers together. She stared at them briefly before raising her head and saying, "I am sorry Alpin got hurt." Her gaze flickered to Saidh's forehead and she frowned and added, "And that ye did as well."

Saidh nodded solemnly. "Thank ye."

"I did no' do it," Fenella added firmly, meeting her gaze. "I heard ye all talking at the tables below. Me maid told me what happened, about the stones falling on ye and Alpin," she explained. "That's why I was in the hall. I was going to go below and see that ye were all right, but when I got to the top o' the stairs I saw that Lady MacDonnell was there and I . . ." She shook her head. "I stopped to wait fer her to leave, and I listened to ye all talking."

She lowered her gaze to her fiddling fingers. "I ken that ye all suspect 'twas me who hurt ye and Alpin."

Saidh waited silently, and when she didn't say anything, asked bluntly, "Did ye?"

"Nay," she gasped, turning on her sharply. "I told ye I did no' and 'tis the truth. I swear it." Frowning, she turned her gaze back to her hands again, adding quietly, "I do no' blame ye fer no' believing me, though. As Alick pointed out, four dead husbands in four years is suspicious, and . . ." She met her gaze apologetically as she said, "I ken I was horrible the other day when I threw the applemoyse at ye. I was hurt is all, and mayhap angry. But I really would ne'er hurt ye, Saidh. Ye're the closest thing I ha'e to a friend or e'en family."

Saidh's first reaction was surprise at the claim.

That was followed by pity and it must have shown in her expression, because Fenella gave a bitter laugh and lowered her head again.

"Aye. Pitiful is it no'? I ha'e seen ye only three times in me life and we probably ha'e no spent more than a dozen days in each other's company. Yet ye've shown me more kindness and support than me own ma or da and are the closest thing I ha'e to a friend now that Allen is dead."

Saidh remained silent, unsure how to respond to that. In truth, it really was just pitiful to her. She had grown up secure in the love and support of her parents and brothers, and while her parents were now dead, she still had her brothers, and now Greer, Aunt Tilda and even Alpin.

Realizing she hadn't included Fenella in that list, Saidh glanced to her guiltily and reached out to pat her hand with a sigh. "If ye say ye're no' behind me being shot with an arrow, and the stone merlon dropping on Alpin and me, I believe ye."

Fenella turned her hand over under Saidh's to grasp it almost desperately. Voice unhappy, she said, "It matters little. The others all still believe 'twas me." She gave a short laugh and then said, "And I can no' e'en blame them. Conran was right. How likely is it to lose four husbands in four years to accidents?"

Saidh merely frowned, unsure what to say or even what to believe just then.

"But I really did no' kill them," she said miserably and then frowned. "Well, I did Hammish, but the others . . ." She shook her head helplessly. "How did this happen? How did me life get so twisted and miserable? I had such high hopes as a child. I dreamed o' the day I would marry Shamus and get out from under me parents—"

"Shamus?" Saidh interrupted with surprise.

"Aye," Fenella sighed miserably. "We were betrothed as children, but our families had a falling out and Da refused to honor the betrothal."

"I see," Saidh murmured, turning that over in her mind.

"And then Hammish offered fer me hand," Fenella went on, shuddering with disgust. "E'en I had heard the tales told o' how he treated women and his unnatural tastes, so when Da at first refused, I thought mayhap he cared for me after all. But it turned out he was just negotiating. He'd refused the first offer, fully expecting Hammish would make a second, larger one." Her mouth twisted bitterly. "And sure enough he did. He offered enough to make e'en me greedy sod o' a father crow with delight. He could no hand me o'er quick enough."

Saidh murmured in what she hoped was a sympathetic manner, then cleared her throat and asked, "Fenella, is it possible this Shamus may ha'e been upset at the betrothal no' being honored?"

Fenella shrugged. "I do no' ken. He may ha'e been, but he died shortly after so it matters little and—" She stopped abruptly and then turned to Saidh, clutching her hands desperately. "I did no' kill him, I promise."

Saidh sighed and patted her hand. "The thought did no' cross me mind," she assured her, and that was true, but the news that Shamus was dead was rather disappointing. She'd begun developing a theory in her head that this Shamus had been so distressed by the broken betrothal that he'd set out to kill Fenella's husbands. Either in a determination to have her himself, or in the hopes she would be blamed and punished for it. If the man died shortly after the broken betrothal, though, then that couldn't be the case.

"What am I going to do, Saidh?" Fenella asked sadly.

"About what?" Saidh asked quietly.

"About . . ." she raised her shoulders helplessly and finished, "everything."

She had no answer for that. Fortunately, Fenella didn't appear to expect one and continued miserably, "Me life is such a mess . . . and yer husband and brothers think I am some sort o' madwoman bent on killing ye."

"Well, we shall ha'e to convince him that ye're not," Saidh said pragmatically.

"How?" Fenella demanded.

Saidh considered the matter and then shrugged. "We shall ha'e to make sure ye and I are both under guard. That way, the next time there is an attempt there is no way anyone can accuse ye o' it."

"Ye mean ha'e two o' yer brothers watch me all the time as me maid says they've been doing with ye since ye took the arrow in the chest?" she asked uncertainly.

Saidh nodded.

Fenella considered that and then said thoughtfully, "That might work . . . At least it will if another attempt is made on yer life."

"Aye," Saidh muttered, thinking it was probably

somewhat bizarre to almost be hoping that another attempt was made on her life just to prove Fenella wasn't guilty, but she couldn't think of any other way to prove it and she did want it proved. She felt sorry for Fenella. Her cousin obviously hadn't had an easy or happy life to date and she'd like to see her get the chance at that.

"But e'en if that happens, what then?" Fenella asked suddenly.

"What do ye mean?" Saidh asked.

"Well, even once the suspicion is raised, me life will still be a mess. I've no husband or home and little likelihood of ever gaining one," she pointed out. "What man wants to marry a woman who has had four husbands drop dead within the first days or months after marrying her?"

None, Saidh thought, but said, "Why do we no' worry about one problem at a time?"

"But what will I do? Where will I go?" Fenella insisted miserably, tears welling up in her eyes.

Alarmed at the arrival of tears, Saidh pulled her roughly to her chest and patted her back. "Ye ha'e a home here as long as ye like, Fenella."

"Really?" She pulled back to peer at her with wide watery eyes.

"O' course."

"Ye would no' mind ha'ing me here?"

Saidh shrugged. "Why would I mind? I grew up with seven brothers, I am used to having a lot o' people around me. Besides, ye could help me run the servants and—"

"Oh!" Fenella cried and threw herself against Saidh's chest, sobbing loudly.

Saidh stilled and stared down at the top of her head with a sort of horror. She'd been trying to cheer the girl and staunch her tears. Instead, the woman was crying fit to die.

"Thank ye," Fenella moaned through her sobs. "Thank ye, Saidh. I promise ye'll no' regret it. I'll ne'er again raise me voice to ye or give ye a moment's trouble."

Saidh suspected that was highly unlikely. She was also beginning to consider that she perhaps should have spoken to Greer ere she'd made her magnanimous offer.

Frowning, she patted Fenella's back and glanced to the door, wondering why Greer hadn't returned. He'd gone to talk to Fenella, but Fenella was with her. Surely he should have returned by now?

"Ye do no' ken how relieved I am," Fenella said, sniffling. The woman did not cry prettily. Her eyes were red, her face blotchy and her nose was running something fierce. "I ha'e lain awake worrying at night, wondering what will become o' me and—" She paused suddenly and slumped unhappily. "I can no' stay here."

"Why?" Saidh asked with surprise.

"Allen's mother," Fenella said grimly. "We got along fine while Allen lived. She e'en seemed to like me, but ever since Allen died she has been saying the most horrid things about me."

"And how ha'e ye responded to those horrid things?" Saidh asked.

Fenella frowned with confusion. "What do ye mean?"

"I mean, I ken she's accused ye o' ha'ing something to do with Allen's death, but did ye tell her ye didn't and ye loved him, or did ye jest burst into tears and run away?" Saidh asked and could read the answer in Fenella's expression. Sighing, she said firmly, "Ye need to tell her that ye had naught to do with Allen's death, that ye loved and were grateful to him, and that ye'll hear no more o' her accusations."

"And what if she does no' listen?" Fenella asked unhappily.

"Then I will speak with her," Saidh said simply, and then added, "But even if she does no' change, she is old, Fenella, and her health has been poorly of late."

She snorted at that. "Her health has been poorly since I married Allen. Goodness, the morning Allen died she was lying in because she felt poorly. Yet she is still here." She grimaced. "I do no' think she is poorly so much as wants attention and sympathy." She blew out an exasperated breath. "E'en does she stop with accusations I do no' think I could forgive and live with her."

Saidh briefly considered suggesting that Aulay might let her live at Buchanan with him and the boys, but then thought better of it. She suspected her brothers would not be pleased if Fenella asked and they learned it was at her suggestion.

"Bowie is handsome, do ye no' think?" Fenella said thoughtfully.

Saidh blinked at the abrupt change in topic and asked with bewilderment, "Greer's first?"

"Aye. He has that fine pale hair and strong features. He is really verra handsome."

"I suppose," Saidh agreed slowly, not understanding where the conversation was going or how it had even got here.

"He was Allen's best friend," Fenella announced.

Saidh stilled and peered at her with more interest. "Was he?"

Fenella nodded. "They were always together, swimming in the loch, going out to check on the villagers, taking off on hunts that lasted for days, and I often found them together in his room at night, just chatting or playing chess," she said, her expression considering as she added, "And he has always been sweet and kind to me too."

"Hmm," Saidh said absently, her mind pondering the possibility that Bowie and Allen may have been more than friends. A man hunting and visiting villagers with his first was not unusual, but the part about Bowie being in Allen's room at night was a bit much. Aunt Tilda had said he preferred the company of men, after all.

"Do ye think if I married Bowie, Greer would set us up in a cottage in the village? That way I could stay close to ye but no' ha'e to live with Tilda."

"Er . . ." Saidh stared at her with dismay. Good Lord! Fenella was like a desperate drowning victim, floating down a river, snatching at every passing branch she saw. First she'd considered Greer, now Bowie. Were Aulay and the boys not Fenella's first cousins, she'd probably be plotting to marry one of them.

"What do you think?" Fenella asked.

Saidh thought that if Bowie and Allen had been

the type of "friends" she suspected, then Fenella was barking up the wrong tree, but she couldn't say that. Instead, she suggested firmly, "I think we should worry about that later. After we've convinced the men ye're innocent o' the attacks on me. 'Tis the most important thing at the moment."

"I suppose," Fenella murmured, and peered around the room. "This is quite a nice room, do ye no' think?"

"Aye. 'Tis," Saidh agreed slowly, suspecting she knew what was coming.

"Much nicer than me own," Fenella pointed out. "Mine is ridiculous small, and the bed lumpy, and—"

"Ye can move here if ye like, Fenella," Saidh said dryly.

"Truly?" she asked, a smile starting to pull at her lips.

"O' course," Saidh said patiently.

"Oh, thank ye," Fenella gushed, hugging her quickly and then pulling back. "I do no' sleep well in the room I'm in jest now. 'Tis no just that 'tis small either. I keep hearing sounds in the wall. I'm sure there are rats in there or something. Large ones too from the sound o' it and I jest lay there worrying they'll chew their way through to me room and—"

"Ye must be tired then," Saidh said on inspiration and stood abruptly. "Why do ye no' lie down and ha'e a little nap?"

"Here?" Fenella asked.

"Aye. 'Tis probably best Aulay and me husband do no' find ye until I can talk to them. They still think ye're behind the two attacks," she pointed out.

"Oh, aye. 'Tis probably best I stay here then," Fenella agreed, swinging her legs onto the bed and lying down. "I really am quite weary."

"Then a nap is jest what ye need," Saidh said firmly, pulling up the furs to cover her.

"Thank ye," Fenella murmured as Saidh tucked the furs around her.

"Yer welcome," Saidh said quietly and turned to head for the door, relieved to be able to escape.

"Yer supposed to be resting," Dougall growled as she slid out of the bedchamber and pulled the door closed.

"Well I'm no', am I?" she pointed out with irritation. "I need to talk to me husband."

"He's down below talking to Aulay and the rest o' the boys," Geordie informed her. "Fenella is missing and they are trying to sort out where she might—"

His voice died abruptly when Saidh turned away and headed for the stairs without waiting to hear the rest. She wasn't at all surprised to hear the clump of both men's feet on the stairs behind her as she descended. They were her guards after all, and she supposed she would have to get used to it, at least until this situation was cleared up. Saidh wouldn't be trying to slip her guard again. She wouldn't risk anyone else getting hurt on her account.

That didn't mean she was happy about having a guard though. The very idea of it chafed at her nerves, actually having her brothers trailing her about like puppies was going to drive her mad, she was sure.

"Wife," Greer said with surprise, getting to his

feet when Saidh reached the trestle tables. "I'm sorry I did no' return. But Fenella was no' in her room when we went to speak to her. Her maid said she'd left the room intending to come below, but no one has seen—"

"I ken where Fenella is," Saidh announced.

The men at the table all rose at this news, looking to her as if they would charge off and tackle the woman the moment they knew where to find her. Saidh scowled at them for it and sat down at the table.

"Where is she?" Greer asked, remaining standing.

Apparently he was as eager to hunt Fenella down as the others, Saidh thought wearily, but merely said, "I do no' think she is behind the attacks on me."

"She may no' be," Greer allowed. "But we need to speak to her to be sure."

"I already spoke to her," Saidh admitted.

"How the de'il did ye manage that?" Dougall asked. "Ye were in yer bedchamber the whole time and we were guarding the door. She did no' pass us."

"The passage," Greer said grimly when Saidh hesitated. He then explained to her brothers, "There is a secret passage that leads to the bedchamber. O' course, as Allen's wife, she would ken about it and how to open it. She must ha'e used it to visit Saidh and then to leave."

Saidh didn't correct him, she simply said, "It does no' matter how she got in. The fact is we talked and I ha'e me doubts that she had anything to do with what's happened. But we both ken 'tis impossible to prove, so she's agreed to a guard to stay with her day and night so that when the next attack happens, we'll ken 'tis no' her."

Greer dropped onto the bench seat beside her, his expression troubled. "The next attack?"

"There has to be a way to find the culprit without waiting fer another attack," Aulay said with a frown. " 'Sides, what makes ye think 'tis no' Fenella?"

"I asked her and she said she is no'," Saidh said calmly, then grimaced and added, "o' course, she could be lying, but . . ."

"But?" Greer prompted.

"I believe her," she said helplessly.

"Ye can no' ken this yet, Greer," Aulay said quietly, "but Saidh generally has good instincts when it comes to judging people."

Her husband let his breath out on a sigh. "If she is no' our culprit, then we are back to sorting out who is."

"M'laird, ha'e ye found her yet?"

Saidh glanced around to see Fenella's lady's maid standing behind them. Seeing the worry on her face, she said, "She is in the room next to the master bedchamber."

"Oh." The maid nodded and turned to hurry quickly up the stairs.

Saidh watched until she disappeared into the bedchamber, then turned back to the table as Greer said, "She may ha'e already used the passage to return to her own room."

"Nay, I suggested it might be good fer me to talk to ye and Aulay ere ye encountered her. She's taking a nap while she waits."

Greer nodded, and then turned to the men at the table. "So . . . if it turns out Fenella is no' the culprit, who else could it be?"

Dougall rumbled, "It would help if we had some idea o' what Saidh may ha'e done o' late to annoy someone."

Saidh clucked with disgust. "Are we back to that then? I ha'e somehow annoyed someone so much they would kill me?"

"Aye," Dougall said simply.

Saidh was scowling at him when a woman's scream sounded from abovestairs. Recognizing the voice as Fenella's maid, Saidh jumped up and charged for the stairs. She heard Greer shout her name over the thunder of himself and her brothers charging after her, but didn't slow. Honestly, it sounded like a herd of stallions were chasing her up the steps, which just made her run faster.

She was nearly at the top of the stairs when the master bedchamber door crashed open and Rory rushed out. He reached her bedchamber first and rushed in just as Greer caught up to Saidh and tugged her behind him, entering the room first. Saidh only caught a glimpse of what waited in the room, before Greer turned and bundled her toward Dougall and Geordie, saying, "Take her to the master chamber and stay inside with her and Alpin."

Saidh didn't protest. She had seen enough.

Chapter 17

GREER WATCHED DOUGALL AND GEORDIE LEAD Saidh to the master bedchamber next door and urge her inside. He waited until the door closed behind the trio before turning back into the room where Aulay and the remaining brothers stood by the bed. All but Alick, he saw. The youngest Buchanan had urged Fenella's maid to a chair by the fire and was trying to soothe her.

Moving to join the men by the bed, Greer stared down at Fenella. Someone, the maid probably, had pulled back the furs and Fenella lay curled up on her side as if in sleep. But she wasn't sleeping. Her face was as white as a spring bloom and the pale yellow gown she wore was blood soaked.

"Someone stabbed her in the neck," Rory announced, straightening from examining Fenella.

"Well, I guess that means Saidh was right and we can discount Fenella as the culprit," Aulay said dryly.

"Damn," Niels breathed. "First they're trying to kill Saidh and now they kill Fenella? Who is next?"

"That's assuming they meant to kill Fenella," Greer said grimly.

"What?" Niels asked with surprise.

"Her face is half buried in the pillow," he pointed out.

"Aye," Aulay agreed, and apparently seeing what Greer did, added, "And she has the Buchanan nose and hair."

"Yer thinking she was mistaken fer Saidh," Conran said slowly.

"Nay," Niels protested. "Fenella's a slip o' a thing and Saidh is more muscular and sturdy. They would ha'e kenned it was no' Saidh."

Greer shook his head. "Not with the furs covering her."

Aulay nodded, his expression solemn. "Under the furs, with just her hair and part o' her face showing, she could easily be mistaken for Saidh."

"Damn," Niels said unhappily.

"Now that that is settled, I'd be most interested in how it was done." Aulay turned to Greer. "My position at the trestle table in the great hall left me facing the stairs and upper landing. I had a clear view o' the door to this room. No one entered or left after Saidh came out. In fact, there was no one up here at all except fer Fenella's maid and she went nowhere near the door until Saidh told her this is where Fenella was."

"Ye're no' thinking Saidh killed her?" Niels asked with dismay.

Aulay reached out and smacked the man in the back of the head.

"That would be a nay," Rory said dryly.

"Aye, I gathered that," Niels muttered, rubbing the back of his head.

Ignoring the pair of them, Aulay turned to Greer with one eyebrow raised. "Who kens about the passage in the wall besides ye and Saidh?"

Greer considered the matter. "I told Alpin about it, and Aunt Tilda probably kens, and then there is—"

"Probably?" Aulay interrupted. "Aunt Tilda *probably* kens? Is she no' the one who showed ye the passage when ye got here to take yer place as laird? Or was that Fenella?"

"Nay." Greer shook his head. "Aunt Tilda and Fenella were both too distraught to be o' much use when I arrived. Bowie was the one who greeted me and gave me a tour o' the castle. He showed it to me."

"Bowie?" Aulay frowned. "Yer first?"

"Aye. He was Allen's first ere he died, and is now mine," Greer acknowledged.

"Why would a first ken about the secret passage?" Rory asked.

Greer glanced to the man with surprise. "Is that unusual?"

"Only family members ken how to find the passages at Buchanan," Aulay informed him quietly.

Greer's eyebrows rose at this news. He hadn't known it was unusual. He'd just assumed that as the laird's first and most trusted soldier he too would know about such things.

There was a brief silence and then Aulay asked, "How well do ye ken Bowie?"

"I only met him when I arrived at MacDonnell after Allen's death," he admitted, but then added, "Howbeit, he's a hard worker and seems reliable. And I really see no reason fer him to wish Saidh ill. As far as I ken, they've ne'er e'en spoken to each other."

"Hmm," Aulay murmured thoughtfully, and then sighed and said, "Then mayhap this time Fenella was the target after all."

"Now ye're thinking we ha'e two killers?" Greer asked with disbelief. "One after Saidh and one after Fenella?"

"It makes as much sense as anything else," Aulay pointed out with frustration. "Alpin was injured in one of the attempts on Saidh and could no' ha'e killed Fenella. He was next door with Rory. Was he no'?" He turned to his brother as he asked question, and Rory nodded.

Aulay turned back to Greer and shrugged. "That leaves Lady MacDonnell and Bowie."

"Aunt Tilda would no' hurt Saidh," Greer said firmly. "Why she has treated her like a daughter since the wedding, letting her wear her dress while we were wed, sitting up with her all night when she was injured." He shook his head, unwilling to even consider that the sweet woman who had been so kind to Saidh might do something so horrible.

"Aye, but she thinks Fenella had something to do with her son's death," Aulay pointed out quietly. "She may ha'e kenned it was Fenella in the bed and killed her fer retribution hoping it would be blamed on whoever has been attacking Saidh."

Greer ran a frustrated hand through his hair at the logic behind those words. He didn't want to believe his aunt could be guilty of murder. But he was of the belief that anyone could take a life in the right circumstances, and Aunt Tilda did believe Fenella was behind the death of her only son.

"Bring her here," Aulay suggested. "None but the maid, Saidh and the lads ken what's happened, so no one could ha'e told her. Bring her here and see what her reaction is when she sees Fenella. She will probably give herself away if she did it."

Greer eyed Aulay, wanting to refuse the suggestion and insist on leaving Aunt Tilda out of this. But, frankly, he was frustrated and exhausted from the constant worry over Saidh's well-being, and who might wish to do her harm, and he was tired of the thoughts rabbiting around in his head as his mind tried to work out who could be behind the attacks. He was desperate to have this matter resolved.

"Fine. Bring her," he said finally. "If nothing else, 'twill cross her off the list of suspects."

Aulay merely glanced to Conran, who nodded and slid quickly from the room. The moment he was gone, Aulay ushered Rory, Niels and Alick to the bedside so that Fenella would not be immediately visible to anyone entering. Then Aulay joined Greer at the foot of the bed when he moved there. It was the best position to be out of the way and be able to see Lady Mac-Donnell's face when the younger Buchanan brothers moved aside to reveal Fenella's body.

They did not have long to wait before Conran ushered in Aunt Tilda.

"Ye wanted to see me, Gr—" she began, but her words died in her throat and she came to a staggering halt as Rory, Niels and Alick stepped away to reveal Fenella. For one moment, she stood frozen, confusion and then shock flickering across her face, and then all the blood seemed to leach from her complexion and she reached out toward Fenella as if to touch her though she was too far away to do so. In the next moment, she pulled that hand back and pressed it to her chest, choking out something incomprehensible before she simply slid to the floor in a dead faint.

At least Greer hoped it was a faint. It was quite possible, however, that they'd given the poor woman a heart attack, he thought with dismay as he stared blankly at her snow-white face.

"What the devil ha'e ye done!"

Greer snapped out of his shock to peer at Saidh as she rushed into the room with Dougall and Geordie on her heels. He was not the only one to begin to move again then. Rory now hurried toward Lady MacDonnell too.

"Ye've killed Aunt Tilda!" his wife accused, dropping to her knees beside the woman to pat her cheek gently. Even as she did, Rory knelt on the woman's other side to examine her.

Greer scowled at the men, who were supposed to have kept Saidh safely in the master bedchamber, and received apologetic looks in response as Dougall and Geordie paused behind his wife. It seemed that, even awake, her brothers could not keep Saidh where she did not want to be.

"She's alive," Rory said soothingly to Saidh. "She just fainted."

"Are ye sure?" Saidh asked anxiously. "I saw her fall, she was grabbing at her heart."

Rory lowered his head to Aunt Tilda's chest and listened briefly. He straightened a moment later, looking less certain. "We'd best get her to her bed."

"She'll want her maid, Helen," Saidh said fretfully, getting up as Rory scooped up Aunt Tilda and stood. "She's trained in healing too. She tends to Aunt Tilda's ailments."

"Alick?" Rory said over his shoulder as he headed for the door with Saidh trailing him and Dougall and Geordie following her.

"I'll fetch her," Alick assured him.

Greer watched silently as the small troupe left, hoping that Saidh would glance back or say something to him. She didn't, however, and he was left standing there feeling like an utter horse's arse for having put Aunt Tilda through that. If the woman died, he would never forgive himself, but worse than that, he suspected Saidh wouldn't either. She might not even forgive him if Aunt Tilda lived.

"Lady MacDonnell was no' faking her shock," Aulay sounded disappointed as he pointed out the obvious.

"Nay," Greer agreed dryly.

"Hmmm." Aulay sighed. "I guess we should talk to Bowie now then."

"REALLY, I'M FINE, DEAR. I WAS JUST A LITTLE OVER-set by seeing Fenella like that," Aunt Tilda murmured, hands fluttering weakly as Saidh finished fussing with the furs she'd pulled over her.

Greer's aunt had woken up as Rory carried her into her bedchamber. She'd at first been confused as to why she was being carried about, and then quiet, but now seemed embarrassed by all the fuss.

Sitting on the edge of the bed next to her, Saidh took her hand and peered at her worriedly. Lady MacDonnell had regained a little color, but was still quite pale and her hand was trembling a bit in hers.

"Are ye sure ye feel all right?" Saidh asked, squeezing her hand gently. "Ye grabbed yer chest when ye fell. How is it now?"

"I am fine," Aunt Tilda assured her on a little sigh. "More embarrassed at fainting as I did than anything, to tell the truth." Grimacing, she added, "Ye'd think I'd ha'e been happy to see Fenella that way after everything that's happened. 'Twas just the shock. I just . . ." She shook her head wearily.

"Greer should no' ha'e surprised ye like that," Saidh said grimly, squeezing her hand again.

"I'm sure he thought Conran would tell me what had happened when he came to find me," Aunt Tilda said quietly, defending the man. She then defended Conran as well, saying, "And Conran probably thought it was no' his place. 'Twas jest an unfortunate set o' circumstances."

Saidh didn't comment to that. She suspected Greer had known exactly what he was doing bringing Aunt Tilda in to see Fenella without warning her first, although she couldn't for the life of her understand why he'd felt he had to do it. Or perhaps she could, Saidh acknowledged. She was sure there were few people who knew about the secret passages. It was probably only supposed to be family as it was at Buchanan. Obviously that wasn't the case, though. Someone outside the family had to know, because she hadn't killed Fenella, and neither could Greer and Alpin have done it. That had left only Aunt Tilda for Greer to consider. Saidh hoped this episode had cleared the woman of suspicion in his mind.

"Oh, Helen," Aunt Tilda breathed in relief as the woman rushed into the room.

"M'lady," the maid said with dismay, hurrying to her side. "What happened? Are ye all right?"

"She had a shock and fainted," Rory explained quietly.

"Aye, but I'm fine now," Aunt Tilda said firmly, struggling to sit up. "And I should get up. We need to tend to Fenella."

Helen straightened with surprise, eyes wide. "Lady Fenella? Is she ill?"

"She's dead," Aunt Tilda announced bluntly as she heaved herself upright. "And we'll need to see to her body."

"Ye're in no shape to tend to anything jest now," Saidh said firmly, urging her to lie back down. "Ye should rest. I shall worry about Fenella."

"But—" Aunt Tilda began, only to heave a sigh and settle back against her pillows. "Aye. Mayhap I should. I *am* weary." Distress crossing her features, she added fretfully, "Though I do no' ken how I'll sleep after seeing Fenella like that."

"I'll fix ye a tincture to help ye sleep," Helen said

at once and bustled over to a chest that sat on a table against the wall. Opening it, she began to retrieve various weeds and medicinals.

"Oh dear," Aunt Tilda breathed, drawing Saidh's attention back in time to see the woman grimace with distaste and mutter, "A tincture . . . vile things."

Saidh smiled sympathetically at her expression. "If it helps ye sleep, 'twill be worth the unpleasant taste."

"I suppose." Aunt Tilda sighed, and then patted her fingers. "Helen has me in hand. There is no need fer ye to stay with me." She frowned and added, "Yer looking a bit peaked yerself, dear. Mayhap Helen should make a tincture fer you, as well. I really do no' think ye should be up running about like this. Ye're still recovering from that arrow."

"I am fine," Saidh assured her, but it was a lie. She felt as if she'd run halfway across Scotland. In truth, she didn't know how she'd run up the stairs when Fenella's maid had screamed. Just going down them had wearied her. She supposed that scream and then seeing Fenella's body had raised her blood, giving her a temporary boost. But that boost was fading now, leaving her feeling weak and a little shaky.

"She's right. Ye've lost all yer color," Rory said quietly, concern on his face. "Ye should be abed too. Besides, I'm sure Lady MacDonnell can no' like her bedchamber being invaded by so many men."

"Oh, aye," Saidh said with realization. She was used to having her brothers around, but supposed it would be unsettling for the poor woman to have the men in her bedchamber. Forcing a smile for Aunt

Tilda, Saidh got shakily to her feet saying, "I'll take me brothers away and leave ye to rest."

"Verra well then," Aunt Tilda murmured, then glanced to the men and said, "Make sure she rests. She does no' look well at all."

Saidh heard her brothers rumble their agreement to the suggestion as they followed her to the door. But she remained silent, her attention on sucking in deep breaths to try to ward off the weakness now dropping around her like a large cape.

"She's right, ye need rest," Rory said quietly once they were out of the room and Dougall had pulled the door closed behind them. "Ye're recovering from a mighty injury, Saidh, and all this rushing about can no' be good fer ye. Besides, I want to check yer wound and apply more salve."

"Soon," Saidh murmured, slowing as she saw Bowie following Alick off the stairs and into the room where Fenella was. Frowning, she asked, "Why Bowie?"

"He is the only one who kenned about the passages besides ye, Greer, Alpin and Lady MacDonnell," Rory answered quietly. "I imagine they want to see his reaction on viewing her body, just as they did Lady MacDonnell."

Saidh frowned at this news and moved a little more quickly up the hall, but only a little. It was a long damned hall and Lady MacDonnell's room was nearly at the end of it. It seemed to take forever for her to reach the bedchamber door. When she did, she found the door open. Bowie had not closed it as he entered. She peered in curiously to see Bowie staring down at Fenella, shock still present on his face. Greer, Aulay, Alick, Conran and Niels all surrounded him.

"And no one entered the room?" Bowie asked slowly.

"Nay. No' from the hall," Greer answered.

"Then they must ha'e used the passage," Bowie said at once, turning wide eyes to Greer.

"Aye, 'tis what we're thinking," Greer agreed grimly.

When Bowie frowned and turned his gaze back to Fenella, Greer added, "Aulay informs me it is usually only family who ken about passages in castles. Yet ye were the one to show it to me. Why would Allen ha'e showed it to ye?"

Bowie glanced to him with surprise, opened his mouth to respond, then paused and closed it again, his gaze turning wary.

"Well?" Greer prompted when the man remained silent.

"I think ye'd get more answers did ye ha'e me brothers leave," Saidh said quietly, moving into the room now.

All of the men turned to peer at her then, and all of them were scowling at her appearance, except for Bowie and Greer. Bowie just looked more wary. Greer, however, looked relieved, though she wasn't sure why.

"Ye should be resting, love," Greer said, striding over to scoop her up into his arms.

"I want to be here while ye talk to Bowie," Saidh protested when he would have carried her out of the room. When that made him pause, she added, "I ken things. I can help."

Much to her relief, her husband nodded and turned to carry her to the chairs by the fire. He set her down in one and would have straightened, but Saidh kept her arms locked around his neck and whispered, "Make me brothers leave. He'll no' talk in front o' them."

Greer met her gaze silently, eyebrows raised and asked in an undertone, "What do ye ken, lass?"

"After me brothers leave," Saidh whispered firmly.

"Why do we ha'e to leave?" Aulay asked by her ear in a whisper of his own, and Saidh jumped in surprise and released Greer to turn to peer at her brother where he now stood behind her, bent at the waist to join the conversation.

Saidh grimaced at the man, then said quietly. "He and Allen were friends like our cook and Quintin."

Aulay considered this news and then nodded and straightened to glance to the other men. "Take his sword and any other weapons he has. We're waiting in the hall, but I will no' leave him armed."

Saidh glanced back to Greer then, expecting him to ask what she'd meant by Bowie and Allen being friends like the cook at Buchanan and Quintin, but instead he asked solemnly, "Is Aunt Tilda all right?"

"Aye." She sighed the word, recalling her anger at him earlier. "And I understand why ye did it, but she is an old woman, Greer. She could ha'e died."

"Aye. I ken," he admitted. "And I regret that it had to be done."

"But ye'd do it again," she guessed, unable to miss the fact that he wasn't apologizing for it.

"In a heartbeat," he assured her solemnly. "I'll do anything necessary to find the killer and keep ye safe, Saidh. I love ye."

That declaration left Saidh gaping at him like a fish out of water. Before she could recover enough to sort out how to respond to it, Aulay paused at the door and said, "We'll be in the hall. Shout and we'll come running."

Greer tore his gaze from Saidh to glance to her brother. Nodding, he murmured, "Thank ye," then shifted his attention to Bowie as the bedchamber door closed behind the Buchanan men. A moment of silence passed and then he again asked, "Why did Allen tell ye about the secret passage?"

Letting out the breath she hadn't realized she'd been holding, Saidh forced her attention to the matter at hand. She would consider how she felt about Greer's claim later, she assured herself as she peered at Bowie.

The man looked like he was battling an inner war, struggling over what to say, or what he dared to say.

"He told ye so ye could use the passage," Saidh guessed and when Bowie glanced to her sharply, but didn't deny it, added, "because ye were his lover."

Saidh had expected Greer to be shocked by this announcement, but the only one who appeared surprised was Bowie. His eyes widened with both shock and alarm now and he began to shake his head.

Wondering why Greer was not amazed at this news, Saidh continued to eye Bowie solemnly as she added, "I ken Allen preferred the company o' men to women. And Fenella told me how the two o' ye were always going off together to swim and taking hunting trips and such. Ye were lovers, were ye no'?"

Bowie stopped shaking his head, and lowered it, his shoulders slumping in defeat. After a moment, he said, "I loved him," in a voice so low she almost couldn't hear him.

Saidh let her breath out on a sigh. She'd suspected Bowie had been Allen's lover after talking to Fenella, but she hadn't been sure. Now that she was, she began to consider all that had happened. "Did ye ha'e a lovers' quarrel at the loch the morning he died? Had he found someone else, or—?"

"I did no' kill him!" Bowie cried, his head jerking up to reveal his shock at the possibility. "I could ne'er kill him. I loved him."

"Did ye think Fenella had done it then?" Greer asked quietly.

"What?" Bowie looked briefly bewildered and then he glanced at the woman's blood-covered body and realization slowly dawned. Expression grim, he drew his shoulders up and turned back to say firmly, "I did no' kill Fenella." Lifting his chin, he added derisively, "Why would I?"

"Out o' jealousy?" Saidh suggested. "She was the wife of the man ye loved."

He snorted at the suggestion. "In name only. They had no' e'en consummated the wedding. I am the one who spent e'ery night in his bed. And I am the one he spent his days with, and talked to and—" He shook his head. "There was nothing to be jealous o' Fenella fer. She was a pretty, brainless child, happy to accept the baubles he gave her and stay out o' his bed."

Saidh pursed her lips and glanced to Fenella. As sad as she was to admit it, that description was probably a perfect portrayal of her cousin during her marriage to Allen. There had been much more to the woman than that, of course. Or could have been, had she allowed it, but Fenella had been so grateful at Allen's kindness and his not bothering her about the bedding, that she'd closed her eyes to everything around her that she hadn't wanted to see. It was the only way to explain how she could live with the man and not realize his true nature.

"I tend to believe ye, Bowie," Greer said, rubbing a weary hand around his neck. "The problem is that whoever killed Fenella had to ha'e entered the room through the secret passage." He let his hand drop and added, "And as far as I ken, the only people who are aware o' it, are me, me squire, me wife, Lady MacDonnell and you." He let that sink in and then asked, "Is there anyone else who knows about it?"

Bowie shook his head slowly. "Nay. No' as far as I ken," he admitted with a frown, and then rallied and added, "But it was no' me, and the boy is in no shape to ha'e done this," he said gesturing to Fenella's body. "So if 'twas no' either o' ye, then ye should look to Allen's mother. She hated Fenella."

Saidh scowled at the suggestion. "I ken she thought Fenella had somehow brought about Allen's death, but—"

"Nay. She hated her long ere that," Bowie informed her. "She blamed her fer no' being woman enough to change Allen's ways, and no' demanding he get her with child. She hated him too fer that. I would no' be surprised to learn she killed them both."

"Nay," Saidh protested. "Aunt Tilda would ne'er harm her own son. She understood and loved Allen."

"Aye, so long as he let her think he would give her the grandchildren she wanted and was no' following his inclinations," Bowie said bitterly. "But when she actually caught us together—" His mouth tightened. "I ha'e never seen such hatred. I thought she'd kill us both right there."

"She caught ye together?" Greer asked sharply.

"Aye. Right here in this room," Bowie admitted, glancing around sadly. "Allen moved to this room after the wedding, leaving Fenella to have the master suite." His gaze returned to Saidh and he added, "As ye suggested, I used the passage to come to him at night. I did that night as well. We were both taken by surprise when his mother barged in."

Bowie shook his head, his eyes growing dim as if he were seeing that confrontation again in his mind's eye. "When she started shrieking, Allen suggested I leave, so I gathered me clothes and did. But I stopped in the hall to dress and I heard him tell her to go to hell. He bellowed that he'd married that little bitch Fenella as she'd insisted, but he would ne'er actually consummate the marriage and gi'e her those damned grandchildren she was always harping on about. She'd jest best forget about it, he said, and leave him be or he'd stick her in a hut on the edge o' the property and she'd ne'er set foot in her beloved castle again."

Pausing, Bowie sighed and rubbed his forehead and then said almost apologetically, "Allen was no' normally like that, but I think she'd pushed him to his limits."

Saidh waved that away. She too would have been upset did someone barge in on her and Greer together. "What did she say?"

"I ne'er heard," Bowie said unhappily. "I was dressed by then and someone was coming up the stairs, so I slipped away to avoid being seen. I returned to the barracks and paced all night, waiting fer Allen to send fer me, but he ne'er did . . . and then the next morn he was found dead in the loch."

Saidh and Greer were silent for a moment, absorbing what he'd said, and then Greer made a frustrated sound. Her eyebrows rose as she noted his expression. Something about the story obviously didn't sit right with him, Saidh realized, and she wondered what it was. She understood when he asked, "Why did she allow ye to stay at MacDonnell after Allen was found dead the next morn? I'd ha'e expected if she was that angry, she'd ha'e sent ye away at once."

"She did no ken it was me," he said with a shrug.

Saidh turned to him with amazement. "How could she not?"

"The Drummonds had stopped to rest on their way north to Sinclair, and the MacDonalds were here on some business, and Allen decided to use that as an excuse to hold a masked ball that night," Bowie explained, and then added with a sad smile, "Allen loved feasts and celebrations."

"I do no' see how that would prevent her—" Saidh began with confusion.

"While we were both naked, we were both still wearing our masks," Bowie explained, flushing slightly. "He liked to do that sort o' thing too."

"Oh, I see," Saidh murmured, but her gaze was on Greer, who was looking at her as if his expression suggested he was imagining making love to her with masks on and nothing else.

"I'd also sooted me hair," Bowie added. "Me platinum hair is very distinctive, so I rubbed soot in it to make me less recognizable," he explained when they both turned blank expressions his way. "It was a masked ball, after all. But if I'd no' sooted me hair, e'eryone would ha'e kenned who I was at once. The game was to see if Allen could find me amongst all the masked men." He shook his head firmly. "Lady MacDonnell could no' ha'e kenned it was me with Allen that night. If she had, I would surely be gone, or probably dead like Allen."

"Ye think she killed him," Greer said and it wasn't a question.

Bowie hesitated, but then said, "She was verra angry. In truth I ha'e ne'er seen her like that. She was near crazed with fury. She could ha'e . . ." He didn't finish the accusation, but fell silent.

"Why did ye no' tell me yer suspicions when I arrived?" Greer asked sharply.

Bowie looked away unhappily. "I was no' sure she

had killed him. I still am no' sure. How could she ha'e done it? I mean, Allen had called fer a bath ere I got there and the tub was still there full o' water. She could ha'e drowned him in that, but then how did she get him to the loch?" he asked helplessly.

When Greer merely shook his head, Bowie added, "And if she did no' drown him in the tub, but followed him to the loch the next morn and killed him ere he was discovered, how did she manage it? Allen was big and strong. There were no signs o' injury to the body." He shrugged helplessly. "So while I suspected it, I could no' see how she could ha'e done it." Bowie paused and then added bitterly, "And I could no' e'en tell anyone why I suspected her without revealing our relationship."

"Which might ha'e seen ye burned at the stake, or mutilated and hanged as a sodomite," Saidh said quietly.

Bowie nodded miserably. "Which I suppose will happen anyway now that I've confessed all to ye."

Much to Saidh's relief, Greer shook his head.

"Nay, Bowie," he said firmly. "Who ye love is yer business. I'll no' go running to the priest or anyone else with tales."

Bowie looked relieved, but then peered uncertainly at Saidh.

"Oh hell, I'll no' tell," she assured him.

Bowie smiled crookedly. "Thank ye, m'laird, m'lady." He hesitated and then straightened his shoulders and said, "I'll pack me things and be gone by morn . . . unless ye still think I had something to do with Allen and Fenella's death?" he tacked on uncertainly.

"Be gone where?" Greer asked with surprise, rather than answer the question. Although, Saidh supposed his question did that. Greer no longer considered Bowie a suspect. Neither did she.

Bowie shrugged. "I'll find somewhere. But I'll leave yer land and ye'll no' ha'e to look on me again."

"The hell ye will," Greer said sharply. "Ye're me first, and yer damned good at the job. And ye swore yer fealty to me, Bowie. I expect ye to keep to yer oath and continue to serve me as ye ha'e."

Bowie closed his eyes briefly. When he opened them again, they were a touch glassy, as if he was fighting tears. Clearing his throat, he nodded. "Thank ye, m'laird."

"There's nothing to thank me fer," Greer assured him. " 'Tis no' as if I'm offering ye light duty with lots o' rest. I'm a hard taskmaster, as ye well ken."

A struggle took place on Bowie's face, and then he shook his head, a small smile tugging at his lips as he said, "Er . . . actually, m'laird, while ye expect hard work and obedience, yer a fair maun. So far I've found ye a rather grand laird."

"Oh." Greer looked uncomfortable and then said, "Well, that's because yer a good worker. I've no' had to punish or rail at ye fer laying down on the job."

"I imagine that's so, m'laird," Bowie agreed solemnly.

Greer nodded. "Go oversee the men in the practice field. I would talk with me wife."

"Aye, m'laird. Thank ye, m'laird," Bowie bobbed his head and turned to leave them.

Chapter 18

"*J* AM QUITE SURE HE DID NO' KILL FENELLA," Saidh said the moment the bedchamber door closed behind Bowie.

"I was about to say the verra same thing," Greer admitted on a weary sigh, and then pointed out, "But that leaves us with Aunt Tilda."

Saidh grimaced at the suggestion. While Bowie had revealed a whole different side to the woman, it was still difficult to believe Aunt Tilda might want to see her dead. Saidh liked the woman. She also thought Aunt Tilda liked her. And, as far as she knew, she'd never done anything that might anger her.

"I find it hard to believe Aunt Tilda would try to kill ye," Greer said suddenly, apparently thinking along the same lines. "She seems quite fond o' ye."

"Aye," Saidh said with relief.

"But I also do no' think Bowie would wish to harm ye, and we ken it was no' Fenella," he added. "And now I am wondering about Allen's death. If she was really so angry that night . . ."

"Just because she was angry, does no' mean she killed Allen. He was her son," she pointed out.

"So, Allen drowned by accident and Fenella was ne'er at risk, but was accidentally killed in yer place," he decided unhappily.

"Perhaps not," Saidh protested, rankling at the idea of someone wanting to kill her. She pointed out, "Fenella could be difficult. Mayhap she made an enemy or two while here and her death has nothing to do with me misadventures."

"So ye think that whoever stabbed her knew it was Fenella and did no' accidentally kill her while attempting to kill you?" he asked dubiously.

Saidh scowled up at him. "Well, ye needn't make it sound so unlikely. 'Tis no' as if I'm such a tyrant fer lady that all and sundry would want me dead."

Greer chuckled at her expression and scooped her up out of the chair and into his arms. He then settled in the chair with her in his lap and kissed her forehead. "That is no' what I mean at all. But Saidh, ye've nearly been crushed by a great huge bit o' the castle fallin' on ye, and took an arrow to the chest. Someone is trying to kill ye. Do ye really think 'tis likely that at the same time someone else jest up and decided to kill Fenella?"

Saidh lowered her head, frustration slipping through her, and then admitted, "I do no' ken. But I came here thinking that Fenella might ha'e been killing her husbands and I was wrong. I do no' want to start doing the same thing to Aunt Tilda."

He pulled back to eye her with surprise. "Ye came here because ye thought Fenella might be killing her husbands?"

"Aye," she admitted, guilt slithering through her. She'd never told him of her part in the death of her cousin's first husband. She probably should have before agreeing to marry him. He might not take kindly to having a wife who was once a party to covering up a murder.

Greer narrowed his gaze on her expression. "Why did ye think Fenella may ha'e killed her husbands?"

Saidh didn't really want to tell him, but felt she had to, and after the briefest hesitation, admitted, "Because I kenned that she killed Hammish."

"What?" he breathed in shock.

Saidh grimaced and then quickly told him the whole story of Fenella's first marriage, the wedding, the wedding night and the following day. She admitted everything, even her aiding Fenella in covering up the murder of her husband and then her worry on hearing of her cousin's other short-lived marriages.

When she was done, Saidh eyed Greer anxiously, unsure how he would take what he'd learned. In truth, she feared he would push her away with disgust for helping to cover up Hammish's death.

"So Fenella stabbed Hammish rather than suffer his abuse," Greer said finally.

"Aye," Saidh breathed unhappily.

He was silent for another moment and then pointed out, "The king had the deaths of the MacIvers investigated and it was decided there was no foul play."

"Aye," she acknowledged.

"Do ye think she killed them?" he asked.

Saidh hesitated. "At first, I feared she had, and then, after talking to Fenella, I changed me mind. But . . ."

"But?" he prompted when she stopped and frowned over the matter.

"In truth, I do no' ken," she admitted, and then added with frustration, "E'ery time I talked to Fenella I came away sure she had no' harmed any but Hammish. But the bit about the feather bothers me still. It seems to suggest she may ha'e killed the senior MacIver as well. But Fenella swore to me that she had nothing to do with the deaths of her other husbands, and . . ." She paused and threw her hands up with exasperation. "Does it e'en matter anymore? She is dead. If she was killing her husbands, she can do that no more, and if she did no' kill any but Hammish, then . . . well, she has more than paid fer it in this life."

"Aye," Greer agreed solemnly. "But what feather were ye talking about?"

"Oh," Saidh waved one hand impatiently. "Aunt Tilda was at MacIver for the wedding to the senior MacIver. She was among the women who helped prepare him fer burial when he was found dead the next morn. As she was cleaning him, she found a feather in his mouth and said as how his eyes were bloodshot. She thinks that may be a sign that he was smothered since her bairns had bloodshot eyes too."

"What?" Greer asked with amazement. "What bairns?"

Saidh frowned at his expression, but then realized he probably had little knowledge of his Aunt's life ere coming to take up the mantle of laird. He probably didn't know about the babies she'd lost.

"Aunt Tilda had three children ere Allen," she explained. "All were smothered in their beds by their wet nurse ere they were out o' swaddling. Aunt Tilda caught the wet nurse killing the last child, and I suppose the woman was probably hung or something," Saidh added with a frown. She hadn't thought to ask what had happened to the wet nurse and Aunt Tilda hadn't mentioned it. Shrugging that concern away, she added, "But Aunt Tilda said she had noticed how the eyes of each babe were bloodshot after they'd been smothered. She suspected it must be something that happens when a body is smothered and since she'd found that feather and Laird MacIver's eyes also were bloodshot, she thought perhaps he had been smothered too." She paused and then added, "Although she also said he was old so his eyes were often bloodshot and rheumy, so Fenella may no' ha'e killed him. And the feather could ha'e got in his mouth some other way. Although I do no' ken—"

"Saidh."

"Hmm?" She gave up trying to work out if Fenella had killed Laird MacIver and glanced to her husband in question.

"Allen was Aunt Tilda's only child," Greer said solemnly. "She had a difficult birth and ne'er carried another."

Her eyes widened, and then narrowed with confusion. "But she said she had three bairns ere him."

"Nay." He shook his head firmly, and then added, "Me uncle's first wife did though, three little lasses who ne'er made it out o' swaddling. The mother threw herself from a cliff after the third bairn died, killing herself," he added grimly.

Saidh blinked. "And then he married Tilda?"

"Aye. She comforted him after his wife died; got with child, and me uncle married her. And," he added, his voice growing hard, "Aunt Tilda was his first wife's sister. She'd acted as nursemaid to each o' the bairns who died in swaddling."

Saidh stared at him blankly, and then muttered, "Ah, hell," and scrambled off of his lap. All her earlier weakness slipped away as blood began to pound through her body, riding a wave of fury. She started to stride toward the door, and then stopped and turned back to peer at Greer as he got to his feet. "She killed those bairns."

"I suspect so," he agreed mildly, and then added to her anger by announcing, "And since Aunt Tilda was the only witness to the death of my uncle's first wife, her sister, I suspect—"

"She killed her sister too," Saidh snapped.

Greer nodded. " 'Tis no' such a leap that she might kill her own son as well, once she realized he was no' like to give her what she wanted."

"Aye," Saidh muttered and then shook her head with bewilderment. "She seemed like such a nice old lady."

"Aye," Greer agreed, walking toward her.

"I liked her. And she told me to call her Aunt Tilda," Saidh said almost plaintively, and then growing indignant, added, "And all the while she's been trying to kill me? Why? What did I e'er do to her?"

"I do no' ken, but I shall find out," Greer vowed, pausing in front of her.

"*We* shall find out," she said grimly, turning toward the door again.

"Nay." Greer scooped her up in his arms and carried her the rest of the way to the door. "I will find out. I want ye nowhere near the woman. Besides, Rory will need to look at yer wound, yer bleeding through yer bandages."

Saidh glanced down and grimaced when she saw he was right. There was a large red circle over her breast on the pale blue gown. They had reached the door now and Saidh glanced around, intending to open it for him, but there was no need. He gave it one healthy kick and then swiftly stepped back out of the way as someone immediately opened it from the hall.

"Me wife needs—" Greer began

"Dougall will take her," Aulay interrupted. "And Rory is already in yer room collecting what he needs out o' his satchel." Grinning, he added, "We heard everything. Yer doors are fair thin here, MacDonnell."

"And our sister is loud," Dougall rumbled as he took Saidh from Greer.

Conran then drawled, "In *all* things. Ye may want to consider that the next time ye're tupping her."

Saidh scowled over Dougall's shoulder at Conran. Not that he even noticed: he and her other brothers were following Greer down the hall toward Aunt Tilda's room, heads together and jabbering away. Discussing how best to approach Aunt Tilda, she supposed unhappily, and heaved a depressed sigh. She really had liked Aunt Tilda. Her turning out to be such a nasty old murdering cow was more than just a little disappointing.

"Sorry, Saidh," Dougall said solemnly. "I ken ye liked her."

"Aye," she muttered unhappily, and reached to open the door to the master bedchamber for him when he paused in front of it.

Dougall immediately started inside, but only got a step or so past the door when he suddenly grunted, stumbled forward, and then crashed to the floor taking her with him. It all happened so fast, Saidh didn't even get the chance to cry out. One moment she was in his arms and the next she was hitting the floor with a soft thud and Dougall was coming down on top of her.

Saidh wasn't sure what hurt worse, her injured shoulder and hip slamming into the hard floor, or Dougall's weight crashing onto her. But the combination was enough to leave her dazed and in agony.

"Oh dear, that had to hurt."

Saidh blinked her eyes open at that comment to see that Aunt Tilda was closing the bedchamber door. When the woman then proceeded to bar it, Saidh forced herself to ignore the pain vibrating through her body and began to drag herself determinedly out from under Dougall. She also opened her mouth to shout for help at the same time, but froze when Aunt Tilda turned back from the door and she saw that she had Alpin in front of her.

The boy was awake, but Saidh suspected held upright only by the arm around his throat. He looked as dazed as she felt in that moment.

"No screaming now," Aunt Tilda said solemnly, producing a knife from the folds of her skirt and pressing it to Alpin's throat. "We do no' want the boy to get hurt, do we?"

Saidh closed her mouth and stopped moving.

"Nay, nay. Do get up," Tilda said at once. "The boys may come running back here any minute to warn yer brothers that I am no' in me room. If they do, and if we are still here, I fear I shall ha'e to kill young Alpin as yer punishment."

Saidh scowled at the woman, and then finished dragging herself out from under Dougall and managed to stagger to her feet. It was a difficult task though, and she knew she was swaying on her feet once she gained them.

"To the passage," Tilda ordered, and then added sharply, "Quickly."

Saidh glanced to Alpin, and then turned reluctantly and crossed the room to the wall beside the mantel. She spotted Rory on the floor on the far side of the bed as they passed it and supposed Tilda had caught him unawares. She'd probably slipped into the room through the passage and knocked him out. Certainly, she couldn't have come up the hall without her other brothers seeing her. They'd been waiting there while Saidh and Greer had talked to Bowie.

"Open the passage," Tilda said when Saidh paused at the wall.

"Where are we going?" Saidh asked as she

pressed the stone Alpin had that afternoon. Dear God, it had only been a matter of hours ago, she realized suddenly. It felt like a lifetime ago now.

"Grab the torch inside and light it from the fire," Tilda instructed, not bothering to answer her question.

Saidh did as she was told, her movements slowed by the pain coursing through her body. She seemed to hurt everywhere, though her shoulder and chest hurt the worst.

"Now in," Tilda ordered when Saidh had straightened from lighting the torch, and then gave her a shove to get her moving.

Saidh stumbled into the narrow passage and glanced back in time to see Tilda turn from closing the passage door. The knife she held was pressed tight to Alpin's throat and a line of blood had sprung up under it.

"Move," Tilda said, her voice cold. "Quickly, child. I would not wish to hurt wee Alpin here to make ye move faster. He's a good lad. Such good manners and always proper."

Saidh ground her teeth together, but turned and started along the passage, holding the torch out in front of her to light the way. But she wished she had her sword. Sadly, she hadn't seen or even thought of her damned sword since waking up in the master bedchamber next to Alpin. What good was having a sword and knowing how to use it if she didn't carry it with her? she admonished herself silently, and then sighed to herself and turned her attention to more useful concerns, like— "Why?"

"Why what?"

"Why did ye kill yer own son?" she asked, and really wanted to know the answer.

"Why do ye think? The lad was always a disappointment," Tilda said grimly. "And after all I did to be able to ha'e him too."

"Killing yer own sister and her bairns ye mean?" Saidh asked dryly.

"Exactly," Tilda said sharply, and then jabbed her in the back with her knife and snapped, "Faster."

Saidh winced at the painful poke, but moved faster.

"Me sister was useless," Tilda announced after a moment as if to justify what she'd done. "She only e'er birthed lasses. I am the one who ga'e MacDonnell his son and heir."

"And then ye killed that son and heir," Saidh pointed out dryly.

"Well, he damned near killed me while I was giving birth to him," Tilda shot back as if that excused it. "And then, after he was born, I could no' ha'e any other children."

"Ye blamed him fer that?" she asked with disbelief.

"He tore me up inside, didn't he? I near bled to death," she snarled, and then sighed and said, "Still, I told meself, I had him. The precious male heir who would ensure me blood would continue down the line." Tilda laughed bitterly. "Little did I ken then. Me sister must ha'e been laughing in her grave at the joke."

Lady MacDonnell was silent for a minute as they

walked and then suddenly squawked, "What man prefers the company o' men to women? How was he to gain an heir that way? He wouldn't," she said, answering her own question. "And he did no' e'en care."

"So ye killed him," Saidh said quietly, slowing as they reached the end of this first passage and automatically starting to turn left as she and Alpin had earlier.

"Nay, turn right," Tilda snapped, poking her in the back again.

Saidh ground her teeth together, very tempted to turn and hit the woman with the flaming torch. But the possibility of hurting Alpin if she did stopped her. Which was what the woman was counting on, of course, she thought as she turned around to head to the right. "How did ye kill Allen?"

"You mean after he finished telling me that he was the laird, and would no longer do as I wished? That he would no' sleep with his wife, or give me grandchildren, and that I'd best jest keep me mouth closed and do as he said or he'd see me in a hovel at the edge of the property?" she asked dryly, and then continued, "After all o' that he ordered me to send fer wine and his first."

"Ye did no' send fer his first," Saidh said with certainty. She already knew that from Bowie. He'd waited all night for Allen to send for him.

"Nay," Tilda said with satisfaction. "I suspected he intended to ha'e Bowie remove me to the threatened hovel that very night. So I did no' send fer him, and I fetched the wine meself. After putting a few o' Helen's weeds in it, I delivered the wine and told him that I had sent a servant fer Bowie and he should be along soon."

"What kind o' weeds?" Saidh asked with a frown, slowing as they came to stairs leading up.

"Keep going," Tilda ordered, and when Saidh started up the stairs, answered, "A combination that made him easy to handle. They worked beautifully," she added with satisfaction. "I had no trouble at all getting him to follow me into the passage and down to the loch. Then I jest had him strip, walked him out into the water and held his head under. He barely struggled. In no time at all I was back in the castle, climbing into me bed."

And slept like a babe, no doubt, Saidh thought grimly, but didn't say as much. Instead, asking, "And Fenella?"

"That was supposed to be you," Tilda said with irritation. "I near to died from shock when I saw it was her instead."

Saidh grimaced to herself. They'd thought her shock because she hadn't done it. Instead, it was because she'd done it to the wrong woman. They should have thought of that possibility, she acknowledged grimly.

"I had intended for Fenella to take the blame fer both yer death and Allen's," Tilda said, bringing Saidh's attention back from her thoughts. "O' course, I can no' do that now."

"Why kill me? I thought ye liked me," Saidh said, and frowned at the plaintive note in her own voice. But truly, she'd come to really like Aunt Tilda. At least the Aunt Tilda she'd thought she was.

"I do like ye, child," Tilda assured her. "Yer verra entertaining. The way ye handle yer brothers impresses me greatly."

"Then why kill me?" Saidh asked with bewilderment, and then slowed as the torch revealed a stone wall half a dozen steps further up.

"Keep going," Tilda hissed, poking her once again with the knife, harder. Feeling a thin rivulet of what could only be blood trickle down her back, Saidh paused and growled, "Poke me with that pig sticker again, m'lady, and I shall turn and shove this torch down yer throat."

"Then Alpin will die," Tilda said coldly.

Saidh ground her teeth together and continued up the last few steps. This time, to avoid giving the woman an excuse to stab her in the back again, she didn't hesitate, or wait to be ordered to pull the lever. She just did it and then stepped out into darkness and cool night air.

"Where are we?" she asked, continuing forward and peering curiously around. They were in what appeared to be a small room. At least it had walls and a ceiling, although all four walls had large openings without any window or shutters, leaving it open to the elements on all sides.

"The bell tower," Tilda muttered, and Saidh glanced back to see her push the stone door closed. Finished with her task, Lady MacDonnell turned to face her, Alpin clamped to her body by her arm again. She'd used her hand holding the knife to push the door closed, but now raised it to press against his throat again.

"There is no bell," Saidh pointed out.

"Nay," Tilda agreed. "No' anymore."

When she didn't explain further, Saidh let the subject go and dropped her gaze to Alpin's face. He looked much more alert, but was still leaning weakly against Tilda. But that might be to their advantage, she thought, and then raised her eyes to Lady MacDonnell's face and asked, "So? Why kill me?"

"That should be obvious e'en to you," Tilda said quietly. "While I like ye, child. Yer no' a lady. In truth, ye're little better than a lightskirt, the way ye lifted yer skirts fer him at the loch and rutted like an animal with him. The things ye let him do to ye . . ." She shook her head. "Yer no better than me sister was. Ye could hear her squeals o' pleasure through the castle too."

Saidh gave a sharp laugh. "So ye killed yer son because he'd no' sleep with his wife, and ye'd kill me because I happily sleep with me husband?"

Tilda's mouth tightened with anger. "A lady suffers her husband's attentions, she does no' revel in them and scream her pleasure like some cheap whore. Besides," she added grimly. "Yer no' good enough to rule MacDonnell. Me people need a proper lady, not a cursing, swaggering lass who thinks she's a lad. 'Tis bad enough that Greer behaves so, yer worse because ye're a woman. Ye merely encourage him to behave badly. Once ye're gone I'll find him a proper wife who'll help me reform him and—"

"Help ye reform him?" Saidh asked with disbelief. "Ye'll be strung up by the neck fer this, no' reforming anything. They ken ye killed Allen and Fenella, and they'll ken ye killed me."

"They may suspect I killed Fenella, but they ha'e no proof and once I explain how Alpin here so cleverly placed a knife to me throat and used the threat o' harming me to make ye do as he wished—"

"Alpin?" she nearly gasped the name. "Ye really think ye can convince them that wee Alpin stabbed Fenella, knocked out both me big strong brothers and then killed me?" She shook her head with disbelief. "He's a stripling."

"And I'm a frail old woman," Tilda pointed out sweetly. "Who has ne'er showed anything but fondness fer ye. While Alpin is a strong lad, with lots o' wiry muscle from saddling his laird's horse, and carrying his shield and such . . . who also complained to one and all that ye were no lady." She put on a sad moue and sighed. "I fear he was horrified at the prospect o' having to serve the poor dear."

Saidh stilled at her words, but then swallowed and said, "Greer'll ne'er believe it. Alpin had no reason to kill Allen."

"Is anyone really sure Allen did no' merely drown accidentally?" she asked. "I am the only one who believed it was no accident. If I was the one who killed him, why would I ha'e squawked about it to one and all, and possibly raise their suspicions that it might ha'e been foul play, when no one thought it anything but an accident ere that?"

Saidh frowned. The woman's reasoning was not completely insane. She might convince . . . Straightening, she said triumphantly, "The arrow. Alpin was sick in bed when I was shot in the woods. He could no' ha'e—"

"Used the passage to slip out by the loch and then go lie in wait fer ye to return before using the passage to return to his bed ere Greer found and brought ye back?"

"Ye used the passage," Saidh murmured. She had no idea where it came out by the loch, but remembered the horses reacting to something in the trees surrounding the clearing. Pushing that away for now, she rallied and said, "They'll ne'er believe Alpin could knock out Rory and Dougall."

"Why not? I did and he is stronger than me," she pointed out. "All he needed was a stool to stand on by the door fer Dougall. I did place one there," she added, and then continued, "As fer Rory, he was bent o'er his satchel on the table when I crept into the room, his head easily reachable to the boy."

"But Alpin can barely stand up," Saidh pointed out. "Those tinctures o' Rory's—"

"He only pretended to take them," Tilda said with a shrug.

Saidh shook her head. "Greer'll ne'er believe it."

"Mayhap, but he'll ne'er be able to prove otherwise," she said with certainty. "And does he prove difficult, I can always kill him and help the next in line to the title."

Saidh stared at her briefly, and then past her as she noted movement in the darkness by the door. She almost raised the torch to see what it was, but then realized doing so might be a mistake if it was help coming, and shifted her attention back to Tilda.

Shaking her head, she said, "Alpin was injured saving me from the merlon ye pushed off the wall."

"Or was he trying to push ye under it?" Tilda asked.

Since the boy couldn't have been pushing her around and toppling the merlon at the same time, that argument would never work, but Saidh merely said, "Ye're such a disappointment."

"Me?" Tilda gasped indignantly.

"Aye," Saidh said firmly. "I actually admired ye and thought ye were a true lady, kind and sweet. Instead, yer naught but a sneaky, brain-addled viper who destroys all she encounters. Yer sister, her bairns, yer son, Fenella . . . is there anyone in yer life who ye've no' killed?"

"Her husband, but I hear she made him so miserable he threw himself on an enemy's sword to escape her," Greer said grimly, appearing out of the shadows behind Tilda and pressing his sword tip to the side of her throat. "Drop the knife and release the lad, or I'll slice yer throat wide open where ye stand."

Tilda froze, fury crossing her face. Saidh suspected the woman might have tried something then, threats or trickery to turn the tables, but the appearance of Aulay and her other brothers moving out into the small room from behind Greer caught her attention, and she closed her eyes briefly. When she opened them again, they seemed as empty as she was and she shrugged indifferently. "Go ahead and slice me throat. 'Tis no worse than what'll happen to me now anyway."

For a moment, Saidh thought Greer might do it. He certainly looked furious enough to, and she couldn't blame him. On the other hand, she didn't want Alpin injured, so while the pair were distracted glaring at each other, Saidh quickly stepped forward and grabbed the woman's hand, pulling it away from Alpin's throat. She then squeezed Tilda's wrist with her other hand until she shrieked in pain and released the knife.

"Thank ye, wife," Greer said grimly as he tugged Tilda's arms behind her to free Alpin.

"Me pleasure," Saidh said dryly, putting out a steadying hand to Alpin when he staggered away from Tilda and toward her.

"Oh, m'lady," Alpin muttered, collapsing against her. "Ye were so brave. And ye did no' scream once, all those times she stabbed ye in the back."

"What?" Greer bellowed. Tossing Tilda toward Saidh's brothers, he rushed forward to catch her by the shoulders and turn her around so he could see her back.

"She only poked me a time or two," Saidh muttered, clasping Alpin close to keep him from tumbling to the floor.

"Nay. She stabbed ye," Alpin said, raising his head to peer at her face from the comfort of her bosom. "'Twas three times I think, and the knife went in an inch at least each time."

"What?" Saidh bellowed now, and tried to twist around to see her back. Unable to, she glanced to Greer and was only alarmed further by his expression. Her voice was shaky as she asked, "She did no' really stab me, did she? It did no' feel like she did more than poke me."

"Yer blood was up," Aulay said quietly, pulling Alpin from her unresisting hands and lifting him into his arms. "Ye'd ha'e felt it eventually. By then ye'd ha'e lost enough blood and been too weak to protect yerself, though . . . which is probably why she was so happy to keep ye talking once she got ye up here."

Saidh stared at him blankly. She'd thought she was the one keeping Tilda talking. Hearing tearing behind her, she glanced over her shoulder to see that Greer had knelt and was tearing strips out of her gown.

"What are ye doing?" she protested.

"I'll buy ye another gown. In fact, I'll buy ye a dozen," he growled. He straightened then to try to wrap the cloth around her waist and back, but she shifted away, scowling.

"I'm no' worried about the gown ye, daft man. I'm worried about ye covering me wounds with cloth that has been dragged through that filthy passage. Rory says dirty bandages are no' good fer a wound."

"O' course yer no' worried about yer gown," Greer muttered, dropping the strips of cloth and scooping her up instead.

"What is that supposed to mean?" Saidh asked suspiciously as he carried her toward the passage door.

"It means—" Greer halted abruptly and swung back when Alick cried out.

Her youngest brother was leaning out one of the

openings, peering down, eyes wide and face pale. Frowning, Saidh asked, "What's the matter?"

"Where is Tilda?" Greer asked at the same moment and Saidh realized the woman was no longer in the bell tower.

Alick straightened slowly, grimaced as he faced them and said helplessly, "She jumped."

"What do ye mean?" Greer asked sharply. "Were ye no' holding her?"

"She just . . ." He waved one hand weakly. "I thought Conran had her other arm. I only let go fer a minute and she threw herself out the opening."

"Sorry. I thought ye had her," Conran muttered. Moving to peer over the edge now, he released a low whistle. "She made a muckle mess."

"And here I thought old bats could fly," Geordie muttered.

Saidh bit her lip at the comment and glanced to Greer's face. His mouth opened, closed, then he just shook his head and turned to carry her into the passage.

The stairway was in darkness, which explained how they'd opened the passage door without drawing attention. Saidh remained silent as Greer traversed the steps, concerned about distracting him and their plunging down the damned things. But once they were off the stairs the entire length of the passage was lit by torches every few feet.

"Look on the bright side," Saidh murmured as he turned down the passage leading to the master bedchamber. "Now we no longer need deal with her."

"Aye," Greer muttered. "And mayhap ye'll stop getting yerself shot and stabbed."

"'Tis no' as if I went looking to be shot and stabbed," Saidh pointed out irritably. "And, she is *your* aunt."

"Was," he corrected dryly.

"Was," she agreed as he carried her through the open passage door into the master bedchamber.

Chapter 19

"SET HER ON THE BED SO I CAN LOOK AT HER back."

Saidh glanced over Greer's shoulder at that order from Rory as they entered the master bedchamber. He and the rest of her brothers were now filing into the room behind them. She hadn't realized the others had followed, but supposed she should have known they would. Turning back as Greer headed for the bed, Saidh protested, "No' the bed. The day after I took the arrow, me new lady's maid, Joyce, told me the maids were squawking about no' being able to get the blood out o' the linens."

"I'll put her in the chair," Greer announced, turning that way, only to pause when Rory protested.

"I'll no' be able to get to her back there."

Greer muttered something under his breath, and walked over to plop her bottom down on the table between the two chairs by the fire instead. "There. Will this please both o' ye?"

"Aye," Rory announced, glancing up from retrieving several items from his satchel.

"Aye," Saidh murmured and then watched as Greer began to pace the room like a caged tiger.

"Something's got into him," Dougall murmured, pausing beside her.

"Aye," Aulay agreed solemnly and then handed Alpin to Niels and said, "Take him to the room next door. Rory can look him o'er there after he tends to Saidh."

Niels hesitated, but then pointed out, "Fenella's still in there."

Grimacing at the reminder, Saidh peered at Alpin's sleeping face and suggested, "Take him to Fenella's room then."

Niels nodded and carried the boy out.

"Geordie," Aulay said now. "Go find Fenella's maid and ask her to select a couple o' women to help her prepare Fenella fer burial."

"I think as lady here, I should probably be helping with that," Saidh muttered reluctantly. It wasn't exactly something she looked forward to. She'd only done it once before, with her own mother.

"Ye're in no shape fer it," Aulay said simply and waved Geordie out of the room, before turning to Conran. "Take Alick and go see what ye can do about Lady MacDonnell."

"Do?" Conran asked dubiously. "She's dead."

"Aye," he said dryly. "So, mayhap ye could get her out o' the bailey?"

"Oh, aye," Conran muttered, and led Alick out of the room. Neither man looked pleased at being tasked with the chore. But since they were the ones who had been lax enough in their duties to let her jump, it was only fair they clean up their mess.

Rory finished fussing in his satchel then and came over to the table where Saidh sat. He scowled when he saw her just sitting there.

"Why are ye still wearin' yer dress?" he asked with irritation.

"Possibly because we are still here," Aulay pointed out dryly.

"Well, get out," Rory said at once. "I need to clean and bandage her back where Lady MacDonnell stabbed her, and then probably sew up her arrow wound again, if the blood on her gown is anything to go by."

"Aye, we're leaving," Aulay assured him. "I just wanted to be sure to tell ye to be quick about tending her. I think MacDonnell needs some time alone with his wife."

"It'll take as long as it takes," Rory said dryly. "I'll no' ha'e her die from this wound jest because I rushed so she could talk to MacDonnell."

"What do me husband and I need to talk about?" Saidh asked with concern, wondering if something had happened while she'd been in Lady MacDonnell's clutches.

"Leave," Rory said firmly, before Aulay could answer. "I need to tend to her."

Saidh scowled at him and then said to Aulay, "Stay. Rory has me so wrapped up in linen 'tis as if I'm dressed anyway."

"Saidh," Rory snapped. "Take off yer dress or I'll cut it off."

"Well, cut it off then," she snapped back, and then muttered, "It hurts to move much anyway."

"Oh. O' course it does," Rory said, calming somewhat. "I'm sorry. I should ha'e realized."

Saidh shrugged and glanced to Aulay in question as Rory retrieved a knife and began to cut away the top of her gown. "What did ye want to say?"

"I jest . . ." He hesitated, looking uncomfortable, and then sighed and asked, "What are yer feelings fer MacDonnell?"

Saidh stared at him blankly and then asked, "What? Why? What're ye—?"

"I think he loves ye, lass," Aulay interrupted, looking truly uncomfortable now.

"Aye," Saidh said.

Aulay raised his eyebrows. "Aye? That's it? Aye?"

"What else should I say?" she asked with a frown. "'Tis no' a surprise. He already told me that."

"Oh." He looked surprised and then asked. "And what did ye say?"

"Nothing," she admitted.

"The man tells ye he loves ye and ye say nothing?" Dougall growled, looking horrified.

"Well, I did no' get the chance to say anything," she snapped. "It was while we were talking to Bowie and—"

"All right, all right. Do no' fash yerself," Aulay soothed, glancing toward Greer. Following his gaze, Saidh saw that her husband had stopped pacing and was eyeing them suspiciously from across the room.

"'Tis no wonder he's so fashed," Dougall muttered, once Greer started to pace again. "He's declared himself and no' yet received one in return."

"Do ye love him, Saidh?" Rory asked curiously

as he worked. He'd sliced her gown away from the waist up, but had tucked a bit of cloth over the little bit revealed of her uninjured breast she saw. Now he moved around to clean the stab wounds on her back.

"Well, do ye?" Dougall asked when she didn't answer right away.

Saidh shrugged helplessly. "I do no' ken. How do ye ken if ye love someone?"

Aulay considered the question and then asked, "Do ye enjoy consummatin' with him?"

Saidh smiled faintly. "I want to punch him e'erytime he kisses me."

"What?" Rory barked, straightening and coming around in front of her to see her face.

"Well, that's how it feels," she said helplessly. "O' course, I do no' do it. 'Tis jest that he fair makes me blood boil with his kisses and I want to . . ." She shook her head. "But I do no' hit him and then he starts in touching and thrusting and me head fair explodes and I do no' want to hit him anymore."

"Ah," Rory said weakly and moved around back of her again to return to work.

Saidh glanced to Aulay and frowned when she saw the amusement on his face. "What?"

"Nothing," he said quickly, clearing his expression.

"So does she like it or nay?" Dougall asked, appearing uncertain.

"Aye," Aulay assured him dryly.

"Then why does she want to hit him?" Dougall

asked. "It seems an odd reaction if she's liking it. And it can no' be healthy fer her head to explode."

Aulay turned to him with disbelief. "Ha'e ye e'er e'en lain with a woman, Dougall?"

"O' course I ha'e," he snapped. "But I ha'e ne'er wanted to hit one while doing it, and me head certainly does no' explode. At least no' the head on me shoulders," he added with a grin.

"She does no' mean she really wants to hit him, or that her head really explodes, Dougall," Rory said with exasperation behind her.

"Well, then why did she say it?" Dougall asked with a frown.

"She means . . . I'll explain later," Aulay said with a grimace, and then turned back to Saidh. "Is there anything else ye like about him?"

"Oh, aye. He's got a pretty . . . arse," she finished, saying *arse* instead of *face* as her gaze landed on Aulay's scars and she recalled his self-consciousness about it.

"What does it matter if his arse is pretty?" Dougall asked with disgust as Rory made a sound that might have been a laugh, or just as easily could have been a cough.

Saidh scowled and rushed on, "And I like to talk to him. He's verra clever. I like the way he thinks. And I like when he fusses o'er me."

"Ye do?" Rory asked with surprise, beginning to bind her waist to cover the wounds he'd just cleaned. It seemed to have gone quickly, and hadn't been too painful, but she had been distracted.

"Ye jest get angry when *we* fuss," Dougall grumbled.

"Aye, well, he does it different," she said dryly. "He makes me feel like he cares, no' like he thinks me weak."

"If the castle was on fire, who would ye rescue first?" Aulay asked suddenly.

"Alpin," she said at once. "He's weakest."

"No' MacDonnell?" he asked with a frown.

Saidh snorted. "He'd already be up trying to rescue me."

Aulay smiled slowly.

"What?" Saidh asked suspiciously.

"Ye trust that ye can rely on him," he said simply and then turned his back and gestured to Dougall to do so as well to give her privacy as Rory began to cut away the bindings around her chest wound.

"O' course I trust him," Saidh said with confusion.

"Saidh," Aulay said solemnly without turning around. "Ha'e ye e'er before met a man ye thought strong and smart and that ye could depend on?"

"Ye mean besides me husband?" she asked and when he nodded, answered promptly. "Da. You. And Dougall, Rory, Conran, Geordie, Niels—"

"Men who are no' Buchanans," Aulay interrupted.

Saidh considered the question. "Mayhap Sinclair. He seems a'right, but most men are puling, lackwitted—Oh," she said with understanding.

Aulay nodded. "Ye like and respect the man, trust him and enjoy him in bed."

"She loves him," Dougall announced, and she saw her brothers grin at each other.

"Aye," Rory agreed with a smile as he finished cutting away the bandages and began to examine her chest wound.

"I am glad ye do. I like and respect him too," Aulay said quietly.

"Aye," Dougall said. "He could ha'e been a Buchanan."

Saidh smiled, knowing that was the biggest compliment her brother could give.

"Ye've made a fine choice fer a husband, sister," Rory murmured.

"Thank ye," she whispered and glanced down as he began to replace the bandages he'd cut away with fresh strips of linen. "I do no' need more stitches?"

"Nay. A couple stitches had torn a bit, but are still holding and already healing. Ye're a fast healer," he added, as though congratulating her on an unexpected skill.

Saidh just shook her head and watched as he finished binding her up. By the time he was done, she was pretty much covered from her waist to her neck in bandages with just her arms and one shoulder still on view. He'd even fully covered her uninjured breast this time, she noted mournfully.

"All done," Rory announced, straightening.

"Then we should leave the two o' ye alone," Aulay announced, then bent to kiss her cheek before saying. "Put yer husband out o' his misery and tell him ye love him."

"Aye." Saidh nodded, and then watched her

brothers leave, before turning to peer at Greer. He'd stopped pacing to watch them leave as well, his expression unreadable, and Saidh bit her lips, wondering how she should tell him she loved him. Should she just blurt it out, or wait for him to say it again? She wondered and then worried that he might not say it again. He might even regret saying it the first time. Or he might be waiting for her to say it herself, ere repeating it.

"What were ye and yer brothers whispering about o'er here?"

Saidh raised her head at that quiet question and found her husband standing in front of her. He looked . . . She frowned, trying to find the word. *Stoic* was the only one to come to mind, but that was not it. It was more as if he were braced for a blow.

"We were no' whispering," Saidh protested, and then admitted, "They were trying to help me sort out if I loved ye."

That had definitely surprised him, Saidh thought wryly as his jaw dropped to hit his chest. Quickly pulling it closed, he raised an eyebrow and asked, "And? What was the conclusion?"

"That I want to hit ye e'ery time ye kiss me, and would no' save ye were the castle on fire," she blurted.

He reacted as if she'd punched him in the gut, stumbling back a step, his face paling. Pulling himself upright, he asked gruffly, "When are they taking ye?"

"Taking me where?" she asked with confusion.

"Home to Buchanan," he said stiffly.

Saidh shook her head with bewilderment. "Why would they take me to Buchanan?"

"Because 'tis obvious I am a poor excuse fer a husband and can no' keep ye safe," he said shortly.

Saidh snorted at the claim, but asked, "That is why ye were pacing so angrily? Ye blame yerself fer me injuries?"

"I am yer husband. I should ha'e kept ye safe," he said grimly.

"And ye did. Ye saved me and Alpin from Tilda in the bell tower," she pointed out with a shrug.

"No' before ye took yet more wounds."

"Me brothers were watching me when Tilda took me," she pointed out. "They were also supposed to be guarding me when Alpin and I slipped away to the gardens and got hurt. So, if ye want to blame anyone, blame them."

"Oy!" The shout came muffled through the door. It was followed by, "We can hear ye! These doors are thin."

"Then stop pressing yer ears to it and go below. I'm trying to talk to me husband here!" Saidh snapped and heard the shuffle of feet as her brothers moved away from the door. Honestly, they were like a heard of bulls the lot of them, she thought and then glanced back to Greer and said solemnly, "This is me home now. Me brothers ken I love ye. They'll no' be taking me anywhere."

Greer blinked as if uncertain he'd heard her right, or unable to process her words. "Ye love me?"

"Aye. Did I no' jest tell ye me brothers helped me sort that out?" she asked impatiently.

"Nay. Ye said ye want to hit me e'ery time I kiss ye, and would no' save me were the castle on fire," he snapped.

"Exactly," Saidh said with satisfaction. "That's how much I love ye."

"What?" he asked with disbelief. "Ye think the fact that ye'd rather hit me than kiss me and would leave me to die in a burning building means that ye love me?"

"That's no' what I meant," Saidh squawked, and then clucked under her tongue. "And I told them ye were clever."

"Wife," he said through his teeth.

Saidh sighed, and shook her head. "I would ne'er leave ye to die in a burning building," she said with exasperation, and explained, "Aulay asked me who I would save were the castle on fire, and I said Alpin, 'cause he was weakest. And he asked why no' you, and I said because ye'd already be up and about trying to drag me out o' the castle." She raised her eyebrows. "See? He says that's a sign that I trust and rely on ye, and I do. Like me da and brothers, ye're a brave, braugh man with a fine head on yer shoulders. I trust that ye'll always be there and ha'e me back. I can count on ye."

"Oh," Greer breathed, relaxing a little. Smiling crookedly, he took her hands. "That is one o' the things I love about ye too, Saidh. I love yer strength and yer stubbornness. The wildness that seems to flow through e'ery part o' yer body," he said with admiration and bent his head to kiss her. It started out a gentle drifting of his lips over hers, but quickly turned into something more carnal and heated as it always did when he kissed her.

Saidh moaned, and wrapped her arms around Greer's waist as desire and need began to bubble up within her, building to the point where she was desperate for an outlet. Something aggressive and physical. Tearing her mouth away, she turned her head to the side and gasped, "About the punching."

"I remember," he growled by her ear.

"Ye do?" she asked with confusion. "What do ye remember?"

"The stables," he reminded her, one hand drifting up her thigh under her skirt and she smiled as she recalled that day. Her telling him that the things he did to her made her want to punch him, and his showing her what she really wanted. How long ago it seemed now. A lifetime, she thought, and then pulled back to peer at him when his hand stilled.

"What is it?" she asked worriedly, afraid she was so unattractive now with all her bindings that he couldn't bear to touch her. Not one to shy from saying what she was thinking, she asked, "It it because I'm wrapped up in linens like a corpse?" Grimacing, she added, "I suppose 'tis hardly attractive."

"Saidh," he said seriously, cupping her face in both hands. "I will always find ye beautiful." He didn't kiss her then as she hoped, but added, "It's jest ye've so many wounds now, I'm afraid o' hurting ye."

"Then keep yer hands below the waist and yer lips above the neck," she suggested pragmatically, and added, "Because I feel like punching someone."

A short laugh slipped from Greer's lips and then he murmured, "As my lady wife demands," and urged her legs apart so that he could step between them. Pausing then, he caught her face in his hands again and said, "I do love ye, Saidh."

"And I love ye too, Greer," she assured him as his lips lowered to claim hers.

Keep reading
for a sneak peek
of Lynsay Sands's next
New York Times bestselling
Argeneau novel

ABOUT A VAMPIRE

Available October 2015
from Avon Books

$\mathcal{J}$USTIN BRICKER ROLLED THE GURNEY STACKED with dead rogues in front of the retort. After kicking the wheel locks to keep it in place, he then glanced to Anders, his partner in tonight's endeavor.

With his dark hair and skin and the black leather clothes he wore, Anders was like a shadow in the white room. He was presently looming over the crematorium technician who stood in the corner. The adult male mortal who had opened the back door at their knock now looked like little more than a naughty schoolboy put there for punishment by an irate teacher. Only the child's resentment was missing . . . the man's expression was blank as Anders worked to remove their arrival from his memories and keep him where he stood, safely out of the way.

When Anders relaxed and turned to walk toward him, Justin raised his eyebrows. "Are we good?"

Anders nodded. "But we have to be quick. His shift ends in fifteen minutes. A new guy will be showing up soon."

"No problem. We'll be out of here by then. As flammable as we are, these guys will be dust in minutes." Justin turned to open the door of the retort, and whistled at the wave of heat that blew out at him. He glanced to Anders as the other man reached his side. "So . . . what did you do to piss off Lucian?"

Rather than answer, Anders asked, "What makes you think I did anything to piss him off?"

Justin grinned. "Well, he gave me clean-up duty because I pissed him off. So I figure you must be in the same boat."

Anders merely grunted and pulled the top body off the stack to send it into the retort.

"Come on," Justin said as the flames shooting into the retort hit the body and it was set ablaze as if it were made of dry straw. "You must have done something."

Anders watched him pick up another body to send it into the retort. Finally, he said, "I might have made some joke or other about his missing so many meals at home since Leigh turned vegetarian."

Justin raised his eyebrows. "That wouldn't bother him . . . unless you said it in front of Leigh."

Anders grimaced, and then started to pick up the next body. "Unfortunately, Leigh came into the room behind me as I was saying it. I fear she overheard me."

"Ah." Justin winced, knowing Anders wouldn't have deliberately hurt the woman's feelings. None of the hunters would. Leigh was a good woman, they all liked her. "Yeah, I bet that— Look out! The head—"

Anders froze with this body half off the gurney, but it was too late. One of the heads had been dislodged and was rolling off the edge of the metal table. Justin made a grab for it, but wasn't in time and the decapitated head hit the floor with a wet splat.

Both men stood and grimaced at the mess, and then Anders nodded toward the crematorium technician and muttered, "I don't suppose we can make him clean this up?"

"You suppose right. It would be hard to erase that from his memory and ensure it stayed erased," Justin said with amusement as he watched Anders grab the head by the man's long hair and toss it into the retort. It rolled forward like a lopsided bowling ball wobbling into the flame jets, where it exploded into immediate flames. Shaking his head, he murmured, "Like kindling."

"Yeah, we're pretty flammable," Anders commented.

"I guess that makes us hot stuff," Justin said and laughed at his own joke. It even brought a smile from Anders as he finished lifting the body he held and sent it into the retort after the head. Anders wasn't known for a sense of humor, so the smile was the equivalent of a belly laugh from anyone else, Justin thought.

A shuffling sound and a moan drew his attention around to a woman standing at the corner of the cooler. She was short and rounded with a wave of raven-black hair pouring over her shoulders and down her back, a shiny black mass against the tan trench coat she wore. She also had one hand pressed against the cooler wall as if to hold herself up, and her complexion was positively green as she stared at the puddle on the floor where the head had been just seconds ago. Justin was pretty sure she'd witnessed the whole head-rolling-off-the-table-onto-the-floor bit. No doubt a gruesome sight for someone not used to dealing with the dead. Hell, he had to do it on a semi regular basis and it had been gruesome to him.

Her eyes lifted reluctantly to him and Anders now and Justin noted that they were a lovely pale blue. She had nice lips too, full and kissable, and the cutest little slightly turned up nose . . . and she was looking at him and Anders with a sort of mindless horror.

"I have the mess on the floor to clean up, so you get to deal with our tourist here," Anders announced grimly.

"Thanks," Justin said sarcastically, but didn't really mind. He loved women, always had, and this one was a cutie. The only shame was that he wouldn't get to play with more than her mind. Once he took control of her and wiped her memories, he'd have to avoid contact with her again to avoid those memories returning. Ah well, plenty more in the sea, he thought, and concentrated his gaze on her forehead, trying to penetrate her thoughts.

"Well?" Anders asked after a moment. "What are you waiting for? Take control of her."

Justin blinked, confusion sliding through him and then said weakly, "I can't."

"What?" Anders asked with surprise.

"I can't read her," he clarified, hardly able to believe it himself. Her thoughts were a complete blank to him.

"Seriously?" Anders asked, eyes narrowing.

"Seriously," Justin assured him, aware that his voice sounded as dazed as he felt. Damn. He couldn't read her. That meant—

"Well, then I'd get after her if I were you," Anders suggested and when Bricker just stared at him in blank confusion, he gestured to where the woman had been just a moment before and pointed out, "She's running."

The closing of the door to the hall told him Anders was right before he could turn to see that she was no longer in the room. Cursing, Justin burst into a run. He'd be damned if he was going to let her get away . . . and not because of what she'd seen. He couldn't read her, and that might mean she could be a life mate for him. Finding a life mate this early in life was pretty damned rare. If he lost her, he wouldn't be likely to find another for centuries . . . maybe millennia, and Justin had no desire to wait millennia to experience what it was like to have a life mate.

She was quick, he noted with admiration on reaching the hall to see her disappearing through the door at the other end. But then panic could be one hell of a motivation and he had no doubt what she'd seen had raised panic in her.

The thought made Bricker frown as he went after her. He would have a lot of explaining to do once he caught up. He'd have to calm her, and then somehow explain that he wasn't some murderous bastard destroying evidence of his dastardly work . . . and all without the aid of mind control. That ought to be interesting, he thought unhappily, and his worrying over that made him move more slowly than he could have. He wanted to work out how to explain things before he caught up. He wanted to do it right the first time, calm her quickly, and gain her trust. He couldn't convince her to be his life mate if she was terrified or suspicious of him. The right words were needed here.

The problem was, Justin didn't have a clue what those right words were and he was running out of time. It did seem a good idea to stop her before she actually left the building, though, and at that moment she was racing through the last hall, flying past the chapels and columbaria, headed for the exit. Letting go of the worry about what to say, Justin picked up speed and caught her arm just as she reached the door. When he whirled her around, she immediately swung her free arm at him. Expecting paltry girly blows, Justin didn't react at first and only spotted the scissors she held a heartbeat before they sliced across his throat.

Justin sucked in his breath and released her as pain radiated through him. He saw the fine mist of blood that sprayed out and splashed across her tan coat and immediately covered his throat. The small amount of blood that had showered her told him it wasn't a deep wound. He was more surprised by the attack than anything else. Still, by the time he turned his attention back to the woman, she'd tugged the door open and was slipping away. Cursing, he ignored his stinging throat and quickly followed.

The woman—his woman—glanced over her shoulder at the sound of the door opening and Justin's mouth tightened at the sight of her wide terrified eyes. So much for winning her trust, he thought and then cried out as she stumbled. She had been looking back rather than to where she was going and that was her undoing. It left her unprepared for the sudden step down in the sidewalk and she lost her footing. She fell flat on her face. It wasn't much of a fall though and he fully expected her to pop back up fighting and with feet moving, but instead she lay prone until he reached her side.

Concerned by how still she was, Justin dropped to a crouch and turned her over. He spotted the bloody gash on her forehead first. She'd obviously hit her head on the sidewalk as she fell. It was a good bump, but not that bad, he noted with a relief that turned to horror as he then spotted the scissors protruding from her chest in the small space where the loosely done up coat didn't meet. Even as Bricker saw that, her eyes opened and then widened with pain and fear of a different kind now. She no longer feared him, at least not as much as she feared for her life. The hell of it was, he was afraid for her life too. It looked bad.

*G*ive in to your Impulses!

These unforgettable stories only take a second to buy and give you hours of reading pleasure!

Go to *www.AvonImpulse.com* and see what we have to offer.

Available wherever e-books are sold.

AVONIMPULSE

IMP 0811